INTERNATIONAL PRAISE FOR *A*

"It grips you from the very first page and won't let you go ..."

—*Cosmop*.

"A journey that you wish would never end."

—*Suddeutsche Zeitung*

"The lively description of the different characters . . . makes this novel an immense pleasure to read!"

—Ursula Drechsler, *Aachener Zeitung*

"Wonderfully written, this is the story of a family and of a woman in search of her roots."

—*Stuttgarter Zeitung*

"A novel which evades and overturns clichés."

—*La Stampa*

"You feel as if you're in an award-winning movie."

—*Nido*

"The most successful debut of the year, competition for Elena Ferrante."

—*Il Deutsch-Italia*

ANYWHERE
BUT HOME

ANYWHERE BUT HOME

A Novel

DANIEL SPECK

Translated by JAIME McGILL

 AMAZON **CROSSING**

Text copyright © 2016 by S. Fischer Verlag GmbH
Translation copyright © 2020 by Jaime McGill
All rights reserved.

Previously published as *Bella Germania* by Fischer Taschenbuch in Germany in 2016. Translated from German by Jaime McGill. First published in English by Amazon Crossing in 2020.

Published by Amazon Crossing, Seattle

www.apub.com

Amazon, the Amazon logo, and Amazon Crossing are trademarks of Amazon.com, Inc., or its affiliates.

ISBN-13: 9781542090124
ISBN-10: 1542090121

Cover design by Rex Bonomelli

Printed in the United States of America

For those who left their native countries
and brought their stories with them

It cannot be surprising that questions about immigration and the immigrant inevitably end up as questions not only about who we are, but who we want to be—the deepest things.

—*Hanif Kureishi,* My Ear at His Heart

PART 1

1

Julia

He claimed to be my grandfather. If he could just tell me his story, he said, I would believe it. He pleaded with me to hear him out, as though his life depended on it. And once he had finished the story, I realized that the life hanging in the balance was actually mine.

But I didn't know that back then, the day he suddenly showed up, a handsome old man gazing at me as though he'd known me forever. It was spring, I was in Milan, and he woke me from a dream—the dream that I'd mistaken for reality.

Clothes make the person. I make the clothes. I give people a second skin, transforming, masking, or revealing what they call their true selves. I watch as they step into the light and expose themselves to the scrutiny of others, while I remain hidden in the shadows. My realm is the atelier, the magic of possibility, the cloth in my hands unfolding from plane into space, from sketch into living sculpture. Materials have personalities; they tell me things about the people wearing them. Silk speaks a different language than wool; linen seeks a different form than velvet. Clothes are alive, they move, they change, they alter the wearer. When I design a new piece of clothing, I see people not only as what they are, but as what they might become.

Since childhood, I've never wanted to do anything else. And there's no greater joy than doing what you love. But talent isn't enough. Fashion is half art, half hard work. What looks like self-realization from the outside actually requires a great deal of self-deception. It's a life devoted to the beauty of other people. There's always a price to pay. My dream of starting my own fashion label was pure megalomania, or worse, sheer naivete. Most of my old London College of Fashion classmates had made peace with their nine-to-five positions, if they hadn't left the industry entirely. They admired and envied my little label, but none of them knew about the nightmares that plagued me, the existential crises, the panicked fear of failing on an epic scale.

I was thirty-six now, but I felt no closer to making it than I had at twenty-six. The lofty goals for which I'd sacrificed the "best" years of my life were still out of reach. Though it sounded glamorous to others, mine was a nomadic existence: living out of a suitcase and making the rounds through the trade-fair circus, driven by chronic debt and a stubborn conviction that talent would prevail in a world that had moved on without me.

My business partner, Robin, was the only person who believed in me unconditionally. He was eight years older and solid as a rock, having already gone spectacularly bankrupt once and recovered in equally spectacular fashion. Robin had everything I didn't: family money, unshakable self-confidence, an endless supply of witty one-liners. And he provided something no one can make it without nowadays: interest-free loans from his parents.

He handled the business; I supplied the creativity. Our company was our family—the clothes, our children. We were two obsessives, mutually reassuring one another that we weren't alone with our crazy ambitions. We shared the sleepless nights, the hopes and disappointments, the dreams of making it big. Everything—except for a bed. We both knew better than to put our start-up at risk like that. Because if there was one constant in my life, it was this: I could always rely on my craft. On men, less so.

Those days and nights we spent in our cramped atelier in Munich weren't about intimate collaboration so much as precisely coordinated processes. There was no sense of competition between us; it was a productive symbiosis. We eagerly awaited our big break without ever asking ourselves what that actually meant. In reality, it was all one long series of successes and setbacks. Somehow, that break was always just around the corner, but it never quite arrived. Like tunnel workers, we went on digging our way forward, taking everything as it came and trusting that one day, we would reach the light at last.

And now that day was here. We were doing our first Milan Fashion Week show, together with fifteen other young designers. There was no prize money involved, but the winner would get a year's worth of help with brand development and marketing from an Italian holding company with several big labels, worldwide distribution, and priceless contacts. After all this time, we finally had a shot at everything we'd been fighting for.

For weeks, we worked like fiends, creating a new collection unlike anything we'd done before: an eclectic mishmash of materials, colors, and epochs. We spent those weeks in a creative frenzy, running on too much coffee and not enough sleep, thinking only of our goal. Milan wouldn't be a home game like Munich or Berlin. Everything was bigger—the venues, the labels, the buyers. The lights were brighter; the rise was faster; the fall was farther. The other fifteen were damn good, and the event hall was abuzz with an air of fierce competition. But everyone kept smiling.

Things didn't quite go according to plan. Seconds before the show, I was rushing around backstage, pinning pants, correcting stitches, fixing makeup, and I jabbed myself in the finger with a needle. At that very moment, the curtain went up. The models switched on their faces and stepped onto the catwalk. And then I was standing back there in the dark, pulse racing while I held my breath, unable to see what was happening out front, unable to hear anything but the music, the clicking cameras, my own beating heart. The thing I'd been nurturing all this time, hidden away, had been cast before the merciless public eye. Now, the judgment would fall. It was too late for changes; there was only triumph or defeat.

Robin and I exchanged glances. In the dim light, his feverish face seemed to glow, while his black-turtlenecked torso disappeared against the dark walls. We'd become ghosts. We tried listening for the audience's reactions, but could discern neither astonishment nor disapproval. Then, the first few models returned, and we dashed over to change their outfits within seconds. Other designers employed more models; we didn't have the money to do that.

The second set was the weirder creations, the ironic references, the optical illusions, the provocative breaks with stylistic convention. After that, silence.

Breath held. And then applause, the first wave of relief, and finally, the moment when Robin took my hand and we emerged from the darkness like moles gazing into the sun. At first, I couldn't make out faces, only a surge of white light crashing over us amid unexpectedly raucous applause. We bowed, laughing, bewildered, intoxicated. All at once, my vision went black. My knees turned to rubber. I collapsed, feeling my body hit the hard stage floor before I sank into bottomless darkness.

2

When I opened my eyes again, I felt sweat and cold night air on my forehead. I was lying in the dressing room, on the cold floor beneath the mirror, surrounded by chairs, racks, and mountains of clothes. The models were all talking anxiously at once, but I couldn't hear them. One was holding my legs up. Robin was nowhere in sight. A young Italian paramedic spoke to the girls insistently as he injected something into my arm, and gradually my world filled with sound again. The worried voices, the booming music next door, a motor scooter outside. The paramedic helped me into one of the chairs.

I glimpsed my pale face in the makeup mirror and, next to it, the face of a stranger. That was the first time I saw him, walking in through the door behind me, an old man among the young models. Tall, slim, energetic. He looked out of place in his elegant suit, his scarf and hat. Nobody seemed to recognize him, but he pushed his way over as though he knew me. I saw his eyes. Clear, blue, and alert. Everyone in the room probably assumed he was here with someone else. Such was the nature of the fashion circus. There was always some stranger running around; nobody knew all the names, and nobody dared ask, for fear it might be someone important.

"How are you?" he asked in German. For a stranger, his voice sounded a shade too worried.

"Okay."

He handed me a glass of water. I took a hasty gulp and ran a hand through my disheveled hair, grateful for the fresh air streaming in through the window. He took the chair beside mine. At first, I thought he might be one of the judges. But no, he seemed too serious for that. You can tell when someone's in the industry. There was something touching about the way he was regarding me. He was moved, troubled, as though he'd known me for a long time. Now, in the neon light of the makeup mirror, I could see that he was probably around eighty.

"Julia," he said softly.

"Have we met?" I asked, growing annoyed at his unwavering gaze.

"Congratulations on the collection." His voice was astonishingly young— not without authority, and yet strangely fragile.

"Thanks."

He cleared his throat. "I'm from Munich as well. I followed you here to see your presentation," he said, as though we were discussing a PowerPoint pitch rather than a fashion show. "My name is Vincent . . . Vincent Schlewitz."

He waited, probably to see how I would react to his name, but it didn't ring any bells. The paramedic interrupted us. I didn't understand a thing, so Vincent translated: I needed to roll up my sleeve so that the paramedic could take my blood pressure. Was I sure I didn't want to see a doctor? I shook my head.

"Just got a little dizzy, that's all," I responded, deliberately failing to mention the cocktail of coffee, adrenaline, and other substances in my blood.

"So, what label do you represent?" I asked the stranger, less out of curiosity than to draw attention away from the cuff around my arm.

He paused, seeming to weigh his words carefully before replying. "You might be surprised to hear this, but I'm here for personal reasons. Once you're feeling better, if we could just speak privately for a few minutes . . ."

He was starting to creep me out. As though reading my thoughts, he added, "I hope you don't think—I'm not some crazed fan, I just wanted to meet you." He was giving me a strange look, almost like he was gazing through me and seeing someone else.

"Not really a good time right now, sorry."

He was undeterred. "This may sound strange, but we're related. Your father"—seeing my reaction, he hesitated—"is my son. I'm your grandfather."

Bad joke. Impossible. Nutcase. The words shot through my mind. The horror must have shown on my face, because he shifted uncomfortably.

"Your father's name is Vincenzo, right?"

Vincenzo. I hadn't heard his name in years. Decades, even.

The paramedic, looking concerned, removed the cuff from my arm and said something else to the man. If my blood pressure had been in the basement a minute ago, it was probably blasting through the roof now. I wanted to leap to my feet, but I was paralyzed.

I'd seen my father once in my life. Vincenzo Marconi, son of a Sicilian guest worker. My mother hadn't told me much else, and what little she'd said about him hadn't exactly been flattering. This stranger who claimed to be his father was obviously German. It didn't make sense.

"You must have me mixed up with someone else," I murmured, and struggled to my feet. I wanted out of there. But standing made me dizzy, and the paramedic caught me by the arm.

"*Piano, signora, piano.*" The paramedic gestured for the other man to leave me alone, but he didn't budge.

"Please. It's very important."

He withdrew a business card from his jacket and held it out.

"I need to explain this to you. Here, this is for you. This is—" He pulled out an old photo and hesitated briefly, as though making sure I was prepared. Then he handed it to me.

The photo was from a different time. Black-and-white, dog-eared. Likely taken in the 1950s, judging from the clothes. A young couple standing by a motorcycle, with the Milan Cathedral in the background. They were holding hands, both looking a bit shy but carefree, beaming with joy. The man was slightly older than the woman, tall and stately, with light-colored eyes full of humor and intelligence. He was wearing a plain summer suit with that straight, slightly square fifties cut. There was something boyish about him, something innocent. I recognized him immediately, even sixty years later.

"This is me, in 1954, in Milan. And that's Giulietta. Your grandmother."

He indicated the woman in the picture. A pretty Italian in her early twenties, short black hair, summer dress, small hat. She looked like me. And not just a little bit. It was like seeing my own reflection. I was shocked. She was younger in the photo than I was now, but she had my delicate figure, my arched brows, that adventuresome, slightly dreamy look on her face that I've seen in photos of myself. Same dark eyes, same wry smile. She seemed full of energy, and yet there was something melancholy in her large eyes. The person I saw there was no stranger; it was an echo of my soul in a bygone world. This was a photo of me as a woman in a different era, in different clothes, next to a man I didn't know. It rendered me speechless.

"That's impossible. My father was Italian. But you're German, right?"

He gave me a slightly self-conscious look.

"What did he tell you about me?"

I turned away so the others couldn't hear.

"Nothing. We aren't in touch."

He seemed startled at the sudden edge in my tone.

"But—?"

"He's dead. Sorry, I can't help you."

"Dead?" he echoed. He looked shocked. "When did he die?"

"When I was little."

"Says who?"

"My mother."

"But that's not true. He's alive."

I stared at him in bewilderment. "No way."

"He is. I know he is. Your father lives in Italy."

Just then, Robin came running into the room.

"You okay?"

Instinctively, I hid the photo behind my back. Robin hugged me. He had to have noticed how distraught I was, but he probably chalked it up to my fainting spell. He shot the uninvited visitor a look of annoyance.

"I'm fine," I said. Before he could ask the stranger who he was, I added, "I'll mail you the autograph, okay? Now, you'll have to excuse me."

The man nodded uncertainly. "Call me. It's important. Please."

I'd never had a grown man give me such a beseeching look. A burden seemed to weigh on his soul, heavier than I could comprehend. As he took his leave with a polite nod, I felt guilty for having sent him away.

"Who was that?" Robin asked.

"No idea."

I'd never lied to Robin before, but I told myself it was nothing—some crazy mistake.

"What's up?" I asked. "What are you grinning about?"

We'd lucked out. At last. Maybe we really had been the best, but it didn't matter—the jury had picked us. I'd finally won the bet I'd made all those years ago against everyone who doubted me. This was it. The big break. The light at the end of the tunnel. And I was still too woozy to stand. I don't recall how I managed to anyway. I hardly remember anything—just loud music and applause, and thoughts exploding through my head like fireworks. Press, jury, investors—everyone pounced on us at once. All of a sudden, we were big.

3

Well after midnight, we were half-drunk outside the venue, paying our models. Robin was keyed up and wanted to go on celebrating at a club, but I didn't have the energy. I'd fallen into a black hole of intoxication, confusion, and exhaustion.

"Are you going to faint again? Should we take you to the hospital?"

"No, I just need some sleep. Go have fun!"

I'd pictured this moment differently. I was the star of the night, but the party was happening without me. And that was okay. I walked across the parking lot to my rusty Volvo station wagon, pulled on the old jeans I'd patched a hundred times over, and rolled my sleeping bag out in back. The collection was piled up beside me. After the models' fees and the gas to drive here, we hadn't had any money left to book a hotel. If we hadn't won tonight, the label wouldn't have existed tomorrow.

I was grateful for the silence. Dance music still thumped in my skull. I curled up and laid my head on the cool leather of my purse. The photo was tucked inside. Why I'd hidden it from Robin, I wasn't entirely sure. The story lived in a place within me to which he had no access, a room in my soul whose door I had long since locked, whose key I'd hidden in a secret location I could no longer remember.

My grandfather—a blank spot on the family map, an undiscovered island no one had attempted to find. His arrival was the answer to a question that had never been asked. His existence meant nothing to me, because my father alone, or rather his absence, was all my mind had been able to grasp. It had never even occurred to me that this stranger might have a mother and father of his own—that was how unfathomable, even inhuman, he'd seemed.

My father simply didn't exist. I had my mother, and that was enough. Had to be enough. I'd seen him once in my life, one single time. Shortly thereafter, my mother had told me he'd died. Car accident. I was a kid, so all I understood was that he was gone, forever. I'd never consciously missed him, because I never had him. But something was missing. And not knowing what or who it was, not being able to put a name to that missing piece, amplified the desire for it. Without an object, a place to direct that indeterminate longing, that unmet need, absence becomes almost like a default condition. You stop questioning its presence. Regardless of how rich and fulfilled your life might otherwise be, you're never satisfied—not with what you have, not with what you are. Something's missing.

Growing up without a dad was nothing unusual in my generation. Couples who stayed together seemed to be the exception. Families were flimsy, temporary constructions built on feelings that fade, hopes that die, and conventions that shatter. What set me apart from my friends was that, unlike the kids with divorced parents, I couldn't visit my dad on weekends; even the kids who planned on tracking down their biological father had someone out there to find. I had no one.

That sense of incompleteness may have been what made me want to design clothing. I wasn't content with the world as I found it. I wanted to fill in the blanks with my own imagination, to project my own colors and shapes onto the canvas of possibility. Why fashion specifically, I don't know. Maybe because it was something tangible I could experience even as a child by dressing my dolls. Dolls were great because they were off-limits. I had to save up my allowance to buy my Barbies in secret, and then hide them under my bed. Barbies were reactionary, unemancipated commercial crap. If I'd been a boy, my radical-leftist mom would have forbidden me to play with toy guns. And I would have ended up marching into Afghanistan.

I fell into a deep, restless sleep. I dreamed we were driving back to Munich. The Alps. A serpentine road. Cool, humid mountain air, wet asphalt, moss on the cliff faces, a sublime landscape of eternal stillness, but I was driving much too fast. Next to me, where Robin was supposed to be, sat a man I didn't know. My grandfather. He shouted something I couldn't understand, a warning, but it was too late: I was racing toward a sharp curve. The rusty guardrail loomed up ahead. I tried to swerve, but the car didn't respond. It smashed hard into the rail, sending shards of glass all around us as the car flipped, careening into the abyss. A fluttery feeling in my stomach as the car tipped forward, plunging into the chasm beneath us. Nothing I could do. I was free-falling into the depths, weightless for a moment that seemed to stretch into infinity. I knew with immutable certainty that my life would be over in seconds.

And then I saw a face. Like my own reflection. The Italian woman in the photo.

I awoke, drenched in sweat. It took me several seconds to realize I wasn't dead. I looked around. The car was fine. It wasn't moving. The sky was growing light outside the fogged windows. Robin still hadn't returned. A few birds were beginning to sing; a bus rumbled by in the distance.

I opened the car door, clambered out awkwardly, and sucked in a deep lungful of the misty morning air. *People die quick as hell,* I thought. One little twitch of your hand on the wheel, brake a few seconds too late, and bam, you're flying off the road. The faster you're going, the less control you have. So, you grip the wheel tight and keep your eyes open, because you've built something for yourself. You have plans. You have a job to do, a calling, a destiny.

You tell yourself there's only one sin—the sin of wasting your talent. Not becoming everything you could be. Talent is a blessing as well as a responsibility, an obligation to use life's undeserved gifts to give back to the world.

I'd always believed that, at a certain point, I'd become the master of my own fate. But who's really behind the wheel? The events of that spring were completely out of my hands, as though set in motion long before.

I was merely part of a greater whole.

4

Our little atelier turned into Grand Central Station. Journalists, buyers, and agents were beating down our door. Barely twenty-four hours after we'd presented our collection, everybody was already asking about the next one. I'd pictured our big break as the moment when we could finally catch our breath. Step off the hamster wheel, rest on our laurels. But now I realized that it actually meant the opposite. More pressure, not less. Yanked into the spotlight, I would have to prove that I deserved the attention, that I wasn't a flash in the pan. And I still felt like I'd been whacked in the head with a wrecking ball.

Robin was firing on all cylinders. Wildly determined to make the most of this opportunity, he was on the phone every day with the Italians, our designated sponsors. I wasn't sure whether they saw themselves as part of our prize or us as their trophies. The company already owned dozens of labels, including several famous houses whose founding families they'd bought out years ago. Robin told them that I'd already designed our next collection. In reality, I had zilch. I was completely burned out. I forced myself back to the drafting table and pumped myself full of coffee, but couldn't come up with a single usable sketch.

Sure, I was happy that we were finally getting recognition for all those years of hard work, but something inside me didn't believe I actually deserved it. I spent hours staring at my sketchbook. My thoughts kept drifting back to Milan—not to the stage, but to the man in the mirror. The meteorite that had crashed into my life.

At night, once I was alone in the atelier, I took out the old photo, brought it over to the mirror, and stared at the Italian woman until her face seemed to melt into mine. Two women in two different eras who looked like twins. Giulietta. Where was she now? Was she still alive?

I tried to imagine what that man had meant to her. And why, near the end of his life, seeing me was so important to him. Were we really related? A grandpa. I didn't know what that felt like. I'd visited my mother's dad a couple of times when I was a kid, but then they'd fallen out. "Old Nazi," she called him.

If it was true that the woman in the picture was my grandmother and Vincent was my grandfather, then I was actually a quarter Italian, not half. Because my grandfather wouldn't have been a guest worker. Not that my "immigrant background" had ever meant anything to me either way. I'd grown up in the complete absence of such categories. My identity was one I'd created for myself, not something passed down to me. Until I saw the woman in that photo. All at once, I understood that the unidentified thing I'd been missing had a human face. And that it wasn't missing anymore.

I looked him up online. Dr. Vincent Schlewitz had been a successful manager at BMW until his retirement twelve years ago. Wikipedia listed him as having developed several cars whose names and model numbers didn't strike me as familiar. He'd been born near Katowice, Upper Silesia, in 1930. Nothing about his biography suggested any ties to Italy, let alone to a specific Italian woman, or to my father.

Somewhere in the depths of the internet, I discovered a photo of Vincent and his wife at a benefit gala. She was blond, blue-eyed, statuesque. Nothing like the delicate, dark-haired girl in the photo. Like he'd said, they lived here. What sane person would go all the way to Milan to meet me when he could have just taken a tram across Munich?

I would have written off the whole encounter—if not for that photo. The woman who was practically a mirror image of me.

Robin noticed. "Where are you?" he kept asking. "You're so out of it!"

He didn't understand how I couldn't come up with anything—especially now, just when we'd gotten exactly what we'd always wanted. I blamed it on the dizzy spell. Why couldn't I just tell Robin the truth? We talked about everything, but we didn't dig too deep, didn't poke at each other's old wounds. Our relationship was based on an unspoken agreement to exclude the dissonant colors from the mosaic of life. But shutting your eyes to things doesn't make them go away. They only grow more powerful and destructive the longer they're ignored.

When I was alone at night, the shadows would emerge to resume our unholy conversations.

Robin was right, though. I was out of it. Maybe I'd never really been entirely in it. Part of me was always somewhere else. I had one foot on the ground and the other in the clouds, as though I didn't quite trust this world.

Work had always been my way of checking out from reality. I could spend nights on end sketching and sewing without seeing another living soul—for an hourly wage barely enough to live on. What for? Why did I keep driving myself to the brink of total exhaustion? Because it was a rush more sublime than any other.

I went to my mother's to pick up my cat. A fashion designer should avoid having pets or houseplants, unless they also have a slightly lonely mother. Tanja—I've been calling her by her first name since I was little—had just moved out of her two-bedroom apartment and into a place she shared with several other aging hippies: a fellow retired journalist, a graying French teacher with a particular fondness for the Western Sahara, and an Afghani asylum seeker who cooked fantastic Thai food. It was sort of an un-retirement home: they were all old enough to leave their day jobs behind, but they were a long way from being done with the world. Having quit her editorial position, my mother was now a freelance journalist for political magazines.

Moving boxes were still piled everywhere, which was paradise for my cat, who ignored me pointedly. Tanja opened a bottle of Prosecco, and we raised a toast to the prize I'd won. Now, all of a sudden, she was proud of her fashion-designer daughter, even if it wasn't the fashion she liked so much as the female-empowerment story. She passionately blocked out the fact that my success was largely thanks to my male business partner's bourgeois parents.

My mother rarely asked about my work—less out of disinterest, more out of contempt for the fashion industry. A woman who drove cars until they were ready for the junkyard, she applied the same philosophy to clothing. The striped green sweater she had on now dated back to the previous millennium. Although she always emphasized how proud she was that I'd forged my own path, she considered fashion hedonistic, superficial, and consumerist. I didn't entirely disagree, but I would still have preferred her to keep her opinions to herself once in a while.

As far back as I can remember, she's always been fighting for something—or against something. When I was a kid, it was the state and nuclear energy; now, it's climate change. And throughout it all, men. She has always had a very clear concept of right and wrong—slightly too clear for my taste, and too unalterable. Granted, you could put it another way: she's stayed true to her convictions.

The only thing she's ever given up is smoking. Nowadays, when I stand near smokers, I can't help recalling the smell of my childhood, of long-haired guys in jean jackets and full ashtrays on the wooden table. She's nice-looking, extremely well read, and no one would ever accuse her of not knowing her own mind.

One thing I have to give her credit for is that she never forced her views on me. She's one of the most honest, upright, incorruptible people I know, and I'm not exaggerating when I say that I wouldn't be where I am today without her. She always encouraged me to go my own way. *You don't have a chance, so use it*—that was her favorite saying. And as different as our lives are, I'm closer to her than to anyone else in the world.

Once the Prosecco was gone, I pulled her into her room—boxes of books, a desk, and a laptop. She didn't need much else.

"So . . . ," I began casually, "my dad . . . Did you ever meet his parents?"

She was completely thrown. We never talked about him.

"Why do you ask?"

"No reason."

She gave me a mistrustful look.

"Mom, come on, just tell me. His parents, where were they from?"

"You already know all of that stuff. Why are you digging up old stories?"

"Doesn't matter. I just want to know."

"Sicily, like I told you."

"Both?"

"Both what?"

"Both mom and dad?"

"Of course. They only marry other Sicilians. That was the big scandal back then—I wasn't one of them."

"Do you remember their names?"

"His mother's name was Giulietta."

"Is that why you named me Julia?"

"That was my idea."

"Did you ever meet them?"

"No. Why do you want to know all of this?"

"What about his dad? What was his name?"

"I can't remember."

"Is there any chance he could have been German?"

"No. They were immigrants. Came here in the sixties. Where on earth did you get the idea he was German?"

I paused. *Should I tell her?*

"You never saw them in person, though?"

"No!" Now she was really starting to get upset.

I hesitated briefly before dropping the bomb.

"Do you know a Vincent Schlewitz?"

"No. Who's that?"

"Showed up in Milan, says he's my grandfather. *His* father." We never spoke my father's name aloud.

I took the photo out of my jacket. The happy couple in Milan. "Do you know them?"

Looking vexed, she put on her reading glasses, and then gaped in amazement.

"That's his mother," I said, then tapped the young man. "And that's the man I met."

Tanja peered at me warily over her glasses.

"What did he want?"

"He said . . . my dad . . . um, he said he's still alive."

Now it was out. She was clearly horrified.

"He's lying."

"He didn't seem like the lying type, Mom. He seemed . . . respectable."

"Then he's mistaken you for someone." Resolutely, Tanja returned the picture, as though declaring the matter closed.

"How old was I when he died?"

"I dunno, eight or so."

"But what if it's true? What if he's still alive?"

"It's not true. And even if it were, what difference would it make? To you, I mean? He left. End of story."

Her wording struck me as odd.

"What do you mean, 'even if'?"

"All I'm saying is, it wouldn't matter. Who you are and what you've accomplished, you did it without him. You're flying around the world, winning awards."

I sensed she was trying to change the subject.

"Did you ever actually see a death certificate? Some kind of proof?"

"No." She took my head in her hands. "Honey, that stuff is ancient history. We did pretty well for ourselves, just the two of us, didn't we?"

She smiled at me. I couldn't help smiling back. If anyone had taught me to persevere in the face of adversity, it was my mother. I took the photo back, found the cat, maneuvered his little butt into the cat carrier, and prepared to leave.

"Ciao, I gotta go. Maybe I'll meet up with the old guy someday, see what he has to say . . ."

I gave her a kiss and walked to the door. But she just stood there without saying goodbye. I turned around.

Tanja looked at me and gestured slowly to an empty chair. "Have a seat."

"Why?"

She pushed the chair toward me and took the one opposite. "We moved when you were eight, Julia. You remember that?"

I sat down. It was a vague memory. We'd moved around a lot.

"To Bernd's place, on Schlörstraße. You remember Bernd, right?"

Yeah. The name gave me a bad feeling. One of the Mr. Wrongs. From the moment we met, I couldn't stand him. That weird scruffy beard of his. He was one of the boyfriends who tried to play dad. And totally failed.

"You wanted to stay at the commune with the other children, and I wanted to finally be alone with you."

"And Bernd."

"Yeah. You were right—he was an idiot, but that's beside the point. Anyway, two days after we moved, you ran away. Remember?"

Now I did. The doll in my little suitcase. The red sandals. The fifty-mark bill I'd stolen from her purse.

"I looked all over for you. And then the cops picked you up at the train station."

The craziest thing I'd ever done as a kid.

"Where are you trying to go?" the cop had asked.

"To Italy. To my daddy."

When he'd asked which city in Italy, I hadn't known how to answer. Italy was Italy.

The memory hurt. I laughed in spite of it.

I can still picture my mother running into the train station. Me standing beside the policeman. My mother scolding me, her fear.

"I was so worried about you," she said. "And the . . . That's when I told you he was dead."

At first, I didn't understand what his death had to do with my running away.

"I was scared, honey. I was afraid you would run off again."

Slowly, the unbelievable truth dawned on me.

"That was a lie?"

Tanja took my arm. "You were so innocent. He would have . . . Vincenzo was unpredictable. You don't know him."

I couldn't get a word out. A world shattered inside me. If there was one person I'd always trusted, it was my mother. Through all the ups and downs, she was my most loyal companion. Or had been.

"I believed you . . ."

"I was just trying to protect you."

"Where is he now?"

"I don't know. Honestly."

The floor felt like it was swaying. She sat there, motionless. I couldn't look her in the eye. Just wanted to get out of there. I got up and left.

"Julia! Wait!" She tailed me down the stairs. "You were eight! What was I supposed to do? Come back! Julia!"

I got in the car and sped away. I'd forgotten the cat. I wasn't sure where I was going. Headed for the atelier as though on autopilot. Not being alone, that was the main thing. I parked around back. Robin was still there. He could tell something was wrong, but I waved him off and sat down to check my email. I had to be okay. And technically, nothing had happened, right? What difference did it make whether some guy I didn't know was alive or dead? Either way, he'd never wanted to see me, so why should I bother with him?

And then a ray of doubt shone through the tear in my worldview: What if he had wanted to see me? What if the whole damn story was actually completely different? Of course, if he was still alive, he could have come looking for me. Did knowing he wasn't dead make it even more painful that he'd never gotten in touch? Was my mother still my ally like always, or was she a liar who had cheated me out of my father? Who was this guy, anyway, and how the hell did anyone have this kind of power over me? My entire existence was going off the rails—and at the worst of all possible times, when I really did have more important things to do.

I took Vincent's business card out of the desk and went out to the courtyard to call him.

"Hi, this is Julia."

"Can we meet up tomorrow?" he asked.

We chose a neutral location, a gelato place in the meatpacking district. I told Robin I had a doctor's appointment.

5

It was one of the first real spring days. The sun broke through with unexpected warmth, signaling that winter was truly over. Everybody was outside. The tables in front of the café were packed with moms and their children, aging-philosopher types, and hipsters with lattes and laptops. People call the neighborhood around the meatpacking district and the market hall "the Italian Quarter," just like they call Munich "the northernmost city in Italy." Waiters here greeted everyone with *"Buongiorno,"* not because they didn't speak German, but because German customers loved replying in Italian.

I didn't understand people who ordered coffee in Italian just to prove how worldly they were. The Italophile intelligentsia and their children, the latte macchiato faction. I'd never seen myself as half-Italian. The three years I'd spent in London had influenced me far more than a bunch of genes. I'd lived in the neighborhood for five years and never set foot in this gelato place.

I made a point of arriving early. As I sat down at the only available table to wait, I suddenly felt like a little girl, angry and insecure. Why was I putting myself through this? *You're a grown woman,* I told myself. *You've made it this far on your own and never looked back. Why rip open old wounds?*

I felt cold sweat on my palms. Something within me was rebelling, telling me to get up and leave. Immediately. Then I saw him getting out of his car on the other side of the street. He was wearing a light, thin suit and beige perforated-leather gloves, which he removed with a practiced motion and set behind the steering wheel. His posture radiated the authority of success. He looked like he'd stepped out of a different era. He locked his car the way nobody does anymore— by hand, using a key. The car itself was a rare gem, a sleek, elegant 1960s model, silver-gray, sophisticated yet unpretentious, with perfect chrome and glittering spoke rims. It was easy to picture Grace Kelly in the passenger seat. His stride was determined, and there was still something boyish about him, but his back was slightly hunched.

Vincent spotted me immediately. I stood up, and we shook hands in a much-too-formal way. When I smiled, he seemed to transform into a young man and back again within seconds. The warmth in his face confused me.

He held out my chair for me. Old school. He and the man in the photo: two parentheses around a life, and between them a question mark that seemed to be eating him up inside. It wasn't until we were sitting across from each other that I saw how choked up he actually was. He cleared his throat, excused himself. To him, this apparently didn't seem like a get-to-know-you so much as an eerie reunion. I felt seen and unseen at the same time, as though he meant it for someone else. But the tender, attentive look in his eyes was so genuine and so overwhelming that a weird feeling of familiarity came over me as well.

I searched for similarities in his features, in his mannerisms. Everything about him seemed organized, grounded, and regulated, while my life was a chaotic puzzle made up of pieces that didn't fit together.

"Please excuse me for catching you off guard like that. I was really only there to see you onstage. But then when you . . . Well, I hope you're feeling better?"

I was grateful for the formal tone he took—somehow it gave me the emotional distance I needed. I nodded.

"So, how long have you been stalking me?" I asked, with a coolness that surprised even me. I sensed that the question hurt him, and maybe I'd wanted it to. A look of regret spread over his face.

"I apologize. It wasn't intentional. I was actually looking for Vincenzo. I didn't even know about you. And then . . ." He was obviously struggling to keep his emotions in check.

"Why did you follow me to Milan? We live in the same city."

"It was a moment of madness, born of nostalgia. When I saw you there up onstage, my God . . ." Now there were tears in his eyes. I did my best to remain unmoved.

"Giulietta would have been proud of your success," he said. "You're living your dream."

I frowned in confusion.

"She was a seamstress as well. She was extremely talented, but she didn't have the opportunities you do. I think your father gave you that name in honor of his mother. He loved her more than anything."

I glanced down and saw a gold ring on his left hand. "Where is she now?"

He shook his head almost imperceptibly, unable to speak the answer aloud: she was gone. But his silence told me that she wasn't dead to him. There are two ways to die. Some people leave this world at peace with themselves. Others go against their will. And an invisible part of them is still here.

The waiter broke the silence. Vincent ordered his espresso in Italian. Unusual for someone of his generation. But his accent was German—that much I could tell—and nothing about him seemed Italian.

"When were you last in touch with your father?"

"I met him once. I was a kid. A few hours. That was it."

"I'm sorry. I didn't know." The look on his face suggested that he wanted to adopt me right then and there.

"It's fine."

"He and I haven't been in contact in a long time . . . He wanted nothing to do with me."

"Hey, we have something in common," I remarked.

He smiled at me shyly and then averted his eyes. We sat in silence, two strangers connected only by a blank space, an absence, an unknown variable named Vincenzo.

The waiter set our cups on the table.

"But you're sure he's still alive?" I asked cautiously once the waiter was gone.

"Positive."

"Why are you looking for him?"

Vincent leaned in and lowered his voice. "I'll be honest with you. I've recently had a death in my family. My wife."

"Giulietta?"

He shook his head. "Giulietta and I weren't married." He watched, checking my reaction. I decided to go with poker-faced for the time being.

"When something like that happens, you realize just how quickly it can all be over. Young people like you are only focused on the future, but when you get older, you start looking back, and you don't want to leave without being forgiven."

He glanced around, apparently checking for eavesdroppers, but everyone was deep in their own conversations. He leaned close again. "I want to have my affairs in order before I go."

"Meaning what?"

"I want Vincenzo to get the inheritance he's entitled to. I have two daughters from my marriage, and . . . Anyway, more than anything, I owe him an explanation."

I raised a questioning eyebrow.

"I should have gone looking for him sooner, but I made a promise to someone . . . It's a long story. Anyway, now I have to break that promise. I hope it isn't too late." He paused and took a sip of his coffee. "After my wife's death, I hired a private detective to track Vincenzo down. So far, he hasn't found him, but he discovered that Vincenzo had a daughter."

He flashed a charming smile. I blinked, startled.

"If we never manage to find Vincenzo, or if he refuses his inheritance, it would go to his children instead."

I leaned back in my chair, confused. "No, thanks, I'm good."

"Don't you believe me?" He attempted to take my hand. I pulled it away.

"It's not really any of my business. My dad is a total stranger to me."

Vincent lapsed into thoughtful silence for a moment. Then he said, "People are only strangers until you've heard their stories."

I considered his words. It was difficult for me to admit, but I'd spent my entire life filling the blank space on my inner map with other things, distracting myself from that pain, substituting a better future for my past. Obviously, it hadn't worked. If it had, I'd be able to just get up and leave without tears springing to my eyes.

Sometimes I think we're inhabited by ghosts. The past is all around. It frightens us, so we run from it. The notion that there had once been a woman who looked just like me, and that her restless ghost was still living inside me, gave me the creeps. I wanted nothing to do with this family. But maybe that wasn't possible. I'd been running for thirty-six years, never turning around. Something inside me was exhausted. That something wanted to stop, to turn around and look the ghosts in the eye in order to be free of them at last.

"How did Giulietta die?" I asked Vincent.

He sat quiet for a long time.

"I've never talked about it."

He gave me a scrutinizing look, as if trying to figure out whether I was ready for his story.

"I have a proposal," he said. "I'll tell you what happened, and you decide whether you believe me. Then, whether we remain strangers or become friends, perhaps we can help each other."

6

Vincent

"It all started in Milan, in the summer of 1954," he began, "a year before Vincenzo's birth. I was an outsider there, and in a way, so was she. Giulietta's family was from the South, a small island near Sicily. Her grave is there as well."

"When did she die?"

"Slow down, one thing at a time. I was living in Munich. I was stranded after the war, a refugee from Upper Silesia. My mother and sister had died on the journey, in Dresden; my father lost his life in Russia. When the war ended, I was fifteen. I enrolled at the university and found a job at BMW. I was young and motivated, but the company was in the red. Our cars were too big. After the war, they only had one car in production—a large sedan, the 501. It was a good set of wheels, but hardly anyone could afford it. Back then, even Volkswagens were a luxury. We were starting from scratch, after all. Still, everyone had work, things were looking up, and people needed a way to get around. They needed small, cheap cars. But we didn't have the financial reserves to develop a vehicle for the masses. We were in danger of going under.

"And then the Italians got involved. At the 1954 Turin Auto Show, our CEO discovered a fascinating little car out of Milan. Tiny and ingenious, smaller than the VW Bug—it even fit into a parking space sideways. It was manufactured by Iso, which normally produced motor scooters, and this was a cross between a scooter and a compact car. The Isetta. Have you heard of it?"

"Yeah, of course. The bubble car."

He beamed. "The bubble car, exactly. With the door in front, like a refrigerator. The CEO came to us in Technical Development and said, 'Boys, we can buy the license to these things for cheap and start building them ourselves.' He wanted one of us to go down to Milan and put the car through its paces. I was the youngest, I didn't have a family, I could leave. They gave me a motorcycle, and off I went."

As he spoke, the years fell away from him. He seemed to grow lighter with every word, and I saw him as a young man on a motorcycle, puttering along through postwar Munich. It was hard to imagine what the city looked like then—halfway-reconstructed buildings interspersed with bombed-out ruins they would still be clearing years after the catastrophe. Thousands of homeless, thousands of trucks hauling the debris of destroyed homes to the edge of town, where the rubble mountains grew, dusty stone monuments to war, an area that would later become Olympic Park. As a child, I went there with my soapbox car, not knowing that the hill beneath my feet wasn't a natural hill at all. That was the day I saw my father for a single afternoon, the first and last time before he disappeared forever.

Vincent left the city behind. The highway was empty. A cool summer morning. It was his first time leaving Germany. Across the Brenner Pass, the gateway to the South: Rimini, Portofino, Tuscany. Places I had only heard about from friends, because my mother had taken me everywhere except Italy. France, Portugal, the former Czechoslovakia, even South America—those were my childhood destinations. Italy, my school friends' first beach experience, was taboo in our house. It didn't bother me, either. I never got why people were always raving about Rome or Florence, never understood how the coffee could possibly taste that much better, how the men could be that much more charming. Until I went to London to study fashion and discovered the Italian designers who embodied the opposites of those clichés: simple elegance, the art of proportion, appreciation for materials coupled with traditional craftsmanship.

Italy was still a mystery to young Vincent, known only through his romantic memories of reading Goethe in school.

Do you know the land where the lemon trees grow,

Amid darkened leaves the gold-oranges glow,

A gentle breeze wafts through the clear blue sky,

The myrtle stands silent, the bay laurel high?

Do you know it well?

'Tis there I'd be gone,

Together with you, O beloved one!

It was cold on the Brenner Pass, a barren, gray lunar landscape with nary a gold-orange in sight. Vincent passed wrecked vehicles with steaming radiators, German tourists in Volkswagens, and trucks struggling up the mountain with whining engines. Armed American GIs stood at the border between Austria and Italy, reminding travelers who was supervising the fledgling democracies in the defeated Axis nations.

The first thing Vincent noticed on the southern side of the Alps was the light. It was as if a veil had been lifted from his eyes, a gray film he was so accustomed to that he had never noticed it. He rode faster and faster down the winding roads, feeling the sun growing warmer on his skin, and when he stopped at the riverwalk along Lake Garda, dismounted, and removed his glasses, the sight took his breath away. He'd never seen a palm tree in his entire life! Palm trees—those were for rich people who could afford tickets on ocean liners or flights to America aboard the Super Constellation. Completely out of reach. But here they were, just standing there like it was no big deal, so close he could touch them. Their fine leaves whispered in the breeze; waves crashed against the quay; shards of sunlight glinted on the endless blue. A sheer excess of beauty. Children were playing in the piazza; the scent of lemon trees hung in the air. Vincent removed his leather gloves, breathed in the mild air, and suddenly understood what Goethe had been trying to say. It could scarcely be put into words, this unexpected, undeserved, overflowing awakening of all his senses.

By the time he reached Milan, the sun was already low in the sky, and rain clouds were gathering. Here, the colors he'd absorbed on the way disappeared into the gray of the urban canyons. Endless, faceless suburbs; fascist residential blocks; six-, ten-, twenty-story office towers; sleek department stores and futuristic exhibition halls, cathedrals to modernity. This Milan was not the *bella Italia* of the old love songs, of quaint fishing boats in the pale light of the crescent moon. It was a sea of motor scooters racing up and down the eight-lane boulevard, a metropolis pulsing to the beat of the stock exchange, the banks, and the factories. Vincent checked his old city map for the address of his downtown boardinghouse. Lost in traffic, with the streetlamps and shop windows blazing to life around him as night fell, he marveled at how much smaller and stuffier Munich seemed in comparison.

All at once, he found himself in the largest square he'd ever seen. The huge, ornate facade of the cathedral dwarfed the surrounding passersby; beside it, no less grand, was the archway to the Galleria Vittorio Emanuele II, with its fashion boutiques beneath a massive glass dome. Brightly lit display-window arcades in perfect symmetry. Genteel waiters in black suits served aperitifs at cloth-covered tables. On the rooftops, gigantic neon signs illuminated the night: Cinzano, Campari, Coca-Cola. Whatever his war-veteran coworkers had said about the Italians' supposed backwardness, lack of discipline, and lousy morale, this panoply of architectural perfection and sophisticated elegance proved them wrong. Families strolled across the piazza, the men in dark suits and the women in evening dresses and coats, with fashionable hats and stoles around their shoulders. They were style-conscious in a way that was as self-evident as it was understated, free of bravado or trendy aberrations, an unbroken tradition incorporating the gloss of modernity with an air of nonchalance. An attitude that had gone extinct in postwar Germany, if it had ever existed there in the first place.

It started to rain. The Milanese opened their umbrellas and walked faster; Vincent stood beside his motorcycle, the only person without an umbrella, a foreigner among locals hurrying into their apartments and restaurants . . . and suddenly he realized that today was his birthday. A day he hadn't celebrated in a long time—who was there to celebrate with? He didn't have anyone anymore. Yet, rather than sadness, he was filled with the simple joy of being alive. The war was over; a new Europe was emerging from the ruins; and he didn't owe anyone a thing. The world was full of possibilities. He drew in a breath of the fresh, humid air. He was twenty-four, young and free, determined to make something of his life.

7

*"Capo ingegnere Ermenegildo Preti! Il progettista Dottore Marco Gobini! Pierluigi
Raggi, capo ufficio tecnico! Gianfranco Sassi, soprintendente della catena di
montaggio . . ."*

Vincent reached out to shake one hand after another as he walked down
the row of engineers assembled outside the Iso factory in suits and ties to greet
the emissary from Germany.

One of them could even speak a little broken German, having fought under
Rommel in the desert. *"Buongiorno, piacere,* nice meet you!"

Renzo Rivolta, the owner of Iso, introduced each man personally. Rivolta
was Italian nobility and an old-school entrepreneur: pin-striped gray suit, green
pocket square, perfectly polished shoes. An energetic and charismatic man.
Vincent could immediately sense that he viewed the company as a family and
the men as his children. A strict but benevolent padrone.

The engineers, all of them older than Vincent, were polite enough to mask
their surprise that BMW had only sent a twenty-four-year-old whelp. One that
didn't speak a word of Italian, to boot. Vincent had barely slept a wink in his
sticky room at the little boardinghouse—he was far too excited. This licensing contract was a major event for his own company as well as Iso; BMW
was urgently in need of a compact car, and Iso desperately needed a win. The
Isetta wasn't selling well in Italy—it was practical but not attractive. And just
as Germans think things are good only if they're practical, Italians think they're
good only if they're beautiful. Even Iso's factory in Bresso, a suburb of Milan,
was a model of modern architecture, with sweeping arched roofs and large bright
windows. As the Italians chatted away to Vincent, discreetly ignoring that he

didn't understand a thing, Renzo Rivolta realized that they would need an interpreter. "Bring me someone who speaks German," he ordered his assistant, who immediately ran off to ask around among the workforce. Without anyone noticing, a short young man broke away from a group of assembly-line workers to address Rivolta.

"*Scusi, Commendatore . . .*"

The engineers looked taken aback at the worker bee's forwardness, but Rivolta turned to listen. Vincent didn't know what to make of the man's rapid speech and gesticulations, but he noticed how different the worker's physiognomy was from that of Rivolta and the Northern Italian engineers. He was smaller, with darker, more olive skin, and his respectful, almost submissive posture stood in contrast to his spirited speech and the roguish intelligence that twinkled in his eyes. Rivolta nodded, and the man ran into an office.

Shortly thereafter, he returned, holding the hand of a young secretary, who hurriedly adjusted her neat, pale-blue suit. She was younger than Vincent, with a bold mid-length hairstyle, yet he saw something unfathomably ancient in her eyes.

"*Ecco, Commendatore!*" the worker announced.

The woman gave a small curtsy, smiling, and Rivolta asked her name.

"Marconi. Giulietta," she replied.

Even to this day, Vincent still remembered how she said her surname first. And he remembered the gleam of her dark eyes; her fine cheekbones; her delicate, but energetically tense body; her voice, clear yet sensuous; and the first German word she said to him, shyly, but with a warm smile and a pronounced but pleasant accent: "*Willkommen.*" She introduced herself as a secretary in the sales office, explaining that she had taken some German as part of her stenotypist course and would be interpreting for him. Their eyes met for a fraction of a second longer than expected; then she looked away again, whether out of shame or courtesy, he wasn't sure. That first glance—was it one second? Two?—contained everything that remained a lifelong mystery to Vincent: how Giulietta's youthful passion and zest for life wrestled with an old force inside her, a dark shadow of melancholy and futility. When we encounter a great love, for one brief moment, we are freed from our imprisonment within space and time. We meet not only the person, but something that shines through them, a premonition that we might be granted the joy of rediscovering the abundance of childhood, back when the world was one eternal summer.

"Giulietta," she said, laughing. "Like Romeo *e* Giulietta."

"Pleasure to meet you. Vincent Schlewitz," he replied stiffly, and held out his hand in a formal gesture. He was trying to hide the impression she had made on him. Was the short worker who had brought her out and was guarding her jealously her husband? Her boyfriend? Neither wore a ring, but there was no mistaking the strong bond.

The Isetta was not a car. It was a ball, a curiosity, an egg on wheels. Ermenegildo Preti, creator of the ingenious design, had constructed planes during the war. Rivolta, then a refrigerator manufacturer, had commissioned him to design the Isetta, and what came out was something like an airplane cockpit with a refrigerator door in front. The back wheels were so close together that, at first glance, it looked like a tricycle. You could either laugh at the egg-mobile or marvel at Preti's ingenuity: no one had ever managed to cover so little space with so much car. So much mobility for so little money. Indeed, the Isetta was an avant-garde design. Since it ran on a nine-horsepower, single-cylinder motor scooter engine, people could even drive it with just a moped license. And with its sensational gas mileage, it was a car for everyone: cheaper than the Volkswagen Beetle, cheaper than the Fiat Topolino, the Isetta was a milestone in mass mobilization.

As Vincent wedged himself onto the narrow upholstered bench alongside Preti, Giulietta translated the designer's brisk engineering lingo as best she could. Inside, the Isetta was surprisingly airy, with its large glass panels and tiny window posts. Preti unrolled the cloth roof, so that Giulietta was gazing down at the two men from above. She let out a laugh as Vincent moved the creaking gearshift into first and the Isetta jolted forward. As Vincent began accelerating, Preti kept right on talking, forcing Giulietta to trot alongside until at last she gave up, gasping for breath. Vincent saw her laughing in the rearview mirror as Preti tried to shout over the noise of the tiny engine. He sped up until the speedometer needle quivered and he was afraid that the clattering frame would collapse beneath him.

"Vai, avanti!" Preti shrieked, and even without his interpreter, Vincent understood that it was an order to stop pussyfooting around. He maneuvered the Isetta in a zigzag, braking, speeding up, circling around Giulietta, who stood there grinning patiently in the sun. It was like dancing on wheels. After he finally brought the Isetta to a halt and Preti swung open the door, Giulietta asked, "How did you like it?"

"Impressive," Vincent replied, squeezing out, as Giulietta translated into Italian. "Just needs a little more horsepower. And there's something wrong with the rear axle." Ermenegildo Preti repudiated the rear-axle remark indignantly. Vincent asked Giulietta to translate that it wasn't a design flaw, probably just an irregularity, slight vibration, maybe a part had come loose.

"Impossibile," Preti retorted, and when Rivolta and the others joined them, Preti ordered his engineers to dismantle the rear axle and check every inch. They didn't want to show weakness in front of the German.

While they worked, Vincent waited near the hydraulic lift in the assembly shop, Giulietta standing tensely beside him. Pointing out flaws to an experienced engineer like Preti in front of his whole team made Vincent uncomfortable, but he was certain he was right. Renzo Rivolta watched in silence as the engineers disassembled the rear axle. Preti himself lent a hand. *"Porca miseria!"* he shouted as he ran a finger along the axle. The others surrounded him, eyeing the axle, but none of them could find an issue with it. Preti, ignoring them, waved Vincent over. At first, Vincent didn't see a problem, either, but then Preti pointed to a hairline crack.

"Come l'ha sentito?" he asked Vincent in astonishment.

Giulietta translated with her delicate accent. "How did you feel that?"

Vincent shrugged. "Butt-o-Meter."

Giulietta gave him a questioning look. She hadn't heard that one in school. Laughing, Vincent pointed to his behind, and once Preti understood, he began to laugh as well. *"Butt-o-Meter! Bravo!"*

He clapped Vincent on the shoulder admiringly. The ice was broken, and the German had a new nickname, "Signor Butt-o-Meter"! Vincent blushed. His eyes met Giulietta's, and she grinned at him mischievously. He realized that she liked him.

Never had Vincent felt himself at home so quickly. Renzo Rivolta invited him to dinner at his villa. The feudal family estate was right next to the factory; he had actually built the plant in the park in front of his home. He introduced Vincent to his wife and children, complained about the workmanship on his Maserati, and told him about his dream: someday, he said, he was going to create a better sports car. In the cafeteria the next day, Chief Engineer Preti and their colleagues showed the German how to twirl those long Italian noodles around a fork rather than cutting them with a knife—which struck Vincent as rather impractical until he got used to it. They drank wine with lunch and ate three-course dinners, and in the mornings, they drank coffee from tiny cups. Giulietta was with them some days; other times, she was needed in the office.

Communication got easier all the time; engineers around the world used the same syntax of millimeters, seconds, and kilograms. As they broke the Isetta down into its individual parts, installed a BMW engine brought in from Munich, logged test results, and optimized the design, the Italians made the German feel like he was a member of the Iso family. Their affection caught him completely off guard. Ever since he'd fled Silesia as a youth, he'd been a loner—not the type to pick fights with others, but not one who made friends easily, either. Work, studies, and career—those were his constants after losing the only people he'd ever relied upon.

Through no doing of his own, he'd become a man who cast his net far into the future, one who never looked back and who wasted no time on frivolities. He gave little thought to marriage and family, despite—or perhaps because of—being an orphan. Though his charm and his blue eyes made him a hit with the ladies, he'd never let any of his dalliances get too close. *A man needs a career first,* he told himself, *a steady income, and a home.*

It wasn't only Giulietta's unconventional beauty that captivated him. Looking back on their first few encounters, what he remembered most was the vague, baffling sense of having just met the mother of his children. Or was it merely wishful thinking? No other woman before or after Giulietta made him feel that way. Vincent didn't believe in destiny; he wasn't religious. In those last few years of the war, he'd experienced too many horrors at too young an age to believe anything other than that humans were on their own, that only rational thinking would save them from the seduction of false beliefs, and from their own spiritual abyss.

The end of the war had been his personal zero hour, the moment when he'd questioned everything he'd ever presumed to be true and become master of his own destiny. Yet now, as he approached the end of his life, it seemed to him that what happened in 1954 in Milan was not his decision, that it was a brief moment in which he was seized by life itself, as a wave in the current, as part of a larger whole. In that carefree summer, seeds were planted that would grow into the love affair of his life, Giulietta's death, and the curse on Vincenzo's soul.

Each evening at six o'clock, as the production staff left the plant and Vincent mounted his motorcycle, he saw Giulietta waiting at the factory gates. She was wearing something different every time: a checked suit one day, a green summer dress the next, and then white pantaloons. Always stylish, but never ostentatious. And one day, instead of riding out to the street, he stopped and asked if he could give her a lift into town.

"I'm waiting for Giovanni," she said.

"Is that your fiancé?"

"No," she laughed, "my brother. We are, how do you say, *gemelli*, born on the same day?"

A secret weight lifted from Vincent's heart.

"Twins," he said.

"Yes, twins." She pronounced it "tweens." He loved her accent.

"Giovanni is a trainee. On the Isetta production line."

Vincent nodded. An awkward pause followed, and they glanced at each other bashfully out of the corner of their eyes.

"Do you like Italy?" she asked.

"I haven't seen much of it," he admitted. "Venice, Florence, Rome—I've never been to any of them."

"Neither have I," she said.

His eyes widened.

"I'd like to go," she said, "but . . ." She shrugged and tried to laugh it off, but Vincent caught something there, in that frustrated laugh. That was the moment he first sensed her ravenous hunger for life, desire rattling from inside her composed exterior, determined to break out.

"I'll drive you to Venice in the Isetta!" Vincent declared, only half joking. She smiled.

"Giulietta!" It was Giovanni, emerging from the factory with his buddies.

"Arrivederci," Giulietta whispered, and hurried to her brother.

Vincent watched her go, admiring her light gait, how it belied the heavy heart that had briefly shone through. She kissed Giovanni on both cheeks, the way people did here with friends and relatives, and then they walked to the tram stop outside the factory gates. Giovanni walked on one side of Giulietta; on the other was another factory employee. He looked Sicilian as well—dark skin, black hair—but seemed quieter than Giovanni, a bear with powerful hands and a solemn expression. Although he didn't touch Giulietta, the way he separated her from the other workers, and the way they instinctively complied, signaled that he saw himself as her protector. Not a guy to mess with.

8

Giulietta would get out early. Instead of six o'clock on the dot, she was out-side the gate five minutes before shift end, waiting for Giovanni and the other man, which gave Vincent a chance to talk to her without interruption. He, too, slipped out of the engineering office a tiny bit before everyone else, and those few minutes before the whistle blew, when they stood side by side at the factory gates making small talk, were the most wonderful of his day. Once, he saw her sketching something in a small notebook, which she stuck in her purse when she saw Vincent approaching.

"What are you drawing?" he asked.

"Nothing," she replied.

But he narrowed his eyes quizzically until finally she pulled out a fashion magazine. The cover showed Gregory Peck and Audrey Hepburn riding through Rome on a Vespa.

"*Roman Holiday*. Have you seen it?"

"No."

"I like this." She pointed to the white, high-waisted skirt Hepburn was wearing. "I stole it," she added, grinning.

Vincent didn't understand until she brought out her sketchbook and showed him a pencil drawing of the same skirt, modified slightly and combined with a jacket and a large hat. Vincent knew only technical drawings, not fashion-design sketches, but he could see that this wasn't the work of a hobbyist—this was a woman who knew her craft.

"You make clothes?"

She nodded. Only then did he notice her new suit, high-waisted like the dress, made of sky-blue material with a subtle diamond pattern. "Did you sew that yourself?"

She nodded again. Modestly, but not without pride.

"Did you study fashion?"

"No, I started because my *mamma* only bought me boring good-girl clothes." She smiled mischievously.

"You're talented!" Vincent exclaimed. "Honestly, everyone here is always dressed so stylishly. Next to you, we Germans look like we're wearing potato sacks."

Giulietta laughed, and Vincent was about to ask her whether he could take her out that evening, when Giovanni clapped him on the shoulder.

"Tutto bene, Signor Butt-o-Meter?" Without waiting for an answer, he said something to Giulietta that Vincent didn't understand. She nodded.

"Giovanni's doing the night shift," she said quickly. "I'll ride home alone. Ciao!"

Before Vincent could reply, she broke away and headed for the tram. Giovanni eyed Vincent searchingly as they chatted, and then politely took his leave once Giulietta had gotten on the tram.

Vincent started his motorcycle. Viale Vittorio Veneto, which the tram line traveled down, was also Vincent's route back to his boardinghouse. He followed the tracks. The sun was already low in the sky, bathing the cobblestones in golden contre-jour light. When he caught up to the tram, he pulled alongside it, and saw Giulietta sitting by a window. She startled when she saw him zip into view. He waved, laughed, and then had to brake abruptly for a tram approaching in the opposite direction. It rang loudly as it rushed past, and Giulietta leaped up to check on Vincent. She ran to the back, past a ticket collector complaining about motorcyclists, to the rear platform, where she peered out the window. Vincent was following close behind. She signaled for him to watch out. He waved in reply, swerving back and forth and releasing the handlebars. She covered her eyes in horror, but then she couldn't help laughing along with him.

Vincent felt like a boisterous kid, as though he'd gone back in time to revisit the forgotten joy of riding his bike through the Silesian summer, racing through the wheat fields, with no yesterday and no tomorrow. He followed Giulietta through intersections and over bridges until she emerged at Naviglio Grande. He stopped beside her and removed his leather aviator cap with an exuberant laugh. A tirade of Italian rained down as she scolded him as if he were a small boy. Vincent didn't understand a word, and he went on beaming at her until her expression finally brightened as well. If he hadn't already fallen in love, his heart definitely belonged to her now.

She glanced around, suddenly worried they were being watched.

"Do you live here?" Vincent asked.

Giulietta didn't reply. Women were washing their laundry at the banks of the old canal that ran perfectly parallel to the street. The red sunset reflected on the water, and on the opposite side of the road, simply dressed waiters were setting up tables on the sidewalk near the tram tracks. The apartment buildings here were plain and not very tall, perhaps four stories. There was a small tobacco shop on the ground floor. Clothes were drying outside the windows, and children were playing soccer among the parked Fiats. It was a small, self-contained world far from the sophisticated boulevard. A *quartiere popolare*. This was where factory workers lived, along with hotel maids, vendors from the market, cobblers and seamstresses with their tiny dark shops.

"Will you show me Milan?" Vincent asked, overconfident.

Giulietta shrugged bashfully. "This is all I know."

"What about the rest? The cathedral? La Scala?"

Giulietta looked around, restless. "Those are for the Milanese. We are Sicilians. We work."

Vincent began to understand. "I'll show you, then. Hop on!" He gave her a provocative smile.

She blushed.

"Giulietta!" A woman's sharp voice rang out from a third-floor window.

Giulietta looked up. Vincent saw a hunched Sicilian woman, old before her time, with country features and black hair up in a severe bun.

"*Si, Mamma, arrivo subito!*" Giulietta called back.

Quick sentences flew back and forth, fascinating melodies Vincent couldn't decipher. As Giulietta turned to leave, she whispered, "Piazza del Duomo. Tomorrow at six o'clock."

Then she ran to her mother.

When the cathedral clock struck a quarter to six, Vincent was already in the square. Punctuality was in his blood, though it was mostly impatience that had driven him out of his small rented room. It was Saturday. The Milanese were strolling along the piazza, clutching shopping bags from the Galleria Vittorio Emanuele boutiques, and Vincent realized why Giulietta had chosen what seemed like the most public place in the city for their rendezvous: this was high-society territory; they wouldn't run into any of her relatives here. Vincent had bought himself some Italian aftershave that morning and put on his best shirt—the only good one he owned, in fact. The evening before, he'd asked his landlady to wash, starch, and iron it. The brown leather bomber jacket he normally wore was back in his room. It was a beautiful day; the air was filled with the promise of summery weightlessness.

He watched a boy chase pigeons across the piazza—and suddenly Giulietta was standing in front of him. She looked fantastic. He didn't notice her dress. All he could see was her smile. It wasn't just on her lips; it radiated from the depths of her eyes, unexpectedly vibrant, shy and yet teasing in a friendly way. She simply smiled away her shame at meeting up with a foreign man behind her family's back. And before Vincent, still mesmerized by her very presence, could offer a handshake or say a word, she asked briskly, "*Allora*, you're going to show me Milano?"

They stepped through the arched gateway leading into the Galleria Vittorio Emanuele. Underneath the gigantic glass dome, sophisticates sat in cafés, the men purposeful but unhurried, the women with cool noblesse. The shop windows were theatrical stages; the clothes, bags, and shoes on display were not mere objects, but works of art. Even the two policemen, casually patrolling in their dashing uniforms, looked as though they'd come straight out of the fashion boutiques. This was a shopping mall transformed into a piazza and a cathedral—not a loud market, but an oasis of strolling, public yet discreet.

Even though the sounds of other voices filled Galleria Vittorio Emanuele, Giulietta instinctively lowered her own voice. She confided that she sometimes came here in secret when the new season began and the shops redecorated their display windows. She never bought anything, of course. She just looked for hours, lost in beauty. Afterward, when she returned home to her little world of Navigli, to her dark room, she felt no envy, no sense of loss—she went to bed perfectly fulfilled, knowing that in her dreams she would wear those clothes, be radiant and carefree.

The next day after work, she would go to the seamstress in the neighborhood, a fat Apulian woman with a beard, a smoky voice, and a big heart, and buy fabric on credit. Signora Malerba didn't carry the fine materials of the London and Paris couturiers, but she had an eye for quality and never let anyone sell her on the cheap stuff—her fabrics were always usable. All Giulietta needed was a pencil, a piece of paper, and her imagination. She'd close her eyes, picture the dress in the shop window, and then sketch it quickly from memory. She'd always change some small detail, whether it was lowering the waist slightly, shortening the sleeves, or playing around with buttons and appliqués. Never would she have dared call any of them her own designs, but adding a personal touch was important to her, no matter how subtle. She didn't need a tape measure to know how much cloth she would require to transfer the drape in the sketch into reality.

When he heard all this, it occurred to Vincent that his work was no different from hers: they both turned two-dimensional drawings into real, three-dimensional objects.

"What about this one?" he asked, pointing to her pastel pencil-skirted dress. "Did you make it, too?"

Giulietta smiled.

"All of them," she said. "I made all of them."

"Why don't you make a career out of it?"

Giulietta walked onward without replying.

"Being a secretary is a waste of your talent!" Vincent insisted.

Giulietta stopped in her tracks. "This is not Germany," she said, suddenly solemn. "You always need a *raccomandazione*. We aren't from the North. We are Sicilians, *terroni, capisci?*"

Without waiting for a reply, she went to the next display window, an elegant hat boutique, and pointed to a red ladies' hat with a wide, curved brim.

"Bella, no?"

Vincent refused to let her distract him. "It doesn't matter where you're from. It matters what you can do!"

Giulietta shook her head, tight-lipped.

"You have reason to believe in yourself," he added.

"You are a dreamer," she retorted. "You don't understand. You're an *ingegnere*, from a good family."

"No," he said. "My family isn't rich. I don't even have a family anymore. My parents and sister died in the war. I'm as poor as a church mouse. But that doesn't matter!" He shrugged, and Giulietta's expression softened.

"I'm sorry."

"You don't have to be sorry. I'm only telling you that because . . . When I came to Munich as a refugee, I was totally alone. I didn't know anyone. But then I said to myself, 'Okay, that also means you're free.' No father whose farm I'm supposed to take over, no commanding officer ordering me around. I needed to make money, so I thought, 'Well, what are you good at?' I've always been interested in cars, so I went to BMW—they were the only ones in the city—and I asked the doorman if they were looking for trainees. Young men were in short supply after the war, so I was in luck. Started earning my own money, and in the evenings, I went to the technical college. The reason I'm telling you all this, Giulietta, is that everyone has a calling, and missing yours would be a tragedy."

His speech made a strong impression on Giulietta. Even so, she didn't see how his experience would apply to her. "You have a different destiny," she said thoughtfully.

"What does destiny matter?" he scoffed.

"It's written in your hand," she said. "Let me see."

Vincent didn't believe in such things, but he liked the idea of putting his hand in hers. He opened his right palm. She didn't touch it, though—she merely studied the lines.

"Strong will," she said. "Long, successful life."

"That's all in there?" he asked with a wry grin.

She nodded fervently.

"I dunno," he replied. "What if another war breaks out tomorrow, and a bomb falls on my head?"

"Fate." She smiled.

He shook his head. "I don't believe in fate."

She went on smiling with a mixture of skepticism and courtesy. "What do you believe in, then?"

"Decisions."

She liked that answer.

"What about you?" he asked, reaching out. "What does your hand say?"

But she kept her palms hidden. All at once, he saw that her eyes were shimmering.

"You talk like my *papà*," she said, suddenly sounding like a lost child. She turned away and stared into the hatmaker's display window.

Vincent felt guilty for having overstepped.

"Come on," he said. "Let's go try that hat."

He smiled at her and opened the shop door. Giulietta stayed where she was, almost fearful. Never in her wildest dreams would it have occurred to her to walk inside such an elegant store.

"Why not?" Vincent asked, as though he didn't know.

"Too expensive," she said, shaking her head.

"So what?" Vincent laughed, and strode boldly into the boutique, hoping she'd follow.

He had never been in a shop of this kind. The realization hit him the moment he stepped inside and felt the genteel stillness settle onto his body like a cool cloth. The carpet seemed to swallow all noise; the air smelled of cold cigar smoke and fine perfume. The hats were arranged on tall shelves made of dark wood. As Giulietta watched from outside, the salesman—a lanky, older Milanese with a polka-dotted pocket square—approached Vincent. The leathery skin of his face was stretched taut across high, arrogant-looking cheekbones. If he was accustomed to a different type of customer, he didn't let it show.

Vincent didn't understand the man's words of greeting, but he gestured to the red hat in the window. The salesman nodded discreetly and removed the hat from the mannequin. Vincent waved Giulietta in. She shook her head, mortified, but when the salesman shot her a quizzical look, she had no choice. Inside, she told Vincent quietly in German that she didn't want the hat.

"Just try it on," Vincent insisted. "That doesn't cost anything!"

The salesman stood there patiently, waiting for a signal. Vincent gestured for him to give Giulietta the hat. The salesman told her something in Italian that Vincent didn't understand and that Giulietta opted not to translate. But she accepted the hat. The salesman pointed to a floor-length mirror framed in dark wood. Giulietta put the hat on cautiously. She looked at Vincent first, not the mirror, as though it were somehow unseemly for her to wear such a thing, as though it wouldn't be real if she didn't see it.

Vincent was enraptured. The hat accentuated her delicate femininity and brought out the inner strength she masked so well. She blushed under his enthusiastic gaze, and her curiosity won out—she had to at least glance in the mirror.

"Davvero bellissimo, signora," the salesman said reassuringly, and when she saw herself in the mirror, she knew he was right.

"Ask him how much it is," Vincent encouraged her.

"No."

She removed the hat immediately.

Vincent turned to the salesman. "How much?"

Stone-faced, the man glanced at the tiny price tag. *"Quattromilanovecentocinquanta lire."*

Vincent cast a questioning look at Giulietta, who gasped and hastily returned the hat.

"Grazie, signore."

She said the word *"signore"* with an almost imperceptible bow, as though this man were her superior, a priest, or some other person deserving of respect. The gesture irritated Vincent, as did the salesman's smug look as he took the hat without comment. He must have recognized her Sicilian accent, and the expression on his face as he carried the hat back to the window made it clear he thought she didn't belong here.

A rebellious voice inside Vincent wanted to tell her not to let this snob intimidate her. Not her, a woman to whom fashion was like oxygen.

"How much?" Vincent repeated more aggressively.

The salesman looked slightly baffled. He paused for a moment, then went to the counter and wrote something on a piece of paper. Vincent read the long row of numbers and, without having any idea how much money that might be in German marks, whipped out his wallet and fixed the salesman with a defiant stare.

"Certo, signore," the snob murmured, and the way he bowed slightly when he said *"signore"* filled Vincent with triumph.

He glanced impishly at Giulietta, who shook her head, blushing, but he could only watch as the salesman retrieved the hat from the window once more.

Vincent laughed as they walked out of the shop. "Put it on!" he said, taking the hat from its elaborate box.

Giulietta exploded. He was *tremendo, totalmente pazzo,* completely insane!

Grinning, Vincent watched her, catching only half of what she said. He wished he could kiss her right there and then. With a huff, she snatched the hat from his hand and put it on. She loved it, of course. Vincent still recalled how they turned toward the display window and gazed at their reflection as though they were a couple. He remembered the way she tilted her head to one side a little and looked so enchanting that he considered himself lucky just to stand next to her.

She held the brim of the hat in one hand, steadying it in the wind, and wrapped her other arm around his waist. He felt her slim body against his back and the warm breeze on his face. The night was glowing; the motorcycle was purring; and when he looked back, he saw her hair flying behind her. The empty evening street belonged to them alone, and he wished the moment would never end.

He dropped her off on the corner of the canal road. He wished he could walk her to her door, but that would be too forward. She removed the hat and placed it tenderly in its box.

"Thank you, crazy man," she said.

He would have kissed her if she hadn't run off. In the yellow light of the streetlamps, he watched her dash across the cobblestones to her building. The tables outside the trattoria were empty. A brightly lit tram rumbled past. Giulietta slipped inside without turning around. Her little world lay under a melancholic spell.

9

On Monday, Vincent waited by the factory gate, even more excited than usual. Yet she didn't come. Shortly after six o'clock, the production workers began to stream out. His searching gaze found Giulietta's brother, standing outside the hall and smoking with a few of his buddies. Giovanni broke away from the group and approached Vincent.

"Buonasera, Giovanni!" Vincent said.

Giovanni took a drag on his cigarette and regarded him coolly.

"Giulietta?" Vincent turned his palms up.

Giovanni tossed the cigarette to the ground. *"È andata a casa,"* he grunted. "Gone home." He stared into the distance as he said it. Giovanni stepped on the cigarette and didn't budge, signaling to Vincent that he was the one who needed to leave.

"Oh, sì, grazie," Vincent said, heading amiably toward the road. *"Ciao."*

Once Giovanni was out of sight, Vincent snuck back onto the property via the side entrance. He approached the office where Giulietta worked, in the side wing of the production hall, and peered through the window. The desks with the heavy typewriters, arranged in neat rows and columns, sat abandoned for the day. Vincent opened an iron door, walked down an empty corridor, and suddenly heard her voice. He sped up, wanting to call out to her, but then he saw that she wasn't alone. A man was helping her into her jacket. She was wearing heels, making her look taller than the man, but he was powerfully built and several years older. It was the guy he'd seen with her and Giovanni. Vincent stopped to watch them from a distance. No kiss, no familiar touches, barely a word exchanged. But there was something watchful, almost paternal in his behavior. She followed him to the door.

The next day, Vincent knocked on the door to the secretarial office, and then walked right in. He'd drawn up a list of extra parts he needed from Munich. Inside, six secretaries were typing and making phone calls; the air was filled with the tap-tapping of mechanical keys. Giulietta spotted him immediately. The other girls watched curiously as he walked over, greeted her cordially, and set the list on her desk.

"These are the parts we need from Munich. Express mail, please."

Giulietta nodded politely and went on typing. Vincent remained standing beside her. She seemed like a completely different person. What had he done wrong? He felt like a schoolboy. Giulietta glanced discreetly at a bag beneath her desk. Vincent looked closer and realized it was the hat box.

"I can't accept the gift." She spoke quietly in German, without looking up. "I'm sorry."

"Why not?"

She didn't respond, but he sensed an explosive mixture of emotions simmering inside her.

"It's from the heart," he added softly.

She went on typing. "People will talk."

He glanced around. The other secretaries hastily turned back to their typewriters.

"I see," he murmured, unsettled.

"No, you don't see," she hissed. "I'm engaged."

It hit him like a punch in the face.

"I u-understand," he stammered.

"No! You don't!"

The secretaries startled. Giulietta got up and ran out of the room to hide her tears, leaving Vincent behind, confused, with all eyes upon him.

Vincent went to assembly, opened the heavy iron door, and stepped into the hall. Metallic noise greeted him, louder and more chaotic than the clacking typewriters in the office. He walked past the large rails used to carry suspended Isetta bodies through the hall, all the way to the front, where they were lowered and screwed onto the chassis assembled on the line. The "wedding," they called that. All day, the men battled against the clock as the conveyor belt rolled onward at a merciless, constant speed. Giovanni worked here. Beside him, deep in concentration, stood the Sicilian he'd seen with Giulietta the day before.

Her fiancé. He performed his duties silently and efficiently, while his coworkers chatted, cursed, and cracked jokes around him. Only once did he pause, pull a handkerchief out of his overalls, wipe his brow, and then resume his toil. An inconspicuous, obedient soldier of labor.

The next day, as Vincent was busy working with the Italian engineers to adapt the four-speed gearbox to the BMW motor, he suddenly saw Giulietta standing in the open doorway. Her demeanor was resolute and withdrawn, but even at this distance, he could sense her agitation. He set down his Allen wrench and went over. "Mail for you," she said with an air of indifference. She handed him an envelope and left. It bore neither a mailing nor a return address. He glanced around, checking whether he was being watched, and then opened the envelope to read the letter. It was typed, in perfect German, with no signature. "I owe you an explanation. Tomorrow, 6:00 p.m., Piazza del Duomo."

They went to a small café where managers often stopped on the way home for an espresso or an aperitif. Men in dark-blue suits debated about the stock market and the weather. The walls were paneled in dark wood; steel signs advertised liqueurs and soft drinks; the barista behind the counter was fumbling with the largest espresso machine Vincent had ever seen. The scent of freshly ground beans filled the air. A summer shower was coming down outside; people hurried across the wide street. Giulietta and Vincent sat at a table near a floor-length window. The glass was fogged; an endless stream of cars drove past. The red hat was in its box under the table.

The waiter brought two servings of espresso.

"Why do you drink coffee in such little cups?" Vincent asked to break the silence.

"Why? That's normal."

He smiled.

"What are the cups like in Germany?" she asked.

"Bigger." He demonstrated with his hands. "About like that. And it's filter coffee. Easier to drink."

Giulietta pondered. "Easier, but is it better?"

Her smile barely concealed her sadness. Then she leaned in. "Enzo is from my family," she said apologetically. "A cousin, but not direct. Distant. He, how do you say, asked of my hand."

"For your hand," Vincent corrected. He fidgeted uncomfortably. "I'm really sorry. I didn't want to cause you any problems."

Giulietta was silent. He was dying to know what she was thinking. "So, when he asked for your hand, you said yes?" He didn't see an engagement ring on her finger.

"I couldn't say no," she replied. "Enzo is a good man. He found the apartment for my mother, my brother, and me. He has a job at Iso, and he gave us, how do you say, *raccomandazione*."

"He recommended you for the job?"

She nodded. "We had nothing left in our homeland. No money, no food, *niente*."

"Your homeland—Sicily, you mean?"

"Yes," she said. "But we're not *siciliani della Sicilia*. We are *eoliani*."

"*Eoliani?*" He struggled to pronounce the word.

"*Sì. Delle Isole Eolie*. Seven islands near Sicily."

Vincent had never heard of them.

"The most beautiful place in the world," she said gravely. "Do you know *Stromboli*? The movie? With Ingrid Bergman?"

"I've heard of it, but I don't go to the movies much."

"Stromboli is one of the seven islands. *È un vulcano attivo!* All the islands were volcanos in the middle of the sea: Lipari, Panarea, Filicudi . . . Our island is called Salina."

"Salina." He let the word melt in his mouth.

"*È la più bella delle isole,*" she said, and the memory made her eyes light up. "But life there is very hard. There's nothing there, only fishermen and farmers. My father worked in the field, for *capperi*—do they have *capperi* in Germany?"

Vincent was confused. He'd asked her a simple question, engaged or not, but she was jumping from one idea to the next. She pulled her dictionary out of her purse and flipped through it until she found the word: "Capers." Vincent didn't know what those were.

"Do you know *caponata*? *Spaghetti alla puttanesca*? *Vitello tonnato*?"

He shook his head.

She smiled. "Someday I'll make them for you!" Then she resumed her story. "My papà and Enzo's papà worked in Don Vittorio's field. Don Vittorio didn't live on the island—he was from Messina. But the land belonged to him. And if the land belongs to you, the people belong to you, too. When Don Vittorio came to the island, you had to kiss his hand. But my papà was *comunista*. You understand?"

He understood. Half of Germany was Communist now. His homeland had become part of Poland. His grandfather's farm had been nationalized.

"My papà said, *'La terra appartiene a chi la coltiva!'* The field belongs to the one who works it. He did the work, in summer and winter, but then Don Vittorio came and took the whole harvest. *No.* We needed a *rivoluzione, in tutta la Sicilia.*" Giulietta's face glowed with love as she talked about her father. "Enzo's father was sick, but he had no money for the hospital. He died. My papà was furious. Did a big strike with other farmers. They wanted *dignità*, how do you say, dignity."

Vincent nodded.

"Papà was a proud man. He said to me, 'When Don Vittorio comes, don't kiss his hand! We are not slaves!'" Giulietta stared into her cup, her voice more and more agitated. "Mamma was afraid. She said, 'We are poor; this is our fate.' But Papà said, 'Fate is not written. We make our fate.'" She fell silent.

"And then?" Vincent asked.

"The don sent men with guns. They shot. Work or death. The farmers were afraid. They went back to work. But my papà didn't want to give up. Better to die with honor than live without honor. He sold everything, took out a loan, and bought *biglietti*. Tickets?"

"Right."

"To America. With the *transatlantico*. For everybody. Including Enzo, his sisters, and his mamma."

"So, you went to America?"

"Almost. We packed our bags. He told us about Boston, about New York—I wanted to go there so much. And then, the night before we were leaving, the men came to our house. Don Vittorio's men. They beat my father. Broke his arms, his legs. Giovanni was a little boy—he couldn't help. I was so scared." She peered up at Vincent, making sure he was following.

"But why did they do it? He was going to leave anyway."

"Question of *onore*," she said.

He didn't understand. "Like revenge?"

She lowered her eyes. "All bones were broken. At Ellis Island, they send the sick ones away. They only take the strong ones into the country. Papà couldn't go. So, we all had to stay on Salina. But Papà was never able to work again. After a year, my papà was dead. Now Giovanni was supposed to work for Don Vittorio. *Capisci?*"

Vincent began to.

"Enzo went to Milan. My mamma phoned him so he would help us. And he asked for my hand."

"He asked your mother for your hand? Over the phone?"

"Yes. For later. I was small—what should I do? My mamma had no choice, and Enzo is an *uomo onesto*, honest, with work. Enzo came down from Milan by train, and during the night, he brought us all to the North. Found us an apartment and work. Enzo saved us."

Vincent was silent, thoroughly ashamed that he'd thought badly of Enzo. Cars continued rushing past outside the window, and the large neon advertisements on the rooftops began to flash. Modern Milan seemed oddly unreal next to the archaic homeland she described.

"Marriage was only *una promessa*. When I grow up. But now . . ." She bit her lip.

"Do you love Enzo?"

Giulietta gazed at him for a long moment, but she couldn't give him an answer.

On the way back, as the motorcycle rumbled down the wet streets, she gripped his waist with both hands. She never let go for a second. Abruptly, unexpectedly, she rested her head against his back. He could almost feel her heartbeat through his leather jacket.

He dropped her off at the corner again. Fog lay atop the canal like down fluff. Somewhere, the shadow of a cat scurried past. She glanced around, checking whether her neighbors were anywhere in sight, and then hurried off without saying goodbye. Vincent tried to sort out his emotions. He wheeled his motorbike around. All at once, he heard her footsteps approaching again. She was coming back. Breathless, she threw her arms around his neck. Then she kissed him, so desperately and passionately that it took his breath away. Before he could return the kiss, she ran off again.

Vincent rode much too fast through the city night. He'd forgotten to put on his aviator glasses; they were hanging around his neck, and the humid summer air slapped against his face. A hundred thoughts raced through his mind; a hundred feelings flooded his body. Lights flew past, and tears sprang to his eyes.

10

When they saw each other at Iso the next day, she was wearing a fire-engine-red dress. Giulietta was there to interpret for Vincent and Renzo Rivolta, who was personally inspecting the Isetta with the BMW engine. As much as Vincent loved her accent, he barely registered her words—all he heard was the sound of what she didn't say. That kiss had heightened the tension between them, growing more and more unbearable, like the electricity in the air before a storm.

He wanted to respect her wishes and put honor before feelings. But Giulietta was clearly torn herself. First, it was indecipherable codes of tiny gestures and things unsaid; then, it was a small pastry Vincent discovered on the dashboard of the Isetta; next, the loose shirt button she sewed for him during her lunch break. Stolen moments like snapshots, burned forever into his memory. Vincent and Giulietta side by side on the rusty guardrail along the test track, exactly as close together as propriety allowed, irresistibly drawn to one another. The way she bit off the excess thread on his shirt button and glanced at him out of the corner of her eye, at his shoulders and biceps, as he sat beside her in his undershirt, his face tanned, his upper arms still pale. The midday sun on their hair, the deafening chirp of the crickets in the bushes, the seconds of hesitation when they had to leave but weren't quite ready to part company. The tacit agreement not to discuss their feelings, and the secret wish that one of them would break the pact.

Instead, they talked about fashion or the future, and while he had a clear plan for his own life—he was determined to design cars himself one day—she said that people's destinies lay in God's hands alone. If there was a God, Vincent retorted, he would want people to make the most of what he had given them. Vincent encouraged her to do more with her talent. He wanted to know why she didn't apply for a job at a clothing company or enroll at a fashion design school. But whatever he said, she always found an argument against it, and it always had to do with her family. She couldn't go to school, because she had to earn money to help with the rent, and she couldn't work at a clothing company, because her fiancé was obviously expecting her to be a mother, just like her mother and her mother's mother and all the generations before. Surely it was no different in Germany.

"True," Vincent replied, "but everything is changing in Germany right now."

"In Italy," she said, "the fashion changes, but under the surface, everything stays the same."

"But Milan isn't Sicily. You live here now!"

She looked at him with that special smile, that mixture of skepticism, irony, and wishing he were right—not condescending, but not believing a word he said, either. She shook her head. "But Sicily is me."

Every day, they got a little closer. Fleeting touches when they said goodbye, hidden messages, and secret dreams were all they had to live on. Every day, they found a few minutes where they could forget the rest of the world, though they never mentioned that kiss, let alone repeated it. In those few, precious moments, they stole back the happiness life had denied them. Giulietta had stalled her engagement for months. Before Vincent's arrival, she'd been trapped between her rational knowledge that Enzo was a good man, and the vague restlessness in her heart, her hope that something else would happen. She didn't know what. But now it was happening. Giulietta was too young to bury her dreams, and with her, far from his country and out of the blue, Vincent found a home.

Once, she telephoned his boardinghouse to play him a German chanson she liked. He stood in the narrow, musty entrance as "*O Mein Papa*" sounded from her gramophone, crackling and distant.

Another time, she told her family she needed to buy fabric from Signora Malerba, but went to the movies with Vincent instead. It was the matinee at a small, packed theater in Brera. Their first time attending a public event together, but in sheltering darkness. Unlike Germans, Vincent learned, Italian moviegoers didn't simply watch the action on-screen—they were lively participants in it. They cursed at the bad guy, warned the commissioner of a trap, and shouted enthusiastic compliments at a particularly beautiful actress. It was a party. The men smoked, the women chatted, the children ran around the auditorium. Only

Giulietta watched the screen in mesmerized silence. She saw Germania: a green Alpine meadow filled with flowers, a happy girl in a dirndl being courted by a dashing young man in a checked shirt. These Germans were nothing like the uniformed Aryans her mother had told her about. They spoke the same hard, unmelodic language. But learning that language had allowed her to discover its hidden beauty, the clarity and precision of its compound nouns, the depths of the German soul. As a child on isolated Salina, she'd never seen *i crucchi*, who had fought against the Allied invasion on Sicilian soil. Her imagination had filled in the details adults had omitted in their descriptions of the tall, blond northerners, admirable and yet frightening in their military efficiency. "They're stronger than we are," one said. "They'll go eventually," the others replied, unconcerned. "Just like the Greeks, the Spaniards, and the Arabs. In the end, they all go home. Sicily will always remain Sicily."

And indeed, the Germans had departed; peace had come; and now she was sitting beside one who'd returned without a uniform and a gun. One who was so different from what she'd expected, yet also unlike Italian men. Giulietta wasn't afraid of the unknown. Quite the contrary: it sparked her curiosity and her desire to cross boundaries. She loved Vincent's courage, his clarity, his sincere smile, and his optimism about the future. And she loved his hands, the considerate way they held and shaped whatever it was he was working with. Practical engineer's hands, but also the hands of a sensitive, sentimental man.

All at once, Vincent felt Giulietta's small hand cautiously seeking his own across the wooden movie seats. He wasn't surprised by the warmth and tenderness of her touch; what surprised him was how her hand responded with such determination when he grasped it. She went right on holding his hand until the lights came up at the end of the movie.

It had gotten late. They were strolling home along the Naviglio Grande. Yellow lights danced silently on the canal surface; the night protected them from curious eyes. Giulietta had her head scarf pulled down low to cover her face and was holding Vincent's arm. She told him that Milan's canal-and-sluice system had been designed by none other than Leonardo da Vinci. An arch bridge spanning the Naviglio Grande soared up out of the darkness.

"Like Venezia," Giulietta remarked.

Vincent recalled that she knew as little about Venice as he did.

"Let's take the Isetta," he suggested with a jaunty grin. "We can be in Venice by morning!"

Giulietta laughed indulgently.

"Seriously," he said. "Why not?"

He expected her to dodge the question the way she always did when he brought up a future any more distant than the following day. But this time, she stopped walking, fixed him with a daring gaze, and declared, *"Andiamo a Venezia!"*

That was the moment he knew he had to tell her the truth. "I have to go back to Germany. My work here is finished."

A hand flew to her mouth. "When?"

"Tomorrow."

The lunch hour on his last day was all they had left. He and Preti had spent the morning loading the reworked Isetta onto an Alfa Romeo transporter, which was already on its way north. Now, he just needed to take the construction plans down from the walls and bring them to the post office, complete his test logs, and say goodbye to the team. He'd grown very fond of Iso, and the engineers were fond of him as well. Vincent was the man who was bringing their baby, their Isetta, to Germany. They prepared a surprise for him in the lunchroom, but the German was nowhere to be found.

That day at lunchtime, Vincent's motorcycle was parked outside the little boardinghouse. Upstairs, he pulled the shutters closed. The honking and rattling of the *motorini* penetrated through the thin windowpanes as he turned toward Giulietta. She stood straight and motionless in the small room with the flowered wallpaper, her eyes fixed upon him. Her body was in flames. When he finally embraced her, melted into her completely, it was as though they had always been man and wife. It was just one time, a stolen lunch hour. That same evening, he drove back across the Alps, and she set the table for her family.

11

Light rain fell on the Brenner Pass. Beneath his leather jacket, Vincent could still feel the heat of Giulietta's kisses, invisible trails on his skin. Around his neck, he wore a red scarf she'd made. It smelled like her. When she gave it to him, they'd made a promise to one another. He was determined to bring her to Germany.

Back home, everything seemed transformed. The world was aglow. It was one of those rare times in life when everything fit together smoothly, deploying its power like a perfectly coordinated gear train. The chief engineer praised his exceptional work, the CEO of BMW traveled to Milan to sign the license agreement, and one full hall of the Munich factory was converted to Isetta production. Vincent got the first raise of his entire life.

He talked to Giulietta on the phone every day, and as they professed their genuine love for one another, he could hear the *gettoni* rattling as Giulietta fed them into the pay phone until she ran out and the conversation abruptly ended. In those conversations, as she stood in the little bar by the tram station outside the factory gate, she first heard him say that long, mellifluous word that echoed in her dreams like a promise: "*Wirtschaftswunder.*" The German economic miracle.

Vincent read newspaper job advertisements aloud to her: "'Seamstress wanted,'" "'Seeking fashion illustrator,'" "'Textile factory hiring.'" He didn't want to bring her to Germany just for his own benefit; he wanted to give her all the opportunities she'd been denied at home. As the days passed, Giulietta's faith in the crazy plan grew. When she closed her eyes and pictured the Germany he described, it was just like her parents' dreams of L'America. She recalled how she and Giovanni had sat in the dark kitchen of their house on the island, the wind shaking the old shutters, as their grandmother told them how over there, on the other side of the ocean, they had pumpkins as tall as a man and buildings that reached all the way to heaven. Everything they lacked on the island—which seemed like everything apart from capers and wind—was available there in abundance. "L'America" had been a magic word then. Now, there was a new magic word, in a new language: "*Wirtschaftswunder.*"

Vincent found an apartment in a new building, not far from the BMW plant. Two bedrooms, kitchen, bathroom. A bit too large for just him, and modern, but with practical, modest décor. He'd been subletting since the end of the war, first a drafty attic and more recently with the Grimms, sleeping in a room that was supposed to have been a nursery. Though some farmers had chased refugees away with pitchforks, plenty of people in Munich had taken them in, even though some had been bombed out themselves. In times of general crisis, kind people looked out for others instinctively. The Grimms, who had remained childless, had treated Vincent like a son. Tears were shed on the day he moved out. Mrs. Grimm gave him a homemade cake, a hunk of sausage, and some cheese spread, and now, here he was, in his own apartment for the first time, with only a few worn suitcases and trunks for company. Mentally, he'd already furnished the whole place: the marital bed, the dining table, the children's room. He slept on the floor the first night. He didn't own any furniture, but he did have a telephone line. As he spoke to Giulietta, his voice echoed off the bare walls. He described every detail of the apartment to her, and they both marveled at how much time one could save with modern household appliances—electric washing machines, vacuum cleaners, bread slicers.

Perhaps, in his euphoria, Vincent had underestimated how difficult it would be for Giulietta to tell her mother what had happened—let alone Enzo. Again and again, she hesitated; something was always coming up, and the longer she put it off, the more uncertain she grew. Her mother was still convinced she would be a virgin at her wedding. Enzo was the only one who knew she hadn't been a virgin since the previous summer. Preparations for the ceremony were already well underway. Vincent urged her to stop lying. Better to get the unpleasantness over and done with, he said. She wrestled with her own emotions—what was the best way to tell them? Confessing that she'd slept with Vincent would mean dishonoring the family, but might it also give Enzo a reason to reject her? Then she'd be free, and he could save face.

No matter how she twisted and turned the situation, she knew it would destroy her respectable family. Her mother would curse her name, and Enzo would never allow her to go to another man. Night after night, she lay awake, hemming and hawing, until finally, she decided not to say anything. There was only one way out: she'd have to pack her bag and run off in secret. Burn all her bridges behind her. But she had to tell Giovanni. He was closer to her than anyone, and he'd only ever wanted her to be happy. When Vincent asked how the conversation with Giovanni had gone, she was silent at first; then he heard her crying softly.

"Molto difficile," she said, "but he thinks it's good."

Vincent heard a note of uncertainty in her voice. Was she telling the truth? He knew Giovanni wouldn't want to lose his twin sister.

"Giovanni said I'm free; I have to decide for myself. It's my life."

"When are you coming?"

"Soon, *amore.*"

Vincent began to worry that Giovanni would talk her into changing her mind. Enzo, his rival, seemed to have far less influence over her than her brother and her mother, the moral force driving the family. Growing nervous, he asked her whether she really wanted him, and she insisted that yes, of course, he was the man for her—how could he ask such a thing? She confessed that she'd been to see a fortune-teller—Milan was full of them—who assured her with absolute certainty that Vincent was the love of her life. Vincent didn't believe in hocus-pocus, but even he saw a kind of inevitability—what Giulietta would call destiny or fate—in the events that had brought them together, in this secure, clear sense of having arrived at a destination.

Which made it all the more difficult to hear her voice without being able to feel her body. His own body was threatening to explode with desire. He decided to travel to Milan, to pick her up in person, to do things properly. He'd come by train because she'd have luggage, and he didn't own a car yet. Giulietta agreed to the plan. He studied the train timetables and then purchased two tickets, round-trip for himself, one-way for her. Giulietta spent two days at the passport office getting her papers in order. On Saturday at 7:00 p.m., Vincent would arrive at Milano Centrale; Giulietta would be waiting for him on Track 15 with her luggage, and before her family noticed her absence, they'd be on the night train headed north.

It was a cold November day. The sun had already set by the time Vincent stepped onto the platform at Milano Centrale. The scent of the city awakened his senses immediately. The odor of coal-fired ovens hung in the Munich air, but Milan still smelled the way it had in late summer, an indescribable scent he forever associated with Giulietta.

The enormous concourse was packed with commuters hurrying to catch their trains to the suburbs. Vincent walked up and down, searching for Giulietta's face in the crowd. He stopped when he reached the front of the track. It would be easy to miss someone in this enormous steel-and-glass hall, but Giulietta had never been late before. Something was off. He waited in the drafty concourse until eight thirty, his feet freezing through the thin soles of the new, low-topped shoes he'd bought the day before, not wanting to turn up in his worn winter boots.

Giulietta didn't show. The night train to Monaco di Baviera left on schedule. Vincent had run up the length of the track and then down through the train itself, making sure he hadn't somehow missed her. All in vain. As the red lights of the last car disappeared into the night, a cold hand wrapped around his heart.

He took the tram to Naviglio Grande. When he got out at the station near Giulietta's building, thick fog hung over the old canal. Not a soul was around. The sidewalk in front of the trattoria, where the tables had stood during the summer, was empty now. The customers were all inside, behind windows foggy with condensation. Dry, brown leaves lay on the cobblestones; no children were playing outside. Giulietta's magical little world had fallen silent.

There was no lock on the building door. Giulietta lived on the third floor; he still remembered the day her mother had shouted to her from the window. Vincent went up the stairs. Broken tiles. A plain, cold metal railing. It was dark in the stairwell; he found a light switch, but the third-floor bulb was out. Only farther up, on the fifth floor, had a dim light gone on. A small, handwritten sign on the door bore their family name: "Marconi." Like the guy who invented the telegraph. Unidentifiable noises came from inside. Giulietta's voice wasn't among them.

Vincent racked his brain feverishly. If he rang the doorbell and her mother answered, or Giovanni, or Enzo, what should he say? They wouldn't understand a word, for one thing. Mathematically speaking, the chances of Giulietta answering the door were one in four. If she was even at home. What if something had happened to her on the way to the station? What if her family already suspected she'd run off? Or maybe, he thought, she just couldn't bring herself to leave. Or they'd found her out before she could get away. If so, then she needed his help now. But once he rang the doorbell, it would all come out for sure. He wanted to protect her, but he also wanted to put an end to all the lying. The truth would have to come out sooner or later anyway, and they'd have to get used to their new, foreign son-in-law. He hesitated for another moment, but then his impatience won out. He pressed the doorbell.

Nothing happened. The doorbell didn't work. He knocked. It sounded more aggressive than he'd intended. Someone opened the door. It was Giovanni. *Lucky break,* Vincent thought; her brother knew about him. But Giovanni didn't seem pleased to see the uninvited guest. Only after their mother called to ask who was at the door, only after Giulietta appeared behind him and froze in horror, did Giovanni shake off his torpor. From one second to the next, his expression brightened, and he greeted Vincent warmly. Giulietta was visibly agitated and extremely tense. She hurriedly said something to Giovanni that Vincent didn't catch.

Then Enzo came to the door, and Giulietta fell silent. She shot Vincent a look, pleading with him not to say anything. Enzo eyed the German mistrustfully. Vincent had always been slightly afraid of Enzo because he spoke so little; today, he seemed more impenetrable than ever.

"You remember?" Giovanni called to him jovially. "This is Signor Butt-o-Meter! The one who brought the Isetta to Germany!"

Enzo nodded and welcomed him. Not unkindly, with a firm handshake.

Giulietta stood in the background. *"Buonasera, Signor Schlewitz,"* she said softly.

Vincent searched for answers in her eyes, but she avoided his gaze. He didn't understand what was going on. Most confusing of all, she looked different. It wasn't anything he could pinpoint. She was wearing a simple house dress; her black hair was up. She was paler than she had been that summer, but that wasn't necessarily surprising. Yet something about her had changed.

When Vincent had knocked, the family had been in the middle of dinner. Without hesitating, Giulietta's mother invited the guest to eat with them. Vincent sensed immediately that Signora Marconi was the head of the household. Her word was law, even for the men. A wiry, resolute woman in a plain checked dress. She had piercing eyes, and her prematurely wrinkled face bore the marks of a hard life filled with sacrifice. A cross hung on a silver chain around her neck.

The entire apartment reminded Vincent of his Silesian grandparents' farm: the crucifix at the family altar, the red-and-white checked tablecloth, the heavy sideboard beside the small dining table, which had a lightbulb dangling above it. The enamel gas stove in the tiny kitchen, the scent of damp masonry, poverty, and onions. The apartment was clean and warm, but something heavy and muted hung over it, the gloomy shadow of a time before the war.

Vincent sat beside Giovanni, separated from Giulietta by the table. He felt uneasy in the glare of the bare bulb. Signora Marconi dished out a large portion of pasta for him, the biggest noodles he had ever seen, and rambled on and on in her high, resolute voice as though he spoke Italian. *"Sono i rigatoni alle acciughe, che buoni! Da noi, non si mangia la cucina milanese! Lì si mangia il riso. Qua no! Almeno una volta alla settimana mangiamo il pesce. Siamo gente di mare!"*

Giulietta didn't translate. She stared at her plate, silent, frighteningly absent.

"Come va la Isetta in Germania?" Giovanni asked, chewing his rigatoni with gusto. The tomato sauce was dotted with small pieces of fish and capers, seasoned with oregano.

Isetta. Vincent understood that. *"Isetta va bene."*

"Ti piace la pasta? È buona?"

Pasta. The noodles. *"Sì, è buona."*

But nothing was good. As Giovanni clowned around, Enzo ate in contented silence, making occasional remarks here and there, refilling Vincent's wine with his huge, callused hands, never impolite, always respectful, but in no way warm. Giulietta seemed to be seething. Vincent stole glances at her, searching for answers, for their true connection, their intimacy and complicity . . . but it was gone. Or rather, it was still there, but something had brutally smothered it.

Giulietta's mother gave her a second helping. She waved it away, and immediately an argument broke out over how she wasn't eating enough. *"Ormai devi mangiare per due!"* Vincent heard, though he didn't know what it meant. Giovanni, laughing, translated using gestures: she was eating for two. For the *bambino!* The little Marconi! Vincent could only stare in reply. Giovanni told him that Enzo and Giulietta were very happy to be expecting. The wedding would be soon! There was no mistaking his simple gesture of sliding a ring onto his finger. Vincent grew light-headed. He struggled to maintain his composure.

"You're pregnant?"

Giulietta nodded. For one fleeting moment, Vincent thought he sensed Enzo's scrutinizing gaze upon him. But when he looked, Enzo turned away, took Giulietta's hand, and smiled at her. He said something affectionate that Vincent didn't understand. Later on, he wasn't sure how he'd managed to keep calm. All he remembered was that dull feeling of having been punched in the stomach and sitting paralyzed in this unfamiliar, musty apartment as the Italians conversed cheerfully among themselves.

Except Giulietta. She was fighting back tears. Giovanni called to his mother, telling her to bring their guest more rigatoni. Vincent gestured to her that he was full. Gathering the last of his strength, he apologized, thanked her for the food, and went to the door. *"Accompagna il dottore alla sua pensione!"* Signora Marconi ordered her son. Giovanni, still chatting away, helped Vincent into his coat. Vincent left the apartment without looking at Giulietta again.

On the way to the tram, Giovanni kept on talking, without worrying about whether the German could follow. Vincent was filled with paralyzing rage at this clown of a man. When Giovanni offered to carry his small suitcase, Vincent batted his hand away. He wanted to be alone. He wanted to know what the hell had just happened.

Why hadn't she said anything? How could he have been so stupid as to believe that there was nothing between her and Enzo, when they lived under the same roof? And how could she be so sure that it was Enzo's child? Part of him was still standing at the train station, in a happier version of the story, with his arms around Giulietta, who had arrived with her suitcases. Holding his wife. His future.

He stopped in the middle of the street and sucked the cold, damp night air into his overheated lungs. Giovanni clapped him on the shoulder and offered him a cigarette. *Keep your chin up,* his silent, knowing gaze seemed to say. *Nothing anyone can do.* For one moment, a glimmer of sympathy seemed to shine in Giovanni's eyes. A second later, the window to his soul snapped shut again.

Giovanni cracked a joke, and the screeching of the tram tore Vincent out of his reverie. The brightly lit car stopped in front of them. The door opened with a hiss. Dazed, Vincent stepped inside. The benches were empty; he was alone except for the ticket collector sitting beside the back door. When the tram started again with a hard jolt, Vincent fumbled out a few lire for the ticket and stared out the rear window, where Giulietta's little world was disappearing into the fog. Giovanni was walking back home. The yellow streetlamps reflected off the canal. Vincent glimpsed a woman gazing out a third-floor window, before the fog swallowed her. He didn't know whether it was Giulietta, and he didn't see her lying awake the entire night, sobbing silently into her pillow.

12

The Isetta was a huge success in Germany. The four-wheeled Italian immigrant became a symbol of the *Wirtschaftswunder*. The fulfillment of the promise that every family, even the smallest, could become part of the new mobile society. Children loved the car's bubble shape; women loved it because it was so practical; and fathers loved how affordable it was. It carried BMW through the crisis. As the first few families drove their Isettas over the Alps to the Adriatic Sea, Vincent was promoted. He got his own office in the development department, and his own secretary. A tall, blond girl from Hamburg who was single and pretty. He wasn't interested, though. He spent his evenings standing in his bare apartment, staring at the wet skeletons of the trees outside the window. He threw himself into his work, trying to forget.

Sixty years later, an entire lifetime later, Vincent hadn't forgotten a single detail. Quite the opposite.

"How do you know it was your child, Vincent?"

I couldn't call him Dr. Schlewitz anymore. His story had become mine. I'd completely lost track of the world around us. I shivered. The sun had disappeared behind the bare trees on the riverbanks. The lights in the buildings were going on, and the waiters started carrying patio heaters outside. It was one of those April evenings when spring is in the air, but not yet strong enough to drive the cold away.

Vincent gazed at me for a long moment. "I didn't learn the truth until later. Until it was too late."

"Did you have proof? A paternity test?"

"No. Something else. It's a long story." He stared at his empty espresso cup.

"So, you never heard from Giulietta again?" I asked.

"Oh, of course I did. She called me from work the very next day. She wanted to explain everything—she felt unbearably guilty. But I didn't want an apology. All I wanted to know was whether the child was mine."

"And?"

"She said no. She said women knew those things." The bitter twist of his mouth suggested otherwise. "I asked how she could marry him if she didn't love him. She said it was a question of *onore*, not *amore*."

"What?"

"Family honor." He bit his lips angrily. "The child was a sign. A sign that she belonged with her family."

"But she could have just—I mean, here in Germany, you and she . . ." I didn't get it.

"It wasn't a rational decision," he said. "She decided against herself. She was scared. Her family protected her. Germany was far away. What if it didn't work out? We didn't have anything, apart from our feelings for each other. It was all still just a dream, and her family was her reality."

"Did she end up happy with Enzo?"

He didn't reply.

"Did you see her again?"

He looked at me and nodded.

"When?"

Vincent averted his eyes with a pensive smile. "It's a long story, like I said. That was just the beginning."

He'd gotten tired. I, on the other hand, was wide awake. I glanced at the photo of Giulietta, trying to understand her through the lens of that time. Why had she decided not to be with the man she loved? All at once, despite our physical similarities, she felt like a stranger. Vincent regarded me thoughtfully and remarked, "Something in her didn't believe that she had a right to be happy."

And at that, I began to understand.

"Can I drive you home?" he asked.

"No need, I don't live far."

I didn't want to reveal that I lived alone and that nobody would be waiting for me. I lived at our atelier; the apartment I had above it was mainly just a place to sleep. Mostly, I didn't want Robin or anyone else to see him and ask a bunch of stupid questions.

"Please." His tone was so insistent that I couldn't come up with a pretext to refuse.

He used a silver key to open the passenger door. The car smelled like a different time, an indescribable scent that reminded me of childhood in the back seat of my mother's Renault. The soft, burgundy-colored leather had a rich patina and creaked when I sat down. I didn't know much about cars, but I did know materials and craftsmanship, and this was exceptional work. The dashboard was a 1960s jewel, with rocker switches and round chrome instruments on a wooden panel. The dials were labeled "*Acqua*," "*Olio*," and "*Benzina*." Vincent sat beside me and pulled on his driving gloves.

"This is an Iso Rivolta. By the same company as the Isetta, named after the founder's family." He pointed to the company logo in the center of the large wooden steering wheel: a silver griffin on black Bakelite. "The family crest."

"I've never seen one of these," I said.

"Only seven hundred ninety-seven of them ever built. Few have survived." He started the car. A deep growl sounded from the engine compartment. "You look so much like your grandmother. She sat there. Where you're sitting now."

His gaze made me uncomfortable. That bottomless pain.

"I could never sell it." Vincent pulled onto the road. "Your dad drove it, too," he added.

My breath caught in my throat. "A Rivolta—or this actual car?"

"This one here. Your mother sat in that seat, too."

That caught me off guard. Listening to a story was one thing, but running my hand across worn, cool leather upholstery that had touched my parents' legs was confusing in its immediacy. My mother had never mentioned this.

"When was that?" I asked.

Vincent dodged the question. "Where do you live?"

I asked him to stop at the corner, far enough from the atelier that nobody would see me. I opened the door immediately, hoping to make it quick. I don't like goodbyes. But it was hard for him to let me go. Maybe he was still looking at me and seeing Giulietta.

"Julia, I—" His voice faltered.

"I'll be in touch. And then you'll tell me the rest, okay?"

Instead of replying, he opened the glove compartment and withdrew an envelope. "I have a request, Julia," he said, and handed me the letter. It was sealed. When I turned it around, I saw whom it was for. Just one word, with no address, in old-fashioned script: "Vincenzo." I went to give it back to him immediately, as though it burned my hand.

"Vincenzo needs to read that," he said quietly. "It's about Giulietta."

"But I—how do you even know he's alive?"

Vincent didn't take the letter back. "Giulietta's brother told me. Giovanni Marconi. He has a specialty-foods shop in the wholesale market."

"Here in Munich? Her twin brother?"

Vincent nodded. "I went to him. He says Vincenzo's alive. In Italy. But he didn't want to give me his address."

"Why?"

"I'm persona non grata there."

I shook my head in disbelief. "After all these years?"

"Your father hates me."

"He knows you're his father, then?"

Vincent nodded briefly. He was hiding something. "He ought to know the truth. I owe him that."

"The truth about what?"

"Giulietta's death ruined his life, and—"

"Was it your fault?"

He shook his head. "I would have given my life for her. Julia, I just have this one request. I know he'd be glad to see you."

"What makes you say that? He and I don't know each other. He's my biological parent. Nothing else."

"If you go see Giovanni and ask him . . . They can't turn you away. You're family."

"They live right around the corner, and they've never been interested in me!"

He fell silent for a moment, gazing into the twilight. "Please don't misunderstand my intentions. I'm not trying to use you for something you don't want to do. I came to Milan because I wanted to see you. And Vincenzo . . . It's simply that, at the end of your life, you don't want to leave things in shambles."

"He's the one who left things in shambles." I placed the letter on the dashboard.

"As you wish," he said.

"Sorry," I said, extending my hand. "But thanks for the story. Maybe we'll see each other again sometime?"

He nodded, looking disappointed, but still made an effort to smile.

I got out of the car and immediately felt guilty. I returned to the car and took the letter.

"I'll think about it."

He beamed in gratitude.

As I crossed the street, I felt his gaze on my back. He wasn't watching me, though. He was watching another woman who had departed this world long ago.

Luckily, I had the atelier to myself for the night. I switched the lights on, made myself some coffee, and sat down with my sketchbook. I read Robin's texts and ignored the ones from my mom. I picked up a pencil and tried to put something down on paper. I still had no idea what to do for our next collection. The ideas we had discussed all struck me as stale. Something completely new had happened. Continents were shifting inside me, trees being uprooted, new impulses forging paths. I stared at the blank sketchbook. If only life were like this. It would be so easy. Just turn to a blank page and start over. But life was made up of thousands of pages, stacked on top of one another, and even though only the top one was visible, the others were all part of it as well, some of the sketches ugly, failed, abandoned. And occasionally, one that was pure gold.

It was only a mile or so to the wholesale market. The other side of my family was within walking distance. I wondered whether my father had ever come to Munich to visit his uncle, knowing that I was in school just a few blocks away. Outside, drizzle began drumming softly against the window. I opened it, breathed in the cool night air, and closed my eyes. All at once, I saw Giulietta's face. Like she was trying to tell me something. When I opened my eyes again, she disappeared. Just the dark, rainy alley. I went back to my desk and tried to picture the dresses she'd made. Wondered what she would think of today's fashion. What she would sketch if she were sitting here now. If she had died before I was born, she couldn't have been much older than forty. What happened? What had her death done to my father? Was that why he disappeared? And why was I resisting the idea of contacting him, now that I knew there was a way to do it? It alarmed me to realize that having a dead father had been easier than having a living one.

13

The doorbell trilled. I jumped, startled. For one bizarre moment, I caught myself thinking Giulietta had come to visit. Or maybe Vincent had returned? I went to the door. My mother was outside, soaking wet and clutching my cat carrier.

"Julia, I'm sorry. Truly."

I just stood there, without inviting her in.

"Let's talk," she said. "Please. I can explain if you'll give me a chance."

"No need. I get it."

"I have something for you. From your dad."

I'm not sure when I'd last heard her say that word. The look on her face was one I'd never seen. Pleading. Insecure. At war with herself. I couldn't just leave her standing in the rain. The cat mewed.

She stood there beside my desk as I opened a can of cat food. I didn't offer her a chair.

"It was wrong of me to lie to you," she said.

"What was it you wanted to give me?"

She rummaged in her purse.

"Sometimes one mistake leads to another, and then another. And then eventually you're there wondering, 'Where did I first go wrong?'"

"You had no right to take him from me."

"He left, Julia. I just wanted you to grow up in clear-cut circumstances."

"Your circumstances were the exact opposite of clear-cut."

"He was dead to me, okay? I needed to bury him. Mentally. So that I could move on."

"Well, you can do that. You're not related to him." I set down the bowl for my cat.

"Blood relations are overrated, Julia. Your real family you choose for yourself."

"No. Family is the only thing you don't have a choice about."

"Honey, you're nothing like Vincenzo. He never got his life together. All he ever did was fail. Look at everything you've accomplished. I know you didn't get that from him."

Almost automatically, I thought about all the debt we'd gone into. The thin ice beneath our feet, the fine line between success and failure. The moments of happenstance that led to one person soaring and another crashing to Earth. How one time when I was a kid, I'd been scared to ride the roller coaster, and my mom had told me to never look down.

"You always had to burn all of your bridges, huh?"

"Times were like that. We had to free ourselves. And I wanted that freedom for you, too. I never stopped you from doing your own thing."

That was true. The one thing nobody had ever shown me was how to keep a relationship intact.

She took a photo out of her purse and passed it to me.

"I found this. Remember?"

It was the only photograph of him and me. My mom took it the day I saw him for the first and last time. I was almost five, and he'd just gotten out of prison, though my mother didn't reveal that part until much later. When I was little, he was "in Italy." That was the whole story. When other kids at preschool asked me where my daddy was, I just said, "In Italy," and that was that. Italy was nice. It was sunny; it had beaches and pizza. Having a daddy in Italy seemed like a good thing somehow, despite his absence. Daddies in Italy eventually came back from Italy. And when the day I'd fantasized about for so long finally came, I was more excited than I'd ever been in my entire life. I still remember how my mother picked me up from preschool one day, and there was a tall man with dark, curly hair standing behind her. My daddy from Italy.

The image was grainy, yellowed, slightly blurred. I was sitting on his shoulders, an unsuspecting, not-quite-five-year-old girl, happy to be sitting so high up, tiny hands clutching his black locks. His eyes were alert, mischievous, penetrating. His body slim and wiry. Tense. An attractive man, slightly too serious for his age, skeptical but enigmatically charming. His smile into the camera was for the woman taking the picture; there was a subtle tension between him and the photographer. He was dressed in seventies clothes: a plaid shirt with a wide collar, a tight leather jacket, bell-bottoms, and worn leather boots. The date on the back of the photo was July 11, 1982. If he was actually Vincent's son, meaning he was born in 1955, he would have been twenty-seven here.

It was hard for me to grasp that this was me, this chubby girl on a stranger's shoulders. Who was I back then? What was left of this tiny creature who knew nothing and had her whole life ahead of her? When I thought back to that afternoon in Olympic Park, it was hard to distinguish between what really happened and what I just imagined. I don't trust my memory. The past is the past; all that remains is an idea of it. The paint we splash onto the canvas of our recollection is steeped in emotions, and emotions are unreliable. Maybe that day was totally different. Maybe I just made it all up so that I would have something to hold on to.

He lifted me up. I remember that. His firm, slender hands around my waist as he hoisted me over his head. I laughed and clutched his hair, which was coarse and wiry, not at all like my mother's. I remember how happy I was when he tossed me into the air. I shrieked in delight, and he caught me again. He laughed. Kissed me. Spun me around so wildly that I lost a shoe. My mother had never done that. I was weightless. The transparent sky, the warm air on my skin—the whole world was summer and light.

He'd brought me a soapbox car made of red-lacquered wood. It was a rickety thing with a hard seat that smacked against my bottom as I raced down the hill. Mom ran beside me, worried, but I squealed in delight. He caught me at the foot of the hill. I don't know how long we kept doing that, but I remember the loving way he looked at me and the huge smile on his face, and how I wished that day would never end.

What followed later—the screaming, the slaps, the blood on the floor—was so awful that I never wanted to think about that day again. It was the last time I ever saw him; he disappeared forever that same evening. Across the border, to Italy.

Even though he vanished from my reality, he showed up in my imagination. There's a world where those absent are more alive than those present. We may believe that the people we're around every day have the greatest influence on us, but it's the invisible ones who shape our dreams.

I gave him a hundred different forms, pictured the house he lived in a hundred different ways, asked my mom a hundred different questions, until finally she got sick of it and decided that he'd died.

"The stuff you told me about that day, was it true?"

"Yes. All of it. I swear."

He'd flipped out, she'd told me. Much later, when I wasn't a child anymore.

"He beat me up. In front of you. I'd moved on with my life by that point. He was locked up for almost five years. And then, when he saw my boyfriend—he just lost it. And the cops came, and he took off. Across the border."

"Was he always that way? What was he like before, when you first fell in love?"

"He was fascinating, but he was also a ticking time bomb."

"What was wrong with him?"

"Those were just crazy times, Julia. We all did things that we—"

"Terrorism, you mean?"

"Well, we weren't in the Red Army Faction—at least, not officially. But it wasn't exactly the peace movement, either."

She didn't like talking about that part of her youth. I've seen pictures of her as a young woman, a furious revolutionary in a black turtleneck and trumpet jeans, a cigarette in her mouth.

The photos made me think of Patti Smith. A woman we always picture in black and white, the way we associate Janis Joplin with flower patterns.

"So that was why he was in prison?"

She nodded.

"Did he kill someone?"

She shook her head.

"What do you know about his mom?"

"Really touchy subject. One wrong word and he'd blow up."

"Was she already dead when you two met?"

"Yeah."

"When was that exactly?"

"Seventy-four."

I counted back. Giulietta hadn't even made it to forty.

"How did she die?"

Tanja was silent for a moment.

"Who's this guy that contacted you?" she asked.

"His dad. He said."

"He hated his father."

"Why?"

"We weren't supposed to talk about it."

"Why?"

"Because he—oh, Julia, do I really have to dredge all this up?"

"Why did he hate him?"

"Because of his mother. Because—I mean, they said his father murdered her."

"What?"

"It was never proven. I never believed it."

"Why didn't you ever tell me any of this?" I was beside myself.

"It made no difference to your life. That was long before you were born."

"How'd he kill her?"

"I don't know the details, Julia. It was all just rumors, and nobody was supposed to bring it up. Totally taboo. He exploded if I even mentioned his parents. Really flipped out."

I searched for the missing pieces to complete the puzzle. "Was his dad's name Enzo?"

"Yeah. That's who contacted you?"

"No. The man I met was German."

My mom threw up her hands. "What did he want?"

"He wanted me to go see Vincenzo."

She looked frightened. "Julia, if he's German, he can't be Vincenzo's father."

I didn't feel like telling her the whole story. Objectively speaking, it was possible that Vincent was just some old guy grieving over a girl he'd loved when he was young. Even if everything else about the family was true, he hadn't offered any proof that he was Vincenzo's biological father. Perhaps Enzo, the Sicilian immigrant and maybe murderer, was my grandfather.

Then I remembered something.

"Hey, did you ever ride in a silver-gray coupé with red leather seats? Sixties model, really snazzy?"

My mother stared at me. "How did you know?"

"I rode in it. It belongs to the old man."

"That was Vincenzo's car. He loved it."

"When were you in it?"

"Before you were born—well, nine months before, to be exact. In a parking lot by the sea, in Italy."

She gazed at me, motionless.

"In that car?"

She nodded. I was bewildered.

"Do you want to visit him—your father?" she asked in a dry tone.

"I'm not sure."

"I'm worried about you, honestly. That was the real reason I wanted to keep you away from him. There's something very, very dark in that family, and I wanted to make sure you didn't get sucked into it. But if you want to go looking for him now . . . You're an adult; I won't stand in your way."

She went home, leaving me alone with the photograph. I sat in the atelier for hours, staring at the image. Bringing it to me had been a magnanimous gesture on her part. I had stolen it from her desk drawer when I was eight. After my big running-away-to-Italy trip ended at Munich Central Station, I'd hidden it under my bed. She never asked about it, because under the unspoken rules governing our world, the photo didn't exist, just like he didn't exist. "He" didn't have a name. We didn't need "him." "He" was dead. And then, one day, after we moved for the third or fourth time, the photo disappeared. She must have taken it from me in secret, just as I'd taken it from her. And we never spoke another word about it.

There were a lot of men in my mother's life after Vincenzo. Some of them were roommates; others were passing through. I didn't trust them, because none of them ever stuck around. I only trusted what was mine. I created my own world from my imagination, using scraps of cloth to make clothes for my dolls, inventing people and families that existed only in my mind, where nobody could take them away from me. I sewed myself my first skirt and gave my friends dresses for their birthdays.

Tanja's world was filled with books, hand-rolled cigarettes, and spelt bread. All things fashion related were frowned upon. She was content with old jeans, a few T-shirts, sneakers, and the same leather jacket. I stood in the supermarket aisle after school reading fashion magazines, and as soon as I had money of my own, I used it to buy an old sewing machine from a friend's mother. My mom let me mess around as much as I liked, but as a die-hard feminist, she found it strange that her only daughter would take an interest in sewing, of all things. My mother lived in a world of ideas and discussions, but I needed something concrete, something that would give me stability as it took shape in my hands. Something that expressed my inner self. Something a person could put on so they wouldn't freeze.

The photograph faded from memory. I forgot all about the strange man and the little girl. Life went on. School in London, my first collection, my first fashion event in Paris, hopping from one trade fair to the next, no money, no sleep, only the clothes in my suitcase, hoping to be discovered. My odds of ending up sitting on a mountain of debt were ninety-nine to one, but I didn't care. I was desperate. More than anything else, I wanted to stand on my own two feet.

Even so, the fear of being alone never left me. I surrounded myself with people at all hours, finding it easier to be strong and self-assured when I had company. Only when I was alone and the bustling background noise faded did she emerge from the eerie silence, as she was doing now. The chubby little girl. I realized to my horror that she was still there, in a dark corner, while I was out onstage, beaming at the world. A child terrified of being forgotten, afraid of starving to death if I failed. A child who longed to be seen and held. Screaming for love. And because I couldn't stand the sound, I shut the door to her hiding place so I wouldn't hear her, because otherwise I wouldn't be able to function out there in the world. I was strong; I was talented; I was good. But the more I tried to plug my ears, the more frightened she got, and the louder she screamed.

There was this popular board game in the 1980s called Life. You put a blue or pink plastic piece into a plastic car, you get some fake money, and off you go. Everyone spins the wheel of fortune, moves a few spaces, and depending on where you land, maybe a little plastic partner joins you in the car, you get little plastic children, status symbols, life insurance, and whoever gets through the fastest wins. The game frames life as an accumulation of things, as though we come into the world as a blank slate, with a little money from our parents, and then set out to increase our fortune. In reality, though, we're born damaged, and everything we do in life is about trying to make ourselves whole again.

14

Robin woke me in the morning. I'd fallen asleep on my sketchbook.

"Where were you yesterday?"

"What time is it?"

"Nine o'clock. Julia, what's the matter with you? I need you. We've got to be in this together."

"Sorry. I was working on the new sketches."

"Let me see."

"They aren't done yet."

He set an open envelope on my desk and went to the coffee machine.

"Just arrived from Milan via courier. Read it."

It was a draft of the contract agreement with the holding company. I skimmed through it while Robin made coffee. Almost immediately, I realized what the deal was actually about.

What they euphemistically termed "patronage" was, in truth, their way of buying up newcomers while they were still small, so that they could build the new brands in a way that fit into their portfolio. From the outside, we'd still look like a young indie label, but in reality, we'd be employees of a company that would no longer be ours, even though it would continue to bear our name.

True, we'd wipe out our pile of debt in one fell swoop, and we'd get a fixed income, but we'd no longer be masters of our own domain. The thought made me uneasy. I'd always resisted anything that smacked of sacrificing independence. Then again, how independent can you be when you're drowning in debt?

"What's wrong with you? You're a star now! They want you. Don't you get that?"

"I'm not sure if I want *them*, though."

Robin struggled to control himself. "It's not a question of whether we want this—it's about whether we can afford not to take it. It's a once-in-a-lifetime opportunity. All our debts erased, just like that."

"And they dictate what we do and how much, where we buy our fabrics, and where we manufacture."

"Their conditions benefit us."

"But I'll have to work with materials I would never use otherwise. And we can chuck our 'sustainable production' label in the garbage if they manufacture in China."

"Bangladesh," he said dryly, setting my coffee on the desk. Then he let the cat out of the bag: his mom and dad wanted us to repay the loan we'd been relying on for years to keep our heads above water. Our ace in the hole. Now that we'd snagged a patron, they didn't see why they should have to keep supporting us. And now that Robin was in his midforties, he didn't see why he should have to keep sponging off his parents.

"Both of us should actually be parents ourselves by now," he added sarcastically. In other words, the only choice we had was handing over our independence or abandoning everything we'd worked for.

Success was a trap. Robin claimed that the contract was just a draft, that he could still negotiate. But he would need something to negotiate with. The new collection. He wanted to see my designs.

"I've barely come up with anything, Robin. One or two sketches, no more."

"We need to throw them a bone. They're flying over to check out the atelier, go through our books, and look at your next collection."

"When?"

"Day after tomorrow."

"Are you insane? I don't have anything!"

"Then we may as well just throw in the towel and drive cabs for the next ten years."

I hated him. I panic when my stuff gets dragged into the spotlight when it's still a work in progress. I'm rarely satisfied, and until something is perfect in my eyes, the mistakes and missing details throw open the door for everyone who feels like they know better to tell me what I did wrong. But to me, it's a process.

A dialogue between my vision and the material. It needs time to ripen. It's always been the same balancing act between creativity and cash flow, but right now, it seemed more impossible than ever: the Milan award had set the bar unbelievably high, while inside, I was falling apart.

Robin laid a comforting hand on my shoulder.

"We're family, Julia. We'll make this decision together, and we'll see it through together."

He knew how to get me on his side. I was about to agree against my will, but my heart began to race, and my palms started sweating—just like in Milan before my knees gave out. I knew that if we signed the contract, the hamster wheel would never stop turning: adjust the drafts, fabric trade show in Paris, sew the first few samples, discussions with the art directors, the marketing guys, the holding company bosses, changes and more changes, adapt and adjust to the point of unrecognizability. Then we'd cancel our contract with our small, fair-trade manufacturing company in Turkey and start producing in Bangladesh, where you never knew whether they were using child labor. Larger quantities, bigger margins, self-denial in the name of market share.

"Sorry, Robin. I just can't."

"Then what do you suggest? Lottery tickets?"

Robin could go from charming to snotty in an instant when he didn't get what he wanted.

"I don't know."

"Just saying no isn't enough. I'll support you no matter what, Julia, but if you don't like what I'm suggesting, you have to suggest an alternative."

"I need time."

"Two days. They'll be here in two days. I gotta go to the bank. Later."

He stalked off, leaving me standing there. I hated how cold he could be when we fought. How he flexed the power that he was normally too easygoing to show. To be honest, I'd found Robin's air of authority appealing in the beginning, but I hated it when people belittled me as a tactic for winning arguments. Outwardly, I fought like a lioness, but it was only a matter of time until the smoke cleared and I just felt abandoned.

I went out into the yard and lit a cigarette to calm myself. I needed space. I got into my car to go pick up the old collection from the cleaners, and as I was loading the clothes into the old Volvo, I came up with a crazy idea.

I didn't want to meet him. I just wanted to see if Vincent had been right, if this twin brother really existed. It was only a ten-minute detour. I took the train underpass in the meatpacking district that separates my hip neighborhood from the not-yet-gentrified suburbs. It's really more of a boundary line than a connection. People who live on the pricier northern side don't cross it. We go to the bars around Glockenbach and buy our vegetables at the organic supermarket even though the same stuff costs half as much at the wholesale market, just a short distance away. And the others stay on their side of the tracks as well, probably because they think those of us who can afford the absurd rent in Glockenbach are a bunch of self-absorbed snobs. They're probably not all wrong, either.

I rolled slowly past the market. This part of Munich was still gritty, full of weird graffiti, backstreet mosques, and mothers in head scarves and polyester coats. A freight train thundered down the tracks. Across from the market entrance, at the head of a row of small shops, was an Italian restaurant. The sign read, "Bussone." Tables on the sidewalk. Italian waiters with gelled hair. Market employees, wannabe hipsters, and Bavarian retirees, defying the April weather by drinking their espresso outside.

Next door was a small store with a blue marquee. "Marconi Fine Italian Foods" was written across the large display window in old-fashioned white script. I hit the brakes and peered into the shop. I didn't see anyone. A cheese counter, hams hung from the ceiling, a red cast-iron slicer, wine shelves, a large chrome espresso machine, and barstools around bistro tables. I waited. People walked past. Italians, Turks, Bavarians. Once I was sure the shop was closed, I parked and got out.

The walls behind the counter were filled with photos. Family, I assumed. Group pictures, too small to make out faces. I found the owner's name on the door. Sure enough: "Giovanni Marconi." A cell phone number. A note written in ballpoint pen was taped to the other side of the pane: *"Chiuso per battesimo!"* Next to that was an announcement clipped from a neighborhood newsletter, with a photo of a cute little girl: "The Marconi family is pleased to announce the baptism of Regina Marconi, daughter of Luca and Barbara Marconi, born March 3, 2012. Baptismal service: April 5, 2014, 4:00 p.m., Italian Fellowship, Saint Andreas Parish Church, Zenettistr. 46."

Five minutes away, if that. And a once-in-a-lifetime opportunity to check out the family without being noticed. If I just waltzed into the shop, I wouldn't have the first clue what to say, but a church would be easy enough to sneak into.

Saint Andreas was one of those unadorned postwar constructions, objective to the point of self-deception. A gray box with a gray door. There was nothing sacred about the building—it almost seemed to reject all things exalted.

I tried to imagine the mentality these architects had in the 1950s, and then considered the fashion back then: the French and the Italians, no longer under German occupation, were ushering in a new era with their confident designs; German fashion houses, meanwhile, were mostly trying not to draw any negative attention. No bright colors, no experiments, focus on practicality. We were decades behind everyone else, and even today, we can't seem to reach that sense of self-evident beauty. How would German fashion have developed without those paralyzing war debts? And why was it that, after being defeated so thoroughly, the Germans have managed to surpass the rest of Europe again with their cars and machinery, yet they've never caught up in fashion, art, and film?

There was nothing going on outside the church. The main gate was locked. I looked around and found a covered side entrance cowering on one side of the building, trying to outdo it in terms of sheer plainness. Announcements in German and Italian were posted side by side in a display case beneath an awning. Apparently, two separate congregations shared this church. Now, I heard soft singing on the other side of the door. I opened it cautiously, and found myself looking into the high-ceilinged interior. It was every bit as gray and no-nonsense as the exterior, but inside, it seemed larger and brighter.

The back pews were empty; the few dozen Italians were all crowded up front. Mothers with puffy hair, grandfathers in suits, kids running around. I slipped inside. Nobody saw me—everyone was facing forward. An older priest in a white robe was leading a Catholic Mass in Italian. I sat down at the far end of the last pew. By the altar, the little girl was crying as her father held her over the baptismal font. The mother caressed the crying child's head, and then the priest gathered the little girl into his arms, said a prayer, and dunked her into the water. The girl fell into shocked silence for a brief moment, only to burst out wailing even louder. The mother scooped her up, shushing her lovingly, and when the father came over to comfort the girl as well, she finally stopped crying.

Gingerly, the father carried his daughter from the altar into the sanctuary, where other kids were dashing around as though on a playground. Nobody called them back. The relatives got up to kiss the little girl. As the priest recited one final prayer, the Italians turned the church service into a family celebration.

I'm not sure when I last went to church. Some Christmas when I was a kid, probably. I was never baptized—my mom left it up to me to choose my own belief system once I grew up. And by the time I turned eighteen, I was well past the age of believing in miracles. God's love didn't interest me as much as love of the carnal variety.

As the family crowded around the child, I remained in my pew, still unnoticed. All at once, a completely unexpected feeling came over me: I felt left out. Even though they were the foreigners in this country, not me. When you're missing something and you don't know what it is, you don't feel sad about it until you see it in front of you. But then it's all the more painful.

Alone on the cold church pew, I started picturing what my life would be like if that little girl had been me, and I began to cry. A statue seemed to be watching me from a nearby wall. It was Mary, holding Christ's bleeding body in her arms. His face was full of suffering and distance; her posture was one of transcendent, inexhaustible love.

I'd been planning to duck out of the church before Mass ended, but when the first few Italians reached the exit, it was already too late. I couldn't bring myself to kneel and fold my hands in prayer to hide my face, so I just stayed seated, staring at my shoes as I heard them walking past. Fortunately, they were all so absorbed in their own conversations that they took no notice of me. Once the chattering throng had passed my pew, I looked up. Too soon.

One man was still standing there beside the priest, thanking him and pressing some money into his hand. He was short and stocky, clapping the priest on the back casually. When he turned to follow the others, our eyes met. He was retirement age, thickset yet agile. He had thinning hair and a gray beard, worn moccasins, beige pants, and an ancient-looking checked shirt covering his ample belly. As he approached, I saw he had mischievous eyes and fine red veins on his cheeks. *Like an aging clown,* I thought. *One who's never lost his childlike curiosity, despite everything.* I'd have liked him instantly if I hadn't been nearly wetting myself in terror at the thought of being recognized.

He gave a friendly nod in greeting, but as he walked past, his eyes remained glued to my face. It was that same puzzled look that Vincent had when he saw me for the first time. I turned away, hoping he would keep moving. He slowed his pace, but then I heard him opening the door. I exhaled in relief. I waited there for a few more minutes as the priest disappeared into the sacristy, and then got up and left.

15

When I emerged through the side exit, I saw the Italians standing in the street, chatting and exchanging gifts and herding their children into their cars. The grandfather with the thinning hair spun the newly baptized girl around in the air, laughing. She crowed in delight until an older woman, perhaps his wife, stopped him and took the child. I kept to one side, rushing toward my car. One of the Italians, younger than I was, swerved around me on his Vespa, but then looked back, stopped, and called out in Italian. A question, that was all I could tell. His body language was clear, though. A total cliché: young Italian guy in sunglasses and an unbuttoned shirt, offering me a ride on his Vespa.

"No, thanks."

When he heard me speak German, his expression turned apologetic. *"Oh, scusa, pensavo che fossi una della famiglia. Sei italiana?"*

"No," I said hastily, without understanding everything.

"Sorry," he said in accented German. "I thought you were with us."

"No problem."

I smiled, and he pushed the scooter aside to let me pass. It took a moment too long. One moment that changed everything. Giovanni came over. He'd put on a flat gray cap that gave him a rakish air despite his age. The little girl was sitting on his shoulders, wearing a gold plastic crown. *"Oh, Marco!"* he called, and Mr. Latin Lover turned. *"La tua ragazza?"* He gestured at me with his head.

"No."

Too late to run. Giovanni eyed me curiously.

"Have we met?" he asked with an inimitable half-Italian, half-Bavarian accent.

"No." I racked my brain for a way to get out of this situation. I felt my face heating up, but my limbs seemed frozen in place.

"Giovanni. *De nonno*, grandpapa of the little beast," he said, and shook my hand.

"Julia. Hi."

I could practically hear the gears turning in his head.

"I thought she was Italian," Marco said. "You look Italian."

I shrugged.

"Where you from?" Giovanni asked.

"Munich." I wondered how much longer I would be able to take this game of chicken.

"But your parents are Italians, no?"

I hated it when people asked me about my heritage. But apart from the fact that guys like him probably asked everyone about their heritage, this was obviously his way of finding out who this person was who had come to his granddaughter's baptism.

"My dad is Italian," I admitted.

It was meant as an awkward attempt to end the conversation, but now he had me on the hook. "Ah, you can see that! Where in Italy is he from?"

I hesitated. What was I supposed to tell him? The truth? If I just said Rome or Venice or whatever came to mind, I'd have to go on lying, invent a name for him, and it wouldn't take him long to notice that I couldn't keep the story straight. And maybe I did want to get to know Giovanni after all—I hadn't decided. At any rate, I was already in deeper than I wanted to be. Something inside me that I didn't have entirely under control came up with a reply. "I don't know."

They both started. Not knowing one's father's birthplace wasn't something that happened in their world.

"Why not? What's his name?"

There was no getting out of this. I didn't even care anymore. The best defense is a good offense. "Marconi. Vincenzo Marconi."

The words hit like a bomb. Giovanni's smile froze. He lifted the child off his shoulders, shaking his head in disbelief. "Vincenzo Marconi?" he echoed.

"Who's that?" Mr. Latin Lover asked.

"Nessuno," Giovanni replied evasively. He couldn't take his eyes off me. I lost all sense of my own body. I wished the earth would open up and swallow me.

"You're Julia?" he asked softly.

I nodded.

"Santo Dio," he murmured.

His wife called him to the car, and when he didn't respond, she came over to us, clutching an armful of flowers, sweets, and a panettone. *"Che c'è?"* She could tell something was off with her husband.

"La figlia di Vincenzo," he said in a throaty voice, pointing to me.

She stared at me. *"Vincenzo?"*

The way she said his name told me that it was a sore subject. A name they spoke only *sotto voce.*

"I just wanted to stop by for a minute," I said with a smile, trying to lighten the mood.

"Macché stop by a minute?" Giovanni exclaimed. "I am your uncle, *Cristo Santo!"*

Before I could reply, he threw his arms around me with tears in his eyes. He was shorter than me, but he made up for it through sheer enthusiasm—judging by his round belly, he ran that specialty-foods shop out of passion. He kept hugging me, and then finally his wife hugged me as well, kissing me on the right cheek, the left cheek, and the forehead. She was a resolutely old-school mamma, plump but firm. More and more family members were glancing at us, sensing that something important was happening. I saw them getting out of their cars, whispering and coming closer.

"Quanti anni?" Giovanni exclaimed. *"Trenta, quaranta?"*

The little girl regarded me with wide, questioning eyes.

"È Julia," he told her affectionately. *"Dai il buongiorno a Julia."*

She hid shyly behind her grandfather's legs but peeped out at me charmingly. I smiled. Other family members came up and asked what was going on. Giovanni fobbed them off with a few lighthearted jokes and then guided me to his car. Apparently, Vincenzo's daughter wasn't everyone's business. He whispered something in his wife's ear. I didn't know what he'd said—all I knew was that, starting today, the world would never be the same. Not for these strangers, and not for me.

They didn't let me go. I never had a chance. We drove to Giovanni's place. He and his wife, Rosaria—a wonderfully warm Sicilian woman who looked like an aging bumblebee in her striped spring dress and her oversized Gucci glasses—lived in an apartment with several of their grown children. In all the commotion, I couldn't tell how many of them there were. It was an old building, not far from the wholesale market. Giovanni's world was a self-contained cosmos revolving around family, business, and food, all flowing seamlessly into one another, within a space of maybe a quarter mile square. Rosaria and her daughters were setting up a buffet in the building's inner courtyard, while the men played with the children. Every ham hock, salami, wheel of cheese, loaf of bread, and bottle of wine was from his shop, Giovanni boasted as he piled food onto a plate for me as though he'd just rescued me from starving to death. He never left my side for a moment. We sat down at one of the picnic tables scattered around the courtyard as the children dashed around us with beeping plastic guns. Somebody had an iPod hooked up to a speaker and was playing Italian pop.

"Buono, eh?" Giovanni asked with every bite I took, as though he'd made the salami himself. "Is with the *tartufo*, the truffles, from Piedmont. *Una favola!"*

It really was *buono. Molto buono.* Rosaria joined us, bearing an enormous plate of her own. "So, tell me," she said quietly, taking a seat beside me, "didn't your papà ever visit you?"

I shook my head.

"Madonna mia," she whispered before giving her husband an accusatory look. *"Com'è possibile che un uomo adulto . . ."*

"Che ne sai tu!" Giovanni snapped, cutting her off. *"Portaci l'album fotografico, dai!"*

Rosaria muttered something in reply, and Giovanni explained that she was going to bring us the family photo album.

"How did you find us?" he asked once she was out of earshot.

I thought for a moment before deciding that it was best to tell the truth. "Do you know a man named Vincent Schlewitz?"

Giovanni's expression darkened. His huge saucer eyes narrowed to slits. "No. More wine?"

Without waiting for a reply, he got up and went to fetch a bottle from the buffet. I sat there by myself, bewildered, feeling like a kid who'd broken the rules. Marco came over with his plate and asked if he could sit. He had a friendly smile, and upon closer inspection, Mr. Latin Lover turned out to be a sweet guy with a wry sense of humor. His relationship to Italy was at least as distant as mine, but for different reasons: he'd come to Germany because he didn't think there was any future in what he called a "cesspool of nepotism and corruption"—at least not for anyone who wanted a legal job earning enough money that they wouldn't still be living with their parents at age thirty.

Giovanni returned and gestured to Marco with the reflexive authority of a patriarch, indicating that he needed to speak to me in private. Marco excused himself and stood up.

Giovanni poured wine for me and himself before taking a seat. "What does he want?" he asked in a low voice.

"Who, Marco?"

"Vincent."

"Is he really Vincenzo's father?" I asked hesitantly. Saying his name out loud wasn't easy.

Giovanni drained his glass. *"Disgraziato,"* he grunted, and then brooded for a while in silence, without looking in my direction. Finally, he turned back to me. "No." He said it with unsettling force.

"I barely know him. He showed up one time. He's looking for his son, and I thought maybe you guys—"

"What does he want?"

"Dunno. Forgiveness, I think."

The good impression Vincent had made on me didn't fit Giovanni's reaction to the mere mention of his name. It wasn't just dislike. It was utter contempt, so deep-seated that it seemed out of character for the friendly Giovanni I'd seen thus far. This had to be the same taboo topic I'd run into with Vincent— something so monstrous that it struck both men mute. And though I didn't know what it was, I figured it likely had to do with the fact that Giulietta was no longer among the living.

Rosaria, suspecting nothing, returned to the table, patting my shoulder as she sat beside me and laid a heavy plaid photo album on the picnic table. "There. Many photo of your papà!" She smiled affectionately. Just like that, Giovanni switched on his fun-loving face again. He grabbed the album and began flipping through page after page of old-fashioned photos in mounting corners, separated by rustling tissue paper. An entire family life within the covers of a single book.

He showed me a page with three photos. *"Matrimonio a Salina,"* it was labeled in flowing, feminine script, *"15 agosto 1968."* The images were slightly faded, with that orangey hue typical of 1960s photos. They showed a bride and groom dancing at a country wedding. Long tables with white tablecloths, arranged in a meadow among the olive trees, the sea in the background, kids running around.

In the second photo, a close-up, I recognized the couple: young Giovanni's hair had been fuller, but he had the same huge eyes. Rosaria had been a bit on the plump side even then, short and smart. A feminine, motherly woman who had her husband firmly under control.

"You were still handsome back then, Giovanni!" she laughed.

Giovanni threw me a wry look. "Look what she did to me!"

The third image was a group picture. I recognized Giulietta immediately. She was standing beside Giovanni.

"She looked like you!" Rosaria exclaimed. *Dio buono! Incredibile!*

The similarity shocked me all over again. She was my age here, midthirties. And she'd changed since the photo with Vincent. Her youthful cheeriness was gone; her horizons had narrowed. She gazed into the camera with a serious expression, holding her son—a curly-haired kid, mature for his age, with a confident expression.

"Your papà," Giovanni said. I could sense his love for Vincenzo. Tender, disappointed love.

"Was a sweet boy." Rosaria shook her head, sighing.

"And you?" Giovanni asked me. "Do you have children?"

"No."

A brief, awkward pause followed. In their world, where marriage and *bambini* came early in life, a woman my age without kids must have seemed hopelessly odd.

"Be glad," Giovanni remarked. "*Sono un disastro.* Make my hair fall out!"

I studied the picture more closely. Giulietta beside Giovanni, Vincenzo beside Giulietta. Where was Vincenzo's father?

Ecco il suo papà! Giovanni pointed to a stoic man with dark skin standing slightly to the back, looking at Giulietta. "Enzo." A strong guy, a shoulder to lean on, the kind of man that hardly exists nowadays. I tried to find similarities between him and Vincenzo. But Vincenzo didn't look much like his mother, either.

Giovanni, seeming to guess what I was thinking about, turned back a few pages and showed me a family photo of Giulietta, Vincenzo, and Enzo, a few years before. Vincenzo, maybe ten, proudly gripping the handlebars of a bike. It was just the three of them, standing in front of a scratched-up Italian house door.

"Those are your grandparents and your papà." Giovanni said it with a decisiveness that made me suspicious.

"Vincent said he was Vincenzo's dad."

I wanted to provoke them. I'm good at that. I'd gotten into hot water with other people's families before because I can't stand leaving things unsaid. Maybe that's another reason why I don't have kids. To me, it seems like every family has an unspoken agreement not to discuss something or other, and usually it's the most important thing. People stick together so that they can tolerate living a lie more easily. Until one person breaks the agreement. Then everything blows up.

Rosaria gave me a shocked look.

"What did he tell you about us?" Giovanni asked.

"That Giulietta got pregnant with his child. Is that true?"

Rosaria lapsed into hurt silence, as though I'd spoken the devil's name out loud.

Giovanni leaned his powerful arms against the table. "Julia, dear, the truth always has two faces."

I explained that I wasn't there to settle some old score, that I'd gotten along fine without a father. That I just wanted to know why he'd left.

"Where is he now?" I blurted out.

Giovanni cast a thoughtful glance at Rosaria.

"Is he still alive?" I added.

"*Sì,*" Rosaria replied emphatically. "*Sì, is alive, certo.*"

For a moment, I wondered whether she was telling the truth—but then, why would she lie to me? She seemed honest. She was about to add something, but Giovanni broke in first.

"This Vincenzo," he said, pointing to the ten-year-old boy, "this *bravo ragazzo* doesn't exist anymore. Different Vincenzo today." He finished his wine. There was a note of shame in his voice, as though his nephew had tarnished the family name, and he couldn't forgive him in spite of all his love. And my mere presence made it impossible for him to keep silent about it.

"Did Vincent tell you what happened to Giulietta?" he asked.

I shook my head. "He told me about how they fell in love. How he came to Milan to take her back with him, and she, all of you, turned him away."

"Nothing else?"

"No, except that then he returned to Germany, and he never forgot about her."

Giovanni raised his eyebrows as if to say, *Well, he certainly kept a few things from you.* Silently, he poured the rest of the wine. Rosaria clinked glasses with him and said something in Italian. I didn't understand all of it, but I got that she wanted me to hear the story.

"È il suo papà!"

That, I understood. Giovanni took a large gulp of wine and paged back through the album. All the way to the beginning, where the photos were black and white.

"Ecco," he said, *"casa nostra a Milano.* He was born there, your papà."

It was a photo of a street in Milan with an old tram line running through it. To the left of the street was a canal; to the right was a row of apartment buildings, with shops and a trattoria out in front. There was a small church on the far side of the canal. Two women in plain dresses were standing down near the water, washing their clothes. This was Giulietta's little world, every detail exactly as Vincent had described. I was filled with the strange sense of having seen the place before.

16

Giovanni

Giulietta's son was born at home on June 11, 1955. She'd wanted to go to the hospital, but Enzo and Giovanni were working the night shift when she suddenly went into labor, so her mother, Concetta, called the doctor to come to them. Together, they brought the child into the world. When Giovanni and Enzo returned home at sunrise, the infant was already there. Enzo, normally unshakable, was moved to tears. He gathered the boy in his arms and kissed him tenderly on the forehead, grateful for this gift from God. Giovanni had never seen his sister so exhausted. It hadn't been an easy birth, and Concetta was sure that the rosaries she'd prayed throughout were the only reason Giulietta had survived. Giovanni managed to make his sister laugh, but a strange feeling crept over him: just yesterday, they'd been young, inseparable twins, sneaking cigarettes outside church and telling each other about their crushes and crazy dreams. Today, she was a mother, and tomorrow, their tiny apartment would be bursting at the seams. Someone would have to go, and Giovanni knew he was that someone.

Concetta made everyone coffee. The neighbors streamed inside, bearing *dolci* and congratulations for the proud new parents. The bride's unmistakable pregnancy at their wedding had set the neighborhood gossip mill churning, but now everything was all right again. When men had sex before marriage, it was silently tolerated, even admired in a way. But a woman not being a virgin at her wedding was scandalous even in modern Milan—and this wasn't really even Milan; this was a little piece of the South inside the city. Still, Giulietta and Enzo had been engaged, which mitigated her offense, and once Concetta had sent them both to confession, joy over the new family member won out. It was a son, which made it an even happier occasion. Sicilian tradition dictated that the firstborn son should bear the name of his paternal grandfather, Vincenzo. Enzo asked Giulietta if that was all right with her. She nodded silently.

The baby wouldn't stop crying. Concetta grasped his tiny hand, put on her glasses, and read his palm.

"A special child," she whispered to the group, "with an exceptional destiny. The kind of child only born once in a hundred years."

That evening, the entire neighborhood was glued to its radios. Anyone who could afford the luxury of a television had a living room full of guests. The Marconis didn't even own a radio. Giulietta, nursing little Vincenzo, missed the commotion entirely, but down in the trattoria, Giovanni crowded around the brown tube radio with the other men. It was terrible news. Not just for the Iso employees, but for anyone who had gasoline in their veins. The accident that had occurred that afternoon was the worst in the history of racing. Shortly after the twenty-four-hour race began out of Le Mans, a German Silver Arrow had veered off the track at 150 miles an hour, flipped, and crashed into the stands, which were secured only with wooden planks and hay bales. The car exploded, sending the hood, the front axle, and the engine flying through the crowd with such force that they tore people's heads from their bodies. More than eighty people died at the scene; nearly two hundred were injured. The wreck continued to burn for hours as the other cars raced past. Although the devastated Mercedes team returned to Germany that same night, the race wasn't canceled; the Maseratis, Ferraris, Jaguars, and Aston Martins went on driving until the following afternoon. The British Jaguar driver who had caused the accident laughed into the news cameras, celebrating his victory.

The old radio Giovanni heard the news on was a German model. And Giovanni silently pondered how, on the other side of the Alps, a German automotive engineer was sitting in front of his own German radio. A man he believed he would never see again.

Vincenzo really was a special child. His little lungs weren't fully developed when he came into the world. He breathed very quickly, and the shortness of breath often frightened him, which was why he screamed a lot. Giulietta watched over him night and day. Sometimes the doctor had to come in the middle of the night with an oxygen machine. Giulietta had stopped working, and although she'd talked of wanting to go back, everyone assumed she would stay at home and have more children like other women did. Losing her paycheck meant they were even shorter on money than before. Enzo took more night shifts, but it was clear that they'd have to stay in her mother's apartment, which they were already paying the rent on anyway. Concetta had stopped receiving a pension when her husband died, and he hadn't left her anything. Enzo built a crib for Vincenzo and placed it beside Giulietta's bed in Concetta's room, but everyone knew that, soon enough, Giulietta and the baby would have to move out of there. Enzo and Giovanni still shared the other room, but their beds would be pushed together to create a marital bed. It was difficult, though. Giovanni loved his nephew, and asking her brother to leave would have been too much for Giulietta to bear. After all, he was her closest friend, whereas Enzo, though a good man and father, simply wasn't equipped to understand the things she kept hidden in the depths of her soul.

One night, as they were secretly smoking near the church wall on the far side of the canal, Giulietta asked her brother, "Do you think you'll find love?"

Giovanni thought for a long time, not wanting to disappoint his sister. "I'm not sure," he said eventually. "You know more about love than I do."

They both knew what they were talking about, or rather, what they weren't. They went on smoking wordlessly, gazing out at the dark canal as it reflected the lights of the tram passing on the other side.

"Do you think it's true that everyone has somebody out there that they're meant to be with?" Giulietta asked into the silence.

"Maybe in the movies," Giovanni said. "In real life, though, it's all just coincidence. Mamma and Papà met in the fields, and there weren't a lot of options on the island. One thing led to another, and boom, they were married. Did you ever see them kiss like in the movies? They had a different kind of love, not the crazy kind with butterflies in your stomach. It's *amore della famiglia*. The one thing you can always count on. Feelings come and go. But no matter what happens, I'm here for you."

Giulietta didn't reply.

"What about your dream of working in fashion?" Giovanni asked.

"You've seen how it is," she replied. "Vincenzo cries the minute I leave the house. Maybe in a year or two, once he's healthy . . ."

Giovanni could tell that his sister didn't believe it herself anymore. Everything he'd always admired about her—her love of life, her crazy ideas and flights of fantasy—had given way to a solemnity that made her seem years older. That evening, Giovanni resolved to wait a while before having children.

Fall came, then winter, and Giovanni moved the coal oven from the kitchen into Concetta, Giulietta, and Vincenzo's room. One night, as Vincenzo was screaming and Giovanni was sitting at the kitchen table, his mother emerged from the bedroom, warmed some milk on the gas stove, poured some of it into a glass, and placed it on the flowered plastic tablecloth. As Giovanni drank his milk, she said, "You need to find yourself an apartment."

"Don't worry, Mamma," Giovanni said. "I'll handle it."

They both knew what this meant for his future: when he finished his apprenticeship, he would not be attending the Politecnico, the famed Polytechnic Institute of Milan, as planned. In order to pay rent, he would have to work on the assembly line with Enzo for the rest of his life. Assuming Iso gave him a job at all. They weren't hiring these days, because although the company was earning money through foreign licensing, the Isetta still wasn't selling well in Italy. It couldn't compete with Fiat and its mass production. The Isetta was more modern than the Topolino, a prewar design from the Mussolini era, but it was still too expensive for poorer families. Giovanni's future was more uncertain than ever.

He went to his room. Careful not to wake Enzo, Giovanni quietly drew back the sheet that smelled of soap and reached into the hidden slit in his mattress. From between the foam and the cover, he withdrew a wrinkled envelope. He opened it and counted the lire hidden inside—the part of his wages he had secretly kept for himself instead of giving to his mother. It would never be anywhere near enough for college, but it was his and his alone. Giovanni remembered what his father had told him on his deathbed: *Do as you wish with your life, but never be a slave to anyone!*

It was just before Christmas when Giulietta found out what her mother had done. Giovanni had never seen his sister so angry. She accused Concetta of driving her own son away, and demanded that Giovanni enroll at the Politecnico.

"But how will I pay rent?" Giovanni asked.

"You'll stay here. Nothing changes. We don't need a bedroom. That will come later."

"When?"

"Once you're finished with your studies! Giovanni, you're smart. You've got more than just a pair of hands—you have a head on your shoulders, too. You have to use that. Look at me! You're still free. You don't have a family to feed. Every door is open to you!"

Giovanni was conflicted. He didn't want to spend his life on the assembly line, true, but were the engineers really so free?

"I saw Chief Engineer Preti at the factory yesterday," he told her. "Commendatore Rivolta ate lunch with him. Then they said their goodbyes; Preti got into his Isetta and the *commendatore* into his Jaguar. Which of them is more clever? The employee or the *capo*?"

"Rivolta is a *nobile*," Giulietta retorted. "Not like us."

"So what? Who says that only people from good homes are smart?"

"That's not what I'm saying. A lot of nobles are dumb as rocks. They only marry each other, like in the tiniest Sicilian villages! But they have money."

"Let me worry about that. You'll see—someday I'll be a *capo*!" Giovanni kissed his sister and left the apartment.

The truth was that he had no idea what to do. And he knew that, as much as Giulietta loved him, she couldn't live like this forever. Even *l'arte di arrangiarsi*, the Italian art of coming to terms with adversity, had its limits. Something needed to give, and it fell to him. Giovanni trudged through wintery Milan. Christmas lights were gleaming everywhere, and the cold seeped through the thin soles of his shoes.

How would his life have turned out if his family had stayed in the South? he wondered. He'd have become a farmer like his father, and maybe eventually he'd have managed to buy his own little parcel of land—a few square feet that nobody could drive him off. He walked to the Politecnico and watched students as they left the venerable old building. They sported nice coats and elegant haircuts—northerners. He occasionally heard the odd Tuscan or Roman accent, but none from the South. If he did enroll, he'd always be *il terrone*, the Sicilian.

He headed to a kiosk and spent a few lire on an issue of *Corriere della Sera*, which he opened to the apartment ads. Why did a person have a chance in this country only if they either inherited money or stole it? And why was it that the poorest of the poor were always fervently religious, like his mother? Was the Catholicism of the South a way of escaping bleak reality, or did his people not have the courage to take their life out of God's hands and into their own, to flout the rules and pursue their own self-interest with ruthless abandon? What was stopping him from robbing a bank—was he too ethical or just too much of a coward?

As night fell, Giovanni passed the Cinema Capitol on Via Croce Rossa. In the bright neon lights of the display window, he saw the placard for *Rififi*. Everyone at work had raved about it. Jean Servais played an aging gangster who cleaned out a jewelry store in Paris. Giovanni loved those film noir guys: trench coats with the collars flipped up, hats pulled low over their foreheads, cigarettes in their mouths. They didn't say a lot, but they knew what was what, and they died at the end. Giovanni bought a ticket and a pack of cigarettes and went into the current showing, already underway. Back then, you could buy one ticket and stay in the theater as long as you liked. Some people watched the same movie three times just so they could keep warm, smoke in peace, or reach under their secret lover's skirt. Giovanni slipped into one of the creaking, red-velvet-upholstered wooden seats just as Jean Servais was getting shot at by another gangster. It had something to do with money. The wounded Servais got behind the wheel of his American convertible, where a small boy was playing with a revolver and wanted to go home to his parents. By the time Giovanni had finished his first cigarette, Servais had brought the boy to safety and then died in a hail of police bullets. With a briefcase full of cash in his car. As the theater lights came up and most of the audience made its way out, Giovanni lit his next cigarette. He wanted to know how Servais had gotten the money.

While an old Sicilian cleaning lady swept her way through the rows, Giovanni went to the men's room. By the time he returned to the theater, the lights were down again, and the *Settimana Incom* was playing. Giovanni enjoyed the weekly news show—unlike most of the factory workers, he was interested in everything that was happening in the world. Whether it was a dam bursting in South Tyrol or the *Andrea Doria* ocean liner setting a new record time to New York, there was something to be learned from everything.

On the screen, Giovanni Gronchi, the new president, was signing an agreement with German chancellor Konrad Adenauer. Giovanni knew about Adenauer; Italians liked him because he was Catholic, and because he took vacations at Lago di Como. Giovanni had never been to Lago di Como, though the Milanese went there to swim. That required a car, and there were two kinds of people in Milan: those who built cars and those who owned them. But the newsreel that evening, December 22, 1955, would change Giovanni's life forever. That was the first time he heard the word "*Wirtschaftswunder.*"

A long, complicated word, hard at the beginning and soft at the end, and the news announcer pronounced it like a magic spell. *Il miracolo economico*, as it was called in Italian, meant chimneys smoking, wheels turning at coal mines, steel forges glowing. It meant places with names like Wolfsburg and Gelsenkirchen. It meant that people who had terrified the entire world just a few years ago, and then been left in complete shambles, had risen from the ashes of war like a steel phoenix. In Giovanni's view, *i crucchi* were Europe's most ambitious people. Maybe not the most fun, but so amazingly disciplined, diligent, and driven that it was impossible not to admire them. Not only were they rebuilding their own country in record time, they were even exporting around the world. Their former enemies were now buying their "Made in Germany" refrigerators, washing machines, and automobiles. The Germans' order books were so full that they had a shortage of workers—on farms, in hotels, in factories, and in coal mines.

The just-signed agreement between Germany and Italy would end up changing the face of Europe forever—but nobody knew that at the time, least of all Giovanni. He didn't even understand the document's complicated name: "Agreement regarding the recruitment of Italian workers for placement in the Federal Republic of Germany." All he knew was that this was the opportunity he had been searching for. He left the theater, his interest in seeing Servais clean out the jewelry store completely forgotten.

"Vita nuova nella Germania Occidentale," read the blue brochure the clerk pressed into Giovanni's hand. Behind him, dozens of southern men with thin, unshaven faces were pushing their way inside, talking loudly in Sicilian, Calabrian, Apulian, and Neapolitan. Their clothing was plain, their wide-legged pants tied around their narrow hips with a cord. They stank of sweat, poverty, and the musty odor of their villages. Giovanni remembered that smell of smoke and mildewed clothes from his childhood, and he hated it—so much so that the first thing he'd done when they'd arrived in Milan was to buy a bottle of cheap perfume, which he shared with Giulietta.

The men here were scarcely older than he was, and like him, they'd come by train to the "German Commission" in Verona, where the Federal Employment Agency had opened an office: a bottleneck for the Italians coming from villages in the South, carrying small suitcases stuffed with clothes and food, hoping to return from the North bearing large suitcases full of German marks. Giovanni didn't have a suitcase with him—not yet. He wasn't some hothead who leaped headfirst into things—he liked to keep his distance and play out all possible scenarios in his head before making a decision. He read the notes on the wall where German companies listed the positions they were looking to fill.

> **POSITION:** Welder, Number: 8, Employer: Rheinische Stahlwerke, City: Essen.

> **POSITION:** Miner, Number: 25, Employer: Zeche Lothringen, City: Bochum-Gerthe.

> **POSITION:** Dishwasher, Number: 2, Employer: Hotel Hirschberger, City: Garmisch-Partenkirchen.

And so on. Dozens of notes dangling before the eyes of the unshaven men, who were conversing loudly and coming together in small groups so they wouldn't be alone on their journey into the unknown. As soon as the right applicants had been found, the German clerks would remove that note and post two new ones. *Like the Milan Stock Exchange,* Giovanni marveled, *except here, they're trading people.* The anonymous work contracts for the German companies were already filled out and waiting. As soon as an applicant turned up, all they had to do was add the employee's personal information. The efficiency of the operation impressed the Italians, who were accustomed to waiting for days and weeks whenever government offices were involved.

Giovanni watched as, one after another, the men entered a room where two Germans in suits and ties were sitting behind a desk, taking notes as the poor saps paraded past. Those who looked reasonably strong were waved onward. Then a doctor would come and look into the guy's mouth and down his pants, and if he didn't have any communicable diseases, they handed him his employment contract right then and there, along with a package of food, ten German marks, and a ticket on the next charter train.

Giovanni was disgusted by the process. A modern-day cattle market. Most revolting of all was the subservience with which his countrymen submitted to it. He saw the mortification in their eyes, sometimes even silent rage, but nobody resisted. They had no choice. Where they came from, there was nothing to eat. Giovanni thanked heaven that he did have a choice. And he was about to turn around and walk out, but then he asked one of the men emerging with a contract in hand about his wages.

"How much is that in lire?" he asked the German clerk. The answer stopped him cold.

Working in a German coal mine, he'd earn almost twice as much as he made on the Iso assembly line. And that was just unskilled labor. If he got certified as a mechanic, they'd pay even more. They had rooming houses for the miners, health insurance, guaranteed union wages. Granted, the thought of toiling away in a dark, dusty tunnel frightened him. He'd seen newsreels about miners being buried alive. He wasn't sure if he'd go crazy down there, with no sun for weeks, months, years. But it would only be temporary. If he lived frugally, in a couple of years, he'd have enough money saved up to return and enroll in college.

"Come with me to Germania," Giovanni said to Enzo after dinner, setting the brochure on the table in front of him. "We'll get rich together, and when we come back, we'll build a house on Salina, for everyone."

Enzo read the brochure in silence. The photos showed beautiful single-family homes. "They give everyone a house?" he asked.

"They take care of everything," Giovanni replied. "*Porca puttana*, are they ever organized!"

"What do they pay?"

"As a qualified mechanic, you'd get two hundred German marks a month."

"How much is that?"

Once Giovanni had converted the sum to lire, Enzo tilted his head thoughtfully.

Giulietta ripped the brochure out of his hand. "No!" she exclaimed. "Never."

"Why not?" Giovanni asked. "They're looking for seamstresses as well. If you want, you can—"

"No! *Basta!* Who would take care of Mamma?"

"I'm not old," Concetta broke in. "Don't think about me. Think about your future. If you're doing well, I'm happy."

"We'll keep paying rent here, of course," Giovanni told her. "Don't worry. And we'll visit, and we'll be back in a few years. Giulietta, look, they even have preschools!" He pointed to the brochure.

"I'm not going up there. It's too cold!" Giulietta leaped to her feet angrily, bumping the table with such force that her plate fell to the floor and broke. Pasta splattered across the tiles.

"Giulietta, what's gotten into you?" Giovanni exclaimed. "Milan is cold, too!"

"What about little Vincenzo, ever thought about him?" she snapped. "He's delicate!"

The commotion woke Vincenzo, who was in the adjacent bedroom.

"What's the matter with you?" Concetta asked. "I can look after him if you want."

Giulietta ran to her bedroom and slammed the door. Enzo, Giovanni, and Concetta exchanged bewildered looks.

Later, Enzo went to talk to her. Then he came back out to Giovanni, shaking his head. "We're not going to Germany."

"Why not?"

Enzo shrugged. "She doesn't want to. And I'm not going without my family."

Giovanni was awake the entire night, smoking and staring out the window. Thick fog blanketed the canal. An adding machine rattled away inside his head. At some point, little Vincenzo began to wail. Giovanni heard his sister get out of bed to nurse him. Then she emerged from the bedroom, holding the baby in one arm; in her other hand was the mechanical sewing machine Giovanni had given her.

"Sell it," she told him. "And keep the money."

"Are you insane? That's your future!"

Giulietta shook her head resolutely. "This is my past. Vincenzo is my life now. Sell it and use the money to start a new life in Germany. That's your future."

Giovanni stared at her in horror. She set the sewing machine on the floor beside him and carried Vincenzo back into the bedroom. Through the half-open door, Giovanni heard her singing the child a Sicilian lullaby, the same one their own mother had rocked them to sleep with. Vincenzo soon drifted off, but

Giovanni remained wide awake. Secretly, he admitted to himself that it would be better if he went alone. He loved his sister more than anyone in the world, but if he stayed here, he'd lose his freedom the same way she had. What spurred him on, even more than the prospect of money, was the desire to be more than just a son, a brother, and an uncle—the desire to finally start living his own life.

Giovanni finished his apprenticeship, and in June 1956, shortly after Vincenzo's first birthday, he burned his army draft notice and bought an old cardboard suitcase at the flea market. As a going-away gift, Giulietta gave him a scarf she'd knitted, to protect him from the cold. Absurd as it was to walk around wearing a scarf in June, he wore it to honor his sister as the whole family escorted him to the train station.

He carried with him his new passport, his apprenticeship diploma, an official letter attesting that he was single, and a police certificate declaring that he wasn't a criminal. Giovanni had never returned to the German Commission in Verona, loathe to subject himself to that kind of humiliation. That meant he didn't have a job lined up, but he trusted that he'd find work once he was there. In Monaco di Baviera, the Bavarian city of Munich, where the trains full of *emigrati* arrived, hiring managers for the German companies were waiting on the platform to welcome those looking for work. People were talking about it all over Italy. They also said that the sky in Germany was always gray, the food was horrible, and the women were spectacularly blond.

Leaving was harder for Giovanni than he wanted to admit. It was six o'clock in the morning; the air was cool. Giulietta had pulled Vincenzo out of bed half-asleep.

"I'll be back, *angelino*," he promised. "And I'll bring you a present from Germany. Take good care of Mamma!"

Little Vincenzo stared at his uncle, wide-eyed.

Concetta slipped a medallion of San Bartolomeo into Giovanni's coat pocket. "He'll protect you on your journey."

"But you always say San Cristoforo is in charge of travel. You call on Bartolomeo when you lose your glasses."

"No, that's San Antonio. Now, be quiet and don't bring me shame, you hear?"

San Bartolomeo was Concetta's favorite saint, and a topic she considered no laughing matter. As an actual apostle of Jesus, he was the undisputed *capo* among the various saints of the Aeolian Islands. According to a legend that had terrified Giovanni and Giulietta as children, Bartolomeo had been skinned alive in Armenia and then thrown into the sea after his martyrdom. By the grace of God, his body had drifted to Lipari, where he was discovered on the beach and embalmed. To that day, a piece of his skin was kept at the sacristy of San Bartolomeo on Lipari. Two thousand years old. The mystery of how the islanders had gotten hold of a skinned man's skin had kept Giovanni up at night as a child, and had ultimately contributed to his semi-estrangement from the masochistic horrors of his mother's religion.

"God protect you!" Concetta gave her son a firm kiss on each cheek and sent him to the train.

"Hurry, before I start crying!" Giulietta grabbed Giovanni's hand when he was already stepping onto the train. She was doing her best to keep herself together, but Giovanni could see the fear in her eyes, the fear of being on her own. He cracked one joke after another, but nothing he said could cheer her up. All at once, she threw her arms around his neck and burst into tears. He tried to comfort her, but her body never stopped trembling, and she only released her brother when the train began to move. As it rolled out of the large station, Giovanni was the one crying—not for himself, but because he felt so guilty about leaving his sister. Through the dirty windows, he watched the passing houses, the ugly buildings of a city that had never become his. When he'd come to Milan from Salina, he'd lost the sea, but not his family. Now, the umbilical cord had been severed at last.

17

Giovanni's old suitcase contained three pairs of socks, three pairs of underwear, three shirts, a sweater. Razor, shaving cream, and a shaving brush—a white one made of modern plastic as he made no compromises in that regard. Toothbrush, mouthwash, nail file. "Always keep your nails clean—women notice that," his mother had told him time and time again. No second pair of shoes, because one was all he had, but he'd polished them the night before with a kitchen towel and olive oil. He was wearing his only suit, since he wanted to cut a *bella figura* on arrival. Plus, a rakish American hat, the kind Jean Servais wore.

The seven ten-mark bills he'd exchanged for lire at an office near the station were stuffed into his socks. At first, he'd thought the clerk was trying to pull his leg—it was ten thousand lire, after all! But then he learned that one German mark was worth a lot more than an Italian lira, and that unequal relationship gave him a small, bitter foretaste of his time in Germany.

He changed trains in Verona Porta Nuova. The station was bustling with southern Italians who didn't know their way around. Like Giovanni, they'd dressed up for the big journey. Most wore cheap summer suits, the pockets bulging with travel documents and provisions; some had ties and pocket squares. One Neapolitan was walking around in pinstripes and white spats. The atmosphere oscillated between public festival and air raid.

Then the charter train to Munich arrived, a brown Italian locomotive pulling a line of dark-green wagons emblazoned with the German National Railway logo. The train had departed from Bari the night before—eight railcars full of have-nots from the South, on their way to the Promised Land. Inside, the compartments smelled of oregano, garlic, and old socks. The toilets were clogged.

Packages of pasta and olive oil, salamis, entire wheels of cheese, were handed through the windows. Everyone had suitcases in their hands, dreams in their heads, fear in their hearts, and patron-saint medals in their pockets. Even the die-hard Communists. San Cristoforo, San Bartolomeo, and the Holy Madonna had to ride along to Germany. Heaven, at least, was fully employed.

Giovanni found a seat in a compartment full of Sicilians from Cefalù. Sicily was just a few hours' ferry ride from his home island, but to him as a child, it had been a completely different world. If an islander had married someone from Cefalù, it would have been a major scandal.

Out here, though, they recognized each other by dialect and greeted one another like family. They were four men, all older than Giovanni, all without formal job training. They shared their bread, showed him photos of their families and their contracts with Rheinelbe Mining Inc.

"What kind of company is that?" Giovanni asked.

"Coal," one replied.

"Where is it?"

The four men shrugged.

"What about you?" another man asked. "Where are you working?"

"I don't know yet."

"Come with us!"

"Maybe," Giovanni said, thinking to himself that they were going to need those medals. The people in the next compartment began to sing.

On the Brenner Pass, everything suddenly went still. German shepherds panted their way through the wagons. Austrian border guards checked their passports as American GIs waited on the platform with machine guns. It was cold up here. Everyone was uneasy, and when the train began moving again, the Sicilians launched into a workers' song. It made Giovanni think of his father. If he'd had the chance, he'd have come to Germany, too. And if there was a heaven for Communists, he was there, looking down at his son, proud of him for taking this opportunity.

The train arrived in Munich that afternoon. There was no choir waiting for the Italians on Platform 11, as some had expected; instead, they were all sent straight to the basement. The German National Welcoming Committee consisted of a gaunt official in horn-rimmed glasses, bellowing something into a megaphone that nobody could understand. Everyone shouted back and forth, passed suitcases through the windows, and then like a flock of sheep, they followed each other one by one down a flight of stairs and into a bare, smelly cellar underneath the platform.

The air was chilly, and the Italians grew anxious. Confusion and outrage spread across their faces. One wall had a long word written on it in old German script, which none of them could quite decipher: "*Luftschutzraum.*" As the official with the megaphone explained, this former air-raid shelter was now their *Weiterleitungsstelle*, whatever that was. The man with the megaphone ordered them all to deposit their suitcases on the luggage rack, take a number, and have their work contracts ready.

Two pudgy German women in white aprons handed out enormous mugs of coffee. Upon displaying their numbers, the new arrivals were each given a brown paper sack containing two hard rolls, a wedge of processed cheese, eighty grams of salami, a packet of shortbread, and a small bar of chocolate. Giovanni and his friends from Cefalù devoured the food in the middle of the jostling crowd as they waited for their numbers to be called. The coffee was wretched, but they took a few polite sips before setting the cups down.

The man with the megaphone sent anyone who didn't yet have a job offer into the next room, where one male doctor and one female were doing examinations, just a curtain to separate the two genders. At that time, nearly everyone making their way up north was male; women only began joining them a few years later. But no one was thinking that far ahead yet, least of all the Italians, who could scarcely imagine calling this cold country home. None of them wanted to stay, and the Germans didn't want them to, either.

That bunker was where Giovanni heard the term "guest worker" for the first time. It meant that he was a guest here for as long as he kept working. *Strange,* Giovanni thought. When they had guests at home, they didn't make them work. The man with the megaphone explained that he would be given a job immediately following his medical exam. Before Giovanni could ask what he would be doing and where, he was swept away by the hundreds of people streaming inside.

Giovanni realized that Platform 11 of Munich Central Train Station was Germany's Ellis Island. But while the Americans had put up a statue proudly greeting their immigrants, Germans sent theirs underground in embarrassment. Granted, the Americans had an equally rigid selection and delousing system. Only the desirable immigrants got in; anyone who had measles or a passport from the wrong country was sent back. But their style of humiliation had more panache: America promised its new arrivals that if they worked hard, they could be part of the country and its collective dream. Germany told its guest workers that they needed to work hard, keep quiet, and then go away. That was the deal: they didn't belong. And the immigrants themselves were equally convinced they'd be back home in a couple of years.

The doctor was a pale, haggard man who had seen better days, and probably better jobs as well. Judging from his movements and his tone of voice, he'd been a military doctor in the war. Giovanni greeted him with a *"Guten Tag,"* one of the phrases Giulietta had taught him before he left. The doctor merely nodded and then, without introducing himself, commanded Giovanni to undress. Giovanni acted as though he didn't understand, and the German repeated the command with gestures.

Reluctantly, Giovanni removed his jacket, then his shirt, then his shoes, and finally his pants. The doctor pointed to his socks. Giovanni shook his head. His money was in there.

"Hands behind your head," the doctor said, sounding annoyed.

He checked Giovanni's underarms for lice, shone a flashlight into his mouth, and handed him a cup to pee in. Giovanni glanced around for a toilet, but apparently, they meant for him to fill the cup right there. The doctor turned his back and began fiddling with a syringe. Giovanni wasn't a nervous person, but standing there on a cold bunker floor with his underwear down, urinating into a cup while a German prepared to jab a needle into his arm, made his imagination run riot. He began to sweat.

When the doctor turned around and started scrutinizing Giovanni's pubic hair, Giovanni decided he had had enough. Besides the fact that his health and hygiene were impeccable, he hadn't come to this country as a supplicant. The Germans were the ones who had recruited their "guests," and although he was glad to offer them his labor, he wasn't about to sacrifice his dignity. He handed the doctor his full cup and dressed again with meticulous care.

"No," the doctor said. "I still need to take a blood sample. Blood! *Sanguis!*"

Giovanni didn't understand a word, but he didn't care anymore. *"Danke schön,"* he said as he turned and left.

He pushed his way through the crowd in the bunker, ignoring the calls of the men from Cefalù as he took his suitcase from the luggage rack and went upstairs to the platform. He had no idea where to go, but any place was better than that subterranean slave market. He walked to the entrance, where he stopped for a moment and took a deep breath of fresh air. He deserved better than coal mining, and he recalled what Giulietta had said to him: *You're smart, Giovanni. You've got more than just a pair of hands—you have a head on your shoulders, too. Make something of your life!* He doubted that he was really quite as smart as his loving sister thought. But he had one thing that those poor saps in the bunker didn't: he knew a German.

For the first time in his life, Giovanni took a taxi. He didn't let on as he—a tram commuter who didn't even own a motor scooter—handed the German driver his suitcase, marveling at how the man greeted him in a friendly, almost obedient tone. So, it wasn't about where you were from, Giovanni thought. It was about what you had in your wallet. Giovanni slid into the back seat of the Mercedes Diesel, caressing the fine upholstery as he settled in. For the very first time, he got to decide where a vehicle went.

Giovanni, the newly self-appointed *capo*, had himself chauffeured to BMW. He marveled at how small the city seemed compared to Milan, almost village-like in its slowness. This wasn't the Germany people talked about in Italy. And he couldn't believe how many Isettas he'd seen on the streets already. He pointed to them to show the driver what he meant by "Bee Emme Vu," the Isetta-maker. The driver understood immediately but corrected him: Giovanni learned that, here, "Bee Emme Vu" was pronounced "Bay Em Vay." And he learned something else: when you were too friendly, the way he'd been with the doctor, people didn't take you seriously.

Giovanni told the driver in Italian that he'd come from Iso in Milano, just like the Isetta had, and that he had an important meeting at BMW. Even though the driver had no idea what he was saying, he nodded politely. Almost like the odd brown plastic dachshund on the dashboard, whose head was constantly waggling. Another lesson: it didn't matter what you said, just how you said it. And a healthy dash of arrogance couldn't hurt. Giovanni laid his left arm contentedly on the armrest, trying to conceal that his right hand was busy removing his shoe and his holey sock to fumble out a ten-mark bill. He rolled down the window so the driver wouldn't smell his feet, and prayed to San Bartolomeo that it would be enough money.

At the factory gate to Bavarian Motor Works in northern Munich, the power dynamics shifted again rapidly. The gateman, a thickset Bavarian, was thoroughly uninterested in what the foreigner with the cardboard suitcase had to say. No appointment, no entry. Anybody could come along and say he was the "*amico*" of "*Dottore*" Vincent Schlewitz, the "*ingegnere della Isetta.*" Giovanni's charm alone saved him from slinking away in defeat. A young secretary, a head taller than Giovanni and blond like a storybook princess, heard him arguing with the man. "Dottore Vincent Schlewitz" was her new boss now that he'd been promoted. She could speak a little Italian, and this particular Italian appealed to her. Giovanni noticed immediately that she wasn't wearing a ring, and he made yet another new discovery: German women liked Italians. She brought him to her boss.

Vincent's eyes widened in shock when Giovanni walked into his office, and Giovanni was fairly astonished as well: the little whippersnapper on the motorbike was now a chief engineer in a suit and tie, with his own office and his own secretary. He looked like one of those guys in American movies, talking about important things on telephones with blinking buttons before taking the train to their suburban homes with white picket fences. An advertising poster for the Isetta hung on the wall behind Vincent's desk. It looked different from the German Isetta. More grown-up, somehow. Vincent was a man who had made it. Giovanni hugged him exuberantly.

"*Amico! Signor Butt-o-Meter! Complimenti!*"

He'd known that Vincent probably wouldn't share his enthusiasm, given the circumstances under which they'd parted in Milan, but he wasn't prepared for just how coolly Vincent would react. He didn't even look Giovanni in the eye. The secretary, Ms. Marianne Kamps, set cups of drip coffee on the desk. Vincent didn't invite Giovanni to sit down.

"I always knew you'd go places in life!" Giovanni said in Italian, and beamed. He simply acted as though all were right with the world—two old friends reuniting after a long absence.

"What happened?" Vincent asked in German, pointing at the suitcase.

Giovanni fixed him with a solemn look and responded in German. "Me." He pointed to himself. "Work."

It took some time, along with Ms. Kamps's interpreting assistance, but Vincent eventually made it clear to his uninvited visitor that he wasn't in charge of hiring. They had a personnel department for that, and to be honest, he doubted BMW was looking for people at the moment. Giovanni couldn't tell whether Vincent was telling him the truth or just trying to get rid of an annoying beggar, and the last thing he wanted was to be viewed as a beggar.

"No problem," he said. "I'll find something. Thanks for the coffee." He got up to leave.

There was one subject they hadn't said a word about. Giulietta was the elephant in the room.

Vincent called him back. "Giovanni, where are you living?"

Giovanni shrugged.

"You want to stay with me for a couple days?"

Giovanni wasn't sure whether to accept the offer. It would mean he'd be in Vincent's debt. But where was he supposed to go? The bunker?

What he needed right now was time.

That evening, as Giovanni and his cardboard suitcase were standing in Vincent's apartment, an uneasy feeling came over him. The two-bedroom apartment in a sensible, newly constructed five-story building was fully furnished, yet it felt unfinished, unoccupied, far too large for a bachelor. As though the sofa set, the yellow Resopal table, the functional wall unit holding the television, the mint-green kitchen, and the white queen-sized bed were relics of a memory of something that was once supposed to happen but never did.

The place was missing a woman's touch, the things that would make it a home. There were no curtains on the windows, no tablecloth on the table, no rugs on the floors, no vases or flowers. The refrigerator was full of cans rather than fruit and vegetables. Vincent boiled water while Giovanni looked around awkwardly.

One corner of the living room exuded more life than the rest of the place put together: there was a picture of the Milan Cathedral hanging above the record player, with Caterina Valente records beside it, and a copy of Goethe's *Italian Journey* on the modern, kidney-shaped coffee table. In the wall unit, to one side of the books, stood a small framed photo of Vincent and Giulietta standing by his motorcycle in Milan. When Giovanni saw it, he knew that the story of his sister and the German had never ended. In fact, it had only just begun.

"You want a Muckefuck?" Vincent asked.

Giovanni looked at him in confusion.

"Coffee substitute. You just stir it right in. No filter, no waste."

Vincent poured some hot water into a cup.

"No, grazie," Giovanni replied.

Vincent drank in silence, and even Giovanni eventually ran out of things to say. Then Vincent suddenly asked in German, "Is she happy?"

Giovanni didn't understand at first.

Vincent pointed to the photo. *"Felice?"*

"Sì, sì," Giovanni replied, hoping Vincent wouldn't see that he was lying. *"È molto felice."*

"And the *bambino*?"

"Vincenzo? È un bellissimo bambino. Molto intelligente!" Giovanni tapped his forehead, but Vincent didn't reply. To bridge the agonizing silence, Giovanni withdrew a photo from his suitcase. It was of the entire family in front of the church by the canal, the day of Vincenzo's baptism: Giovanni and Giulietta in the middle, Enzo beside Giulietta and Concetta next to Giovanni, with Giulietta holding the little boy. Vincent studied the photo as though trying to find an explanation for the situation that had been torturing him all this time: Why had she left him?

Giovanni studied Vincent's face, picturing his nephew and searching for an answer to the question he had never dared ask Giulietta.

When Vincent couldn't stand looking at the photo any longer, he gave it back to Giovanni.

"Vincent," Giovanni said, *"Giulietta è una mamma. È finita. Basta, ciao, capisci?"*

No reply.

Vincent went into the kitchen and spread margarine on two slices of bread. He topped each with a slice of cooked ham, fished two slices of sweetened pineapple from an open can in the refrigerator, and placed the pineapple on top of the ham. Then he draped each one with a slice of processed cheese from a plastic package.

"Practical," he said. "The cheese always stays fresh, and you can portion it out exactly."

He put the whole thing in the oven. His favorite meal, he said, something a little exotic. He explained to Giovanni that it was supposed to have a maraschino cherry in the middle, but he hadn't had time to go shopping. Instead, he added a few shakes of a seasoning Giovanni had never heard of. Fondor, it was called.

"For fine flavor," Vincent said.

Giovanni kept silent about the fact that this was the first time he'd eaten pineapple, and he marveled at the Germans' culinary imagination. Italians would never have come up with this idea of layering ham and cheese, sweet and salty, right on top of each other. It was very practical: *primo*, *secondo*, and *dolce* all in one bite, which gave you more time to work. Maybe Toast Hawaii was the secret to the German economic miracle.

After they ate, Vincent showed Giovanni his black-and-white television. "There's even advertising on TV now!" he said proudly.

In the television commercial, a cheerful housewife made pudding with some sort of magic powder from a package. Then the husband came home from work, ate his pudding and was happy, and his wife was relieved that she'd made him happy.

The next commercial showed a German family eating lunch while a chef in a large hat checked the tastiness of their food with a strange apparatus called a "Yum-o-Meter." The mercury on the device measured just "medium-tasty" on the father's roast, but then the chef seasoned it again, and the Yum-o-Meter went up to "perfect." Giovanni recognized the yellow-and-red shaker—it was the powder that Vincent had sprinkled on their toast. "Fondor for fine flavor!" the housewife exclaimed, smiling, and everyone beamed. Vincent handed Giovanni a cigarette, and they smoked in silence, watching the television women make their husbands happy.

The next day, Vincent spoke to a personnel manager that Giovanni never saw. That evening, over Toast Hawaii, Vincent explained that BMW wasn't hiring anyone at the moment, not even Germans. The Isetta was selling well, but that was only enough to keep the company barely treading water and prevent them being taken over by Mercedes. Before they could start manufacturing in larger numbers again, they'd need to develop more moderately priced models, this time of their own design, and Vincent was in the middle of it. Young engineers were in high demand, but no production workers. Not yet.

"Go to Wolfsburg," Vincent told him. "The VW assembly lines are running full speed. Last year, they broke the one-million mark."

A million Volkswagens. When Germans went for something, they really went for it—whether cars or Stalingrad. Yet again, Giovanni was impressed by these people, who had risen to greatness out of rubble and ruin, armed only with diligence and technical expertise.

"VW's success won't last long, though," Vincent grunted. "The Beetle's an outdated prewar design. By 1960, nobody will be buying those things anymore."

Vincent seemed to consider the subject closed, and Giovanni understood that it was time for him to leave. *Guests are like fish,* they said back home. *After a couple of days, they start to stink.* And Vincent didn't exactly owe him any favors.

That same evening, Giovanni picked up his suitcase and left. Vincent didn't ask him if he wanted to stay, or where he planned to sleep. He simply wished him luck.

Giovanni didn't sleep anywhere. By midnight, he had found his way back to the train station, back to the catacombs beneath Platform 11. Another charter train had arrived; even at this hour, the bunker was filled with people looking weary after their long journey. Some were sleeping in chairs; a few had been given bunk beds. Giovanni asked the other Italians, "Anyone headed toward Wolfsburg?" But nobody had a job with Volkswagen. Wolfsburg was expanding, but since it was close to the East German border, they had enough laborers coming over from there for the time being.

The only offers Giovanni could find now were the ones his countrymen had passed up: pit worker in Duisburg, trash collector in Ennepetal, dishwasher in Husum. The bottom of the barrel. After his brief detour into a better world full of televisions and Toast Hawaii and blond secretaries, Giovanni was back to cold, ugly reality. That night, he understood that his dreams weren't worth a damn, that he was no better than his compatriots, just one poor bastard among many who had to work in order to survive. In this world of masters and slaves, he might never make it to the other side.

A guy from Palermo told him that they were still looking for people at the wholesale market right here in Munich. He'd found something there for eighty-five pfennigs an hour. So, Giovanni followed the man and signed on. For seventy pfennigs an hour. He lived in a wooden barracks in a field outside the city, a single room with seven other Italians. They shared a washbasin, a gas stove, and an immersion heater. Every morning at four o'clock, Giovanni got up, walked to the wholesale market, and carried crates of Sicilian oranges through the rain.

18

Monaco di Baviera,
30 settembre 1956

My dear sister,
Germany is wonderful. Here, anyone can make it, no matter
where they're from, no matter who they know. All that counts is
what you can do. They offered me a position at BMW, on the Isetta
production line, but I turned it down. I'm working at Mercedes;
they pay better there. Plus, their cars are bigger. Their customers
are high-society people. Soon I'll have enough money to come back
and start my own company. How's little Vincenzo? Give him a
kiss from me!
    Hugs,
    Giovanni

Milano, 16 ottobre 1956

Dear brother,
I was so happy when your letter arrived today. Not a day goes by
when I don't think about you and miss you. I'm so glad you're
doing well in Germany! I'm proud of you for making your own
way in the world. Look—I knitted these socks for you, to keep
you from freezing in the German snow! Vincenzo is growing so

fast, you'll hardly recognize him when you get back. It seems like he grows more every day, like he's taking extra-big steps now to catch up on his delayed development. He uses his little arms to pull himself up on all the furniture, and wobbles around the room on his own two feet. He's a real explorer, always has to be in motion, investigating everything. I don't want to keep this from you—after you left, he got sick again. His eyes. Dottore Scattà says it's an infection, and he mustn't look into the sunlight or his retinas might detach. So, I sewed dark curtains for us to hang in the windows. Of course, he's so curious, he's always going to the window, trying to peek outside. I really have my hands full keeping him safe.

Brother dear, there's so much to tell you. I often think about how, when we were children, we went down to the sea and sat on our rocks and told each other our little secrets. You know me better than anyone else on Earth. Sometimes I talk to you in my mind, wondering whether you can hear me. I wonder whether you have enough to eat, whether you've made friends, whether you miss us. And then I tell myself that I have to let you go, that you've got to go your own way, without me.

Love,
your sister, Giulietta

PS: Enzo says Mercedes is in Stuttgart.
Are you not in Munich anymore?

Monaco di Baviera,
24 dicembre 1956

Buon natale, dearest Giulietta.

My first Christmas without you. I'm sorry I can't come, and I'm sorry it's been so long since I wrote.

There's a German on this postcard. They eat white sausage with mustard, but not spicy mustard—theirs is mixed with sugar. They eat the sausage without knives or forks.

Picture it: they suck the meat right out of the casing with their mouths!

Hello to Mamma, Enzo, and Vincenzo!
Giovanni

PS: I'm still in Munich. Mercedes has a big dealership here, and I have a job in the workshop. I'll be a master mechanic soon.

Milano, 24 aprile 1957

Dearest brother,
It's a spring without sunshine. Outside, the trees are in bloom and the streets are full of people, but Vincenzo and I live behind closed curtains. I still haven't returned to work, because I can't leave Vincenzo alone with Mamma. Enzo, fortunately, is a devoted husband, so we don't want for anything. Vincenzo's eyes are the only thing I really worry about. Dottore Scattà says we need to be patient, but I get the feeling that even he's not sure anymore. Mamma thinks someone put the evil eye on him. You know how she is. She went to one of her friends, you know, and they did a coffee-cup reading for him. Guess what she said? He's going to be healthy. He's more sensitive than other children, because he has the fire of God in him. The talent to change the world. He'll go far with it, farther than any of us. But she says the fire is dangerous: people who have it in them and don't learn to control it will destroy everything they create.

Do you think that's true, Giovanni? Please call. I miss your voice.

Love, Giulietta

Milano, 27 dicembre 1958

Dearest brother,

Thanks so much for your Christmas present. Vincenzo loves it. And the best news of all: his eyes are healthy again. But the infection left a permanent scar: one of his eyes has turned brown, like mine; the other one is still blue-green. Dottore Scattà says it has to do with pigmentation, but he can see just fine.

At last he's allowed to go outside again. Up until now, he was living in his own little dream world, but now he's discovering the world outside the house, and he never stops asking questions: "Why can't we fly to the moon?" "Because it's too far away." "How far?" "I don't know. Far enough that there's no air to breathe." "But the Russians shot a dog into space." "Yes, but it died, unfortunately." "Why didn't they build him a better rocket?" "Because there aren't any better rockets." "Why not?" It goes on and on like that, constantly. The world isn't good enough for him the way it is.

Like his father, he loves cars. He wants to know all of their names, and he can already tell them apart better than I can. When we went shopping yesterday, a Mercedes drove by, and he recognized it immediately—it was just like the toy you sent him. He's proud to have an uncle who works for Mercedes.

How are you? When are you coming to visit us?

Love, Giulietta

A gust of wind blew through the courtyard, sweeping the old letters off the table. Giovanni bent to retrieve them.

"Why did she give back your letters?" I asked.

"She didn't," Giovanni murmured uncomfortably. "I went to get them myself. *Ancora un bicchiere?*"

He opened another bottle and filled my glass without waiting for an answer.

A little blues band was playing now, with Marco on guitar. He winked at me.

I suspected Giovanni had taken the letters after Giulietta's death, but it was clear he didn't want to get into that with me. We drank his wine, and I answered a few discreetly phrased questions about myself. Then there was something else I simply had to know.

"If you two were so close, didn't she ever confide who Vincenzo's father was?"

Giovanni was silent for a moment. "She knew that I knew that she knew."

"Why didn't you ever talk about it?"

"Wasn't important," he grumbled.

"But when you saw Vincenzo, you must have realized—"

"That was over. Past. Now she was a woman, a mamma. You have to forget. Life goes on."

I gave him a skeptical look.

"What was I to do?" he cried. "Take a boy's papà away? They were a *famiglia*. What right should I have to destroy them?"

I understood it wasn't my place to question his decisions. I decided to steer the conversation onto less dangerous ground. "She only ever talks about Vincenzo in her letters; there's nothing about her. Did she go on making clothes?"

Giovanni raised his eyebrows. "Vincenzo was her life. *Solo Vincenzo. Sempre Vincenzo.* He was her little prince."

"What about fashion?"

"She was talented. The way she worked with the fabric, it was—but she gave it up. I called her. I said, 'You have to start making clothes again. You have a thousand times more talent than me. If I can do it, so can you.' But she said, 'Giovanni, we are *gemelli*; the two of us are one. You have a career; I have a family. That's how we divide it up.'"

19

In the summer of 1962, as drivers were rolling down their windows to show passersby that they could afford a car radio, Giovanni traveled to Milan for vacation.

It was six years since he had left for Germany, and he decided he was old enough to tell his sister the truth at last. He knew his mother would ask him again when he was moving back to Milan for college. Surely, he had earned more than enough money by now. He'd learned to duck the questions, and sent photos of himself leaning against a Mercedes that wasn't actually his, because his wages were barely enough to survive on. He'd painted himself into a corner; the engineering degree he'd dreamed of was now well and truly out of reach, and no matter how hard he tried to curry favor with his German boss, no matter how much he joked around with his German coworkers and drank beer with them at lunch, in the wholesale market hierarchy, he would always remain the *maccherone*, an eternal member of the caste who did the dirty work at the very bottom of the food chain.

Although Giovanni was well liked, he was farther than ever from owning a Mercedes, or even lying beneath one as a mechanic. Maybe he lacked ambition, or what people referred to as a "calling." Giovanni simply struggled along, enjoying little adventures with his German girlfriends, and suddenly six years had passed.

People can get used to any lies, especially their own, but eventually they need someone they can tell the truth to. Even after his six years in exile, his sister was the only person he could think of. He had to confess to her. And she needed to help him tell their mamma.

He took the train over the Alps, a large heavy package sitting beside his cardboard suitcase. A gift for Giulietta. He was wearing a plaid jacket and the flat cap that had become his trademark. Sitting across from him was an elderly couple from Hamburg who told him that Italy was a beautiful country, but the coffee there was too hard on the stomach, which was why the wife had packed milder Nescafé, which the husband would prepare for them in the hotel using an immersion heater from home.

The apartment on Via Lodovico Il Moro still smelled of garlic, onions, and damp, reminding him of his childhood on the island. The old furniture and the wallpaper hadn't changed. Giulietta was starting to look more like Mamma, though. She'd gained weight, and she'd developed those fine worry lines around her mouth that distinguished all mothers from the young women they were before.

Vincenzo was already finished with second grade; he'd started school earlier than the other children, having taught himself reading and math at home. He was lively and hungry for knowledge, and he loved his uncle from Germany who told funny stories that seemed like they must be made up. He didn't care, just loved hearing about things like Mercedes world records, crazy race car drivers, and beer glasses the size of buckets.

"Will his eyes always be that way?" Giovanni asked his sister.

"Yes."

"How strange."

"Mamma says it's a sign."

"Of what?"

"That he sees more than we do."

Giovanni didn't believe in his mother's Sicilian hocus-pocus, but he found it hard to pretend that the boy's eyes didn't bother him. When you look into someone's eyes, you really see just one eye. When he looked from one of Vincenzo's eyes to the other, it was like looking at two different people. *But what can the boy do about it?* Giovanni thought, and dropped the subject.

At dinner, Giovanni set his large package on the table, grinning. "Open it!"

Vincenzo helped his mother unwrap the present.

"It's a Singer," Giovanni said. "Like Grandma's, do you remember? But this one's modern! All electric!"

He'd been expecting Giulietta to be pleased with the elegant white sewing machine, but her response was muted. She thanked him politely, placed the machine on the floor, and set the table.

Giulietta had changed. She was still a beautiful woman, but the sparkle in her eyes, while not entirely gone, seemed to have turned inward. Her face was more serious now, her movements mechanical. Everything about her seemed focused on fulfilling her duties as a housewife and a mother. She smiled as she brought the pot of pasta to the table, but her brother suspected she wasn't happy with her life.

Vincenzo leaped out of his chair to inspect the curious machine. The delicate little toddler had become an intelligent, boisterous child. Enzo called him back, but in vain—Vincenzo had completely forgotten about his pasta and wanted to plug the sewing machine in immediately to start it up. But the plug didn't fit the Italian socket.

"Papà, we have to rebuild the socket!" he called.

Giovanni lured him back to the table by handing him his own gift—a model car. Silver, with gull-wing doors. A Mercedes.

"Mamma, look, a Mercedes. An SL! Do you have one like this, Giovanni?"

"No."

"But you said you had a Mercedes!"

"Sure, but mine has four doors. So you can get in and out more easily, you know?"

"But then, why did you come by train?"

"Italian streets are hard on the chassis, you see. In Germany, they have the Autobahn, straight as an arrow, no potholes!"

"Didn't you hear?" Enzo piped up. "We're building the Autostrada del Sole, from Milano to Napoli, across the Po Valley, over the mountains, straight on through. They're relocating entire villages for it!"

"Sure, but the German Autobahn is even straighter."

Enzo fell silent.

Giulietta kissed Giovanni on the head. "I'm so proud of you, brother dear! I always knew you'd go far in life."

"He only has one mouth to feed," Enzo retorted.

Giovanni was startled by the resentment in his voice. Though Enzo had never spoken of it, Giovanni knew he'd always been jealous of the bond between the siblings. No matter how he tried, his wife would never confide in him the way she did in her brother.

"Show your uncle your pictures, Vincè," Giulietta said to change the subject.

Vincenzo jumped up and returned with a stack of paper. "Look, these are my creations!"

Giovanni laughed in delight. They were pages of graph paper torn from his school notebook, and he'd drawn cars on them. Not just any cars, though—cars that didn't actually exist.

"This one's a rocket car!" Vincenzo explained. "The gas tank is up front. The driver sits in the middle, and the rocket engine is in the back."

"Bravo, Vincenzo, bravo!" Giovanni said as he thumbed through the drawings: a car with wings, a car with a helicopter rotor, and a submarine car.

"Why don't you build something like that, Papà?" he asked Enzo.

"Because it doesn't exist."

"So what? That's not even true—rocket cars exist. In Germany. Didn't you see those in Germany, Uncle Giovanni?"

"Nonsense," Enzo grunted.

"Is not, I read it!"

"You should be reading your schoolbooks instead. Did you do your homework?"

Vincenzo dashed off to retrieve a book. He opened it and pointed to a photograph of a black iron cigar on wheels, with flames coming out of the back. White letters on the side read, "OPEL." "See?"

"You're right, Vincenzo," Giulietta said.

"See, Papà? I was right!"

"Go do your homework."

Vincenzo stuck out his tongue.

"Don't do that to your father," Giulietta scolded. "Now, do your homework."

He obeyed his mother. Enzo was silent.

"*Allora*, Enzo," Giovanni said to lighten the mood, "tell me about Iso! Still at the same job?"

Enzo nodded.

He'd lied. Unlike Giovanni, however, he'd downplayed his success. The following day, Giovanni accompanied Enzo to the factory to visit his old friends. It was Saturday, but Enzo had a weekend shift. Vincenzo came with them, running through the halls as though he lived there. The workers clearly knew the boy and liked him. When they walked into the hall where Enzo and Giovanni had once assembled Isettas, Giovanni stopped dead in his tracks. The bubbly minicars were gone, replaced with big brand-new GTs, so beautiful and modern that Giovanni was rendered speechless.

"Commendatore Rivolta used the money from the Isetta licenses to invest in a new design," Enzo said. "The Iso Rivolta GT. Didn't you hear about it at Mercedes? The *commendatore* presented it at the Turin Motor Show."

Giovanni shook his head. He couldn't take his eyes off this exquisite beauty. It was more than a car. It was an artistic montage of all the best that automotive engineering had to offer.

A chassis by the ingenious engineer Bizzarrini with a De Dion rear axle, topped with an elegant Granturismo body by Bertone, designed by Giorgetto Giugiaro, with a German five-speed transmission, the finest hand-sewn leather interior, and under the hood, an eight-cylinder American Corvette engine. With more than three hundred cubic inches and three hundred horsepower, it was poised to topple Ferrari and Maserati as king of the Autostrada. Renzo Rivolta, who had been laughed at for manufacturing the smallest car in Italy, was now creating the country's finest sports car. And Enzo, the quiet, modest mechanic from the assembly line, was building it. Giovanni gaped silently.

"You're rich, Uncle Giovanni," Vincenzo called. "Why don't you buy yourself one?"

That night, Giovanni and Giulietta sat out on the old wooden bench in front of the church on the far side of the canal, smoking in the same spot they had as teenagers, far from their mother's eagle eyes. Giovanni tried to find the right words to tell Giulietta that he was an *imbroglione*, a liar, a charlatan. But she beat him to it.

"Giovanni, I lied. In my letters. I'm not doing well."

Giovanni hesitated.

"My marriage to Enzo—we live together, but—Mamma always said love develops over time, but it's been more than seven years, Giovanni."

Once Giulietta started talking, she didn't stop. The words poured out of her, everything she hadn't told another living soul for years, not even the priest at confession.

"Enzo's a good father, but I'm afraid Vincenzo is more than he can handle."

"In what way?"

"He has such a lively spirit. He has so many questions his father can't answer. Fathers should be smarter than their sons, shouldn't they?"

"But they get along, they have the same passion, he brings him to the factory . . ."

"You don't understand. They're different. They fight. Vincenzo is always contradicting him, sometimes for good reason, sometimes not. One of these days, and it won't be long, Vincenzo will surpass his father, and Enzo knows it. It pains him. Have you ever felt superior to Papà?"

Giovanni considered the question. No, their father had been an authority no one could challenge. Even now, long after his death, nobody was allowed to speak ill of him.

"No, that would have been hard," Giovanni replied. "I mean, Papà was a hero, right? A tragic hero, one who paid for his own stubbornness with his life."

"He wasn't stubborn. He was true to himself."

"Yes. He was. But what's that got to do with Enzo? Sons always chafe at their fathers—that's normal. You worry too much, Giulietta."

She was silent, staring out into the night.

"Enzo's jealous," she said at last.

"Of who?"

"Nobody."

"Nobody, how?"

"He follows me when I go shopping. He's always asking where I've been and who I was with. He's obsessed with the idea that I'm having an affair."

"Are you?"

"Of course not! I swear, Giovanni, there's nobody else. He's my husband!"

Giulietta paused for a moment to get her voice under control.

"A few days ago," she continued, "I went down to the trattoria because we were out of parsley. He came after me. I saw him peeking in through the window. When he realized I'd spotted him, he hid. So, I went out and said, 'Enzo, what the hell are you doing here?' And he actually asked me if there was something going on between me and the padrone. *Madonna mia*, where would he get that idea?"

Giovanni took Giulietta's hand and squeezed it. "Why don't you two make more *bambini*?"

"We're trying, but—" She shook her head. "It's not meant to be. Maybe it's my destiny to be there for just Vincenzo. He's doing well in school, you know. He's ahead of the others, even though he's younger. They all envy him."

"What if you go back to work?"

Giulietta shrugged. "What would that change?"

"Are you still making clothes?"

"I quit."

"Why?" Giovanni squeezed her hand again. "You were so good at it. Come with me to Germany! Bring Enzo and Vincenzo! They need workers. I'll find you something in the clothing industry!"

Giulietta stared at the canal bridge in front of the church. "You always said you'd come back, Giovanni. Why don't you come back?"

"Because—" Giovanni couldn't get the words out.

Giulietta gazed at him for a long moment. "You've changed."

"So have you," he said.

She got up. "Come on, Mamma's waiting."

Giovanni took her arm to hold her back. "Do you really want to waste the best years of your life by this smelly canal? What's wrong with you? You used to want to travel, you learned languages, you always wanted to see Venice . . ."

She turned away, weeping silently.

"You're right, Giovanni," she said, looking at him. "But I can't come to Germany."

The next day, Giulietta left the apartment early and returned at noon with a bag full of material. Instead of preparing lunch, she sketched a pattern, put it in the bedroom beside her new sewing machine, and began making a dress. When Enzo came home that evening, he found Vincenzo on her lap, watching in fascination as the thread traveled across winder, looper, and shuttle. Enthusiastically, he explained the interplay of the upper and lower threads to his skeptical father, and when Giulietta finally got up to fix dinner, Vincenzo disassembled the machine into its individual parts.

Enzo sat silently during dinner as Giulietta described the dress she'd begun: an asymmetrical white sheath dress with straight, black appliqués and large buttons. Like the ones Coco Chanel made in Paris.

"And who's going to wear it?" Concetta asked.

"Me, Mamma."

"What will people say?"

"Why should they say anything? I'm not doing anything wrong."

"But they'll envy you. You'll draw the *malocchio*! The evil eye!"

"I don't care! I'm not buying it. I'm making it with my own two hands!"

"You think you're better than us?"

"Leave her alone, Mamma," Giovanni protested. "She could earn a little extra money, sewing for people."

"She doesn't have to," Enzo grunted. "I earn enough. We may not be able to afford a Mercedes, but we're not lacking for anything."

"If it's God's will, he'll give you another *bambino*," Concetta declared resolutely, and the table abruptly fell silent. Vincenzo looked at his parents questioningly, but they avoided his eyes. Every family in the neighborhood had at least two or three children. Their failure to conceive was like a blot on the family.

Enzo laid his large, hairy hand on Giulietta's arm. "It's okay," he said affectionately.

At the end of August, Giovanni headed back across the Alps, never having told the truth about his life in Germany. He had less sense than ever of where he belonged. Unlike Giulietta, he didn't even have a spouse, let alone a child. And though his sister was conflicted over her talent, she still had one, which was more than he could say. There had been no prophecies in his childhood, no promises, no predestined path. He'd just been put into the world and left to his own devices on the broad slopes of the island, which he'd combed with scraped calves, searching for firewood or berries or lizards, between the volcanic rubble and the endless sky.

If he was being honest, he thought, he wasn't ambitious enough to make anything of himself. He liked eating and drinking, and instead of pursuing an education in the evenings, he preferred to go out dancing and enjoy the effects of his charm on German women. Maybe it was too late for him to ever return to Italy. Maybe he'd never own a Mercedes. *Everyone,* Giovanni thought, *is unhappy in their own way.* The only person who never complained was Enzo. Because he'd never wanted to become anything more than he already was. A solid, down-to-earth man for whom work simply meant fulfilling his duty to feed his family. One who had never thought that his career needed to be a calling, and was thus free of any presumption, perfectly content with himself and the world.

"You use the oil on salad, right?"

The friendly voice of the German woman in his compartment jolted Giovanni out of his reverie. The brown faux-leather seats beside his were occupied by a family in flowered shorts on their way back from vacation in Rimini; the children were wearing straw hats, and all four had sunburned faces. The woman gestured to the assortment of boxes and bottles Giovanni had stuffed into the luggage rack: olive oil, salami, cheese, pasta, pesto, and wine.

"We cook with it," Giovanni said. "Meat, fish, vegetables. In the pan."

"It's pressed from olives?"

"Yes. It's very good." Giovanni picked up the bottle of oil and showed it to the woman.

"Look, Gerhard." The woman handed the bottle to her husband.

"Nocellara olives from Messina," Giovanni explained. "Not very well known, but—"

"My wife uses margarine," the man grunted. "Top-quality margarine."

Upon arriving in Munich, Giovanni distributed the goods to his countrymen, who were standing on Platform 11 of the drafty station as usual, waiting for news and food from home. They paid him in German marks, cigarettes, and empty promises.

Twilight descended over the courtyard behind Giovanni's house. Lanterns hung over the empty picnic tables; most families had already gone home.

"I'm the only one in the *famiglia* with *nessun talento. Zero.*" Giovanni grinned. "But you know what? Only stupid people are happy. The smart ones see the world for what it is—*un macello. Un disastro.* A nuthouse. And then they go crazy themselves."

Rosaria gathered up the used plates. "Good thing you're not a genius. Move over."

Giovanni winked at me. "Sure I am. I'm just so brilliant that I don't tell anyone."

"A closet genius."

"*Ecco.* See? You understand me." Giovanni put an arm around his wife. "You know she owns a company? She's a famous artist!"

"Hardly," I said. "I'm in debt up to here."

I was embarrassed by his making a fuss. Secretly, though, I would have found it even more embarrassing if I were meeting my dad's family for the first time without having achieved anything. I kept silent about the thing that truly filled me with shame: the fact that I was about to lose control over my company.

"*Brava!*" Rosaria exclaimed. "Your *nonna* is looking down at you from heaven!"

I wondered whether I would have chosen the same career path if I'd known my grandmother, and if so, what I would have done differently. Probably nothing, but it still gave me the sense of not being alone in my passion, of having a like-minded person at my back, someone who understood me and supported me.

"Did Giulietta sell the clothes she made?" I asked.

Giovanni nodded. "*Sì*. But she didn't have a big business like you do."

"Enough for her to live on?"

"It wasn't for the money," Giovanni replied. "For Giulietta, making dresses was like breathing."

I tried to picture what it was like for her back then.

"You're lucky you grew up in Germania. In Italia, without a *raccomandazione*, you're nothing. Here, you pursue your *passione*."

If this was genuinely my calling, I thought to myself, then why wasn't I happy? I'd grown up confident that if you just stayed true to yourself, you'd make it. But since Milan, I wasn't so sure anymore. Maybe, I thought, this family's real heritage was failure.

"So, didn't you have another papà?" Giovanni asked with unabashed indiscretion.

"I had a lot of papàs, but really I didn't have any." I paged through the photo album, looking for a way to change the subject. Vincenzo, maybe ten years old, in the production hall with his father, next to a half-finished sports car. It was the same model as the one Vincent had driven me home in.

Another photo: Vincenzo, sitting at the dining table and drawing a futuristic car with tail fins and wings. Upon closer inspection, it wasn't a picture like other kids draw—it was like schematics, a kind of exploded diagram where Vincenzo had sketched each part separately, from the frame to the motor, the doors, and the mirrors.

"When did you find out that Vincenzo was Vincent's son?"

Giovanni was silent. He didn't appreciate the question, and he made sure I could tell. Then he slid the album toward himself and flipped through until he found a picture of himself and Giulietta on a white motor scooter. She was wearing a breezy summer dress, her arms wrapped around him from behind. Giovanni, in lightweight white slacks, an open plaid shirt, and that same rakish flat cap, was riding through Milan; perched between his legs was eleven-year-old Vincenzo. Underneath, it read, *"Agosto 1966."*

"It must have been then. On vacation."

Although Giovanni acted as though it was none of his business, he remembered every detail of that summer day . . .

20

It was a summer of long hair and short skirts, of transparent chiffon blouses and silver space-age pantsuits. The Beatles played their last concert. Revolution was in the air. Giovanni was in his early thirties and still a bachelor, which prompted his mother to increase the frequency of her prayers to San Bartolomeo. Giovanni, who had by now magically ascended to managing director of Mercedes Munich in the minds of his family, was with his sister and his nephew, riding an Iso motor scooter through Milan's streets now depopulated of Milanese. It was a hot summer, and Adriano Celentano, that spindly, Milan-born southern Italian in white flared trousers, was tootling from the car radios. Uncle Giovanni had come down from Munich on the night train. They were on their way to visit Enzo on his lunch break. Giovanni had brought him a can of Vienna sausages and a bottle of wheat beer.

Vincenzo had changed. Now that he was on the verge of adolescence, his childlike sensitivity had given way to greater confidence. He'd seemed distracted and restless before, but now he showed astonishing concentration and determination. He'd skipped a grade at the *scuola elementare* and graduated early to the *scuola media*, where he'd passed his first year with flying colors. He'd discovered the world of books and now spent entire afternoons in the school library. While his friends read comics, he devoured everything he could find on Leonardo da Vinci, the man people said had awakened early in a time of darkness, while everyone else was still asleep. Vincenzo pored over every detail of his sketches and copied them himself. The anatomical and artistic works didn't interest Vincenzo as much; his enthusiasm was for the ingenuity of da Vinci's machines—airplanes, submarines, automobiles, all well before their time. What others had only managed to realize centuries later, he'd done calculations for back in the fifteenth century.

Vincenzo learned that the world wasn't shaped by mysterious forces but by natural laws, which humans could discover and apply, transforming their existential vulnerability into mastery. He learned that everything started with an idea, and that sketches translated those immaterial concepts into two-dimensional images, which could then be converted into three-dimensional reality.

He rode his bike along the canals and sluices da Vinci had designed, putting himself inside the mind that had invented Milan's first system of trash collection by boat. He peppered his parents with questions they couldn't answer. He wanted to know the names of the people who had invented every object: toasters, coffee grinders, aqueducts, rockets. He asked himself what his own contribution could be to the world, what things no inventor had ever invented. It was obvious to him that the world was incomplete, and he thought of inventors and engineers as a society of visionaries who, equipped with the secret knowledge of the sciences, set out to fulfill the world's boundless potential.

"Guarda che bella!" Inside the factory, before they found Enzo, Vincenzo ran to a nearly fully assembled car and waved his uncle over. *"Che macchina!"*

Giovanni had to agree with his nephew; he'd never seen a more beautiful car than this one, the Iso Grifo, waiting in the semidarkness of the production hall for its first drive, like a predatory cat poised to strike. Unlike the company's first coupés, which had followed a noble, purist philosophy, this new creation looked like an erotic dream in sculpture form. An endless, curved hood, flowing lines atop muscular flanks, and a tight tail. Pure sex. A high-performance sports car from the mind of Giorgetto Giugiaro, who combined the casual largesse of American muscle cars with the elegance of Italian Granturismo.

"Trecentocinquantacinque cavalli, cinque virgola quattro litri, otto cilindri, cambio a cinque marce oppure automatico . . ." Vincenzo rattled off technical details as though he had designed the car personally.

Giovanni ran his fingers along the chrome window bars. "How much does it cost?"

"Forget it, Giovanni," Giulietta laughed. "It costs as much as a Ferrari."

"And it's just as fast!" Vincenzo added. "But far more reliable. It's the best car in the world!"

Giovanni avoided thinking about why, in this society, the best things were only affordable for the few, and whether that made them better than others. He glanced around for Enzo. Just then, he heard a voice outside.

"Signor Butt-o-Meter! Che piacere!"

And then a second male voice that made Giulietta stop dead.

"Signor Preti!"

Outside the gate—silhouetted against the glare—two men were embracing after many years. *Ingegnere* Ermenegildo Preti, the father of the Isetta, and Signor Butt-o-Meter, Vincent. Before Giovanni could ask his shocked sister what the German was doing here, she grabbed Vincenzo's arm and pulled him away.

"Come on, Giovanni. Let's go to the cafeteria."

Giovanni followed, but before they reached the door, Preti called after them. "Giulietta! Giovanni! Look who's come back! *Oé!*"

Little Vincenzo turned around.

"Ciao, Vincenzo. Come va?" Preti called.

Giovanni saw Giulietta turn to stone. When she heard Preti's approaching footfalls, she quickly put Vincenzo's hand in Giovanni's and gave him a stern look. "You stay with your uncle. I'll be right back."

Then she took a deep breath and walked toward the gate. Giovanni remained behind, holding the hand of the bewildered boy.

"Guess who's come to visit!" Preti exclaimed as he led Giulietta to the door. "Look what became of our Butt-o-Meter! He's picking up his new car!"

From across the factory floor, Giovanni watched Giulietta and the German shake hands. He couldn't hear whether they said anything. Time seemed to stand still.

"Who's that?" Vincenzo asked.

"Nobody."

"Why nobody?"

"Because . . ."

"Did you see the car?" Vincenzo freed himself from Giovanni's grasp and ran to the gate. Giovanni hurried after him, but Vincenzo was faster. The silver-gray metallic lacquer of a new Iso Rivolta GT glittered in the sun. The subtler, more understated of the company's two sports cars. It was a particularly fine specimen, with gleaming Borrani spoke wheels, a sunroof, and burgundy-red leather seats.

"Ciao, Vincenzo. How are you?" Preti called.

Giulietta, who hadn't seen her son coming, whirled around in alarm.

"Vincenzo, go to the lunchroom!" she snapped.

Vincenzo startled, but he couldn't drag himself away from the Rivolta.

The stranger asked Giulietta a question in a language Vincenzo didn't understand. Giulietta nodded curtly.

"Ciao," the man said in a friendly tone, and extended his hand to Vincenzo.

Like everyone who saw Vincenzo for the first time, he did a double take to make sure that the boy's different-colored eyes weren't an illusion. Vincenzo looked uncertainly at his mother, silently asking permission.

"Did you find Papà?" Giulietta asked instead.

Vincenzo shook his head without taking the stranger's offered handshake.

Then Vincent saw Giovanni standing by the gate. "Giovanni."

"Ciao, Signor Butt-o-Meter!"

They shook hands, and Giovanni gave Vincent a friendly clap on the shoulder to mask his discomfort.

"What are you doing here—looking for work in Italia?" Giovanni joked in German.

"No, just here to pick up my car."

"*Macché*, are you a millionaire now?"

"No, no," Vincent said in a reserved tone. "But I registered a couple of patents."

While the adults conversed, Vincenzo took the opportunity to peer inside the car through the open driver's side window.

"Hands off!" Giulietta exclaimed.

"It's okay," Vincent said in German. Then he turned to Vincenzo. "Want to sit inside? *Dentro la macchina?*"

The boy nodded politely.

Giovanni saw the panic in his sister's eyes.

"Come, Vincenzo. We're leaving," she said.

But Preti smiled obliviously. "Oh, let the boy sit. He won't break anything."

Vincent opened the driver's side door and removed his perforated leather gloves from the seat. Vincenzo's eyes filled with reverence. Only high-society people and race car drivers wore those. He clambered into the driver's seat, sweeping his gaze across the dashboard's brilliant chrome, the wooden steering wheel, and the black Bakelite toggle switches. He breathed in the scent of the leather and ran his hand over the gleaming silver griffin on the steering wheel, the mythical cross between a lion and an eagle, the Rivolta family crest. He was in another world, a world where everything was fine and elegant, where men had everything under control.

"Start the engine! *Il motore!*" Vincent smiled and stuck the silver key into the ignition. "Put it in neutral."

Vincenzo understood in spite of the German words. He engaged the clutch and turned the ignition, and the eight-cylinder sprang to life, rumbling low. The car vibrated beneath Vincenzo's body, and his foot gently touched the gas pedal until the engine was running smoothly. Giulietta grew increasingly nervous with the way Vincent was observing the boy. His gaze was friendly and attentive, but searching as well.

"How are you?" she asked Vincent, trying to distract him.

"Good. You?"

"Good."

Between words, they regarded one another, peering out of their own invisible armor, looking for an unprotected spot in the other's defenses. They studied the fine lines that had formed in each other's faces, searching for twelve years of untold stories, as images preserved in memory bubbled to the surface as though not a second had passed.

Impulsively, Giovanni sat down in the passenger seat to distract Vincenzo. They twisted the knobs and switched the car radio on. Some station was playing Fabrizio de André.

"Are you still in Munich?" Giulietta asked.

"Yes."

"Do you have children, too?"

"No."

Her gaze darted to his hands. No ring.

"I've been working a lot. Time just flew by. How everything changes . . . Back then, just riding a motorcycle over the Alps was an adventure. Today, you can fly to New York in eight hours."

Giulietta nodded without replying. Though outwardly composed, inside she was overwhelmed with a torrent of shame, guilt, and helpless rage.

Vincent turned to the boy. "Want to take a little drive?"

Vincenzo didn't understand and turned to Giovanni for translation.

"Come on, *figlio mio*, out of the car—we have to go."

Vincenzo reluctantly obeyed.

Vincent took Giulietta aside. "Can I talk to you alone for a moment?"

Giulietta hesitated, but feared that Vincent was willing to speak his mind in front of the others if need be, so she walked a short distance from the car with him.

Giovanni watched closely. He couldn't hear what they were saying; he knew only that Vincent asked her something and Giulietta shook her head, and then a sudden, brief argument erupted, in which Vincenzo's name was mentioned.

"No!" Giulietta cried, stomping away to grab Vincenzo's hand tightly. "Come on, hurry up! Giovanni, we're going home!"

She hurried away without waiting for her brother. The boy turned to look back at them one last time, but then disappeared into the hall along with his mother. Vincent glanced at Giovanni and the confused Preti. Then he slipped on his gloves.

Preti turned to Giovanni. "Tell him Renzo Rivolta has invited him to lunch."

Giovanni translated. Vincent thanked Preti politely but said he needed to get back to Munich. Another time.

"Dottore, you can't refuse the *commendatore*'s invitation!"

Vincent apologized, got behind the wheel of his new car, and drove off.

Giovanni exhaled in relief. But an uneasy feeling in his stomach told him that these few minutes would have far-reaching consequences.

"Did you see his gloves?" Vincenzo exclaimed loudly. "With holes! For ventilation!"

They were sitting at the trattoria beneath their apartment, the asphalt gleaming yellow in the light of the streetlamps. It was a humid evening; smog hung over Milan like a bell jar, and hardly a breath of air rustled the red-and-white checked cloths on the small tables. "Giovanni, when I grow up, I'm going to come to Germany and work at your company!"

Enzo cast a scrutinizing glance at Giulietta. She avoided eye contact.

"Bring us a bottle of red," Giovanni called to the waiter. "But not the house red—it's no good. A nice French wine, okay?"

"Mamma, why don't we go to Germany?" Vincenzo tried again.

"Don't you like it here?" Giulietta asked as Enzo brooded.

"Sure I do. But in Germany, they're rich."

Basta!" Everyone jumped when Enzo suddenly smacked his palm against the table. Giovanni's glass fell over. He barely managed to catch it before it could shatter on the asphalt. "Germany this, Germany that. Don't you two see you're making the boy crazy?" He bent toward Vincenzo. "What, isn't Italy enough for you? It's the most beautiful country in the world!"

"How would you know?" Vincenzo retorted. "You've never been anywhere else." Unlike his mother, he didn't get intimidated when Enzo raised his voice. Quite the opposite, in fact.

"Your family is here. And if everyone runs off and leaves it for the bandits, this country will go to the dogs. You want to build cars? You can build them here. Like your father. We make the best cars in the world! Why do you think that German came down here instead of spending his money on a German car, huh?"

Giulietta took Enzo's hand to placate him, but Vincenzo refused to drop the subject. "What good is it to build cars if you can't buy them?"

Enzo grabbed Vincenzo's ear. "Listen here, Son. We aren't fancy snobs with leather gloves. I work with my hands! See that? That's the feel of hands that are worth something!"

"Let go of him!" Giulietta cried, horrified.

Enzo ignored her. Vincenzo shrieked in pain, and Giovanni stepped in. "Enzo, leave him be!"

"You stay out of it, millionaire!" Enzo yanked his son close and looked him dead in the eye. "We're Sicilians. *Terroni.* We get our hands dirty, but we're honest people."

Vincenzo kicked his leg furiously. "Asshole!"

Enzo slapped him across the face so hard that Vincenzo nearly fell out of his chair. "You talk like that to your father?"

"Enzo!" Giulietta shrieked, and smacked his hand away. Her glass crashed to the ground and shattered. The other customers glanced over uneasily and whispered among themselves.

Vincenzo stared at his father in silence. His body was quivering; his eyes were shimmering; he was fighting back tears but didn't want to let his guard down. Not a word passed his lips, but in that moment, Giovanni saw something break inside him. Something that would never be whole again.

Abruptly, Vincenzo turned and ran across the street to the bridge.

"Vincenzo!" Enzo shouted. "Come back!" He got up to follow his son, but Giulietta held him back.

"Leave him," she said. "It's too late."

Giovanni chased after the boy.

He caught up to him on the far side of the canal near the church wall. "Vincenzo! Stop!" He put a hand on his shoulder. Vincenzo averted his eyes, trying to hide the tears.

"Sit," Giovanni said, gesturing to the little bench. "This is the Bench of Sighs, did you know that?" He sat down, lit a cigarette, and waited. "This is where your mother and I always came when we were young. We smoked in secret and told each other everything."

Vincenzo slowly came closer.

"Your papà loves you, you know."

"He's an idiot."

"No. He's just afraid to lose you."

"He's an idiot, Giovanni!"

"You can't talk that way about your father."

"Says who?" Vincenzo shot back, snuffling and then spitting on the dusty ground.

"Says me."

"Who are you, anyway? You're a liar."

"What the hell are you talking about?"

Vincenzo gave him a defiant look. "You say you're the boss at Mercedes, but you know nothing about cars. And if you drive a big fat Mercedes, why do you always take the train?"

Giovanni hesitated.

"You know what, Uncle Giovanni? You don't own a car. And you don't work for Mercedes!"

Giovanni didn't know how to respond. He'd always been quick with a retort, but the boy was staring at him with such unmistakable clarity that he knew there was no point trying to keep up the lie. They saw Giulietta coming across the bridge toward them.

"Don't worry," Vincenzo said, plucking the cigarette out of Giovanni's hand, taking a drag, and handing it back. "I won't rat you out."

Vincenzo didn't speak another word to Enzo for days. Enzo tried in his own way to make things right—he bought cannoli, brought design plans home from the plant, made clumsy attempts to get Vincenzo to laugh. Eventually, they started exchanging a few words here and there, but things were never the same. Vincenzo's cheek didn't hurt for long, but the wound in his soul was slower to heal. It was the pain of being misunderstood, at his very core, by the man who was supposed to be his role model.

The following weekend, Vincenzo and the neighbor boys organized a bike race on the street. Barefoot on racing bikes much too large for them, with the saddles screwed low, they zipped along the canal in the gleaming sunlight. Some of them stood on the pedals. The course was up to the next bridge and down the other side of the canal. While Enzo was at the factory and Concetta cooked, Giovanni and Giulietta stood outside in the doorway and watched the boys. Vincenzo pumped all of his rage into the pedals. He wasn't the strongest, but he was tough, and he hated losing. He'd spent days working on his bike, oiling the gears, inflating the tires as far as they would go. And sure enough, he caught up to the bigger boys between the two bridges.

It was a neck-and-neck race, with the girls on the other side of the canal cheering them on.

"I did everything wrong," Giulietta said out of nowhere.

Giovanni blinked. "What?"

"I'm afraid for Vincenzo."

"Oh, you don't have to worry about him. He'll be fine. He's so talented."

"That's just it. I mean, the whole world admires people who do something special, the ones who have talent. The movie stars, the fashion designers, the inventors, the race car drivers. Because they're pursuing their dreams."

"But if he has a dream, that's a good thing."

"Talent is a curse, Giovanni. It drives you. It never lets you rest. It controls you. And sometimes it kills you."

Vincenzo was the first one across the finish line. He braked hard, skidded around the curve, and threw his arms up in the air before the second-place boy arrived. Giulietta and Giovanni applauded. *Bravo! Bravissimo!*

They were the only ones clapping. The girls stuck by their brothers, and their brothers had lost. But Giovanni noticed one of the little princesses sneaking glances at Vincenzo as he savored his victory with feigned nonchalance.

Giovanni high-fived his nephew. "Good job, big guy."

Giulietta proudly kissed him on both cheeks, though he fended her off gruffly.

"Enough of that." Giovanni pulled his sister away.

At that moment, Enzo rode up on his motor scooter. He looked despondent as he dismounted and approached Giulietta.

"What's wrong?" she asked. "Why aren't you still at work?"

"Did you hear?"

"What?"

"Commendatore Rivolta is dead."

Everyone froze.

"Heart attack."

"But he was so young!" Giulietta looked distraught.

"What will happen to the company?" Giovanni asked.

"Piero, his son, is taking over."

"Isn't he still in college?"

"It's his destiny," Enzo replied, and glanced at Vincenzo, who was standing beside his fallen bicycle, looking lost.

After the funeral, which the entire company attended, all grieving their *commendatore* like a father, Giovanni headed back to Munich. It was a cool September day, and a harsh wind blew on Platform 11 as he distributed the goods he'd brought as usual.

He shivered, feeling miserable. The only things he owned were those he sold—the scents and flavors of Sicily, his indestructible trove of childhood treasures that he could bring with him anywhere in the world. But besides that? He was thirty-three now. If he dropped dead as suddenly as the *commendatore*, he wouldn't have a son to continue his life's work. Not to mention that he didn't have a life's work. He didn't have a single thing that was his—no home, no calling, no possessions. Giovanni needed to change something.

Moglie e buoi dei paesi tuoi, goes the Italian saying. *Take wives and cows from your own country.* On his next vacation, he went not to Milan, but south to Naples. From there, he boarded a ship going even farther south, to the island he grew up on, and Mamma arranged the rest. Rosaria was the daughter of Concetta's younger sister, Maria. Giovanni's cousin. Her father, who owned the only grocery store in the village, had recently died of a lung infection, and on his deathbed, he'd made his wife promise him to find his stubborn daughter a husband at last. Rosaria was neither dumb nor ugly—she simply had no interest in marrying any of the local fishermen's sons just so she could scrape by on this godforsaken island, her life not one iota better than that of her parents.

Enter Giovanni, the wealthy cousin from Germania!

21

Salina

It was the summer of '68. Giovanni wore a white suit like the ones in 1930s American movies. Rosaria wore the most elegant gown of her entire life. She'd commissioned it from Giulietta so that she wouldn't have to get married in her mother's wedding dress, like her older sister had done. Milan couture, so to speak. The kitschy ruffles and appliqués she had insisted upon against Giulietta's advice underscored her personality, which was a little loud and extravagant, but always generous.

The entire family had come together on the island for the first time since their father's death. Salina had hardly changed in all those years. Still no streetlamps, no newspapers, no tourists. There were a couple of Fiats and Ape three-wheelers, but no gas stations. Instead, there were wrecked cars rusting by the roadside, wild cactus, moss and gorse among the stones scattered throughout the fields, whitewashed houses, and the grandiose expanse of sky above the sea. On the horizon, Stromboli, the eternally smoking volcano. Some nights you could see it spitting fire. The rocks were black, the men untamed, the women superstitious. And the sirocco wind blew in from the deserts of Africa.

They'd set up long tables in the field beside the old farmhouse Giulietta and Giovanni were born in. Today, it was a ruin with a caved-in roof, surrendered to the winter storms. The damp stone walls were collapsing; the plaster had crumbled away years ago. The windows and doors were nailed shut, and wild weeds had sprouted up all around. A haunted house without ghosts. Their parents had once worked the field at the edge of Malfa, the green heart of the island. Salina was best known for its capers, but a few grapevines had once grown here as well. Now, the whole thing was fallow, since the owner, who lived somewhere near Messina, hadn't found anyone else to lease it. After searching the village for a wedding venue and coming up empty-handed, Giovanni decided to revive the enchanted garden of his childhood, even though it didn't belong to him—an act of defiance against the old don and the passage of time. His father would have appreciated it.

Giovanni went all out. He wanted the tables buckling under the weight of the food, so he could show everyone what he'd accomplished while in exile. Not just for himself, but also for his father, whose death—and the curse upon his wife and children—was still discussed in whispers. Some people admired the man's bravery, while others felt he had gone too far and gotten what he deserved. But now his son was back from the North, a radiant hero who had worked his way out of poverty and restored the Marconi family honor. They had left in defeat; now they were returning in triumph.

Of course, nobody, not even Giovanni's bride, knew his true financial situation. He'd told Rosaria's mother that he was an *uomo d'affari*, a businessman with a *grande casa moderna*, and the mere mention of the word "Mercedes" was enough to earn looks of admiration and respect from the villagers. He began hinting to his future wife that he'd started selling more than just cars, that he was expanding into the field of food import-export. His plan was to prepare her for the reality awaiting her in Germany gradually, fully confident that an island girl still living in her parents' moldy cottage would view even a one-bedroom in a new building in the Munich suburbs as moving up in the world.

Giovanni devised the dinner menu personally. He spent weeks refining it, wanting to express respect for tradition by using local products and his grandparents' recipes, while also bringing a touch of the big wide world to the island. Surely such care would ensure that nobody would accuse him of forgetting his roots, and everyone's jaws would drop in amazement.

If the Sicilians have one thing that sets them apart from other Mediterranean cultures, it's their food. Sicilian cuisine is undoubtedly the best in Italy, because over the centuries, they learned to incorporate influences from all the neighbors who conquered them and then left again. The Greeks brought olives, wine, and honey; the Romans, ice cream; the Normans had dried cod and rolled roast; the Spaniards knew how to make chocolate; the Arabs contributed lemons, almonds, and pistachios.

ANTIPASTI: BUFFET DI TERRA
Melanzane ripiene
Caponata alla siciliana
Peperonata in agrodolce
Formaggio maiorchino
Parmigiana di melanzane

PRIMO DI MARE
Risotto alla marinara ai gamberetti di nassa e patelle
Pasta Margherita con pesce spada alla ghiotta

SECONDO TERRA E MARE
Brodo con polpette di manzo
Ventre di pesce stocco alla ghiotta
Involtini di pesce spada grigliati con insalata verde
Acciughe ripiene

DOLCE
Bianco e Nero
Piccola Pasticceria
Frutta fresca
Formaggi nostrani

Giovanni brought the rice from Milan, since there was none on the Aeolian Islands. Same with the spumante, because the dry Franciacorta preferred among the Milanese hadn't yet arrived in the South, where everyone still drank sweet Asti or Cinzano. The pasta was from the *pastificio* Triolo in Messina, handmade from Sicilian grain—not that industrial stuff that was on all the shelves these days. The wine was from a vineyard in Lipari, a barrel wine that was neither red nor white, the kind nobody makes anymore. Back then, winemakers in the Aeolian archipelago combined different grapes, both red and white, based on instinct and family tradition. Fruit, carob, and honey were sometimes added before fermentation. A particular highlight was the Malvasia, the amber-colored dessert wine from Malfa.

But he would save the real showstopper for last. Giovanni had asked around, and everyone who knew anything about food was in absolute agreement on the *dolce* of the year: *Bianco e Nero*. All of Sicily was buzzing about it; rumors had reached the Aeolian Islands, but nobody on the island had yet tasted the legendary dessert. Only one *pasticceria* in Messina made it, and it had to be eaten within an hour or it would melt in the heat. It was fluffy fried beignets filled with a special *crema* and then bathed in *gianduia*, a dark chocolate nougat whose ingredients were a family secret. The strawberry-sized beignets were stacked into a pyramid and then topped with wafer-thin leaves of chocolate, creating a sweet, melty shell you had to break open with a spoon. Giovanni brought the two *pasticceri* in all the way from Messina, the master and his apprentice, so that they could prepare *Bianco e Nero* fresh. The night before the wedding, the islanders stood gawking on the old pier as the legendary pastry chefs clambered off their ship and into the little boat used to row passengers ashore, bearing innumerable packages of secret ingredients and an enormous pan. Finally, the deckhands used a crane to lower a cow into the water. They tied a rope around its neck so that the animal, pulled along by the rowboat, swam toward its fate as part of the wedding buffet.

Word that the legendary *Bianco e Nero* was coming to the island spread like lightning, and everyone who wasn't on the guest list made a last-ditch effort to get into the bridal pair's good graces by bringing over a gift and their best wishes, hoping to score an invitation in exchange. It was then that Giovanni knew he had won. He didn't care that it would take him a year to pay off the debt.

His mother took command of the kitchen, of course—they didn't want anyone suggesting she'd forgotten traditional *cucina siciliana* up in Milan. For three days, she was in there from six o'clock in the morning to eight o'clock at night, along with her sister and Giulietta, and when Giovanni came in on the morning of the feast and presented his white wedding suit, she gave her son a tender kiss on the forehead and said, "This is the most wonderful day of my life!"

For her part, Giulietta seemed oddly absent. She cooked and set the tables, but her soul had a life of its own, one that even her twin brother could hardly access anymore. Maybe she was jealous of Rosaria, he reasoned. She'd always been his only confidante, and that position was now being threatened. But Giovanni didn't expect his wife to replace his sister. He hadn't picked Rosaria because he wanted a woman he could talk to about anything. He already had that. In truth, he wasn't madly in love with Rosaria at the time, and the German women he'd amused himself with wondered why he, the freedom-loving hedonist, was choosing to marry a girl from a remote island. In fact, that was exactly why Giovanni wanted Rosaria: she was everything the women in the big city weren't. He wanted her because he knew he'd never find a better mother to his children anywhere on Earth. Decades later, with his countless grandchildren on his lap, he realized to his great satisfaction that his instinct had been spot-on.

Vincenzo explored his ancestors' island like it was some magnificent open-air playground. That summer, he was no longer a child, not yet a man—a fully formed person who didn't want to be controlled by others anymore, yet who also had his whole life ahead of him. It was his first trip outside of Milan, since travel wasn't something the Marconis did. When school was out, the family simply got together, and the children were left to their own devices in the city. Vincenzo loved that.

Unlike his classmates, who looked forward to spending time away from books, Vincenzo was excited about having time for the books *he* wanted to read. He spent hours at the city library, reading about da Vinci's heirs, the inventors of the modern age: from Thomas Jefferson to Isambard Brunel, Karl Benz and Ferdinand Porsche to Wernher von Braun, who was building moon rockets for the Americans now. Men who weren't satisfied with the existing world, so they created things that had never existed before. Men who left something lasting behind. Vincenzo had brought books with him now as well, but as soon as they arrived on Salina, the island's wild beauty drew him like a magnet, and he spent his days outdoors.

He swam in the sea or trekked through the hills with Uncle Giovanni, who let him in on the secrets of his own childhood. How to split a sea urchin open with a knife and spoon it out raw, for example. He showed Vincenzo the *gamberetti di nassa* in the fishermen's traps, with neon-blue eggs on their stomachs. Or the *velelle*, whose bright-azure shells had a transparent sail to carry them along the waves. Most fascinating of all, though, was the *aliscafo* that had recently landed on the island: a hydrofoil with a turbine engine that lifted right out of the water at higher speeds, gliding across the waves on wings alone. A majestic sight, a triumph of technology.

That was how Vincenzo pictured his own life: no longer subject to the elements, but conquering them thanks to modern technology, defying the laws of nature, transcending the ordinary. Engineers in Messina had developed the hydrofoil; it was the pride of Sicily, and for the old islanders who still remembered the days of sailing ships, the *aliscafo* bordered on a miracle. All at once, the world had gotten smaller. On the islands themselves, things had hardly changed since Giovanni was a child; the most recent sensations were television, a power plant, and the phone at the bar on the piazza. But here, on the far side of the moon, Vincenzo encountered a phenomenon that turned everything he knew about life on its head.

The father of this phenomenon, Don Calogero, was one of the Cifarellis, who were related to the Marconis by marriage. They were better off than the Marconis; they'd gone to college and lived in Palermo. Don Calogero had a law office there, and what brought him to Salina today, besides Giovanni and Rosaria's wedding, was business: he owned land on the island, just outside Malfa.

He'd been one of the first to realize the untapped potential that lay in vineyards. For centuries, Salina had been known for a unique wine only grown and pressed in Malfa on Salina, Malvasia delle Lipari. "Nectar of the gods" was what the ancient Greeks had called the elegant golden dessert wine, and as recently as the last century, it had fetched exceptionally high prices in Naples, Paris, and even New York. But then, around the turn of the century, a vine pest brought in from America had destroyed most of the vines, forcing more and more people to leave the island. Initially, they'd boarded the same ships that had brought the pest, the ones heading for America and Australia; later, they'd gone north to the Italian automobile factories, as Enzo, Giovanni, and Giulietta had done.

A handful of farmers still cultivated the few remaining vines, selling the wine in Sicily and on other nearby islands, but it was no longer competitive on the international market. They needed visionaries like Calogero, who saw Malvasia as a slumbering treasure. One by one, he purchased the fallow fields around Malfa, whose soil and vines were just waiting to be revived. In a time when the island was populated almost exclusively by the elderly, while younger people were striving toward exile, he paid ridiculously low prices.

But Vincenzo didn't know about any of that—not yet. All he saw was an impressive-looking man striding down the gangway of the *aliscafo*. Despite the summer heat, he was wearing an elegant, pin-striped three-piece suit, from which the silver chain of a pocket watch dangled, plus a hat and hand-stitched shoes that gleamed in the sun. Deckhands heaved his countless enormous suitcases ashore. The contrast between the futuristic, air-conditioned hydrofoil and the Palermo lawyer's aura of cigar smoke and old money could not have been greater.

Still, it wasn't Don Calogero who captured Vincenzo's attention. It was the woman beside him. Not his wife, who was busy berating the deckhands about not ruining her suitcase. The woman he was leading down the gangway was fourteen years old. His daughter, Carmela.

She was wearing a straw-colored summer hat, a white linen dress, and leather sandals. She was unusually tall, almost taller than Vincenzo, and her catlike eyes were an infinitely deep turquoise green that reflected the sun and the sea. When Giovanni, who had come to the harbor with Vincenzo to welcome the Cifarellis, introduced the two of them, Vincenzo could barely get a word out—her powerful floral scent was too intoxicating. He didn't notice that it was the same perfume her mother used, nor that she wasn't half as bored as she was acting. Vincenzo was hypnotized by her eyes, her pouty lips, the lithe movement of her long limbs. She was categorically unhurried; everything about her received and waited. She was the summer and the sea.

Once they had loaded the luggage onto a pair of donkeys, Vincenzo helped Carmela into the open bed of the rickety Ape truck Giovanni had borrowed to ferry guests into Malta. Carmela's older sisters were already studying abroad; she was the only one who'd come with her parents. Giovanni slid into the driver's seat of the three-wheeler, and Signora Cifarelli squeezed into the tiny cabin beside him. Don Calogero would wait at the harbor until Giovanni returned, since one couldn't ask a man like him to dirty the back of his fine suit in the bed of a dusty truck.

"Take good care of her," Calogero told Vincenzo half-jokingly, half-threateningly, as Giovanni drove off.

Vincenzo and Carmela leaned back against the driver's cabin. The potholes jostled them around, shaking their bodies. They couldn't help bumping against each other as they rode around the tight curves, and Vincenzo couldn't take his eyes off her bare legs, peeking out beneath her summer dress.

Carmela's skin was dark, sun-drenched, and Vincenzo briefly spotted a tiny scar on one of her knees. As Giovanni rattled down the windy road along the blue coast, her perfume mingled with the scents of motor exhaust and the rosemary growing on the roadside. Carmela's hair danced in the wind, stinging Vincenzo's neck and cheeks. He didn't pull his head back, for fear he would lose this thrilling and confusing feeling that took his breath away.

They say that Sicilian weddings never bring just one couple together. Giovanni was so busy with his preparations that he didn't even notice Vincenzo and Carmela getting closer, below the adults' radar. Only after the Mass, as they were celebrating in the field and Giovanni was able to relax for the first time in days, did he notice that Vincenzo and Carmela had slipped away from the banquet and were sitting by themselves on an old stone wall. A sea breeze blew in, making the white tablecloths billow. "A ghost!" some children giggled.

The older islanders sat in their chairs, perfectly stuffed, tirelessly praising the sensational food, the cooks, the pastry chefs from Messina, and of course, the man who had put it all together. They'd eaten and drunk from one o'clock in the afternoon until six o'clock in the evening, and if anyone still had anything left to criticize after the *secondo*, the *Bianco e Nero* shut them up right away. Giovanni scraped his foot across the dark earth, remembering how he'd played in this field as a kid, stomach growling with hunger, never complaining, because he didn't want to embarrass his parents. Now, his mother was sitting happily at the table, surrounded by the people she loved most, and Giovanni's new wife was at his side.

Catastrophe struck out of nowhere. It started when one of the musicians, Sergio the accordionist, went up to the bridegroom, pulled a rusty pair of scissors out of his baggy pants, and snipped off a piece of his tie, laughing. The other guests, roused from their digestive stupor, laughed and applauded as Sergio reached into his pocket and stuck a hundred-lire bill into Giovanni's shirt pocket. Now, one after another, people began rising from their chairs and weaving their way over to shorten Giovanni's tie bit by bit and then reimburse him generously for the insult he had suffered. Men and women, old and young. Giulietta got the last piece. Enzo gave his brother-in-law a proud clap on the cheek, and Vincenzo grinned down at him from his wall. Sergio struck up a tarantella, accompanied by a man on an out-of-tune guitar and an elderly mandolin player.

Within minutes, the sleepy afternoon became a boisterous dance festival. First, the old women rose to their feet and clapped their hands. Then the children followed, then the men. Toothless fishermen and hunchbacked farmers' wives suddenly grew young again and, spurred on by music and wine, began demonstrating the tarantella to the young people. Rosaria pulled Giovanni out from behind the table, and Giulietta went over to the musicians and shouted something to them. They stopped the tarantella and launched into an exhilarated, driving rendition of "*Tu vuo' fa l'Americano*." Giulietta sang along, to the dancers' great delight. When they were young, Giovanni and Giulietta had heard the hit day after day on the radio. Everyone loved it. Giovanni was amazed at Giulietta's beautiful voice, which he had nearly forgotten. Giulietta sang with her entire body.

Sergio set his instrument down and, as the guitarist started the next verse, he invited Giulietta to dance. She didn't have to be asked twice. Suddenly, Enzo was on his feet.

"Did you ask first?"

Sergio stopped, confused. "Of course I asked her."

"You should have asked me."

Giulietta grasped his arm. "Enzo."

He ignored her. "Have you forgotten your manners?"

"*Scusa*, Enzo. I didn't know that you—"

"What, that I'm her husband?"

"Oh, I knew that. I just thought, you two live in Milan, and—"

"Leave him alone, Enzo," Giulietta said, more firmly this time.

"And you thought that in Milan, we've forgotten how to act around other men's wives?"

Sergio spread his arms out apologetically. Before the situation could get too tense, he returned to his chair and set his accordion on his lap. Enzo took Giulietta's arm, but Giulietta remained rooted to the spot, glaring at him.

"What was that?" she demanded.

"Come on, let's dance."

"Enzo, I'll dance with whomever I want to."

"You'd rather dance with him?"

"That's Sergio! We went to grade school together!"

"So what? Can't you be happy with your husband?"

"When are you going to quit that? When?"

All at once, Vincenzo was at his mother's side. "Leave her alone."

"This is none of your business," Enzo told him.

"It's okay, Vincenzo," Giulietta said.

"No."

"Stay out of it," Enzo growled.

"Don't tell me what to do."

"I'm your father, *cazzo*. Show some respect."

Now the other dancers had stopped as well. The musicians went on playing.

"What is there to respect?" Vincenzo nearly spat in contempt.

Everyone held their breath. A son who dared disrespect his father in front of everyone—that was unheard of. It didn't happen. It simply couldn't be.

Enzo wound up to slap Vincenzo. He didn't want to hit him too hard—it wasn't about causing him pain so much as showing everyone else who was the man of the house. Which was why he hesitated briefly, and Vincenzo used that fraction of a second to duck deftly out of the way. Enzo missed. Giulietta shrieked, and before Enzo could haul off again, Vincenzo punched his father in the face. Enzo stumbled. He didn't go down, but everyone drew away in horror.

"Vincenzo, are you insane?" Giulietta shrieked.

Enzo and Vincenzo stared each other down, motionless. Enzo's lips trembled, but he didn't let the pain show. Everyone was expecting him to beat his son to a pulp, but he simply stood there. He waited until Giulietta smacked her son on the back of the head and snapped, "What's the matter with you? Have you lost your mind?"

Vincenzo pushed her away and ran into the field, looking furious.

Giovanni chased after him, thorns tearing his wedding suit. "Vincenzo! Come back!"

But Vincenzo disappeared behind the withered bushes.

"Porco Dio!" Giovanni cursed.

The banquet was ruined. It was meant to be unforgettable, and now it was. The musicians packed up their instruments; the guests whispered; the pastry chefs from Messina discreetly gathered their dishes. Concetta berated Enzo, who was sitting silently in a chair. Giovanni and Giulietta stood apart from the others, in the fallow vineyard.

"Come on, Giulietta. Go to Enzo."

She shook her head.

He gave his sister a handkerchief. "He means well."

"He never stops! He's blind with jealousy!"

"But why?"

"Who knows. He sees ghosts!"

"You're not being fair to him. Jealousy is the sister of love."

"I can't take it anymore, Giovanni. Not for my sake, I don't care about that, but for Vincenzo. One of these days, they're going to kill each other."

"But why?"

"I don't know, Giovanni. I don't know."

Late in the evening, when the other guests had gone home and Giulietta was scrubbing the kitchen with Rosaria and the two mothers, Giovanni returned to the field to clean up. The moon shone pale on the white tablecloths, which rippled lethargically in the night wind. Giovanni stepped behind an olive tree to relieve himself. As he undid his trousers, he saw something through the branches: Vincenzo and Carmela were back on the old stone wall. She whispered into his ear, and Vincenzo took her hand. He looked bashful, uncertain, and thrilled. Then they kissed, shy and overcome by a desire greater than they could comprehend. The stars glittered above them, and the dogs howled in the hills.

The following morning, Giulietta shook Vincenzo awake. "Get dressed!"

"Why?"

"Don't ask questions. Just hurry."

Giovanni blinked in surprise when Giulietta came running out of the house with the half-asleep Vincenzo. He'd spent a short, restless wedding night, and now he was busy heaving gifts, suitcases, and his wife's dowry—bedsheets, embroidered pillows, tablecloths, and her grandparents' china—into the back of the Ape. They needed to get their household effects back to his apartment in Germany, and then they'd take a honeymoon. He'd promised Rosaria.

Enzo had gone into the field with Concetta to clear the tables.

"If we hurry, we can make the nine-thirty ship," Giulietta announced, tossing her bag into the back of the truck.

"But—"

Rosaria came out of the house and gave Giovanni a look of bewilderment.

"Rosaria, I'm sorry," Giulietta said.

Vincenzo squatted beside his mother in the overfull truck bed as it rumbled toward the harbor. Giovanni was behind the wheel, silent.

"Mamma, where are we going?"

"Shh, not now."

"But I want to stay here!"

"You can come back later."

"Where's Papà?"

She stared out at the road disappearing behind them.

"Are you leaving him?"

She didn't answer.

"Where are we going, *cazzo*?"

"Germania."

Vincenzo gave her a look of incomprehension. Giulietta took his hand and squeezed it. "I love you. No matter what happens."

Just as the ship put out to sea, Enzo leaped from an approaching Ape and ran to the quay wall, where waves were crashing in the wake. Vincenzo, at the ship's railing, saw him standing there, watching in utter disbelief. A small man, growing progressively smaller. Suddenly, he felt terribly sorry for him.

22

"Without that *incidente*, your papà would never have come to Germania. And you would never have been born." Giovanni gave me a mischievous smile.

It was dark and quiet in the courtyard. Rosaria, Giovanni, and I were the only ones left, apart from Marco, who was tearing down the stage. The wind picked up; a light drizzle began to fall. Rosaria shut the photo album, and Giovanni opened an umbrella. I considered what he'd said. The events leading up to my life had been a series of breakups. Men and women who weren't right for each other. And it had always been the women who had the courage to take control of their own destinies. The children paid the price.

"Where does he live now?"

"Italy."

"Where in Italy?"

Giovanni pondered. Rosaria looked at him. "Do you want to visit?" he asked.

I wasn't sure. I thought about Vincent. Giovanni seemed to read my mind.

"Or does someone else want to visit him?"

His hesitation annoyed me. Why couldn't he just say, *Your dad lives on Via Such-and-Such in Milan. Here's his cell number. Sorry you had to wait thirty-six years for this.*

"Didn't you guys ever wonder where I was? We live in the same city. You knew he had a daughter, right?"

That one stung. I could sense Giovanni's shame.

Rosaria broke the silence. "He lives in Naples." She gave Giovanni an expectant look.

He defended himself, gesticulating feverishly. "She can't just go down there and say, *Ciao, I'm your daughter*. Vincenzo has *famiglia*! This requires *discrezione*!"

"Giovanni," I broke in, "I don't want anything from him. He has his life, I have mine. Maybe it would just be nice to get to know him."

Rosaria took my hand and gazed at me with more empathy than I was comfortable with. I didn't want to burst into tears. "Call him, Giovanni," she said.

"Eh, and what should I say?" He gave me a questioning look.

"Tell him I'm here."

Rosaria lurked beside her husband like a watchdog as he stood at the hall telephone, nervously dialing a long number. She gave me a supportive look. Clearly, she'd noticed how uncomfortable I was. What right did I have to barge into these people's lives, no matter how friendly they were? Not to mention barging into the life of a stranger who coincidentally happened to be my father.

I stood there, paralyzed, as the line beeped on the other end. I wished I could have just slunk away there and then, back to my old life, uncertain as it was. At least that would have been a familiar uncertainty, not like this new and deeply unsettling variety.

Giovanni and Rosaria's apartment contained an unbelievable mishmash of Italian neobaroque décor and old Ikea furniture. I would never have imagined such a spectacular confusion of taste could exist in my town. Gold sofa armrests with linden-green pillows fringed in red cord; an old-fashioned sideboard beside an overstuffed Billy bookcase; kitschy wood-framed images of Neapolitan fishing boats at sunset and a smiling Padre Pio with stigmata on his hands and a halo around his bald head. *The clichés about Italians are true*, I thought to myself.

"Carmela? Oh! Sono Giovanni da Monaco. Tutto bene?" Giovanni launched into a long monologue I didn't understand. Then a question, then disappointment—or was it relief?—and then a mollifying, *"No, non c'è problema."* He held one hand over the receiver and turned to look at me. "Not there."

I was relieved, too. If Giovanni had handed me the phone, I wouldn't have had the first idea what to say. *Hi, Dad*? No way, I couldn't call him that. *Hello, Vincenzo*? Calling a total stranger by his first name seemed odd, but then again, Giovanni had described him so vividly that I could picture him—as a thirteen-year-old. How old was he now? As I was doing the math in my head, something happened on the other end of the line, and Giovanni tugged my sleeve.

"He's just walking in the door!"

All three of us held our breath.

I heard a faint male voice through the receiver. *"Pronto?"*

"Oh, Vincè, come va? Tutto bene?" Giovanni started off in a jovial, chatty tone, but then lowered his voice and turned away from Rosaria, as though it would prompt Vincenzo to turn away from his own wife down in Naples. Then he said my name. In the silence, you could practically hear the bomb dropping. Rosaria and I exchanged an anxious glance. Giovanni listened for the impact, waiting for sounds of surprise, disbelief, joy—and heard nothing.

"Vincenzo? *Pronto!* Vincenzo!"

He lowered the receiver and gazed at me with large, apologetic eyes. "Hung up."

How could I have expected anything else? I was alone again, walking past the wholesale market to my car. Some rain had fallen, and the cold light of the streetlamps reflected on the wet streets. Giovanni's shop was dark; a refrigerated truck was turning into the market gate, and a truck full of cows rumbled toward the meat-processing plant.

A dark cloud settled over my mind. The feeling of not being worth anything. That everything was futile, no matter how hard you tried. Knowing that you didn't really have any business being in this world, that your existence was just a whim of nature, that nothing made any sense.

But now that I had heard his voice, I knew it wasn't actually a whim of nature that had put me here. That man, that specific person, had brought me into existence just so he could abandon me. Again. Before I could even ask him why.

As I got into the car, I checked my phone, which I'd left in my purse all day on silent. Two texts from my mother asking whether everything was okay. As if she could smell it. Three texts, two calls, and four emails from Robin. I left them unread and drove back to the other side of the train tracks. The better side. Crawled back to the safety of my apartment; felt like a stranger in it. I curled up in my cold bed and tried to sleep, though my entire body was shaking.

How little it takes to pull the rug out from under someone. I hadn't lost anything; nobody had taken anything away from me; I was still the same person. The mere silence of a stranger on the phone was enough to open up a hole beneath my feet that hadn't been there just moments before. Apparently, the membrane separating happiness from unhappiness was a thin one. Now it was torn, and I'd fallen through.

At two o'clock in the morning, I gave up trying to sleep and made myself a double espresso. I dug out my colored pencils and my sketch block. Best pain medication—obsessive work. The only place I felt safe. I turned on some music and began to sketch, losing all track of time. Maybe I'd come up with something presentable and wouldn't have to disappoint Robin. At sunrise, I got up from my chair and realized that all I'd drawn were the clothes from Giovanni's story: his plaid shirt and flat cap, the wedding dress Giulietta had sewn for Rosaria, Giulietta's own linen summer dress, Carmela's hat. Vincenzo was the only one not present. The others were all there, uninvited guests in my apartment.

Vincent's letter was still sitting on the kitchen table, untouched. I needed to give it back to him. To close the sluice he had opened.

"Where have you been, goddammit?" Robin asked when I came into the atelier the next morning. "Wow, you look like hell," he added before I could reply.

"Thanks a bunch."

"Where were you?"

"Why? What's the matter?" I made myself an espresso.

"Oh, nothing, just shitting bricks."

"So, business as usual." I drank the coffee, avoiding Robin's eyes.

"I scheduled dinner with the Italians. I know, I know, but do you have any better ideas?"

I raised my eyebrows and shook my head.

"You need to come. Tomorrow evening. We have to do this."

I was too weak to object. Every cell in my body hated this plan, but I had no choice but to play my part. "Fine, whatever."

"Bring your sketches."

Over my lunch break, I snuck away to call Vincent. Whatever he'd written his son, he would have to tell him himself. Not for all the money in the world would I venture into that lions' den.

"Hello?" a female voice answered.

"Sorry, I was trying to reach—Dr. Schlewitz?"

"Can I give him a message?"

"I'd rather talk to him myself."

"I'm afraid that isn't possible." The voice cracked.

"Why not?"

"Who is this?"

"This is—Julia. His granddaughter."

There was a discomforting silence on the other end of the line.

"Did something happen?" I asked.

When I reached his room, she was standing beside the bed Vincent was lying in, connected to a confusion of tubes and cables. Private insurance, private room. A tall, slim woman in her late forties with pale brown hair in a ponytail and thin lips. She was wearing a beige suit, as though she'd come straight from the office. Her open purse was on the windowsill. Louis Vuitton.

She came over and extended her hand. "It's a pleasure to meet you, although these are less than ideal circumstances. Clara Strobel." His daughter. She made eye contact, but her smile wasn't genuine. I wanted to go see him, but she planted herself directly in front of me, like a guard dog.

"How is he?"

"He needs to rest right now."

"Julia," he called out to me, sounding weak but determined. "Come in."

Clara reluctantly stepped aside. Vincent was shockingly pale, and it hurt to see him in a hospital gown, lying helpless in bed. Apparently, they hadn't even had time to bring him his pajamas. He held out his hand and drew me closer. I sat on the edge of the bed, clasping his hand and struggling to hold back the tears that sprang to my eyes. He was no longer a stranger to me—he was a person whose story I was part of.

"I'm tough." He smiled, trying to play down the pain in his chest. "But . . ."

"Dad, don't overexert yourself," Clara interrupted, adjusting the pillow beneath his head. "He had a serious heart attack," she told me. "Just lucky I happened to be at the house. I found him in the living room."

I nodded and went on holding his hand, since he seemed not to want to release mine.

"The doctor says he isn't out of danger yet. Please don't agitate him." Her face was hard. She wanted me out of here.

"I dreamed of the day when you two might meet," Vincent remarked.

I gave Clara a slightly pained smile. So, this was my aunt.

He clutched my hand more tightly. "Did you find him?"

"I visited Giovanni, yes."

His eyes brightened.

"We called Vincenzo. He lives in Naples."

"And?"

"He hung up."

The news pained Vincent. The wheels in his head seemed to turn feverishly.

"Dad, you need to rest!"

"I'm fine."

Clara took my arm and drew me to the door. "Can I just talk to you alone for a moment, Ms.—uh, Julia? We'll be right back, Dad."

I followed her out.

In the neon light of the hospital hallway, Clara seemed even harder than before. "I want to be completely honest with you. This isn't a pleasant subject to bring up, but—my sister and I know that he tried to change his will. However, it's not that easy. And before we put all of that on him now, in his condition . . ."

"I didn't know anything about that. Honestly. And don't worry, I don't need money." That was a lie, but it was true that I didn't want anything from him.

"Well, then, everything's fine. In that case, I suggest we just draw up an informal waiver, and—"

"Why are you assuming he's going to die?" I asked, and returned to the room, leaving her standing there.

I sat down on the chair beside Vincent's bed and pulled the letter out of my jacket. Clara followed me. I tried to decide how to tell him. How to say I hadn't been able to grant his wish. He took my hand before I found the words.

"Please tell him to come. I need to speak to him."

"I know how much this means to you. But me and Vincenzo, that was never a good idea."

"There must have been some misunderstanding. Don't give up. When he sees you, he won't turn you away. He can't possibly." Vincent gazed at me tenderly, equal parts insistent and fragile.

"He already has." I set his letter on the nightstand.

"If you don't go to him now, that will never change."

"I wish I could have done that for you, but—"

"For you," he said. "You have to do it for you."

"I don't need to see him," I lied.

"If Giulietta were still alive, she would want you to. She didn't get to go peacefully."

I don't think I've ever seen anyone so fixated on something. Making amends with Vincenzo was the only thing he still wanted; he wasn't clinging to life so much as to that idea.

"I don't have much time left," he said, and tried to smile.

"Dad, that's enough," Clara declared. "We're going now."

He gave me a pleading look before shifting his gaze to the letter on the nightstand.

I don't know what made me do it. Maybe it was to spite his nagging daughter. Maybe it was empathy for the heartbroken young German in Giovanni's story. Maybe it was some invisible presence guiding my hand. Or maybe it was my own injured pride, refusing to be denied by a father—sperm donor, more like—who hung up when I called. Something in me wanted to look him in the face and say, *Here I am! Even if you don't want me, I still exist!*

I took the letter.

"I'll bring him to you. Promise. But you have to promise me something, too. You have to wait for us."

He nodded. I'll never forget his grateful smile.

Rosaria answered the door with an apron tied around her plump body and a telephone to her ear. When she saw me standing outside, she looked pleased and immediately ended the call. "Julia! Come in! Giovanni's at the shop. Are you hungry?"

"I need Vincenzo's address."

She looked at me thoughtfully. "Wait for Giovanni. Maybe he can go with you."

I shook my head. "There's no time."

That evening, I went to the train station. Small overnight bag, Vincent's letter in my purse. Platform 11, the night train to Naples. The same platform where Giovanni had arrived, the same platform he'd stood on to distribute his salamis to his countrymen. Now, it was bustling with German backpackers and young Italians who had no idea that there was an old bunker beneath their feet, through which millions of guest workers had been funneled into the country.

A couple was kissing in an open train door. I pictured Giulietta arriving on Platform 11, wearing a homemade dress and holding the hand of a thirteen-year-old boy who would eventually become my father. As though she were secretly peeking over my shoulder now. And if she could see me, I sensed, a smile would flicker across her face.

As I was about to board, I heard a Vespa rattling up behind me. I turned around. Handsome Marco was veering across the platform like a madman, and Giovanni was on the back, holding two plastic bags. Marco stopped beside me, grinning and shrugging as if to say that he hadn't stood a chance against Giovanni—who hopped off with surprising agility for his age and his belly.

"Oh!" Giovanni said. "And where are you going?"

"Timbuktu," I replied sarcastically.

"That's convenient—I'm headed there as well. Business calls. Ciao, Marco." Quickly, he boarded the train and then held out a hand to me with a gallant flourish. "Signora Marconi?"

PART 2

23

Giovanni didn't even have a train ticket. Plenty of travel provisions, though. He pushed his way into an empty compartment, heaved his bags onto the seat beside him with a sigh, and offered me the seat opposite as though he were my host. Then he took out a salami and began slicing it with a pocketknife.

"*Mannaggia la miseria*, you didn't even leave me time for dinner!" He handed me a piece. "*Mangia, è buono, del suino nero dei Nebrodi!*"

Resistance was futile. Before the train even departed, Giovanni had his delicacies spread across the small table near the window as though it were the most natural thing in the world. The scent of salami, sheep's cheese, and marinated olives filled the compartment. It was as if Giovanni felt at home here, as if he'd always eaten in this compartment, as if riding trains to and from Platform 11 were etched into his soul, as if this food and this train line constituted his personal *Gesamtkunstwerk*. Marco grinned at us through the window until a conductor shooed him and his Vespa off the platform. Our train pulled away into the night.

"Giovanni, I must be insane," I said with an uneasy glance at the clock. I was supposed to have been at Robin's eight minutes prior to show him my sketches for tomorrow's meeting.

"Why?" Giovanni opened a bottle of red wine and sniffed the cork.

"I'm supposed to be saving my company right now."

"The craziest ideas are usually the best ones," Giovanni replied, and poured me a glass of wine. No crappy paper cups for him, of course. "It's a Rosso di Salina. Nero d'Avola *e* Nerello Mascalese. Brought it just for you. What's wrong with your company?"

"It's about an investor."

He leaned forward. "I saw you on the internet—Marco showed me. Madonna, what a life you have! London, Paris, Milano, New York! And your own company! If only Giulietta could have been half as successful!"

"Giovanni, we built all of that on credit. We're broke. Either we give up control to a huge corporation, or we go bankrupt."

He gave me a look of incomprehension.

"Um, it would be like if McDonald's bought your store and said, *Don't worry, everything will be the same as before. You can do what you want. But let's just do the math . . . What if we put our yummy burger patties in your panini instead of your Parma ham? Then we could work much faster and make a lot more panini.*"

Now he understood. "Criminals. Those *multinazionali*, they're destroying the small businesses! Everywhere you go, it's just chain stores. Our children, *mangiano delle schifezze*, they don't know what good chocolate tastes like anymore, *quello buono*, not these *industriale*! I still know how they made *caponata* in the old days. But the children? And the politicians, all criminals. We need a revolution!"

I didn't know much about slow food, but the things that upset him were totally applicable to the fashion industry as well: disappearing craftsmanship, globalized production, the dictatorship of the masses, trivialization of taste.

"*E allora*, what are you going to do?" he asked.

"No idea."

"Sometimes you just have to wait, and the solution presents itself."

I couldn't imagine how.

"Did Vincent promise you money?" he went on.

"No."

"How much do you need? I'll give it to you." He made a generous gesture, as if wiping away all of my concerns.

"No, Giovanni. It's too much."

"Oh, come on, nothing is too much."

"Three hundred thousand."

He stared. "Are you crazy? All that debt? I don't have that much."

"It's okay. You know what? I'm a lot like you. I always wanted to be my own boss. And I did it, but it doesn't mean more freedom—it means you work all the time and you're constantly worried about money."

"*Eh sì*, what can you do?" He shrugged. "And besides that? What do you do other than work?"

I scoffed. "Nothing."

"You need a family," he said, and cut another hunk of cheese. "Work is just work, but when you come home to your children, nothing is more important. Look, I've had the store for forty years. Always the same one. Never expanded, no partners, no investors, because it's enough to live on. I make my own decisions about what I sell, only good stuff, *niente roba industriale*, and *basta*. Am I rich? *No.* So what? *Che me ne frega!*"

"I'm not trying to get rich, either. I just want to do my work without having to wait tables at night, you know? I can only do one thing, and it's fashion."

"You're like Giulietta. But *più fortunata*."

"What does that mean?"

"Luckier."

I grinned crookedly. "If there's one thing I don't have, it's luck. Diligence, maybe. Stubbornness, yes, naivete, yes. But it's like I was always just on the verge of my big break, and then—it's like a curse."

"Maybe you have the *malocchio*."

"What?"

"That's what my mamma would say. The evil eye is following you. Did you make someone envious?"

A cold chill ran down my spine for a brief moment, and I had the absurd idea that maybe Giulietta envied me. From beyond the grave. I hurriedly discarded the thought.

"*Macché!* I'm just joking!" He laughed and passed me a hunk of salami. "*Dai, mangia.* Why don't you make babies?"

I shook off the blunt question. "Look, a designer in London I studied with once told me that there's a two-out-of-three rule. Life is mainly about three things: career, children, relationship. And you can have any two. One of them, you have to sacrifice."

Giovanni pondered. "Are you married?"

I shook my head.

"And your—boyfriend, what does he say to two-out-of-three?"

"I'm single. One out of three."

"Ah. And if you go bankrupt, then zero out of three!"

We exchanged a wry grin.

"Dumb rule, you know," he said, refilling my glass. "Three or zero doesn't matter. Life is always a *gran casino*."

"A what?"

"*Casino*. Problem. Mess." He raised a glass to me, and then abruptly asked, "So, why do you have to go see Vincenzo now?"

"Maybe I'm running away."

"You are like Giulietta." He smiled at me with sad eyes.

"What about you?" I asked. "Why did you come with me?"

He gave me a cryptic look. "Maybe you're curious to hear what happened to Giulietta in Germany. And your papà."

"Did she manage to become a dressmaker here?"

He tilted his head. *"Sì e no."*

"How do you mean?"

He picked up the second plastic bag and withdrew a worn, green-and-brown plaid photo album. "I'll show you."

It was a different album from the one with the pictures of Italy. A wedding picture of Giovanni and Rosaria was attached to the photo mount on the thick cover, and it was obvious which of them had chosen it: Rosaria stood in the middle of the image, a beaming bride in white; Giovanni was to one side, looking slightly overwhelmed. He opened the album and paged through countless variations of the same motif until he found the first picture of Giulietta: She was standing on Platform 11 beside Giovanni. Thirteen-year-old Vincenzo was wedged between them as though he were their son, peering at the camera with a look of uncertainty, defiance, and weariness. Giulietta was smiling and holding her suitcase. Rosaria must have taken the photo when they arrived. I imagined how she must have felt, a newlywed following her husband into the Promised Land, with his sister and her son unexpectedly in tow. And Vincenzo, a teenager newly in love, suddenly thrown into a foreign country due to his parents' marital crisis.

"He didn't get off to a good start in Germany, hmm?"

"Vincenzo hated Germany."

"The only one of you who was half-German."

Giovanni dropped his eyes. He obviously didn't want to hear that.

"Did Giulietta want to stay in Germany, or did she just need a break?"

"Even she didn't know. Nobody knew anything. It was a *gran casino*."

24

Monaco Di Baviera

Giovanni, the extraordinarily successful head of Mercedes Munich who moon-lighted as a food import-export wholesaler, brought his bride, his sister, and his nephew home. He didn't take a taxi the way he had when he first arrived twelve years before. He took the tram. Last stop: Hasenbergl.

Their journey from the central station to the outer perimeter of the city was long enough that Giovanni had time to gently prepare his family for the reality awaiting them. Whereas Rosaria slowly began to realize that her husband had a different status in Germany than at home, Giulietta just gazed out the tram window, taking in the sights. She'd been worried it would rain all the time in Germany, and she was amazed at how warm the summer was. The women were taller, with shorter hair and lower heels. Among the stodgily dressed office work-ers, she spotted men with short pants and long hair, hippies with thick necklaces and inside-out Afghan sheepskin jackets over their bare torsos; the girls wore minidresses or long, flowered Indian skirts. Everything was more anarchic than Milan, and perhaps more tasteless as well: the cuts were less elegant, the colors and materials combined wildly, but with amazing vibrance—everything was possible here.

"*Un grande palazzo*, you said!" Rosaria screeched when they reached the entrance to the ugly, gray high-rise in the middle of a housing project. Beautiful Munich, with its Renaissance and baroque treasures designed by Italian archi-tects, was nowhere to be seen.

"It is a *grande palazzo*. Would you call that small? Nine stories! And it's state-of-the-art! Made of solid concrete! Would you rather live in a crumbling old house? Like your parents' place, with the leaky roof and the broken windows? I got central heat!"

Giovanni unlocked the door and led his clan, along with their packages and suitcases, to the state-of-the-art elevator. Rosaria, the island girl, had never ridden in an elevator, so she opted to trudge up the stairs to the seventh floor rather than squeezing into that narrow cabin that might be the death of her. Giulietta joined her out of solidarity, and Vincenzo rode the elevator with his uncle.

Giovanni had just rented the one-bedroom apartment, and it was fairly expensive, given his circumstances. He considered himself lucky that he, a "southerner"—which was what they called anyone even halfway dark-skinned back then, except for the really dark ones, the "Negroes"—had been able to get an apartment at all. The only reason he'd been accepted as a tenant was because his boss at the wholesale market knew the landlord, and because Giovanni could prove that he had a full-time job. The high-rise community in Hasenbergl, advertised as modern social housing, was a win for both sides: the increasing numbers of immigrants, many of whom were arriving with their families, had an affordable place to live on the edge of the city, while the Munichers living in the city center rarely had to see the foreigners. Two worlds, connected by the Number Eight tram and separated by an invisible curtain of money and mutual prejudice.

When they reached the apartment door, Giovanni picked up his wife and carried her across the threshold. After setting her down on the other side, he went back to retrieve the suitcases.

"What are you standing around like donkeys for?" he barked at Giulietta and Vincenzo, who were lingering in the stairwell, looking somewhat lost. "Come in!"

Giulietta pushed the reluctant Vincenzo into the apartment, and the man of the house gave them a tour. It had a living room, a bedroom, a kitchen, a bathroom, and even a balcony. An electric stove, a large refrigerator, a bath, and a modern toilet. Carpet, yellowish-brown wallpaper, and a bulb dangling from the ceiling. Giovanni had bought a marital bed made of modern compressed wood, with white veneer, plus a dining table and a television. Proudly, he switched on the large oak box, and the black-and-white test pattern for German Channel

Two slowly faded into view. "Fantastic, isn't it? It's actually all in color—they broadcast in full color in Germany! The technology's very expensive, but we'll buy ourselves a color TV in a couple of years!"

Vincenzo swept his skeptical gaze over the shelves constructed from fruit crates. He'd had an inkling about all this for a long time, but asked no questions to avoid humiliating Giovanni in front of his less-than-enthusiastic wife.

And Giulietta? She simply chose to like it. For years, she'd closed her mind to this Germany, never visited her brother even once, and nobody knew why. But now a switch had flipped in her head. Something in her saw that this country, which she'd visited so often in her fantasies, was her chance to turn her life inside out.

"*È ossigeno, Giovanni,*" she said. "Germany is oxygen. I can breathe here."

That evening, Giulietta laid the embroidered bedding from Rosaria's dowry on the living-room couch. She set the pillow on the floor to make a second bed. Vincenzo leaned against the wall and watched mistrustfully.

"It's just for summer vacation," she insisted. "When school starts again, you'll be back with your friends."

Giovanni was standing in the kitchen with Rosaria, who was washing up after dinner. "Where is our baby supposed to sleep?" she whispered, and Giovanni laid a comforting hand on her belly, whose roundness no one could have possibly seen underneath the wedding dress.

"It's only temporary. Don't worry. Hey, it's kicking!"

"*Macché*, nobody's kicking. Did you tell her?"

Giovanni shook his head. Of course he'd told her when she'd asked about the measurements for the wedding dress. When Giulietta came to the door, Rosaria turned away, and Giovanni removed his hand from her stomach.

"I'm sorry, Rosaria," Giulietta said softly.

Enzo called that same evening. As soon as Giovanni answered the phone, he was buffeted with the rage and disappointment of a husband who had suffered utter humiliation in front of the entire family. A man who let his wife run off wasn't worth much in Sicily, where women are the real epicenter of the household.

"Enzo, calm down. Your wife is fine! Nothing's decided yet. She's just a little confused. Hang on, I'll give you to her!" Giovanni held the receiver out to Giulietta, but she shook her head vehemently. "*Scusa*, Enzo, I'm not sure what to do."

On the other end of the line—the pay phone in the bar on the piazza, if the background noise was any indication—Concetta yanked the receiver to her own ear, and the Day of Judgment thundered down upon Giovanni. Hellfire, sin, damnation—she pulled out all the stops at her shrillest volume, as though she had to scream in order to be heard in Germany. Giovanni was mortified at the thought of half the villagers pushing their way into the little bar to witness the drama, as though it were a Greek tragedy or a Puccini opera. Exasperated, he shoved the receiver into his sister's hand.

Giulietta tried in vain to interrupt the torrent of accusations. "Mamma, I'm okay! So is Vincenzo!" But she never got a chance to make her case. "I don't know!" she exclaimed in response to Concetta's incensed query as to what would happen to her marriage and child. "Mamma! I don't know!" Angrily, Giulietta slammed the receiver into its cradle. Vincenzo, in underwear, with his blanket around his shoulders, padded in from the living room and gave his mother a questioning look. The TV played in the background. Somewhere in America, astronauts were preparing for their first flight to the moon.

Giulietta didn't have a plan. All she had were emotions. She, who had always been the more sensible of the twins, suddenly had no idea what she wanted anymore. She only knew what she didn't want, and that was to look back. Late at night, Giovanni and Giulietta stood on the balcony, smoking the way they had in Milan, except there was no bench and no church on the balcony—only a gray apartment building with a handful of windows still illuminated. The air was humid; a summer thunderstorm rumbled in the distance.

"Am I a bad wife?" Giulietta asked. "Am I a bad mother?"

"Of course not," Giovanni replied. "All marriages go through a difficult phase."

"For thirteen years? Giovanni, I spent thirteen years waiting for love to come."

"What's so important about love? Feelings come and go. You're a family—that's what counts."

Giulietta blew cigarette smoke into the night without replying.

Giovanni took her arm. "Listen, I'm here for you. Whenever you need me. But think of Vincenzo. He has to go back to school after vacation."

Giulietta spun around angrily. "I always think of Vincenzo! And Mamma! I do everything they expect of me, and still I'm doing everything wrong!"

She was near tears. Giovanni put his arms around her. "Giulietta, sister dear, you're not doing anything wrong."

"For the last thirteen years, I've felt like I was living under a dark cloud. Sunshine was for everyone else. Giovanni, there's a revolution happening out there on the streets, and what am I doing? Cooking, washing, ironing, shopping, taking Vincenzo to the doctor. You know what? That dark cloud is Mamma's shadow!"

"What do you expect her to do?"

"She carries old Sicily around with her like a cage—we're the little people. The poor farmers. The victims. Who don't deserve to be happy! She can't let me be happy, because she was never allowed happiness herself."

Giovanni looked at her thoughtfully. He had to admit it was true. He cast a glance into the living room, where Vincenzo was staring at the television. He could hear the whole conversation. Giovanni shut the balcony door.

"And I always have her voice in my head," Giulietta went on. "Anytime I get up the courage to do anything, the voice says, 'You can't do that! You're not allowed! Stay where you belong—you're safe there!'"

"So, what are you going to do now, Giulietta?"

"Have you ever read Marx?"

"What the hell does Marx have to do with it?"

"I bought his book. In Milan. *Das Kapital. Social being determines consciousness.* Don't you see, Giovanni? That's Sicily. In me, in you. I don't know a lot about politics, but I do understand one thing: either we take our fate into our own hands, or we die. A little more every day."

"But what do you want to do?"

"If the Americans can fly to the moon, I can at least make it over the Alps."

"Germany isn't paradise."

"I don't need paradise. Just being allowed to live is enough."

25

The air was sticky, and uniformed policemen stood at the ends of the rows, making sure none of the long-haired audience members lit up a joint. Onstage, the actors rolled around beneath a blanket with the word "Censored" printed on it, and then got up with their breasts exposed.

Rosaria had to avert her eyes—she was ashamed for these people who had obviously lost all sense of shame themselves. Giovanni had invited *la famiglia* to the theater in order to prove his own worldliness and lift Giulietta out of her melancholy. *Hair*, the scandalous American musical, was premiering in Germany, with German text and actors. They'd had to leave Vincenzo back at the apartment, watching a TV show in a language he didn't speak, because the musical was only for age sixteen and up.

Giulietta had never been to a musical, nor to the opera, though she frequently listened to opera music. This, though, was beyond the limits of her imagination. Initially skeptical, she soon let herself get swept up in the music, which unexpectedly pierced her straight to the heart. She loved the crazy costumes as well: an explosion of colors, an experiment with no respect whatsoever for tradition and morality—as though someone had thrown open a door nobody had noticed before, letting a whirlwind of light into a musty house.

Fashion here was apparently about personal expression rather than harmony and balance. It didn't matter whether the proportions were right or which materials were combined how, as long as it was emotionally authentic. For Giulietta, who'd grown up somewhere between Milanese refinement and Sicilian tradition, this spectacle was equal parts shock and liberation.

"What's the song about?" Rosaria whispered to her husband.

"Bah." Giovanni shrugged. "They want free love. Everyone screws everyone else."

"And this is the country where you want to live?"

"Oh, they're just joking around!"

"Did you live this way before we were married, this free love?"

"*Of course not,*" Giovanni lied, taking her hand affectionately. "Who do you think I am, dear?"

Giulietta tapped her feet in time to the songs, barely able to stay in her seat. The sweaty German guy with horn-rimmed glasses beside her seemed to find it disconcerting.

"Giovanni, do you understand these Germans?" Giulietta whispered. "They're sitting here as stiffly as parishioners in church. Are they always this way?"

Giovanni shrugged. "That's just how they are."

By the end of the evening, Giulietta and Rosaria agreed that Germans were strange people, albeit for different reasons. Giovanni took them to Leopoldstraße and showed them an Italian ice cream shop run by people from Veneto. The tables outside were filled with students with matted hair and solemn faces, talking as though the worldwide revolution were beginning in five minutes.

Giulietta noticed that the Italian café was the only one with tables and chairs on the sidewalk; people at the German establishments all sat indoors. When she risked a peek through the window of a Bavarian pub, there wasn't a single long-haired man inside—just fat guys with strange brushes on their hats, and a waitress in a dirndl carrying four unbelievably large beer steins at once. It was exactly like that movie she and Vincent had seen once. When they returned home on the last tram, they found Vincenzo asleep in front of the white noise of the TV.

Vincenzo hated Germany. He missed his friends, his bike, his books. He wanted to go home—but not without his mother. And since he was all too aware of her unhappiness with Enzo, he didn't want to make her even more miserable with his own unhappiness. So, he toughed it out, waiting for summer vacation to end, while Uncle Giovanni conducted telephone diplomacy. He advised his brother-in-law not to pressure Giulietta for the time being. He'd talk to her himself, he said, and she'd come to her senses by the end of the summer. Enzo could barely stand waiting, but ultimately, he was wise enough to keep his own passionate emotions in check and follow Giovanni's advice—though he did make

Giovanni swear not to let Giulietta out of his sight. If Giovanni didn't protect her like he would his own wife, Enzo would murder him with his bare hands. "You can count on me, Enzo," Giovanni said. "I love her just as much as you do."

Along the way, Giovanni explained to Rosaria that, due to various delivery, quality, and export issues at Mercedes, he'd decided to move into the food industry full-time. She didn't need to worry, he said; he had everything under control and a brilliant vision. With the international Communist revolution close at hand, there was no future in luxury cars, whereas everybody needed apples, oranges, and bananas no matter what party they belonged to. He even brought her with him to the wholesale market; she spoke no German, and his boss, Mr. Riemerschmid, didn't speak Italian, so Giovanni was able to present him as his "business partner." He explained that good old Riemerschmid was plagued with health issues and preferred to remain in the background while he, Giovanni, was on the front line of sales.

Giulietta went out for a haircut one evening and returned home with a short bob and blond highlights. She was also wearing straw-colored sandals and a sunshine-yellow minidress she'd bought at a boutique in Schwabing, near the university. Men on the street turned to look at her. She looked years younger, and she felt that way, too. She was visible again. She wanted to live. Her own life, not other people's. And then she did something Giovanni only found out about later.

She went to the German Technical Museum with Vincenzo. And as Vincenzo, with ever-growing enthusiasm, discovered the famous planes he'd seen only in books—the steel Messerschmitt Bf 109 in war paint without the swastika and the Junkers Ju 52 with its gleaming aluminum skin—Giulietta left him alone briefly and went to the entrance. She stepped into the yellow payphone booth outside, pretended she was calling someone, and paged through the phone books hanging beside the apparatus. She found the name she was looking for. And she found his address.

During all Giulietta's years of marriage, a secret life had existed inside her, alongside her real one. There was no Enzo in that second life, no guilt for having taken a father from his child and a child from his father. There was only a blooming suburban garden with rustling pine trees. In that garden was a house with green shutters and a red-tiled roof, and in that house was an oak table with a checked tablecloth, where Vincenzo and his siblings sat to eat dinner. She was vivacious in that other world, in the prime of her life, even as she wilted in the Milan apartment. Not because she and Enzo had to pinch pennies, but because she wasn't the woman she could have been.

She was purely functional, a shell that existed only for others. But her second self had kept going all those years, developing a life of its own. The other Giulietta bought a new couch for the living room, took the children to piano lessons, went out dancing with her husband, took summer holidays in Venice, and opened a tailor's shop in Schwabing, where she sold an Italian tourist a sunshine-yellow minidress.

Now, all at once, this life that had been tucked away in her soul was right in front of her, tangible, filled with the sounds and smells of the city—his city—and a shiver went through her every time she saw a man on the street who looked like him. There was nothing left for her to fear, and nothing she desired more than the moment when their paths would cross. Her other life was just a tram ride away, and she had to visit in order to know whether it really existed or was merely a dream. Whether, thirteen years later, there was a way for her to become the woman she'd never been, to fill those lost years with love, to live backward, back to the moment where she'd taken the wrong path and, against all reason, to start again from scratch.

The gardens in the wealthy neighborhood of Bogenhausen smelled even more wonderful than she'd imagined. The villas were larger, the fences taller, the streets more sedate. The birds twittering in the trees were the only sound as Giulietta stepped out of the tram in her new dress and made her way through the elegant neighborhood. She didn't hear children playing in the yards. The revolution sweeping the streets of Europe, shattering old customs, was but a faint echo here, a passing breeze that bounced off the self-satisfaction of the bourgeois walls and died away as though it had never happened. New Mercedes sedans were parked outside the front gates, alongside older Borgward convertibles and a futuristic Ro 80. Giulietta looked around for the silver-gray Iso Rivolta with the red leather seats, but there was no sign of it. Maybe he'd sold it—maybe he'd banished everything from his life that reminded him of her. Maybe she deserved it.

The address was right, but the house wasn't what she'd expected. The big pine trees were missing. There was no white picket fence, just a wire one in front of a deep-green thuja bush that separated the property from the street. Behind it, in the shadow of two Wilhelminian-era villas, was an inconspicuous, newly built bungalow, all stark straight lines and glass surfaces and slate-gray window frames. It wasn't a particularly romantic structure, but she decided it suited him. It was an engineer's house, precise and advanced. Even so, a faint sense of disenchantment crept over her. The nameplate above the doorbell told her that it was the right place. His last name, nothing else. She squinted at the window but couldn't make out anyone inside. There were no toys or tricycles in the yard. Beside the house was a two-car garage. The front gate was locked.

It took her an eternity to work up the courage to press the round white doorbell. She heard it jangling inside the house. Her heart nearly leaped out of her chest. But nothing happened. The front door remained shut. He wasn't home.

Giulietta decided to wait for him. She'd waited thirteen years; a few more hours were nothing. It was Saturday afternoon; he might return from shopping at any moment. She took a pocket mirror out of her purse and fixed her hair. Clouds gathered in the sky, and a gust of wind stirred up flower petals; the air was electrified. Giulietta glanced around. No covered bus stops or stores to take cover in. She loitered by the gate, not sure where to go.

The cloudburst came suddenly, fat droplets thundering down onto the parked cars and dancing on the curbs. Giulietta held her purse over her head and took shelter beneath a chestnut tree. Then she heard his car approaching. She could distinguish the deep rumbling of an Iso Rivolta from any other car. The car approached, drove past her, and stopped at the driveway. Despite the torrent of water streaming down the window, she recognized his silhouette.

Vincent opened the door, jumped out of the car, ran through the rain, hurriedly opened the gate, and trotted back to the car, all without noticing Giulietta. She came closer as he drove the Iso through the gate and stopped in front of the garage. The red brake lights reflected off the wet ground. Vincent got out again, jogged around the car in the pouring rain, and opened the passenger door. He removed his beige jacket and held it out over the woman, who climbed out slowly. She was tall and elegant, with a dark bob that was obviously dyed and a short Mondrian dress by Yves Saint Laurent. The loose cut of the dress wasn't enough to conceal that she was pregnant. She opened her umbrella so he wouldn't have to keep his jacket up.

Suddenly, Vincent's gaze fell upon Giulietta, who was frozen in place. Bewildered, he stopped and stood there in the downpour. His wife, who had already unlocked the front door, looked to see why he hadn't followed. Giulietta whipped around. Under no circumstances did she want to be seen by him now, and certainly not by her. She hurried away.

"Giulietta?"

She heard him approaching behind her on the wet sidewalk. Her heart was pounding in her throat. She turned around slowly. Her wet dress clung to her skin, as did his shirt. They gazed at each other, overcome. How could she have been so stupid to show up here, a foreign object? How could she have been so presumptuous to think there would still be a place for her in his world?

"What?"

"Sorry."

"What are you doing here?"

"Nothing. Visiting my brother. Summer holiday."

Seeing him in the flesh shocked her. Not because the old feelings were back, but because something was missing. He wasn't looking for her anymore. He had lost his youthful restlessness, that insatiable longing that had still filled him when they'd seen each other two years before in Milan. This was a man who had come into his own—not just in his career, but in his heart as well.

"Vincent?" His wife had stepped into the street. She went to him and held her umbrella over his head. Not over Giulietta's.

Vincent introduced the two of them in a tone that was awkwardly formal. "This is Giulietta. From Italy. This is—my wife." He didn't say her name. As though he were trying to prevent Giulietta from getting too close to their life.

"Oh, Italy," his wife said amiably. "Sunny there." She was attractive; she was clever; she'd been his first secretary at BMW. A woman who knew what she wanted: him. "Don't you want to come in, Giulietta? You're going to catch cold."

"Y-yes, of course, sorry," Vincent stammered.

"No, thanks," Giulietta replied. "I have to go. Ciao."

Avoiding his eyes, she turned hastily and walked away. Somehow, though completely soaked to the skin, she managed to maintain her dignity until she got to the end of the block. Only once she was around the corner did her entire body begin trembling. She wished she could die right there and then.

Giovanni and Vincenzo stood in the doorway to the living room. They didn't know what was wrong with Giulietta. She was lying on the couch, weeping, softly at first, then racked with deep sobs, then screaming angrily into a pillow. Vincenzo sat down beside her and put a hand on her shoulder.

"Mamma? What's wrong?"

"Nothing, honey. Go back to sleep!" She buried her face in her hands. Alarmed, Vincenzo looked to Giovanni, but he was equally bewildered.

After a few minutes, Giulietta sat up and wiped her eyes. Vincenzo embraced her cautiously.

"Mamma, what happened?"

Abruptly, she burst into tears again and buried her face in Vincenzo's arms. He held her tightly, as though he were the parent and she the child. Then, composing herself, she gripped both of his arms and stared straight into his eyes. "Vincenzo, promise me you'll do something with your life! Whatever you do, follow your passions! Don't think of anyone else, not even your mother!"

Giovanni watched as the young man nodded gravely.

26

Our train stopped on the Brenner Pass. It was midnight, but I was wide awake, staring at the photo of my father. I was starting to see the similarities to Vincent: the inquisitive gaze, the delicate lips, the slim build. At thirteen years old, he'd already been taller than his Sicilian mother.

"When did she tell you?"

"That same night. She told me everything."

"Including who Vincenzo's father was?"

Giovanni hesitated and then shook his head. "But she knew that I knew."

"And Vincent?"

"The next day, he came to the wholesale market, looking for Giulietta."

"What did you tell him?"

"Nothing. He gave me his business card. He wanted her to call him. At the office."

"So, did you give her the card?"

He shook his head disdainfully. "I saw the ring on his finger." He reached for his plastic bag and pulled out a small Thermos. *"Vuoi un caffè?"*

I nodded, deep in thought.

"You know," he said, "that summer in Milan with Vincent, 1954, that was the only time Giulietta was *completamente viva*. Alive. Once you've tried good wine, *quello buono*, ordinary wine won't taste good to you anymore. And every time you drink it, you'll be searching for that first time."

He poured the coffee into two espresso cups.

"But memory is a ghost. You have to forget it. The past is gone. That guy in the photo there, that was me once, but that isn't me anymore. That's someone else."

He handed me a cup. I pondered. I'd spent my whole life not turning around, not looking back. I just kept moving forward.

"Without your past, you're missing something, though," I said. "I mean, maybe I'd be a different person today if I'd met you guys sooner. If I'd known who—" I caught myself about to say "we." Who we are, not who you are. Was there a "we" connecting me to people who had been strangers just a few days before?

"Maybe it was better that way," he said. "You were free. You could do what you wanted, *no?*"

My phone rang again. This time, I picked up.

"Hi, Robin."

"Where are you? Why aren't you returning my calls? I've been sitting here waiting for you for hours!"

I was silent.

"Do you have the sketches finished?"

"I'm on my way to Naples."

"Wait, what?"

"I'll be back in forty-eight hours. I'll explain later. It's a family thing."

"Um, you do understand what's at stake here, right?"

"Yeah."

"You can't just abandon me now. Are we a team or not?"

"Sorry."

"What am I supposed to tell them tomorrow?"

"I don't know, Robin. No clue. I really don't know."

"You always know exactly what you don't want. But I need a 'yes' from you right now."

"Robin—"

"A 'yes' to us. To whether we're still a team."

He hung up.

I knew how deeply I'd disappointed him. I knew how impossible I was being. Though I instinctively resisted the deal, I didn't have a plan B.

In the meantime, Giovanni had taken his own phone out of his jacket and called his wife. I didn't catch everything he said, but it sounded like it was mostly about food and grandchildren. The important things. When he hung up, he proudly showed me the pictures his wife had sent him—the newly baptized princess photographed from all angles.

"Bellissima, no?"

I wondered what would have become of me if I'd grown up in an environment like that, surrounded by noise and love and people who spoiled me. And then I realized that, for the first time in ages, I wasn't functioning the way everyone expected me to. That I was prioritizing my family—could I call them that?—over my career. How many times had I missed my mother's birthday? How many Christmases had I spent working to meet some deadline? I clung to my job like it was a matter of life and death, as if I would cease to exist without it, lose the *right* to exist. Everything had come second—my freedom, my love life . . . to say nothing of children. Being creative and independent was a privilege, sure. But was I driven by desire for personal fulfillment, or was I simply obsessive?

Amid all the chaos of those few days, the one thing I was sure of was that I belonged exactly here, in this shabby night-train compartment in the middle of the Alps, with Giovanni and the invisible others sitting beside us. If it's true that part of us lives on after death, then Giulietta was here, too, and she wanted nothing more than for me to bring her son to his real father, and to find my own father in the process. I was scared as hell, but deep down, I knew I couldn't run any longer.

Dogs suddenly barked on the train platform, and there was a cacophony of male voices, shouting in Italian and Arabic. Border-control police yanked frightened people out of a train bound for Austria. Men with large rucksacks. Women and children. An argument turned physical; the police herded the refugees toward the station. An undignified, ghostly scene under the fluorescent lights. No one else bore witness; no one intervened. Our train started up again. A small girl in an anorak, clutching her teddy bear and holding her father's hand on an unfamiliar train platform—that was the last thing I saw.

"Poveracci." Giovanni shook his head. "This world is a mess."

Nobody checked our passports, a privilege we owed solely to having not been born in the wrong place. Giovanni handed me the photo album and refilled our wineglasses.

"So, what did Giulietta do?" I asked. "Did she go back to Enzo or stay in Munich?"

27

The night Giulietta saw Vincent, she told her brother everything. Almost everything. Afterward, when he crawled into bed with Rosaria, he heard his sister crying in the living room. Neither he nor Rosaria slept a wink. They lay awake until dawn broke and Giovanni's alarm was about to ring.

"Basta," Rosaria finally declared, and rolled over in bed. "I can't take it anymore."

Giovanni embraced her. "Just ignore it, *amore.*"

Rosaria sat up and switched on the bedside lamp. "Do something, Giovanni! You're the only one she listens to!"

"What am I supposed to do, *porco Dio?*"

Rosaria rose to her feet with determination and padded to the living room in her nightshirt. "Giulietta, stop crying," she commanded, and planted herself in front of the couch Giulietta was lying on. Vincenzo, who hadn't slept, either, sat up from his pillow encampment on the floor, rubbing his eyes. "You have everything, an apartment, a husband, a great son . . . You even have amazing talent! And what do you do? You complain about how unhappy you are, how cursed your life is! Don't you hear what you're saying? What arrogance! You think you're so special?"

Giovanni, who'd followed close behind, tried to rein his wife in, but she was on a roll.

"It's everyone else's fault, right? Society, imperialism . . . *Porca miseria!* Do you know what you sound like? Like a whiny old Sicilian woman! Like your mamma!"

That hit home. Giulietta fell silent. Then she wiped her tears from her face, looked up at Rosaria with red but sober eyes, and said, "You're right, Rosaria. You're right."

Outside, the morning sky blazed above the high-rises.

From that day forward, Giovanni never heard a single complaint pass his sister's lips. Giulietta pulled herself together once and for all. She decided that she had no right to what people called love, not in this life. If you expect nothing, she reasoned, you can't be disappointed. Simple as that. But rather than returning to Milan, she did something that surprised everyone.

"Giovanni," she announced when he returned home with meat and vegetables for dinner, "I'm going to make clothes."

"How do you mean?"

"I'm opening a boutique."

"A boutique, hmm? Where?"

"Here."

Giovanni started. "Here, in my kitchen? Giulietta, you can't simply open a boutique! You need start-up capital, you need a space, you need a work visa."

"I know. I'll work and save money. It's like you always say, if there's anywhere people can make it without connections, it's Germany."

It was too much for Giovanni. He felt guilty for having put ideas in his sister's head. He needed to come clean with her. They weren't children anymore.

"Tomorrow, I'll take you to work with me," he said, "and show you how far a person can get here in twelve years."

The next morning, Giulietta woke up at a quarter to four with Giovanni. They made some espresso before leaving the slumbering apartment block and taking the first tram. Forty-five minutes later, they reached the wholesale market; the area outside the halls was already a hive of activity. The light of the streetlamps reflected on the wet asphalt, and dozens of diesel trucks trundled through the gate. Giovanni got a guest ID for his sister and led her past the guard and into the "Belly of Munich." If the metaphor was accurate, then Munich was an insatiable, ill-tempered giant who devoured unbelievable quantities of beef and bananas. The fruits and vegetables were from all over the world, as were the men and women carrying, cleaning, sorting, and selling them. Besides the Italians, there were Spanish and Portuguese, Yugoslavians and Greeks, Arabs and Turks.

"My realm," Giovanni declared ironically, almost a little contritely, and gestured to a small vegetable stand in the middle of the loud hall swarming with yellow forklifts. "And this is my boss, Mr. Riemerschmid."

Giulietta gave her brother a look of confusion. The heavyset, cantankerous Bavarian shook Giulietta's hand without smiling and spoke German to her in an accent she could barely understand. At first, he thought she was Giovanni's wife. Then he gave his employees their daily instructions, complained about how the price of apples was falling, and headed over to the next stand—he owned several.

Giulietta looked into Giovanni's eyes and understood everything. His shame. His lies. And the tiny scrap of self-respect they had allowed him to preserve. He didn't have to say anything else. It was a fate all too familiar; things had never been any different for the Marconis.

"Why did you lie to me?" Giulietta asked over Giovanni's breakfast break. She drank coffee; he wolfed down a knuckle of pork. Beside them were the stand's other employees, eating blood sausage and *Münchner Teller*, a mix of ground innards in a greasy sauce topped with bread dumplings. They washed it down with *Weissbier*. Foods Giulietta had never seen before, and that filled her with dread.

"Because it was impossible."

"For twelve years?"

"Have you taken a look around? All the stores belong to Germans. We foreigners might get work hauling crates, or selling stuff, or driving forklifts, but we don't own anything. Those are the rules of the game."

"So, change them."

Giovanni gave her a tired smile. It wasn't like he hadn't tried.

"How much does he pay you?" she asked.

"Three marks fifty per hour."

She converted it to lire. "That's less than Enzo earns at Iso!"

"I know."

"Your boss is cheating you."

"So? Everybody cheats everybody here." Giovanni concentrated on his pork knuckle. "Giulietta, that's just how it is. You'll never open a boutique in Germany. I might be able to get you a job selling fruit, seeing as you speak German . . ."

"I'm not a fruit seller!" she exclaimed with a vehemence that amused Giovanni.

"Do you have something against fruit sellers? Your brother happens to be one."

"No, I don't. And I'm not upset with you just because you don't work at Mercedes. I don't care what you sell. But it hurts my heart to see what's become of your dreams. You wanted to become the *capo*. You wanted to do better in life than Papà. For him."

"That was a long time ago. And you know what? Maybe I really will do better than him. Because he could never accept the idea of working for someone else. If he'd been smart and accepted it, he'd still be alive today."

Giulietta didn't want to hear that. "I believed in you, Giovanni. My one ray of hope was that you'd been successful."

"Why would things be better for me than anyone else?" her brother grumbled, wiping his mouth with a napkin as he stood up. "Come on, I have to get back to work."

"Wait!" Giulietta got up and took his arm to stop him. "I know what we can do."

Giovanni didn't want to hear any more.

"You have a visa, right? You have work, so you're allowed to stay?"

"Yeah. Why?"

"Start your own company! And hire me, then I can stay, too. I'll do your bookkeeping."

Giovanni rolled his eyes in annoyance. "Number one, sister dear, I told you what the rules are around here. And number two, bookkeeping? Didn't you want to make dresses?"

"I'll make them in my free time. I can do that in my sleep. But, Giovanni, I'm talking about a company out in the city, not here in the market. Out there, you can make your own rules!"

Giovanni sighed. "What kind of company would I start? I didn't go to college; I don't know how to do anything; and I'm going to be a father soon. *Mannaggia*, Giulietta, stop it, please, be reasonable!"

"Just do what you've always done, Giovanni. The thing you do best."

He gave her an inquiring look.

"How many tons of cheese and wine have you brought over the Alps over the past twelve years, hmm? That's something you know about—food. But not this disgusting slop here." She gestured to the bones on the plates of the other workers, who had gone back into the hall. "Italian stuff. Good stuff."

"I just sell that on the side, to our people. You can't make a living on that. Germans don't know anything about proper food, and the ones who have money buy cheese and wine from France. Can you imagine, they've never even heard of mozzarella!"

Giulietta wouldn't budge. "I was at that corner store on your street yesterday. Do you know what they're selling there? Canned ravioli! And *sugo* in a jar! It's called Miracoli. And then the ice cream: Capri. All Italian names! The Germans are copying our food. They come to Italy on vacation, and then they want to eat that stuff at home, too."

"Have you ever opened one of those cans? It's dog food!"

"Exactly! And you'll sell the good stuff. Real ravioli, handmade, not industrial."

Giovanni brooded. It wasn't like he'd never considered it. Honestly, he'd just never had the courage. Not because of the food—he knew all about food. Because of the Germans. "And Vincenzo?" he asked. "When he goes back to Milan for school, how are you going to live without him?"

"He'll go to school here."

"Here?" Giovanni couldn't believe his sister's naivete. "How will he manage that? He doesn't speak a word of German! Do you have any idea how hard that was for me?"

"He's smarter than you." She smiled wryly.

Giovanni made a face and lit a cigarette. His sister had lost her mind.

When Rosaria caught wind of Giulietta's idea, she set in motion an avalanche that would roll unstoppably toward Munich: First, she called the bar back on her island and asked Alfredo, the barista, to take a message to her mother. Soon thereafter, Rosaria's alarmed mother showed up at the bar to call Concetta, her sister in Milan. The two women decided it was high time to take matters into their own hands. Giulietta needed to see reason.

When the doorbell rang, Giovanni and Giulietta exchanged surprised glances. They were in the middle of dinner, and they weren't expecting visitors. Vincenzo shrugged his shoulders as well. Rosaria alone suspected the truth. Giovanni answered the door and nearly jumped out of his skin: his mother and Enzo were standing in his stairwell. Accusation incarnate. They were sweating in coats and winter shoes—though it was the middle of summer, they were dressed for the North Pole. Enzo was holding two old suitcases. Before Giovanni could get a word out, his mother shoved him aside resolutely and pushed her way into the apartment. No power in the world could have stopped her. Enzo gave Giovanni a brief, contemptuous glance before following his mother-in-law.

"A scandal!" Concetta bellowed, wheezing as she removed her coat. "What's happened to you two, that your aged mother has to put herself through such a long trip? Have you gone out of your minds?"

Giulietta's bite of food caught in her throat. She got up from the table and stared into Enzo's silent, dark eyes. He was exhausted from the journey, exhausted from waiting, exhausted from the rage he'd been swallowing every day. He wanted his family back.

"Vincenzo!" Concetta embraced her blindsided grandson, covering him with kisses. "*Amore!* The things she's put you through! What kind of mother would do that? Pack your things—we're going home!"

Enzo set the luggage down and stood with his fists clenched.

"Leave him be, Mamma," Giulietta said, but Concetta ignored her. She glanced around the tiny kitchen.

"So, this is your *palazzo!*" she exclaimed before stomping down the hall and opening the door to the tiny bathroom. "What did I do to deserve such punishment from God? That my own children would lie to my face!"

"Mamma, calm down. Have a seat," Giovanni insisted.

Enzo tried to draw Giulietta aside to talk to her, but she resisted.

Concetta resumed her aria. "What did he do to you? Enzo is a good husband. You should be thanking God every day for him! Look at me, I don't have anyone. Who do you think you are, Princess Soraya?"

Enzo took her aside. "Mamma, I'll talk to her."

Concetta went right on berating her daughter. "Think about other people for a change! Who will take care of me in my old age?"

Giulietta, who had been standing there with trembling lips, finally found her voice. "I've only ever thought about other people! But you, maybe you could think about me for a change?"

"For shame! Oh, if your father could hear you now!"

"Mamma!" Determinedly, Enzo pushed Concetta aside. She acquiesced, granting him the floor. He took Giulietta's hand and gazed into her eyes decisively, almost threateningly. "Come home."

Giulietta's body quivered.

"Think about your son!" Concetta called.

At that, Giulietta tore away from Enzo. *"Basta!"* she shrieked at her mother. "It's my life, Mamma! Mine!" Everyone flinched, even Vincenzo. Firmly, Giulietta dragged Enzo out to the balcony and shut the door behind them. The others stood there, staring out through the glass, dazed.

"Amore mio!" Concetta cried, affectionately stroking Vincenzo's head. He turned away; he hated being treated like a little kid.

"You're my wife," Enzo said. "Have you forgotten that? For better or for worse!"

Giulietta fought back her guilty conscience. Leaving Enzo in the middle of an argument hadn't been difficult, but looking into his eyes now, physically sensing his anger and injury, was another matter.

"It's not your fault, Enzo. It's mine. I thought love would develop eventually, but—we have to stop pretending."

The words broke Enzo's heart. He really did love her. He just had a hard time expressing his strong feelings. He was a man of action, not a man of words. A bear with broad shoulders and firm hands.

"Maybe love is just a fantasy, Enzo. I don't know. But if I go back to Milan now—you don't deserve to be anyone's second choice."

"What do you mean? There's someone else?"

"No."

He eyed her suspiciously. Then he glanced through the window into the living room, where Vincenzo was standing and staring outside. "Vincenzo comes with me."

"No." Giulietta shook her head firmly.

Enzo grabbed her arm roughly. "Who do you think you are, that you can just take a boy away from his father?"

She tried to shake him off, but he was stronger. "Enzo, he needs me."

"What he needs is a home! You're robbing him of his country, his family, his friends. Only thinking of yourself! And now you want to stick him in school here, where he doesn't know anyone? Where he doesn't speak the language? At home, he gets the best grades in the class. What would become of him here?"

Vincenzo opened the balcony door and stepped outside.

Enzo released Giulietta. "Pack your things," he commanded his son. "We're going home."

Giulietta planted herself between them. "You can't separate us, Enzo. He'll find friends here. He'll get good grades no matter what school he's at! What do you think, Vincenzo? You like it here, right? You want to stay with me, don't you?"

Vincenzo glanced back and forth between his parents uncertainly. His mind raced. Whatever he said right now would be the wrong answer. Not because he had to choose between his mother and his father, but because choosing his mother—and there was no question of that—meant renouncing his own desires.

"But didn't you say we were going home after summer break?"

It broke Giulietta's heart to see Vincenzo suffering. But this time, she was wildly determined to hold on to the tiny scrap of freedom she'd grabbed hold of. She couldn't stand by and watch herself shrivel day by day. She wanted to live.

As Concetta boarded the train to Milan on Platform 11, she didn't deign to glance at her daughter. A handful of Hare Krishnas in orange robes sang and danced their way through the station. Enzo, bleary-eyed and unshaven, stood beside her with the luggage, a powerful man with the face of a lost child.

"You won't be happy in Germany," Concetta declared. "And Vincenzo will come back home to us." Her razor-sharp tone made it sound like a curse.

"Mamma, stop!" Giovanni cried. "You're just making everything worse. Give her a kiss, come on!"

Concetta remained implacable. "What God joins, man may not separate. God will punish her."

Giulietta turned away and buried her face in her hands.

"What kind of God is that?" Giovanni exclaimed. "As if she weren't suffering enough already!"

"Come, Enzo," Concetta ordered.

Enzo set his suitcase down and went to Vincenzo. Neither of them knew what to say. Enzo hugged him so hard that Vincenzo could barely breathe.

"I love you, Son."

Giulietta's heart shattered.

Enzo avoided her gaze. He didn't want her to see the tears in his eyes.

"Will you call me?" Giulietta asked.

He nodded, picked up the suitcase, and boarded the train.

28

Naples

Naples was a smack in the face. The light was too bright, the sun too powerful, the heat oppressive even in the morning. The humidity pressed against my skull like thick soup. The train platform was full to bursting; a jackhammer rattled somewhere nearby. It seemed like the air smelled of the harbor, moist and putrid, but maybe it was just the stench of the overflowing trash cans. Voices flew around, loud, aggressive, singing. The air vibrated with vitality, but a shadow hung over it as well, the hounded malaise of a country in permanent crisis.

Nothing, not one face, fit the cliché of cheerful Italians. These people weren't even well dressed, or at least most weren't, clutching their briefcases as they streamed out of commuter trains into the city. It was less a question of style than a question of money. If Southern Europe ever went bankrupt, the mobile phone companies would be the only ones to survive. Giovanni walked ahead; I followed him through the ocean of voices. We passed through the surprisingly modern station hall and stepped out into an enormous square that was one giant construction area. Fences, excavation pits, overwhelmed traffic cops, all surrounded by the old palazzi of a more noble era.

"*Cazzo,*" Giovanni groused, "*hanno cambiato tutto!* Where's the damn bus?"

He trotted across the street, where a dented little Lancia braked abruptly, honking, and maneuvered around him. Here, they didn't seem to honk to warn people. They honked to say, "Here I am!" while completely ignoring the traffic laws.

There probably wasn't a single German whose parents didn't drag them to the beach on Rimini, through Roman ruins or Tuscan trattorias when they were kids. Except me. Sure, I'd seen the movies. I knew the Marcello Mastroiannis and Monica Belluccis, the Latin lovers and the Mafiosi. I could keep up with the conversation; I had an image of Italy in my head. But images are there to protect us from reality. My mind lacked a category for this, and it caught me completely unprepared. Naples was enormous, damaged, beautiful, and ugly to a degree I had never thought possible. It was a cauldron of exhaust and noise—greedy, indifferent, fast, dirty, and opulent, life continually triumphing over death.

Suddenly, the strap of my handbag wrenched my shoulder forward; I lost my balance and slammed hard against the asphalt. The two boys on the scooter drove off at a maniacal speed. Giovanni ran after them, cursing wildly, but they disappeared into traffic. Giovanni ran back to me, breathless. I tried to get up, but my knee hurt like hell. My jeans were torn and bloody. I'd heard stories about this, of course, but it was one of those things that only happened to other people.

"Porca Madonna!" Giovanni groaned. "Are you hurt?"

I rubbed my scraped elbow. Only then did I realize what they had stolen from me. The bag contained not only money and my passport, but also Vincent's letter. I felt suddenly naked.

"Dammit."

"Benvenuta in Italia!" Giovanni pulled a sarcastic face.

He helped me to my feet. My shoulder hurt.

"Everything okay?"

"Yeah."

No. Nothing was okay. I was in the wrongest place in the world. I wanted to leave, to catch the first train home. There was no way I could go see my father like this. Not because of my torn jeans, but because now I had nothing for him. What was I supposed to say to him without the letter? For some absurd reason, I felt like I was only worth his time if I brought him something. Without the letter, I was nothing. I hated myself. Why did I come here? How could I have been so naive?

"This was a stupid idea. There's no point. I'm going home."

"Ma no! Does your arm hurt?"

"It's fine." I turned around and walked back to the train station.

Giovanni caught up. "Julia! Don't do anything stupid!"

"The letter was in the bag!"

Giovanni shrugged. "*E allora?* You don't need a letter. Not important. What's important? You. If you run away now, you'll regret it."

I shook my head. He took my arm in a fatherly way, and a wave of pain and despair crashed over me. I couldn't hold back my tears any longer. He put his arms around me, and I sobbed uncontrollably until his shirt was soaked.

"Why do I have to be the one to come to him, anyway?" I hissed furiously.

Giovanni smiled at me, doe eyed. "Because you're braver."

I don't remember how long it actually took to get there, but it seemed like forever. The bus jolted up and down the badly maintained streets, past crumbling palazzo walls black with exhaust. I stared out the dirty window, trying to sort my thoughts and get my emotions under control. Street merchants hawked cheap bedding; laundry fluttered in the wind outside the windows. Chic women in business suits wove their way through the traffic on Vespas; black-framed death announcements hung on the walls, showing the names and photos of the deceased. Dozens, hundreds. The blue of the sea flashed into view behind an urban canyon. His city.

My gaze latched onto every man who was around his age. Late fifties. Would he have gray hair? Or no hair? Had he stayed slim and sinewy like in the photos, or was he heavy and stout like that guy in a suit, barking into his phone as he drove? Was he successful, happily married, or did he look back on his own life in horror? Would I remind him of my mother, and if so, would that be a good or bad thing? Could I speak German with him? Did he still remember the language? What was I supposed to call him?

"Did he ever ask about me?"

Giovanni's voice was soothing. "He loved you. You were his family."

"Then why did he leave?"

Giovanni raised his eyebrows knowingly. And didn't reply.

Vincenzo's building was on a dark, narrow street not far from the harbor. It was an old apartment complex whose best years had been sometime in the century before last. The once-grand facade was now filthy; the ocher paint was peeling; a confusion of electric cables hung over the door. Giovanni pressed a buzzer on a doorbell panel that hung crooked in the wind, once unscrewed and never correctly secured again. "Cifarelli," it said. Not Marconi.

"Cifarelli? Wasn't that the rich uncle from Palermo?"

"Not quite an uncle. More distant."

"So, the girl at your wedding that he—"

"Pronto?" The intercom crackled. A woman's voice. Dominant, sensual, smoky. I reflexively pictured a badly aged Brigitte Bardot.

"Pronto, Carmela? Sono io, Giovanni!"

"Giovanni? Ma che ci fai qui?"

"Vincenzo c'è?"

The buzzer sounded.

"Is he here?" I whispered.

Giovanni shrugged and pushed the heavy door open.

The stairwell smelled cool and musty. It was unexpectedly ample and radiated the morbid charm of faded elegance. Yellow sunlight glowed through clouded windows. We walked up the sweeping wooden stairs, whose beautiful wrought-iron railing was broken in several places. I grew slightly woozy; I hadn't had breakfast.

"Listen," Giovanni said, and drew me closer conspiratorially. "We'll tell his wife you're a friend of mine. *Va bene?"*

"Why?"

"It's more discreet. It's a touchy *situazione."*

I stopped in my tracks. "Giovanni, I'm not interested in lying. I'm not doing him that favor. He's just going to have to deal with it. He has only himself to blame."

I started walking again, leaving Giovanni where he stood. My heart was hammering in my chest, but I had to see this through.

Giovanni caught up to me at the top, gasping for breath. He seemed almost as nervous as I was. A massive, dark-green door was open a crack. I fixed my hair as best I could, though it was already a wreck from the night on the train. Giovanni knocked, and a woman appeared.

She was wearing a green silk robe that was somehow garish despite its cosmopolitan elegance. She was on the far side of fifty, perhaps even sixty—one of those women who had once been spectacularly beautiful, whose full lips had taken on a derisive twist as her glory faded. She had dark hair tinted red and sensuous green eyes. The nails of her slim fingers were freshly painted. She smelled like Chanel and menthol cigarettes.

"Giovanni, che ci fai qui?" she asked, glancing quizzically at me from the corner of her eye.

"Bella come sempre!" Giovanni embraced and kissed her.

She laughed away the compliment and turned to me. *"Buongiorno."* It sounded like a question.

"Buongiorno," I replied without extending my hand.

Giovanni explained to her that I was German and didn't speak Italian. Then he introduced us clumsily. "Julia. Carmela."

She shook my hand with a friendly smile. So, this was the girl who had enchanted Vincenzo on the island so long ago. The first love of his life, before my mother—and after her.

"Vincenzo c'è?" Giovanni asked.

"No."

She beckoned us inside and closed the door quietly.

The apartment was surprisingly bright; unlike the musty stairwell, the rooms were airy and modern. Designer furniture with occasional baroque accessories that would have been kitschy in Germany, but fit Carmela to a *T*: a glass chandelier on the ceiling, paintings of lush flower bouquets, a colorful throw over the couch, pillows with playful patterns and gold fringe. A large picture window drew the eye to a sun-drenched roof terrace. Giovanni and Carmela chatted, and I didn't understand a word. Then she looked at me in shocked silence. I felt like an intruder, horribly guilty and self-conscious.

"La figlia di Vincenzo?" she whispered.

Giovanni nodded. Her eyes searched my face for something. Then she asked him something I didn't catch, something about a *ragazza* and a *telefono*.

"Sì." Giovanni nodded.

Suddenly, she burst out laughing.

I blinked at Giovanni, who didn't know what was going on, either.

"Scusate," she said, and explained to Giovanni with a sheepish smile.

He laughed as well. "When we called, she thought you were Vincenzo's lover."

"Sorry," Carmela said to me in English. "I am sorry!"

Giovanni asked her where Vincenzo was now. She responded with an energetic torrent of words before reaching for her phone.

In a low voice, Giovanni translated for me. Apparently, Vincenzo and Carmela had gotten into an argument after I called. He'd insisted that the woman on the phone wasn't his lover; she hadn't believed him, and he'd left. She didn't know where he was now. Judging by the laconic way Giovanni explained the situation, I figured it wasn't the first time this had happened. Carmela sounded agitated as she spoke into her *telefonino*. I tried to figure out what she was saying, caught only the words "Giovanni" and "*ragazza*," and realized she'd gotten his voice mail.

I glanced around the living room timidly. The family photos on the sideboard were the first thing to catch my eye when we walked in, but I'd avoided looking at them closely. More family I'd never had. It was shocking to see Vincenzo older; he'd been younger than me in all the pictures I'd seen of him until that point, but these photos were of a father. There was still that searching restlessness in his gaze, the sharp features, the dark hair, but he'd lost that wiry, lanky look—well fed by his Sicilian wife, no doubt—and he now seemed more sure of himself.

It wasn't the same self-assurance he'd had in that one photo with me, a twenty-something's sense of boundless horizons. It was confidence founded upon achievement, wounded by setbacks, but strengthened by having overcome. I saw a man proudly embracing his children, a son and a daughter. One picture showed the family on the beach, in the late 1980s or so. The children had sand on their skin and clam shells in their hands; Vincenzo was lying beneath an umbrella, with Carmela beside him in a bikini. She was blindingly beautiful. Then, maybe twenty years later, there was the family outside the entrance to an Italian university, the son holding a diploma, and Vincenzo, already gray, gazing solemnly into the camera, deeply moved. Eerie how much the son looked like him. And then a photo of the daughter, sitting on the sofa in this apartment with a baby in her arms. Vincenzo and Carmela were laughing beside her—proud grandparents, young to be so. My little half sister was already a mother. I tried to make out any similarities to me, but she seemed to take after Carmela. The baby's father wasn't pictured.

Carmela hung up, trying to collect herself. "*Bevete qualcosa?* Drink something?"

I shook my head, feeling equal parts drawn in and left out, still mesmerized by the photos. I stared at framed experiences that weren't mine, wondering whether he ever thought about me. And my mother. The other family that could have been. Or whether he secretly knew that the essence of a life lies not in the still images capturing its progression, but in the things that can't be seen.

"Vincenzo will come. Don't worry."

I didn't want to wait around. I didn't trust Carmela. There was something disingenuous in her eyes, something shadowy; I didn't know whether she was friend or foe. She went to the kitchen to fetch water for Giovanni.

"Why would he argue with his wife instead of just telling her the truth?" I asked Giovanni in a low voice.

"Let me tell you something. *Vincenzo è schizofrenico.* Split *personalità.* When he came back from Germany, he washed his hands of the whole place, like it never happened."

I wondered whether it had made him happier. Giovanni, seeming to read my mind, pointed to the white wall unit on the other side of the living room. The top shelf was lined with silver and gold trophies; beneath it were model cars, framed certificates, and photos scattered among the books: an attractive man in white racing coveralls, getting out of a sports car with sweaty hair, helmet in one hand. I moved closer.

"He was famous, your papà," Giovanni said.

I was confused. "Famous" was the last thing I'd have ever called him. To me, he'd always been a phantom. The word "was" caught my ear as well. Sure enough, the certificates were all from the 1980s and '90s, and the framed photos were of a man in his thirties, around my age, lively and focused, yet wise beyond his years.

"He was a great *pilota.* Look, this photo, this was when he won—1986, the European Cup, with Alfa Romeo."

Vincenzo on a podium. Up at the top, clutching a large silver trophy. The same trophy that was on the shelf now. I gaped. I would have believed almost anything about him, but how did the criminal my mother had described end up a racetrack hero? How had that gifted child become a violent radical, and how had that violent radical become a winner?

I drew nearer to the grainy photo, trying to discern the story behind the face. His features had little in common with the weedy, uncertain boy in Giovanni's album. Only his eyes were the same—narrow and searching, seeming to challenge the photographer.

He wasn't like the slick racing stars you see today. He reminded me more of Paul Newman, Steve McQueen, that type. Daredevils with sideburns, fuel in their veins, and groupies for breakfast. White coveralls with a round collar, stripes and advertising logos on the sleeves. The pictures showed him in his cockpit, surrounded by colleagues and mechanics, near the stands. Always surrounded by people, yet somehow lonely, his thoughts elsewhere. He radiated more than just a determination to win—there was a melancholy light in his eyes, as though he knew every race might be his last. I had to admit, my father had been sexy.

Giovanni pointed to the base of the trophy on the shelf and made a face that was supposed to express something like pride. The small plate was engraved in black: "European Touring Car Championship 1986." And his name: "Vincenzo Marconi."

I stared. My stomach was doing flip-flops in a way that made me even more light-headed, while my brain tried to assemble this person's different modular components into a logical whole. It didn't work. Giovanni was trying to get me to admire Vincenzo, but what I really felt when I looked at these devotional objects was that I'd been lied to.

1986. That was the year I ran away. To Italy, with fifty marks in my pocket. Until my mother caught up to me at the train station and told me my dad was dead.

The truth was that those were the years when Vincenzo was genuinely successful. Because he'd made a timely escape from a woman who obviously hadn't made him happy. I was angry at him. I wished he could have stayed faceless. I didn't want reality to force me to understand him.

"Happy guy," I remarked sarcastically.

"No." Giovanni waved the idea away. "Vincenzo's always a little sad."

"This doesn't exactly strike me as a failed existence."

"It's an invisible unhappiness. Everyone in the country is a master of *fare bella figura*, but inside, *tanta depressione*. Come on, let's go see the *terrazza!*" Giovanni put his arm around my shoulder to lead me outside. *"Che bello, eh?"*

Up here, a fresh breeze blew in from the sea. Palm trees, lemon trees, and bougainvillea in terra-cotta pots lined the expansive terrace. The view was breathtaking—out across the tiled roofs, the dockside cranes and ships, all the way to the shimmering blue Mediterranean. The rattling of the *motorini* echoed from below; swallows flew through the air; children played soccer on neighboring terraces.

"*Quant'è bella, Napoli!*" Giovanni exclaimed. "It's terrible how they're ruining this country, *'sta banda di criminali!*"

Carmela came out to the terrace, bearing a white tray. "*Accomodatevi.* Please, sit down."

Giving me a pleasant smile, she set crystal glasses, a carafe of water, and three espresso cups on the large table. Her courtesy seemed affected, and I wasn't sure if it was to conceal aversion to me or merely uncertainty.

We sat down around the table beneath the white awning, and she picked up a book from the tray. It was a German paperback from the 1970s, faded and tattered. *The Sorrows of Young Werther*. Goethe. Carmela opened the book and withdrew a small photo.

"This is you," she said. It was a statement, not a question.

I startled. The photo showed Vincenzo as a young man in a leather jacket and bell-bottoms, next to a laughing little girl in a red soapbox racer. The Munich TV tower was in the background. The girl was me.

Giovanni, looking surprised, asked where she'd found the picture. She tilted her head back and forth in silence. I asked her in English whether she'd known I existed. She smiled. Vincenzo had his little secrets, she said, but after twenty-five years of marriage, she knew him better than he realized.

I stared at the image until it seemed to come alive in my mind. This was yet another Vincenzo, a boisterous, laughing man with none of the thin-lipped distrust he showed in earlier and later years. It was as though a window to his soul had opened on this one day, only to snap shut again a short time later. Why had he left his family in order to start another?

Giovanni seemed to guess what I was thinking. "Vincenzo is sometimes one way, sometimes another," he said thoughtfully. "Way up one day, way down the next. Win or lose, no middle ground." Then he added, "But he wasn't always like that."

Out of the corner of his eye, Giovanni cast a scrutinizing glance at Carmela, who lit a menthol cigarette. Once she had hers going, she offered me one. I turned it down. Giovanni brought out his photo album, laid it on the table, and asked Carmela if she'd ever seen it.

"No."

She opened it and flipped through the photos with a mixture of interest and distance. I couldn't see the images, which made me feel almost jealous. Giovanni noticed, and turned the album to face me. There he was again, the thirteen-year-old with the skeptical expression, leaning casually against a Fiat 500 in front of a small shop with a sign, "Marconi Italian Foods." He was wearing a T-shirt, jeans, and low-top shoes.

"Vincenzo was the only one of us with German blood in his veins. And ironically, it was his neck that Germany broke."

"How so?"

29

Vincenzo

An Italian teenager, leaning against a wall, smoking. He didn't understand what the German kids were shouting to each other as they played soccer in the field between the high-rises. His mother and his uncle were at the store, so he hung out alone. They'd told him he ought to help them, but he didn't feel like it. Instead, he roamed through the streets of the housing project, people-watching.

He hadn't chosen this country. It belonged to other people. He didn't belong here. An older woman walking her dachshund gave the foreign boy a mistrustful look as she passed. Vincenzo felt like Germany was a country where everyone avoided everyone else, and nobody dared laugh. He didn't laugh, either. Just wandered around in the glow of the streetlamps, kicked a dumpster, wished his orange racing bike weren't back in Milan. As the night grew cooler, he peered into a German living-room window. A family was eating supper. The first live broadcast from space flickered on their black-and-white television: snowy images, broadcast interruptions, garbled audio transmissions in English. Three American astronauts left gravity behind.

His mother had enrolled him in a German school, a concrete building right there in Hasenbergl. It was the *Hauptschule*, the general secondary school, the one that took everyone, even the foreigners who didn't speak German. Attendance was compulsory. Vincenzo had never thought of school as "compulsory." In Milan, he'd been preparing for the *liceo*, the school for those who hoped to attend college. *Gymnasium*, they called it in Germany. But he couldn't go there because he didn't speak German. People could switch from the *Hauptschule* to the *Gymnasium* later, his mother said. Later.

Vincenzo was given a seat in the back of the class, beside Pedro, a Spanish kid whose German was stronger than his. Vincenzo had brought notebooks, but couldn't follow anything the teacher said. So, he doodled airplanes and tanks. Math was the only subject he excelled in. Numbers knew no language barrier. But when the teacher handed back his first corrected test, he asked Vincenzo which classmate he'd cheated off. Next time, he said, Vincenzo would sit by himself.

They smoked cigarettes in the schoolyard during breaks. Vincenzo didn't have any, so he went to the nearest supermarket and stole some. Just like that. It was wrong, of course—his moral compass was as razor-sharp as his mind. But did the rules of his neighborhood in Milan, where everyone knew everyone and there was always a chance you were stealing from a relative, also apply in a foreign country whose people didn't follow the same rules of common decency toward you? When the cashier, a fat woman with short hair, saw him, he ran off. Faster than she could catch him.

Running, he was good at. He'd always been faster than everyone. Couldn't stand anyone beating him. In Milan, his friends had marveled at how he could calculate the circumference of the earth or the distance to the moon in his head. Vincenzo, the best in the class. Vincenzo, whom everyone wanted to sit beside during exams so they could copy his answers. Vincenzo, his mother's little prince. Here in Germany, he was just the foreigner, the immigrant's boy, the spaghetti kid.

The Milanese girls had been impressed by his charm and eloquence, but here, robbed of speech, he was nobody. As the German boys pulled out all the pubertal stops to get the attention of the opposite sex, Vincenzo was but a footnote at the fringes of the girls' perception. He scorned their plebian behavior, their rituals, the jokes he didn't get. He remained an outsider, and only his fellow outsiders—the ones who'd been held back, and the other immigrant kids, Greeks, Spaniards, Turks—had any interest in his company. But he didn't understand anything they said, either, and he wasn't trying to make friends, because he secretly felt they were beneath him.

But how was he supposed to prove his superiority? Without words, all that remained was the language of fists, and that had never been one of his strong suits. Vincenzo was tough and wiry, but not particularly muscular. And he was alone. He didn't have a chance against the German kids' cliques, and they never passed up an opportunity to show him where he belonged, which was at the bottom of the pecking order.

And finally, to add insult to injury, he'd been forced to say his last name in front of the class, which had immediately earned him a nickname. Since then, the other kids had taken to shouting, "Hey, Macaroni!" every morning when he came in, or, "Go away, Macaroni!" when he approached them in the schoolyard to bum a smoke. And when he had cigarettes of his own, they refused to take any from him because he was a thief, stupid and devious and all the other traits they ascribed to foreigners because they couldn't recognize them in themselves.

One afternoon, he surprised Giovanni at the wholesale market and asked, "Uncle Giovanni, what's a *Gastarbeiter*?"

"That's us," Giovanni replied. "Guest workers."

"Us, you mean the Italians?"

"Take a look around. Everyone that isn't German is a *Gastarbeiter*."

Vincenzo swept his gaze around the large hall filled with noise and loud voices. There was Ivo, the skinny forklift driver with a sociology degree; Pepe, the heavyset butcher with the sick mother; Ali Moustache, who sometimes snuck his coworkers a fish or two; and the Turkish women whose names nobody knew, who swept the floor when everything closed for lunch.

That's us.

"But I'm not a guest worker," Vincenzo pointed out.

"No. You're a *Gastarbeiterkind*." Giovanni laughed. "A guest worker child."

Vincenzo tried to repeat the long word after his uncle, but his tongue got tripped up.

"The Germans take words that are normally separate and smash them together to make new words. '*Ausländerbehörde*,' immigration office. '*Straßenbahnschaffner*,' tram conductor. '*Weltraumrakete*,' space rocket. No 'of,' no 'with,' not even a space in between. A minimum number of letters, very efficient!"

In Giovanni's view, compound nouns were a little like Toast Hawaii. He broke down the word that Vincenzo had picked up in school. It encapsulated everything his thirteen-year-old nephew didn't want to be: *Gast*, guest; *Arbeiter*, worker; and least of all *Kind*, child. That afternoon, Vincenzo realized that his life was headed in the wrong direction. He understood that his family's Germany was not the land of inventors and opportunity he'd read about in books. It was a country for people who obeyed the Germans.

"Now do you understand why I want my own shop?" Giovanni said, tapping his nephew sharply on the chest. "Never be a slave to anyone else."

Vincenzo nodded thoughtfully.

Giovanni lifted a crate of lemons from the stack and handed it to Vincenzo. "Someday, we'll all go back south."

"Stop lying, Giovanni."

Giovanni startled.

"You'll never go back."

"How would you know, kid?"

Vincenzo shrugged disdainfully and lit a cigarette. "Anyway, the stuff you said about the Germans isn't true."

"Hey, since when do you smoke? Does your mother know?"

Vincenzo ignored the question.

"What isn't true?"

"They don't like us. They're completely prejudiced."

"Oh, and you aren't?" Giovanni retorted. "What you just said, that was prejudiced! You'll lose your prejudices when you get older."

"But obviously, you're not prejudiced at all, right?"

"I work around the clock, smart-ass. I don't have time for prejudices. Now, help me."

Giulietta was largely oblivious to what Vincenzo thought. He kept his feelings quiet because he didn't want to upset her, and she was too focused on herself to sound him out. She loved her little prince more than anything, no question, but for the first time in her life, she was putting herself ahead of others. Awakening from the slumber of her unwanted housewife-and-mother existence had her imagination firing on all cylinders—her life was hers again. At last, she could stop standing in the shadows. At last, she believed in herself. Whereas Vincenzo wandered aimlessly through the neighborhood after school, Giulietta had a goal once more. And this time, it wasn't just a diffuse dream. It was her big opportunity.

The little store across from the wholesale market that would someday become one of Munich's best specialty-foods retailers was a dusty hole-in-the-wall.

Giulietta had discovered it by chance. Since the death of the locksmith who had once occupied the place, the roller shutters had been at half-mast, quietly rusting away. Teenagers had smashed the windows; the place was crawling with wood lice; the walls were mildewed; and rusty water dripped from the pipes. Never in his life would Giovanni have considered setting up shop there.

But Giulietta had a vision. She had a gift for seeing a place not as what it was, but as what she could turn it into. She asked around in the neighborhood and found an address for the owner, the locksmith's widow, Erna Baumgartner. She turned out to be a recluse who had no interest in renting the space: it had belonged to her Herbert—God rest his soul—and she knew she probably ought to sell it, but she was just too attached. If only the Lord had blessed them with children.

Giulietta drank coffee with her, that watery German percolator stuff, and something happened. Maybe Giulietta was the first person who really listened to her, this wiry little Municher who'd lived behind closed curtains since her husband's death. Maybe that was why Giulietta understood her so well, since she herself had lived behind closed curtains for years. At any rate, a miracle occurred: Mrs. Baumgartner, known in the entire neighborhood as a hateful old cow, agreed to rent to an Italian from the wholesale market. For one year, no more. One never knew with foreigners, after all. They might not pay; they might cause problems; they might leave and never be seen again.

Giulietta scrubbed until her knees and fingers were raw. She felt like she was ready for anything. Ready to make up for all those lost years. Rosaria admired her sister-in-law's toughness and sometimes toiled by her side even though she was already six months along. Giovanni, who worked at the wholesale market from four thirty in the morning until three o'clock in the afternoon and then renovated the store until late at night, worried more about his sister than about his pregnant wife.

But nobody heard a single word of complaint from Giulietta. Far from it. Others had come to earn some money, send it home, and then go back where they came from. But Giulietta couldn't go back. She was damned to move on. She set up her fashion atelier in the shop's back room, which was scarcely bigger than a closet. A small table, a single chair, a clothes rack. Nothing else would fit. Rosaria lent her an iron.

Having spent every last penny on the Wedding of the Century, Giovanni couldn't buy her a new sewing machine the way he'd been planning, so the table remained bare for the time being. They hauled a large, used, refrigerated display counter into the sales area out front, mounted shelves on the freshly whitewashed walls, and hung up pictures that Giovanni carried over from his apartment: colorful fishing boats, the Naples harbor at sunset—gold-framed high art. And to Giulietta's confusion, Giovanni set a plastic Madonna on the shelf. Tucked discreetly into the corner, but not without a colorful, blinking halo, so that his mother would be pleased if she ever ended up visiting.

"What's that for?" Giulietta asked.

"It's pretty," Giovanni said.

"You always say you don't believe in that stuff."

Giovanni shrugged. "You never know."

He went on working. Rosaria put a water glass full of daisies she'd picked on the sidewalk beside the Madonna.

When they finished five weeks later, an exhausted Giulietta tugged off her dirty smock and clunky boots, and slipped on her flared jeans with flowers on them. It smelled like fresh paint, floor polish, and the October rain outside the door. A bare lightbulb dangled from the ceiling. It was Sunday, shortly before midnight, and all at once, unfamiliar music pierced the silence, electrifying the room along with every fiber of her being. It was a sound so new, so unbelievably nonchalant and sexy, that it seemed like it had come to Earth from a different dimension.

It was "All Along the Watchtower," and Giulietta was enthralled despite not knowing what most of the words meant. Her body understood the music and began to dance. Barefoot, arms spread wide, she laughed and reached for Giovanni's hand. He was sitting on a wine crate, too tired for Jimi Hendrix. His legs leaden, all he wanted to do was sleep.

Giulietta turned to Rosaria, who stood polishing the counter. She grabbed her hand and refused to let go until Rosaria finally set her rag aside and allowed Giulietta to pull her away. Rosaria was bashful at first—she had a child in her belly, after all. But Giulietta's joy was infectious. She danced through the shop, spinning around and around like an oblivious girl. She abandoned all shame, closed her eyes, began to fly.

Giovanni watched his two nearest and dearest in amazement. Then they took his hands, one apiece, and dragged him to his feet. He capitulated to their charm, forgetting his tired legs, forgetting his debts, and thanked the blinking Madonna for the two best women life had ever given him—besides his mamma, of course. Without them, he'd have been far too much of a coward to make this miracle possible. His own realm, where nobody could tell him what to do, and nobody could chase him out.

Nobody except Mrs. Baumgartner. The landlady. All at once, she was standing red-faced in the doorway and waving her umbrella around. She'd thrown a coat over her nightgown, put on a head scarf, and trotted through the rain to put a stop to the action next door.

"Where do you think you are? This is a respectable neighborhood! Shut that yowlin' off, or I'll call the police on you for disturbin' the peace!"

Giovanni could already see his virgin rental contract circling the drain. Germans didn't mess around, he'd come to understand. They had the horrifyingly un-Mediterranean habit of actually meaning what they said. No meant no. And stayed that way.

There was no calming Mrs. Baumgartner down. The neighbors had probably lit a fire under her behind, upset that she was renting to foreigners. The stench of garlic, the end of nighttime peace and quiet, the start of criminality. She'd ignored their prophecies of doom at first, then developed a guilty conscience, and now all her fears were coming true. Giovanni laid the charm on thick, but she went right on berating them, talking a blue streak. Blustering past, she discovered the back room and decided on the spot to evict Giovanni because he'd only mentioned sausages, not seamstresses. The words "sneaky," "underhanded," and "conniving" were used.

Giovanni was livid. He had half a mind to throw the keys at the xenophobic old bag's feet. Let her keep her overpriced dump! But Giulietta remained calm. And then the second miracle happened. With angelic grace, she managed to steer things in a wholly different direction. As Giovanni was still trying to placate the enraged Rosaria and her injured Sicilian pride, Giulietta told the old woman about how long she'd been making dresses and working toward opening her own boutique. Maybe the unvarnished truth of the story was what pulled Erna Baumgartner back from the edge. At any rate, a few minutes later, Giulietta was measuring her waist and promising her a new winter coat, and in the end,

Mrs. Baumgartner ended up sitting with them at the counter as Giovanni let her taste the difference between an industrially produced sausage and a real mortadella from Bologna. In truth, she hadn't cared one way or another about the finer points of Italian meat production, but she went on and on about how she'd eaten every meal alone since her husband's death, with only the parakeet for company, and how it was so much nicer to have company. Just like in the good old days during the war. The Madonna in the corner blinked.

The next day, Mrs. Baumgartner schlepped an old cast-iron sewing machine into the shop. A black monster, Hungarian made, probably smelted down from armor steel. Giulietta had her first order.

30

During the day, while Giovanni worked at the wholesale market, Giulietta held down the fort, selling Parma ham and pecorino. At night, she sat in the back room and sewed. Sales were slow at the store; few Germans ventured into the little space where Italian rang out. Guest workers came by for the freshly ground espresso, but bought their groceries at the supermarket, where they were cheaper. Giovanni's wages from the wholesale market were the only thing keeping the shop afloat, and at home they were short on everything.

Rosaria, now well into her third trimester, was worried. Giulietta, on the other hand, was filled with unshakable optimism. While the others slept, she could finally do what she loved. Free and unhindered, she let the fabric glide through her hands, fabric that grew and became the dresses she had already fashioned in her mind. It happened without effort or worry, almost as if by magic. Giulietta worked as though she knew she was running out of time. At sunrise she got up, made herself a coffee, and went outside. She inhaled the fresh autumn air, the scent of the wet leaves on the sidewalk, and smiled at the Turkish street sweepers. She felt rich, though she didn't have a penny to her name. She was living her dream at last.

One afternoon, Vincenzo came into the shop with a bloody nose. His shirt was stained red, and he was cursing like a sailor. Giulietta was shocked. She tended to him lovingly, while Giovanni tried to sift through the ranting and raving to figure out what had happened. It seemed Vincenzo had gotten into a fight with some other boys at school. In the classroom, right in front of the teacher. Him against three others. His teacher had asked him something about the Holy Roman Empire of the German Nation, saying surely he would know about that as a descendant of the Romans, but Vincenzo still didn't speak enough German to understand the question.

One of the German kids slipped him a crib sheet. Vincenzo read it out loud without knowing that the words meant "Shut up, pussy!" The class roared with laughter. Vincenzo didn't understand why. The teacher smacked him upside the head. Humiliation made Vincenzo see red, and he climbed over his desk to yank the kid who'd passed him the note out of his chair. A wild fistfight broke out. Vincenzo didn't have a chance. He was alone; the other boy had friends. And in the end, the guest worker child was the only one who got suspended.

Giulietta felt guilty for having neglected him. Against Vincenzo's wishes, she went to his school the following morning, where she dragged the teacher out of the room in front of the whole class and told him off. Vincenzo was thoroughly mortified, because now he was a snitch and a mamma's boy on top of everything else. The teacher merely smiled in response to Giulietta's outburst. Boys will be boys.

Of course, he was far too clever to admit to the slap. He was one of those men who kissed up and punched down. Besides, he went on, Vincenzo had no business being at school anyway until he spoke proper German. Where else was he supposed to go? Giulietta asked. The teacher shrugged. Home. Italy was nice; he'd been to Rimini on holiday. Seething, Giulietta went to the principal and asked where all the guest worker children could learn German. The old man shrugged. His hands were tied, he said. Resources were tight; the teaching staff was at capacity; and the public education system didn't have the means to provide special treatment. She could always try a private school, he suggested. As if she were Jacqueline Onassis.

"What kind of country doesn't teach its kids the language?" Rosaria asked over dinner. "Don't they have any national pride?"

Vincenzo ate his *zuppa di fagioli* in embarrassed silence.

"Why do they send for us, but then refuse to care for our children? If you ask me, they don't like children. Have you seen that sign by the playground? 'No playing after 6:00 p.m. Keep off the grass. No bicycles permitted!' *Dio mio*, this whole country is a barracks yard!"

"Calm down, Rosaria," Giovanni snapped. "The Germans were all children once, and they survived. He'll learn the language, one way or another."

Giovanni had also learned it, one way or another. His German lessons had come from *Bild*, a tabloid newspaper with nice big print that cost only ten cents. Of course, he knew that his accent was unmistakable and his grammar was catastrophic. The people who worked at the wholesale market skated by on a simplified German peppered with Bavarian dialect and colorful curse words. Whoever shouted the loudest got their way. And the Germans spoke to their foreign coworkers as though they were part Neanderthal. "You, work!" "Don't eat!" "Get lost, ya dumb bastard!" That was the German they learned from the Germans. And Rosaria, confined to her own four walls as a housewife, didn't even watch German television.

Giulietta wasn't content to sit around and fret. Once again, she took matters into her own hands. If the school wouldn't teach her son, she'd have to do it herself. What had she learned German for, if not this? She understood the logic behind German grammar; she loved the precision of the words; and behind the hard sound many people found off-putting, she sensed a sentimental depth that remained hidden to others. Maybe it was Vincent's voice echoing in her head when a thought in German plucked a string inside her that she'd shared with no one else.

Every afternoon, Giulietta sat down with Vincenzo at the small kitchen table and taught him his father's language. While the other kids played soccer outside, he learned that *la macchina* was neutral in German, neither masculine nor feminine: *das Auto*. He learned the difference between an *A* and an *Ä*, and how to pronounce the word *Streichholzschachtel* without making a fool of himself.

Soon they were joined by another Italian boy, a slowish kid from Bari named Pippo, and then Vasilis from Corfu, who was always repeating German curse words and laughing his head off, and then a shy Turkish girl named Neylan, who learned faster than the boys, which awakened Vincenzo's competitive spirit. Giulietta suspected the girl had a secret crush on her son, but Vincenzo's self-esteem was so far gone that he didn't even notice.

Those were cheerful afternoons, where they often giggled at the sounds of the words, and the children were happy that someone was finally looking out for them. Their parents were all at work, both fathers and mothers. When Giulietta discovered how neglected the other students were, she began cooking for them as well. It delighted her to see them thriving, growing progressively more confident, but between the shop and the tutoring sessions, she found less and less time to sew. Yet again, she put her dreams off for the future. But that was just how things went: two steps forward, one step back. She remained optimistic that she would succeed in Germany eventually.

All at once, the sun vanished. It rained for days; a leaden gray sky swallowed all color. The November chill crept beneath their skin and through the gaps in the windows. Giulietta made Vincenzo a duffel coat and knitted wool socks, because their two suitcases had been full of light summer clothes. Rosaria caught cold and lay in bed, coughing, her due date approaching fast.

Then she went into labor. Giovanni brought her to the hospital. Not the one in Hasenbergl—no, his child would come into the world in a beautiful place. Schwabing was a well-to-do neighborhood, but not far by taxi. As long as he showed his insurance card, which covered his wife as well, the hospitals would treat them the same whether they were Germans or foreigners. He liked that about this country. Never set foot in a public hospital without making a will first, they said in Italy. Giovanni knew his wife was in good hands with the German doctors.

He was standing in the corridor, feeding ten-cent coins into the telephone, when it happened. Rosaria had been brought into the delivery room, and he wanted to call his sister at the shop. Back then, men didn't hold their wives' hands as they gave birth; they stood out in the hall, chain-smoking. At the exact moment Giulietta answered, Giovanni turned around and saw him. He was waiting in one of the chairs, in a gray coat with his hat on his lap. When he spotted Giovanni, he blinked in surprise. Then he got up and came over to him.

"I'll call you later." Giovanni hung up. "Butt-o-Meter!"

"Giovanni," Vincent said cautiously. "Are congratulations in order?"

"Not long now. Yours?"

"Might need a C-section."

Giovanni withdrew a pack of cigarettes from his pocket and offered one to Vincent. He took it and flicked his lighter.

"Your first?" Giovanni asked.

"It is. Better late than never."

They smoked in silence. Neither of them mentioned the woman they were both thinking about. Giovanni watched Vincent out of the corner of his eye. Did he know? He seemed anxious to say something but unable to find the words.

211

Then a nurse emerged and smiled at Vincent. "Congratulations. It's a girl. Everyone is healthy."

Vincent clapped his hands to his face, hardly able to contain his joy. He got up, laughing, and tears spilled down his cheeks. His hat rolled to the floor as he threw his arms around Giovanni. "A girl!"

Giovanni clapped him enthusiastically on the shoulder, while the nurse stood there watching. Then he leaned in closer. "Stay away from my family," he hissed, softly and unmistakably into Vincent's ear. *"Capisci?"*

Vincent startled.

Giovanni smiled at him. *"Auguri, Vincent, auguri!"*

Vincent picked up his hat, perturbed.

"Come with me," the nurse said. "You can see your baby now."

Vincent followed her without saying goodbye. Giovanni, puffing his cigarette, watched him go.

Rain drummed on the hospital windowpane as Giovanni peeked outside two days later, humming a Sicilian lullaby as he rocked his daughter. Rosaria lay in bed, exhausted and proud. "We'll call her Marietta," she said. "After my mother, Maria."

"Anything you want."

Through the curtains, he watched a couple hurry through the rain outside the hospital. Vincent held his umbrella over his wife, who got into the Iso Rivolta, holding their newborn. Vincent cast a brief glance up at the building, pausing for a moment. Then he got into the car and drove off.

Giovanni was the happiest father on Earth, but as soon as they got back home, the thing everyone had warned him about—all the men, anyway—happened. Giovanni was no longer the man of the house. Now *la mamma* was in charge.

"Later, later, all you ever say is 'later'!" Rosaria screeched as she sorted dirty laundry in the bedroom with the baby in one arm. "I can't take it anymore! This isn't a home; this is a temporary arrangement!"

"I know, I know. Everything in life is a temporary arrangement!" Giovanni protested, wishing he were far, far away.

"You know what? I'm going back to Salina! Me and Marietta!"

"Not so loud! What will the neighbors think?"

"Maybe you should care more about your own child, hmm? You need to make a choice, Giovanni. Who is your family?"

Giulietta opened the bedroom door. Rosaria and Giovanni fell silent. They exchanged an embarrassed glance. Giulietta's voice was clear and calm.

"Don't go back to Salina."

Giulietta bought an evening newspaper and studied the apartment ads. Vincenzo sat beside her, learning abbreviations: ZH for *Zentralheizung* (central heat); MB for *Mitbewohner* (roommate); KMB for *Küchenmitbenutzung* (shared kitchen). It didn't get more efficient than that. They were building new apartments all over Munich, yet most of them were either out of her price range or "went off the market five minutes ago, sorry." How it went was, Giulietta would call the landlord, and as soon as he heard her name, someone else would coincidentally have just taken the place. Then, she tried calling without giving a name, but her accent gave her away. And finally, one landlord told her straight out that he had nothing against foreigners; he simply didn't rent to them. Giulietta was about to hang up, but then, in a moment of brash impulsivity, asked, "Why not?" Baffled silence at the other end of the line, followed by a thundering sermon about the stench of garlic in the stairwell, the loud music, the Southern Europeans' payment practices. "And then the sick grandma moves in with 'em, and the uncle with no job and five kids!"

"Now you know why I live at the ass-end of nowhere." Giovanni grimaced sarcastically and refilled Giulietta's Chianti. He confessed to her that he'd found his own palazzo only with the help of his boss, who knew the landlord personally. Germany's being free of nepotism was a fairy tale he'd stopped believing in long ago.

"Goddamn Germans!" Vincenzo got up and walked out, slamming the door behind him.

"I'll talk to Rosaria," Giovanni told his sister. "You can stay here as long as you want."

"Giovanni, I didn't come here to end up dependent on someone else all over again. I'm going to find a place of my own, even if I have to live in a phone booth!"

Giulietta found something. Giovanni could barely believe his eyes when he accompanied her to the "no-pressure, get-to-know-you session," as the young man on the phone had put it. It was larger than a phone booth but smaller than an apartment. It was a room. In a *Wohngemeinschaft*, another one of those long compound nouns—a shared apartment, a commune. With three students who described themselves as undogmatic Trotskyites, not Leninists, and who viewed taking in a real member of the working class as an act of international solidarity. Double points because she was an underprivileged foreign woman. Apparently, it made them feel like they were doing something useful, though Giovanni got the impression that they didn't have much else useful in their heads.

It was in a run-down old building on the west side of town; the apartment stank of beer and hashish, and they hadn't scrubbed the toilet in a very long time. Everything they said in Italy about German cleanliness and Prussian discipline, this generation was enthusiastically throwing overboard. The walls were purple, the floorboards crooked, the shelves mere plywood planks atop bricks; the only serious piece of furniture was the record player with homemade speakers. A look inside the refrigerator—canned beans, a squished tube of tomato paste, and a bowl of cherry Jell-O—told Giovanni everything he needed to know about what sort of people these were.

Refrigerators like these, thought Giovanni, were a clear sign that the Communists would eventually lose the Cold War, as well as the reason that Europe couldn't give in to them without a fight. If they won, everyone would be eating borscht with tomato paste from morning to night. At any rate, Giovanni could see that these long-haired wannabe intellectuals were interested in his sister purely for political reasons, not erotic ones. Besides, one of them was female, a woman of perhaps twenty in a sweater with elks on it, with a young daughter who shared her mother's mattress. The woman's name was Alex; the other two were Roland and HP—yet another abbreviation. It wasn't obvious which of them was sleeping with whom.

"What will Vincenzo say?" Giovanni asked his sister quietly.

"It'll inspire him."

"Inspire him to do what?"

"Stop being so pessimistic all the time!"

Giovanni took a deep breath and then made his financial contribution toward global revolution: three months' rent in advance.

Giulietta spent two full days cleaning. She hung a bedsheet across the room, dividing it in two, one half for Vincenzo and the other for herself. Each of them got a mattress. Other than that, there was a clothes rack. That was it. Giovanni hauled in bags full of cheese and claimed the refrigerator in the name of Italy. The Trotskyites' resistance faded the first time Giulietta made pasta—not college-kid spaghetti soaked in canned tomatoes, but a *vera puttanesca* with Sicilian anchovies, fresh thyme, and Salina capers. Over dessert, a tiramisu with fresh-ground espresso, Giulietta was voted the kitchen authority. The working class was even permitted to assume dish duty.

Later that night, Giulietta sat on her mattress and knitted a scarf by the light of her nightstand lamp while Vincenzo crept around the apartment, sleepless. Alex and Roland made out on one couch; the little girl had fallen asleep on the other. HP sat beside the child, smoking, as the evening news flickered on the TV screen. Demonstrators tipped over a police van. HP offered Vincenzo a drag on his hand-rolled cigarette. Vincenzo shook his head. Aimlessly, he rummaged through the record collection, marveling at the psychedelic covers as he tried to work out the English text on the back sides. A chill ran down his spine as he studied the men's spaced-out faces. He realized that the authenticity these flower children brought into the world lay not in their colorful messages of peace but in a darker subtext, a tortured, furious cry of the soul that was just as violent and destructive as the wars they were protesting against.

Vincenzo drew a single out of its sleeve. Janis Joplin. "Summertime." He braced the record between his palms, placed it on the turntable, and guided the needle onto the vinyl. It crackled; then an electric guitar sounded from the speakers softly, almost tenderly, before the room was conquered by a female voice completely different from any he had ever heard. Crystal clear, deep and throaty, then ascending to hoarse heights until it became a penetrating scream disconnected from words that terrified Vincenzo and filled him with unsettling desire.

The little girl awoke and blinked at Vincenzo with large eyes. Her blanket had slipped off the sofa. HP had fallen asleep next to her. Vincenzo got up, went to the girl, and gently tucked the blanket around her.

31

Enzo

By early December, Italy is already thinking about Christmas. All of Italy, including the Italians in New York and Sydney and Munich-Hasenbergl. Rosaria set up a colorful, blinking wooden crèche in her reclaimed living room. Her mother had shipped it over. She missed her daughter. And as the temperature dropped, Rosaria's homesickness grew.

"Giovanni, let's celebrate Christmas at home."

"At home" wasn't their apartment. Home was Italy. And Italy was Salina.

"How are you expecting to travel down there with the baby?"

"The same way we came. By train."

"It's a two-day trip. And if the weather's bad, there won't be any ferries."

"My mother hasn't seen her grandchild yet. Neither has yours. It's a disgrace!"

"What about Giulietta? Should we just leave her here by herself?"

They knew Giulietta wouldn't even consider going. It wasn't home to her anymore.

"What about Vincenzo?" Giovanni asked her. "You want him to celebrate Christmas without his *nonna*? Without his father?"

"I'm not going back, *basta*."

But *la mamma* was determined. And so, Giovanni found himself glued to the telephone, trying to save Christmas through loud diplomatic negotiations among Salina, Milan, and Munich. Christmas meant family: *Natale con i tuoi, Pasqua con chi vuoi.* And maybe if they could get Giulietta to go, she and Enzo might reconcile. Giovanni secretly hoped so, anyway. But his good intentions died in the cross fire of mutual accusation. Concetta was categorically on her son-in-law's side, and she had Giovanni pass along the message that Giulietta was no longer her daughter. Giulietta didn't show anyone how hurt she was.

"What do I do, Giovanni?" Enzo asked over the phone. "What good is a family if you can just take it off like an old dress? Why doesn't she love me anymore?"

"I don't know, Enzo. I don't know."

On December 9, 1968, a rainy Saturday evening, the doorbell rang. Nobody heard it, because the commune was having a party. The Stones were blaring from the speakers; thirty college students were standing around the candlelit living room, drinking beer, smoking grass, and dancing. Most of the guys were wearing bell-bottoms and button-down shirts without ties; the girls were more open to experimentation. There was a little of everything, from ultra-short leather skirts with fringed jackets to Indian saris. Giulietta wore a brightly colored minidress with a psychedelic pattern. "Free your mind!" someone painted on the wall. Vincenzo stood to one side, watching. He'd become introverted and taciturn, with only his penetrating, concentrated gaze connecting him to the outside world. His hair had gotten longer—he'd simply stopped letting his mother cut it. His dark locks hung into his eyes. Someone offered him a bottle of beer. He hesitated for a moment, then accepted. Took a sip and stared at the girls' legs. He thought about Carmela. Her small breast in his hand. The doorbell rang again. He heard it this time, went to the door, opened it. Enzo was on the other side. He was holding a suitcase in one hand, Vincenzo's orange racing bike in the other. Vincenzo's jaw fell open. At first, he was afraid Enzo would storm in and smash everything to pieces. But then he realized—to his far greater horror—that Enzo looked like a ghost. Emaciated, hollow-cheeked, pale. His eyes, which Vincenzo had so often feared, had lost all trace of anger. They were the eyes of an abandoned child.

"I brought you your bicycle."

Vincenzo didn't know how to respond. Enzo's lips trembled. He let his suit-case fall to the floor and threw his arms around the boy, hugging him so tightly that he could barely breathe. When Vincenzo felt his father's body and smelled that familiar mixture of sweat, oil, and aftershave, he realized for the first time how short Enzo was. Vincenzo had grown taller than his father.

Giulietta was dancing. Then she saw Enzo and froze. He stood in the living room in his work boots, looking lost and glancing around with a disconcerted air. The college students ignored him; only the little girl peered at him curiously from her mother's arms. Giulietta was overwhelmed with shame. She felt too old for the minidress, and the high heels that made her taller than him embarrassed her. And then she got angry with herself for being embarrassed.

"What are you doing here?" Giulietta's tone sounded sharper than she'd intended.

Enzo didn't reply. He just stood there, gazing mutely at her. Tears ran down his cheeks. Only then did Giulietta realize that there was no accusation in his gaze, only longing and love. She fought down the emotion welling up inside her.

"Just listen to me, please," he said gently. His voice was nearly lost beneath the booming music. "Don't send me away."

Giulietta glanced at Vincenzo. He shook his head to say he didn't know what was going on, either. Someone bumped into her.

"I can make it without you," Enzo said, "but I don't want to. I want *us* to make it. You and me. And him. All of us, together."

"Enzo, I'm not coming back."

"But how can you provide for Vincenzo on your own?"

Giulietta turned away from the college students' curious eyes and went to the window. Enzo followed. Vincenzo stayed where he was and watched. Enzo touched Giulietta's arm tenderly. She stepped away.

"I'm doing fine! I'm working! I can breathe here. Do you understand that?"

Enzo wiped his brow. He was sweating. "But you can do that in Milan, too. You should see it. Everything's changing. All of Italy. Same students as here. Nothing's sacred to them anymore."

"No. Italy never changes. It's too old for that. They go out to the piazza, shout, 'Ho Chi Minh,' then they come home and say, 'Mamma, where's my pasta'!"

"You think the Germans are any different?"

"*I'm* different! People can reinvent themselves here, because the whole country is reinventing itself."

Enzo looked around nervously. He glanced at Vincenzo, who was standing alone amid the dancing girls.

"Then I'll come to you. I can reinvent myself, too."

Giulietta blinked. "What's happened to you?"

"I want you, Giulietta. You and our son. Everything's changing. The whole world's falling apart; and you're all that I have. I'll always protect you both."

Giulietta felt her knees going weak and fought against it. "No. Who would take care of Mamma?"

"You're asking me that?" Enzo retorted. "She's *your* mother!" His loud voice frightened the little girl, who ran over to ask Vincenzo who the man was. Vincenzo picked her up and carried her away.

Enzo took Giulietta's hand lovingly. "I want you just the way you are. I've always admired your strength and talent. You should do what you want to do. It's my turn to change now."

Giulietta was speechless. Tears sprang to her eyes.

"Everything okay?" Roland came over to her, regarding Enzo with suspicion.

Giulietta nodded, and he backed away.

"Is there someone else?" Enzo asked.

Giulietta shook her head, anger flaring again.

Enzo grasped for words. "I—it's like a sickness. Jealousy eats me up inside, and I don't know why." He kissed her hand uncertainly. Only now did she sense just how ashamed he was, how much agony he was in.

"You really have changed," he said. "God has switched on a light in your eyes. And I want to watch over it, to make sure it doesn't go out."

Giulietta turned away. She didn't want him to see the tear rolling down her cheek.

Vincenzo watched his parents slip out of the living room, leaving Enzo's suitcase right where it was. They went to the bedroom and closed the door. The little girl ran after them. Vincenzo caught her and picked her up again. He carried her into her room, laid her on the mattress, and tucked her in. Then he went back into the hall and stared at the closed door, trying to decide what to do. A student he didn't know stepped out of the bathroom and offered Vincenzo a joint. Vincenzo took it.

Long after midnight, when Enzo emerged from the room to fetch his suitcase, he picked his way across the floor, around empty beer bottles, overflowing ashtrays, and sleeping young people. The record player was looping endlessly around the last groove. A woman moaned somewhere. Enzo discovered Vincenzo among the sleepers. He scooped him up in his powerful arms, as though he were still a child, and brought him into their room.

32

Enzo stayed. Vincenzo didn't know what to make of it. Enzo was unbelievably nice to him, bought him little gifts, helped him work on his racing bicycle. Giovanni and Giulietta watched them through the front window as they rode the orange bike around through the wet leaves in front of the shop, bundled up in their thick coats.

"I'm just not sure," Giulietta said.

"What else do you want?" Giovanni asked impatiently.

"I don't know whether what I can give him is enough."

"Have you talked about it with him?"

"He says he can give enough for two."

Giovanni fixed her with a penetrating gaze. "You don't know how good you've got it with him. And you're not exactly young anymore. Maybe we expect too much from love. Maybe we listen to too much Adriano Celentano!"

He grinned wryly. She tried to smile. She knew he meant well. Enzo came to the door; an icy breeze blew through the shop. He rubbed his hands together to warm them.

"Giovanni, can you find me a job?"

They went to the train station. Platform 11. Giovanni hadn't been back down to the bunker since that first day. Very little about the place had changed in all those years, except the new arrivals themselves. Southern Italy had been picked clean; now Germany sought workers from the vast expanses of Anatolia and the deserts of North Africa. *"Ey, Arkadaş!" "Labès?"* Giovanni had picked up a few words of Turkish and Arabic at the wholesale market, which helped him push his way through the crowd, with Enzo in tow, toward the German officials who were freezing down here along with the new immigrants.

"Your passport, Enzo."

Enzo handed his passport to the German from the employment office, who was standing under the fluorescent lights in a wide tie and horn-rimmed glasses, and Giovanni explained that his brother-in-law was no mere unskilled laborer—he had been assembling the finest automobiles in the world for years.

"We've got something at VW."

"In Munich?"

"No. Wolfsburg."

"No, my brother-in-law must stay here. He has a wife and child."

"This isn't the tourist bureau."

"The what?" Another one of those long, winding phrases Giovanni didn't understand. Enzo asked him what was wrong. Giovanni translated. "He wants you to go to Wolfsburg."

"Where's that?"

"Far away."

Enzo shook his head. "Munich."

The official adjusted his glasses, looking annoyed. "Listen, the German companies tell us how many people they're looking for, and if you want to work in the automotive industry, all we have right now are Volkswagen in Wolfsburg and Ford in Cologne."

"Munich."

"Oh, get out of the way and let me do my job. A lot of people are waiting. Next!"

The official gestured to a young Tunisian of perhaps twenty-two. He stepped forward quickly and set his papers on the podium. "Volkes-wagen." His one and only German word. The official held out a stamp and sealed the destiny of a man whose name he couldn't pronounce. Perhaps he would meet the love of his life in Wolfsburg and start a family. Perhaps he'd build a house there, join a soccer club, and end up buried at the city cemetery. It was all decided with a flick of a stamp.

Enzo clenched his fists in frustration. "First, you tell us you're looking for millions of workers," he snapped at the official in Italian. "Now I'm here, with two good hands, and you don't want me?"

Giovanni shushed him and pushed him to the side. "Sorry, but isn't there any other work here in Munich?"

The official had made up his mind to ignore the irritating duo. There were so many new arrivals flooding in from the platform that he didn't have time for special requests.

That was the moment when Giovanni first realized things would eventually change. Work wasn't infinite; supply and demand would soon equal out. And from there, it wouldn't be long until there were more job seekers than jobs.

Giovanni spoke to his boss. Two days later, Enzo had a job at the wholesale market. As a forklift driver. It took Enzo longer to learn how to pronounce the word than how to operate the vehicle. A week after his arrival in Germany, he sent Iso a letter of resignation. He'd spent his life handcrafting the most beautiful cars in the world, only to end up stacking fruit crates in a cold country where he didn't speak the language. But he didn't mind. He was with his family, and that was the main thing.

"If you still doubt he's a good husband, there's no saving you," Giovanni told his sister as they unpacked a freshly delivered wheel of Pecorino.

"Maybe I wasn't completely fair to him."

"You weren't. Give the man another chance. You took Vincenzo's friends from him—don't take his father as well."

"What if it doesn't work out?"

"We're not sixteen anymore, sister dear. Love is a choice."

The students held an extraordinary general household assembly to discuss whether Enzo was allowed to move in. Just the question of whether Giulietta and Vincenzo got one vote or two led to an endless back-and-forth over women's and children's rights, before they launched into a contentious discussion weighing international solidarity with the oppressed classes against the needs of the commune residents. The vote was close, but ultimately their political idealism had its limits, and Enzo was permitted only visitation rights; he would have to register Giovanni's apartment as his place of residence. Enzo bore it all with surprising stoicism. He knew it was only temporary—soon he would find his family a home of their own. Knowing that his wife was cleaning up other people's messes was an affront to his honor as it was.

"No!" Rosaria said to Giovanni when she learned of the new roommate nobody had asked her about.

"Don't be so heartless!"

"Me? Heartless? Who cooked for your sister all that time?"

"It's just for the time being! He'll spend some nights here, some there, until they can rent their own place."

"Everything's just for the time being with you, hmm? You know what? I'm going back home for the time being."

"But Rosaria, *amore mio!*"

And as if that weren't enough, Giovanni had to explain the whole situation to his mother in Milan as well.

"Shouldn't you be happy?" he exclaimed into the telephone. He had to raise his voice; Concetta's hearing was getting progressively worse. "They're back together, just like you wanted!"

"But not in Germany! Tell him to bring her back!"

"Mamma, he tried. You know Giulietta. Stubborn as a Sicilian donkey."

"What about me?" Concetta complained. "What will happen to me?"

"We'll work something out. It's only temporary."

"You said that when you left! And when did you come back? Never!"

"Someday, Mamma. Once we have enough money, I'll build a house on Salina, and we'll all live there. Including you!" It was hard to believe his own words. Though he still clung to the dream, it seemed to fade farther into the distance with every passing year.

"What have the Germans done to the two of you that you'd even abandon your old mother? What kind of people are they? What has the world come to?"

"Mamma, I promise we'll spend Christmas together. All of us. *Va bene?*"

He knew Giulietta wouldn't come with them—Concetta's rejection had hurt her too deeply. But promises were the only currency he had left.

Then came the snow. Giovanni had told them about it, and of course his winter fairy tales were filled with magical, powdery fluff, mulled wine at Christmas markets, and children on sleds. But the new arrivals weren't prepared for just how cold it would actually get. Rosaria least of all. The three who'd lived in Milan had seen snow once—it had stayed on the ground for several days, gradually turning to gray slush—but Rosaria had only heard of it. The winters on Salina were chilly, since the air was damp and the houses were only heated by gas stoves or fireplaces. But snow, that was as exotic to her as palm trees were to the Germans.

It snowed nonstop for two days, falling so thick and fast that they couldn't see their hands in front of their faces. The snow swallowed the hydrants, the cars, and the sound. Heavy snowplows struggled through the streets, piling the stuff into enormous white walls. Nobody dared go outside; schools canceled classes.

Giovanni took Enzo to the forest to chop down a Christmas tree.

"You mean they really have a tree in every single home?" Enzo asked, amazed. "Madonna, how many million Germans are there?"

Giovanni shrugged. "We have the sea; they have the forest."

They dragged the dripping monstrosity into Giulietta's apartment, where they were met with vociferous opposition. HP set his Adorno down and got up from the sofa. In his white wool sweater, with his long hair and beard, he reminded the Italians of Rumpelstiltskin. "No Christmas trees in this house."

"Why not?" Giovanni asked.

"They're a symbol of the bourgeoisie."

Giovanni translated for Enzo, who gave HP a look suggesting that real members of the proletariat ate milk-faces like him for breakfast. The standoff lasted only a few seconds before HP stepped aside, and Enzo carried the tree into Giulietta's room. Giovanni heard HP run straight to Roland's room. "Can you believe this guy? Wake up, man! The Mafia killed Kennedy. Martin Luther King. What if Enzo's working with the CIA?" So much for the xenophilia of the enlightened Left. Meanwhile, Enzo contentedly set up the Christmas tree. It was the first he'd ever had.

Vincenzo was very quiet as he saw his uncle off from Platform 11 before Christmas. Too quiet, Giovanni felt. He knew his nephew wished he could come along to Italy. But if everyone went to Italy, it would force Giulietta to choose between facing her mother's wrath and staying in Germany on her own. Vincenzo was all too aware of that, and he remained loyal to Giulietta. The three of them would spend their first Christmas by themselves in Germany, while Giovanni and Rosaria brought their baby daughter to meet her grandparents: first to Concetta's in Milan, and she'd travel with them to see Rosaria's mother on Salina. Giovanni had worked at the shop right up through the twenty-third, supplying vast quantities of panettone to his fellow Italians; Giulietta would take over while he was gone. After all, the last thing his fledgling business could afford was to close during the time of year when people ate the most. Giulietta embraced her brother tenderly, but without shedding a single tear. Now he was on his way south, and she remained in the North. Each of them secretly wondered when the family would be together again. And both had begun to realize that the temporary arrangements they kept making had become the norm; the only thing really changing was how they felt about their dreams.

On that December day, Giovanni had no way of knowing that Giulietta's life would be turned upside down once more while he was on vacation—this time in a way so devastating and irreversible that he would wish he'd never left her alone.

His idea when getting married had been to start a kingdom of his own, a realm where everything finally revolved around him for a change. A wife who respected him and children who admired him. But he hadn't expected the force with which Rosaria had distanced herself from him the moment she arrived in Germany. And when the young Marconi family stepped off the ferry on Salina in the cold December wind, bearing suitcases full of gifts and with his seasick mother in tow, Giovanni realized that the center of his universe had shifted elsewhere.

Rosaria's mother, Maria, wrapped in a thick woolen coat and scarf, cuddled her tiny granddaughter in delight, showering her with blessings. Then she threw her arms around Rosaria, the lost daughter, and hugged her sister, Concetta, with a heavy sigh. Finally, she greeted her son-in-law with, "*Bentornati!* This time you're staying, you hear me?" Rosaria held the baby as the women headed for the taxi, whose toothless driver was smoking a hand-rolled cigarette. Giovanni followed behind, carrying the luggage.

How do you say gravity in Italian? *La mamma.* All others are mere satellites in her orbit. And though it takes some Italian men decades to escape their mothers' gravitational pull, it requires only nine months to catapult them into a new orbit. Italian machismo isn't a true expression of patriarchy—it's merely a pubescent rebellion against domestic matriarchy. Women have always known that; men have always realized it too late. As Giovanni stepped onto the island of his birth, he felt trapped. It was more than a feeling of childish helplessness: he was a grown man, but he'd become superfluous. Not in his role as family representative and breadwinner, but in his opinions and all the ideas he'd grown accustomed to in Germany.

"Can you smell the thyme, Giovanni?"

Salina in winter was the salt of the churning sea in the clear air, mingled with the herbs whose healing power was only known to the old women. But it was also the cold smoke in the alleys, the mildewy scent of damp stone walls, and the silence of abandoned houses.

Old women stepped into their doorways as the Marconis trundled into the village in two Ape vans. It was a sunny December day; the old men sat outside the bar in the piazza with hunched backs and wrinkled faces, drinking coffee, playing cards, and calling out greetings. Nothing had changed; nothing would ever change. The clotheslines between the buildings, the scrawny cats in the roads, the "*Vendesi*" signs outside boarded windows.

"This will do you good. This is home!" Rosaria's mother told Concetta.

Rosaria was silent.

Everyone knew that Concetta couldn't remain alone much longer in Milan, and there was no way Enzo could keep paying rent for both her and his family in Munich. Her only remaining option was her sister Maria's house, and Maria was more than happy to have her. Two widows whose children had gone to the North. Neighbors emerged from their homes. *"Auguri, auguroni!"*

Later, as they were eating on the terrace among the old olive trees, Rosaria abruptly announced, "Giovanni, I'm staying here."

He smiled. "Yeah, yeah, I think that every time I come back, but then—"

"You can eat proper food here," Maria broke in. "The good stuff."

"Germany has the good stuff now, thanks to us!"

Nobody was interested in his new business.

"Giovanni. It's not the food. Or the cold. It's the people."

"The Germans are good people. They just take longer to warm up. You'll see."

"Maybe, but they're only good to their own kind, not to foreigners. We'll always be outsiders to them."

"You just need to learn the language. You have to go out like Giulietta does. Then you'll—"

"Who are we to them?" she exclaimed with surprising vehemence. "Guest workers? When I have guests, I don't make them work, I invite them to dinner! But up there, I've never even met our neighbors. Can you imagine?"

Maria shook her head.

Rosaria began feeding little Marietta. "I want my daughter to be respected in school," she went on. "Not like Vincenzo."

"Vincenzo's a special case," Giovanni protested, but she interrupted.

"You said one day we'd come back and build a house!"

"Yes, someday. Later. How am I supposed to afford a house right now?"

"Giovanni, the house is already here. It's big enough for everyone. We just have to renovate it."

Her mother nodded. "It'll belong to you one day anyway."

"But you wanted to get away from here!" Giovanni exclaimed.

"You promised me a palace! But guess how we really live?"

Now things were really getting dicey. She was going to ruin his reputation.

"How do you expect me to earn a living out here, in the middle of nowhere?" he broke in. "There's no work!"

"Giovanni!" his mother exclaimed in a sharp tone.

"Your father's fields aren't being cultivated," Rosaria's mother pointed out. "That's still good soil."

"Those fields never belonged to us."

"Buy them. They'll be cheap; nobody wants them anymore. You're rich!"

"But I'm not a farmer," Giovanni retorted angrily. "I'm a salesman!" The argument fell flat, because here it didn't matter what a person was—everyone did whatever work there was at the moment.

"Well, then, go back to Germany," Rosaria said. "I'm staying here. And so is the baby."

"Are you joking?"

She rose resolutely to her feet and cleared the dishes. Giovanni would have thought her capable of many things, but not this. The wind rustled the silvery leaves of the *olivi*. *Some people are like trees,* Giovanni thought. *Dig up their roots, and they wither.* He should never have uprooted Rosaria.

Later, a sulking Giovanni walked to the piazza to call his sister from the bar. Vincenzo picked up.

"Where's your mother?"

"At church. With Enzo."

"What about you? Why aren't you at church?"

"I'm watching TV."

"On Christmas?"

"You never know about anything that's going on, Giovanni!"

"What do you mean?"

"Don't you have a TV on the island? Apollo Eight! The Americans are flying to the moon!"

"Today?"

"Right now. They're broadcasting from space. Live!"

Giovanni waved the barista over. "Turn the television on! And bring me more coins!" He fumbled another thousand-lire bill out of his pocket—the coins were tumbling through the pay phone like sand. The man switched on the old television, which was sitting in the corner atop a crocheted blanket alongside a statue of the Virgin Mary. Snow filled the screen.

"Do you see it, Uncle Giovanni?"

"No!" Giovanni exclaimed. "The goddamn TV is broken!" he snapped at the barista, who was fiddling with the reception knob.

"Bad weather in Messina, we don't get a signal."

"Shit. And they're landing on the moon?"

"Jeez, Giovanni. No, not yet. They're taking photographs and filming. They're flying around to look at the far side of the moon."

"The moon's ass?"

"Just look at everything you're missing out there at the ass-end of the world!"

"So, what does it look like? Is it pretty?"

"It's a desert. Totally barren. Gray."

"No way! The moon is white!"

"What's he saying?" the barista asked.

"Shh!"

"Now they're showing—oh, wow. That's unbelievable."

"What are they doing?" The barista was beside Giovanni now, listening to the receiver as well.

"They're filming the earth. It's rising, like the sun. Over the moon. That's—"

"Our Earth? Behind the moon?"

"Yeah."

"What does it look like?"

"Like a marble. Tiny. Nothing but darkness all around it."

"What color is it?"

"I dunno. The television is black and white."

"Green," the barista piped up. "It's green. Like the forests."

"No, it's blue. Like the sea. Haven't you ever seen a globe?"

"A what?"

Giovanni grew exasperated. The Americans were flying to the moon, and he was stuck in the middle of nowhere.

The first images of Earth from space weren't the only thing Giovanni missed. Later, after his *gettoni* had rattled away, the astronauts read the story of creation live from space. "Let there be light, and there was light." Then Vincenzo heard the doorbell. At that moment, Giovanni was standing in the clammy church of Malfa, where the priest had a cold and was coughing nearly as often as the old women. It wasn't until much later that he learned of the events taking place in Munich.

Vincenzo got up from the threadbare couch and went to the door. The adults had all gone out, leaving him and the little girl, who now considered him her best friend, alone in front of the television. At first, he thought it was his parents returning from Mass, but then he opened the door to discover a stranger. A German. He was wearing a blue trench coat over a gray suit, with a hat and fine leather shoes. He was perhaps forty years old, high forehead, clear blue eyes. Under his arm were two wrapped presents—one large, one small.

"Hello."

Faces are like windows. Some are open; some are closed. This German was different from the others. His window was wide open.

"Is your mother home?"

Vincenzo knew the voice from somewhere. "No."

"When will she be back?"

Vincenzo shrugged uncertainly. The man glanced into the apartment, looking indecisive. Then he looked Vincenzo over in a bashful and overly curious way that Vincenzo found creepy.

"You must be Vincenzo?"

Vincenzo nodded.

"Would you mind giving this to her?" He handed Vincenzo a small envelope wrapped in green paper, with a golden bow.

"And this . . . is for you." The larger gift. Vincenzo blinked. The man smiled warmly. "Just take it. Merry Christmas!"

He tipped his hat and started down the stairs. On his way down, he cast one final glance back at Vincenzo, who was standing in the open door, bewildered.

The man's smile was gone, and Vincenzo saw a shadow of sadness descend over his face.

He set the package on the couch. There was something off; it was too big not to be significant somehow. He resolved not to open it without asking his mother first, but then his curiosity won out. He cautiously peeled away a piece of the wrapping paper, and then ripped the rest open in astonishment once he realized what was inside.

It was a racetrack. Even back in Milan, he'd dreamed of having one, but his parents' presents were always useful things—warm socks, school notebooks, winter boots. And now, unexpectedly and undeservedly, he had one. The package contained a white Porsche and a red Ferrari. He knew them from television. The cars were perfect reproductions, down to the last detail. Plus, controllers and countless black curves and straight pieces for recreating famous racetracks. Monza. Silverstone. Hockenheim.

When his parents walked in, Vincenzo was sitting cross-legged on the floor. He'd set up the track in the living room, and now he and HP were racing feverishly. Vincenzo had the red Ferrari, of course. At first, Giulietta and Enzo thought HP had brought it home. Until Vincenzo showed his mother the other gift. The small one. It was still sitting unopened on the couch.

"Who's it from?"

"Dunno. Some German guy. He said to tell you Merry Christmas."

Giulietta gave Enzo a confused look. He shrugged. She opened the envelope, and the color drained from her face.

"What is it?" Enzo asked.

"Where did you see him?" Giulietta barked at Vincenzo.

All at once, Vincenzo felt like he'd made some colossal error. "Here. He rang the doorbell. Who is he?"

Vincenzo saw his mother seem to shrink from Enzo. Enzo didn't move.

"That was a customer," she told him hurriedly. "He was interested in me. Last summer. But I said no."

Enzo remained composed.

"Put that back in the box," Giulietta ordered Vincenzo. "We're returning it!"

"But why?"

"Now!"

Vincenzo obeyed.

"You don't have to explain anything to me," Enzo said. "What happened, happened. Just tell me one thing: Do you want to start over with me?"

It was snowing heavily as Giulietta waited at the end of the tram station near the English Garden, wrapped in her red winter coat and scarf. She had the two gifts under her arm. It was already dark out; she was shivering in the cold, and her heart was in an uproar. She'd come to their arranged meeting place ten minutes early, and she was determined not to get into his car. She recognized the sound of the Iso's engine before she saw it. No German cars made that deep rumble. Vincent stopped near the sidewalk and opened the passenger door. Giulietta stayed where she was.

"Get in?"

He looked different in the winter. Older, more serious. She'd only ever seen him in the summer. Really, she told herself, she hardly knew him at all. She'd only seen one tiny cross section of his life. But then where did that inexplicable sense of familiarity come from? She placed the racetrack on the passenger seat. And carefully laid the envelope with the opera tickets on top. Venice. He hadn't invited her to the National Theater in Munich; he'd invited her to La Fenice in Venice. The very idea!

"Thank you." She'd resolved to leave immediately. Not to spend too much time chatting. Not to answer any questions.

"Giulietta," he urged, "it's cold."

She managed to avoid his eyes, shut the door, and walk away. Behind her, she heard him accelerate. The long car slowly pushed past her. He rolled down the window.

"Giulietta, please. What did I do wrong? I just wanted to make you two happy."

Giulietta stopped walking. He opened the door. She didn't get in.

"Why are you following me?" she exclaimed. "You have a family!"

"Didn't you get my letters? Back then?"

He sounded vulnerable now, which she somehow found both repulsive and touching, because she felt like it was her fault. She took a quick glance around and then got in. Inside, it was warm. As soon as she closed the door, they both fell silent. The only sounds were the purr of the engine and the ticking of the hazard lights. The car vibrated smoothly.

"Did you read them?" he asked again.

He had the same delicate lips, the same clear eyes, the same honest expression. A man she could never imagine having ever done anything unethical in his entire life. Everything she'd fallen in love with was still there.

"Vincent. You have your life. I have mine."

"Why didn't you ever write back?" he insisted. He wasn't the type to beat around the bush. It was that German penchant for getting to the bottom of things even when it was pointless.

She was silent at first, but then the words came tumbling out. "I read them all, over and over. But what do you want from me now, Vincent? Everything's been decided."

He didn't say anything. Took her hand. His skin was warm. She recognized it again instinctively. She wanted to pull her hand away, but she couldn't make herself do it. He leaned over and kissed her cheek tenderly. She froze. She smelled his scent. He kissed her again, seeking her lips this time. More cautiously than before, less urgent, but bewilderingly familiar.

"We can't," she said.

He breathed in the scent of her hair. Abruptly, it all came rushing back, as though they'd parted ways just yesterday: memories of that summer in Milan, of the dry grass and the starched sheets in his boardinghouse. Fat snowflakes settled onto the windowpanes of his car and enveloped them in a white cocoon, isolated from the hushed outside world.

"Why did you come to Munich?"

"Vincent, you have a family."

"I kept asking myself, Was I wrong, was I deceiving myself back then? Did I misjudge you? How could you do that, just break everything off like it never happened? I tried to forget you, I tried, but—"

She cast her eyes down in shame. *"Al cuore non si comanda."*

"What's that mean?"

"You can't command the heart."

At that moment, he knew that he wasn't alone in his feelings. She wanted him to know that. She clutched his hand more tightly.

"But it's too late now, Vincent."

"We can't go on acting like there's nothing between us."

She felt trapped, like a caged animal. Why did he always have to be right about everything? It drove her crazy, because he still didn't understand anything.

"Do you love your husband?" he asked.

"It's not because of Enzo!"

"Why, then?"

Suddenly, she realized she'd said too much. She fumbled for the door handle. He grabbed her hand. "Because of Vincenzo? He's old enough, he'll understand." He held her tighter. "Look at me, Giulietta."

She tried. Without blinking. She hoped he wouldn't ask, and she could see him wrestling inwardly with himself.

"I have to go, Vincent."

"Is he . . . Is Vincenzo our son? Tell me the truth."

Giulietta was paralyzed. She wanted to shake her head, but her muscles refused the command. She averted her eyes, but he took her face in his hands and fixed her with a penetrating gaze. All she could do was meet his eyes, mute and motionless. Then she felt the pressure of his hands slowly subsiding, bit by bit, as he gradually understood what she could never say out loud. She remained perfectly still, though tears of desperation stung her eyes.

It was the single most horrible moment of her entire life. She shattered inside, strangled by shame and guilt. Somehow, she managed to get her hand on the door handle, shove the door open, and stumble out of the car. She ran blindly across the street. Cars braked and honked. Giulietta fell, got up again, and ran toward the bus pulling up on the opposite side of the road. Vincent jumped out of the car and ran after her, shouting her name through the blizzard. The bus barely managed to avoid hitting her. She banged on the glass; the driver opened the door; she got in. As Vincent came running over, the bus trundled off again, spraying dirty water on his pants.

"Giulietta!"

He jogged after the bus as Giulietta stood at the illuminated back window, staring out as though hypnotized. Then he stood there, alone in the street, a shadow receding into the distance until the thick snow swallowed him.

Giulietta returned home, soaked to the bone. Vincenzo was lying on the sofa, scribbling in his German notebook by the light of a small lamp. Giulietta threw her wet coat onto the floor, hurried to Vincenzo, and threw her arms around him so tightly that it scared him.

"I love you, Vincenzo. More than anything in the world. You know that, right?"

"I love you, too," he stammered, caught off guard. "What happened?" Her hair was tangled and dripping; her scarf was as wet as a sponge. Giulietta burst into tears. It made him uncomfortable. He pushed her away cautiously, trying not to hurt her feelings. "Mamma, who was that guy?"

"That was somebody I used to love. A long time ago. Before you were born."
She studied his face, looking for a reaction. He was thoroughly confused.

"But now I'm married to Enzo. To Papà. He's always been a good father, hasn't he?"

"Yeah."

They heard Enzo walking across the creaky floorboards in their room. Giulietta clung to Vincenzo desperately, as though doing so could hold back the avalanche headed toward them both.

33

Giovanni shut the album. The evening sun bathed the Bay of Naples in a light almost surreal in its beauty. Vincenzo's place at the head of the terrace table was still empty. I was exhausted and wired. Wanted to get up, to quit waiting, get away from here, be alone so I could sort all of this new information into the mosaic of the past several days. I needed to restabilize the wobbling house of my own identity, because it felt as though its entire structure had been based on inaccurate calculations, and now it was threatening to collapse.

I'd been fascinated by how much Giulietta and I were alike, but the more I learned about Vincenzo, the more surprising and disconcerting similarities I noticed between this Italian boy in Hasenbergl and the girl that I'd once been. I had a German passport, a German mother, a German identity, but deep down, I felt as stateless as he did—an outsider carrying something inside that separates them from everyone else, an invisible difference preventing them from truly belonging.

It had taken me years to reinterpret that differentness, to attribute it not to some deficiency of mine but to what one might call talent. When I drew or dressed my dolls in the clothes I'd sewn, I didn't imagine it was anything extraordinary—if anything, I'd have been surprised to hear that not everyone had a knack for it. Only when I saw how other people reacted did I become aware that it was special, something like my personal identity: it was me, the thing that separated me from other people. And that was what helped my young, uncertain self make peace with being different and start seeing it as something I didn't have to fear. The price, however, was that I gave up what every child yearns for: belonging.

I can still recall the day I showed my mother a Barbie doll wearing the outfit I'd made for her. I'd saved my allowance to buy the doll and used fabric from my old worn-out clothes to make the dress, and to me she was absolutely special, completely different from all other Barbies. At first, my mother didn't even realize the clothes were handmade, and remarked disdainfully about American plastic crap indoctrinating an entire generation with impossible beauty ideals. In short, Barbies were bad, and I was a victim of the toy industry, not a girl expressing her innate creativity for the first time.

On that day, the close ties that had always bound us tore a little, and we never quite patched them again. At the time, it hurt my feelings and added to my loneliness, but today I realize it was actually a kind of rebirth, the start of a new self, the severing of an umbilical cord. Later, though, when fashion had become my life and my career, I discovered something: that sense of being "flawed" hadn't really gone away. It had merely shifted to a different level, unnoticed. I couldn't trace it back to anything specific, because the source of that torturous feeling lay in the unknown.

The other trait that linked me to young Vincenzo was his inner conflict. I've had it since I was a kid. Before, I'd always attributed it to my mother and her restless lifestyle. The agitation that came over me when I spent too long in the same place or with the same guy, the desire to travel, the deep-seated feeling of being rootless and on the run—they all made me feel strangely connected to the Italian boy. As though people from the same clan were linked by fine subterranean currents and could recognize each other instinctively, by a smell, a melody, a secret code indecipherable to anyone else. An immaterial heritage passed down like a gene, a virus, a whisper, from one generation to the next.

All at once, we heard someone open the front door and walk into the apartment. I glanced inside, but the windows only reflected the three of us on the terrace. I looked ragged and weary. On the other side of the glass, a pale shadow moved through the living room. My father probably saw me now, though I couldn't see him yet. Suddenly and completely unexpectedly, a sense of absolute calm came over me. The anxiety I'd felt when picturing this encounter over and over again was gone—like when you finally step into the spotlight after hours of stage fright, and once there's no turning back, everything runs like clockwork.

Vincenzo stepped onto the terrace, and aged decades within seconds. A stranger who was nothing like the kid in Giovanni's stories. He was wearing a light-colored bomber jacket, a half-open shirt, and dark-blue suede shoes. Gray curls framed a delicate, tanned face and those unsettling eyes—one brown, one blue green. Under one arm, he had a pair of dirty racing coveralls plastered with advertising logos. Looking closer, I realized they were covered in blood.

When Carmela saw his face, she jumped to her feet, looking worried, and asked what had happened. He gave her an evasive reply, which Giovanni translated for me: he'd flipped his car and briefly ended up in the hospital. A few scratches, nothing serious. Giovanni stood as well and inspected Vincenzo's scraped hand with concern. I alone remained seated. From the very first moment, it was all about him, not about me. He avoided looking at me, though there was no mistaking how tense he was. I stayed in my seat. Just when I was starting to feel completely invisible, he turned to look at me.

"When did you arrive?" he asked me in good German, which he seemed to be digging from the farthest recesses of his memory.

"This morning."

His question was really why, not when. We hadn't even introduced ourselves. But why would we? Our roles had already been assigned. Which meant so had the question of blame—which was precisely what I wanted to avoid.

No, I wanted to come to him as an independent adult woman. Exactly the opposite of how I currently felt. Carmela filled the unbearable silence with rapid patter, plucking the coveralls from his hands and telling him to sit. He remained standing. Giovanni said something to him. The only word I understood was "Giulietta." My presence on his terrace was obviously more than he could handle, and I could only guess what he was thinking. The silence stretched into eternity. No "Hello"; no "How are you?"; no hugs; no nothing. I was an uninvited guest in his realm.

"Your father wants to see you," I said, as if to show him that coming here hadn't been my idea. "Vincent," I added, so he would know which one I meant.

"What's he want?"

"He had a heart attack. He's in the hospital. Not doing well."

"So?" He shrugged.

I was shocked at his coldness. "There's something he wants to tell you."

"Why didn't he just come himself?"

"He came to me."

"Ah." It sounded pejorative, almost jealous.

"He wants you to come see him. Now. He doesn't have much time left."

"He's no concern of mine."

He turned away and disappeared into the apartment. We heard him shut the bathroom door. So that was that. My reunion with the father I'd thought was dead. We sat there, exchanging distressed looks. Carmela gave me a friendly, apologetic glance, as if to say, *He doesn't mean it. Give him time.* I'd seen enough, though. I got up, grabbed my little suitcase, and left.

Giovanni tried to hold me back, but I was outside before he could stop me. Under no circumstances did I want anyone to see that I was about to start bawling like a child. Whatever the situation was between Vincent and Vincenzo, whatever had turned Vincenzo into a man incapable of saying hello to his own daughter, I no longer cared. I'd kept my promise to Vincent; now I was done. I called a cab and jumped in before Giovanni could catch me. I told the driver to take me to the train station. Maybe another train was headed north tonight. We were halfway there before I remembered that I didn't have a cent to my name.

34

The driver threw me out in the middle of a large street. Fortunately, I didn't understand his tirade about the *tedeschi*, so I returned the favor by withholding my opinions on Italians. The sun had set. I was standing on the center line of the ugly harbor street. Cars sped past; a ship's horn blared in the distance. Just behind the road, the neon lights on the enormous vessels gleamed against the night sky. I wondered how I was going to get home. My suitcase had nothing in it but an extra pair of underwear, jeans, a blouse, and a fanny pack. My phone rang. It was Giovanni. I ignored it and crossed the street toward the sea, where it was quieter.

I stopped at the shore to collect myself. The dark water lapped against the quay wall; the cool evening breeze smelled of algae and oil. I called Robin. It went to voice mail. He was probably at dinner with the investors.

"Hi, Robin. I'm in Naples. You were right. It was a crappy idea. I'm coming back. I need a little money for a ticket. Call me? Thanks. And sorry." I didn't mention the thing with the holding company. I didn't have a solution. I was standing by the Mediterranean Sea, and I was completely screwed.

"Oh. Signorina! Americana?"

I startled. A guy stepped out of the darkness. Mean voice, slightly drunk, filthy jeans.

"Dove va?"

Instinctively, I returned my phone to my pocket and walked away. He followed me, shouting something. I started running. His grimy voice at my back. I didn't shake him until I reached the road. He was the type who kept to the shadows. I ran down the loud street, so packed with cars and motor scooters that it seemed as if every single person in Italy must be there in a dented compact car—entire families, groups of friends, all prepared to spend the night in traffic. I found a spot that was sufficiently lit to keep the shadowy figures at bay.

Robin didn't return my call. Suddenly, I worried that he was using my absence as a chance to close the deal on his own. But he couldn't do that; we were equal partners. He needed me just as much as I needed him. I had to get home. Not wanting to wait any longer, I dialed the only person on Earth who always caught me when I fell—no matter how badly I screwed up or how many times we argued. My mother.

"Honey, where are you?"

"You were right. He's impossible. There's just no way."

"What happened?"

"Nothing. Absolutely nothing. Can you send me some money?"

What she really wanted to do was come straight down and save her child in person, but fortunately, I managed to talk her out of that. She promised to look up wire transfers online and call me back. I would just have to hold out until the banks opened in the morning. I could sleep at the train station or wander around all night to keep myself awake.

"Thanks."

"You know I'm always here for you."

The words brought tears to my eyes, and I hated myself for it. I gazed into the night sky over the dark sea and felt pretty damn lonely. People start families just so they don't have to feel like this. Maybe it's the most existential of all emotions, and nobody wants to admit to themselves that, no matter how many children or parents they have, they're completely alone inside.

At a brightly lit bar on a dirty street corner, a group of guys crowded around the television. Soccer. Battle cries. But not drunken ones. Just as I was about to go in, Giovanni ran over, sweaty and outraged. He'd been looking for me for hours! He grabbed my arm and launched into an accusatory tirade about how scared he'd been that he'd lost me, that he'd failed me as a protector. I shouted right back at him. After a few minutes of yelling at each other, we reached an agreement that we both considered Vincenzo a *deficiente*. I didn't know the exact translation, but it sounded about right.

"*Allora*, are you coming with me? I'm going to talk to him."

"And say what? There's nothing left to talk about. You saw that yourself."

"Oh, don't be so huffy. Give him a little time, *no?*"

"Giovanni, thank you for everything, really, but I'm going home."

He was silent. It took a lot to silence Giovanni.

"*Vabbè*, you need money? No more trains tonight—you'll have to stay in a hotel." He whipped out his wallet.

I didn't want his money. The one thing I wanted to avoid at all costs was owing that family anything.

"I'll be fine. Ciao, Giovanni."

His phone rang. He fumbled it from his pants pocket with some difficulty and answered the call.

"Oh! Vincenzo!"

He held the phone out to me. I shook my head. He insisted. I waved it away energetically. Giovanni told Vincenzo that he'd found me and that he had damn well better apologize. Then he jammed the phone against my ear.

"Julia!" Vincenzo sounded worried. "Julia?"

I didn't respond.

"I'm sorry."

I went on not responding.

"It's a story from way back. It has nothing to do with you."

Giovanni pressed the phone into my hand. I took it so he would leave me alone.

"I can explain. Come back. Please."

I hung up.

Giovanni puffed up his chest in indignation. "You can't do that. He's your papà!"

"Listen. You give him Vincent's number, and let him do whatever he wants with it." I took out my phone to find Vincent's contact information.

"He's a difficult guy, but you're a bit difficult yourself, *eh?*" He grinned at me wryly. "You know, he may not be the best papà, but he's the only one you've got."

I made a sarcastic face. "Here's the number. Write this down."

Giovanni plucked the phone from my hand. "When you have children, what are you going to tell them about their grandpa? Come on, go back to Munich with him, just a few hours, and he'd better behave himself, that *imbecille*, and you two get to know each other a little. After that, *tanti cari saluti!* What have you got to lose? Your Sicilian pride, *eh?*"

Four eyes of a sleeping animal slowly coming to life. It growled, vibrated, and roared hoarsely before lifting its eyelids, and the headlights shone out at me. I stepped aside as Vincenzo maneuvered the sports car out of its spot in the labyrinthine underground garage. I could tell just by looking at him that there'd never been anywhere he would rather be than behind the wheel. He slipped on a pair of perforated brown leather driving gloves and got out. The gesture reminded me of his father.

"Che bella macchina!" Giovanni murmured reverently.

The car was straight out of a different age. With its long, flat hood and sensuous curves, it exuded something from every pore that modern vehicles no longer had: character. There was nothing mainstream about it, nothing accommodating, no compromises in the name of mass appeal. Guys who drove cars like these only really existed in movies from the 1970s—featuring sideburns, unfiltered cigarettes, dangerous blondes riding shotgun. Anyone who drives a car like that today has a lot of money or a lot of style, or else they're stuck in a time warp.

"An Alfa Romeo Montreal. You hear that engine? *Che bestia!*"

Honestly, I didn't care about the engine one way or another. I was more worried I'd lose my nerve. Vincenzo took my suitcase and set it in the trunk beside his own leather bag. He held the passenger door open for me, and I got in. Inside, it smelled like vinyl, tobacco, and gasoline. Black rocker switches, gleaming steel, and a cassette radio. Everything about it looked the way people used to picture the future, back when they still believed in the future. I took out my phone and called Germany. Clara, Vincent's daughter, answered.

"He's not doing well," she said.

"What's going on?"

"He's still conscious, but—" Her voice faltered. "Excuse me."

"Tell him we'll be there in twelve hours, okay?"

"I will. Hurry."

Giovanni opened my door and slipped me something with a conspiratorial gesture. It was a package wrapped in German newspapers. "I kept it," he whispered. "Don't open it until you're on the road, *va bene? Ciao.* And watch out, he's a miserable driver!" He said that last part loud enough for Vincenzo to hear. Then he smiled at me with his huge doe eyes. I set the package under my legs, in front of the seat, and took his hand.

"Thanks, Giovanni."

He softly shut the door. Vincenzo tossed his cigarettes and his sunglasses onto the dashboard and got in.

"Listen—" he said.

"We should get going."

He looked at me for a moment, and then put the car into gear. With precise, controlled movements, he steered the car out of the narrow garage.

It was well after midnight, maybe around one thirty, and the side streets we took were eerily dark. We didn't talk much. He drove with calm concentration. I rolled down my window so I could breathe.

"How old is he now?" Vincenzo asked out of nowhere.

"I dunno. Eighty. Older, maybe."

He fell silent again and turned onto the city highway.

I took Giovanni's package out from underneath the seat and opened it quietly. From among the newspapers, I withdrew a gray book, like a school notepad or a diary. It was already fairly yellowed and worn, with a practical, sixties-style cover. It had a small box in the middle for people to write their names, but it was blank. I opened the notebook. In the top left corner of the first page, "Giulietta Marconi" was written in delicate blue ink. It was a woman's handwriting, with sweeping, almost exuberant curves, but very straight within the lines, correct and legible. The cursive of a woman who had learned how to write beautifully. I turned the page. A date and an entry: "December 30, 1968."

"What's that?" Vincenzo asked.

"Giulietta's diary."

He hit the brakes and pulled off to the side of the road. Then he stared at the notebook in shock. Took it from me and flipped through it. Among the entries, there were dress designs sketched in colored pencil. Late 1960s, early 1970s.

"Where'd you get this?"

"From Giovanni."

"And where did he get it?"

"I don't know." The notebook was written in German. Of course. So that Enzo couldn't read it.

Vincenzo stuck the notebook into his leather jacket and hit the gas.

"Hey! Giovanni gave that to me!"

244

"Did it belong to him?"

"Give it back!"

Vincenzo was stubbornly silent. Drove through the concrete labyrinth of bridges and arterial highways, past ugly apartment blocks and billboards. Then he took the book out and handed it back.

"It doesn't belong to anyone," he said. I caught a fleeting glimpse of an unfathomably deep, irremediable pain in his eyes. He turned onto the Autostrada del Sole, toward Rome. I set the diary in my lap and opened it.

35

Giulietta

December 30, 1968
Nothing has been the same since that kiss. Vt. wants to see me.
Wants to know everything about his son. How long can I keep
him away?

E. would never forgive me. Neither would V. I feel like a
traitor.

January 14, 1969
His letters are getting angrier, his calls more frequent. Now he's
even calling in the evening, when E. is here. I hang up, lie to V.
I don't know how long anyone can live a lie without drowning
in it. Now, of all times, when V. and E. are starting to get along
again. They fixed his bike together yesterday. I watched. Any other
mother would have had only joy in her heart, but mine cramped
as though choking on shame.

February 19, 1969
I have to meet with him. If he tells E., or V., our lives will be
ruined.

Fragmented thoughts, flashes of emotion from which I tried to reconstruct the rest of the story. Giulietta's entries were a quarry of snapshots, nightmares, and hasty self-assurances, written in fear of being discovered, in perfect German and elegant handwriting as though she were trying to cling to proper form even as the guilt, the self-accusation, and the dread of the inevitable consequences of her decisions threatened to devour her.

She was less ashamed of having loved another man than of having kept her son from knowing his father. She cooked, ironed, and sewed for her family as though nothing had happened, intercepting Vincent's letters before Enzo checked the mailbox, rushing to pick up the phone so she could claim it had been a wrong number. She knew that, sooner or later, Vincent would ambush his son. She had to meet up with him in order to dissuade him from trying. She was prepared to do anything.

On a windy morning in March, while Enzo was working at the wholesale market, Giulietta took the tram to the other end of town, where nobody would recognize her. Even with the weak tram heater rattling beneath her wooden seat, she shivered. The damp cold of this accursed, unending winter seeped into her shoes. Though she took great pains with her clothes, there was never enough money for good shoes. She always held off until Christmas so that she could grab a pair while they were on sale, but then she always ended up deciding that spring was just around the corner, and she could make it in thin shoes until then. But spring took an eternity to arrive. And this year, the wait was even longer than usual.

As she exited the tram, Giulietta caught herself murmuring the Lord's Prayer. "And forgive us our trespasses, as we forgive those who have trespassed against us." As a child, she'd mumbled it hundreds of times in muted singsong along with everyone else as they stood packed into the small, clammy church. The women's gloved hands and dark winter coats, the lowered gazes and the breath in front of their faces—she hadn't forgotten any of it, least of all the sound of Concetta's voice as she watched her and Giovanni from above so that she could read every single word from their lips. Thy will be done, on Earth as it is in heaven. We are nothing, we sin, we surrender and plead for our daily bread. As we forgive those who trespass against us.

Even back then, she'd wondered how she was ever supposed to forgive the men who'd killed her father, and if she couldn't, then how could God forgive her sins, or rather, the things she considered sins at the time: lying to her mother, not washing her feet, having aspirations beyond the tight circle their mother defined as "we." And that "we" had always been as small and clammy as the church beside the canal. Giulietta had thought she'd left the past behind once and for all, but now here it was, as present as ever, burned into her soul.

Vincent had chosen their meeting point. It was the most modern building in the city, and the tallest, plus, it was a public place that assured Giulietta maximum discretion, since no guest workers ever ventured inside, even though they'd helped construct it. The TV tower was an enormous concrete pencil whose point was touching the clouds when Giulietta arrived and looked up. It made her dizzy.

The structure was a daring contrast to the beery sluggishness of the Bavarian state capital: here, atop the rubble mountains of Oberwiesenfeld, they would be holding the Olympics, showing Germany's bright, cosmopolitan face to the world. An optimistic vision of the future, rising from the ruins of the war.

She was alone in the elevator. The building had only recently opened, and everything still smelled new. She thought back to the day they'd arrived in Munich, when Rosaria hadn't had the nerve to take the elevator to the seventh floor. This elevator catapulted her hundreds of feet into the air in seconds, and hardly vibrated at all. Still, her stomach did a flip-flop, reminding her of a German expression, *Mir rutschte das Herz in die Hose. My heart slid into my pants.* Her own language had the saying *il cuore in gola, one's heart in one's throat,* which she could feel. Why Germans thought their hearts fell southward when they were afraid, she'd never understood.

Vincent was standing at the observation-deck window with his hands stuffed into his coat pockets, next to one of the telescopes that worked only if you put coins in. Despite everything that stood between them, the first thing she felt when she saw his handsome profile was love. Pure, unadulterated love. But it lasted only a fraction of a second before shattering. When Vincent turned to look at her, there was nothing familiar in his eyes. He didn't say hello. He was a wall of ice. Giulietta was alarmed. She had to pull herself together, had to avoid looking out the window so she wouldn't feel like she was falling into a chasm. She'd expected him to take her to task angrily, even contemptuously, with the moral superiority of a man who had the luck and the freedom of doing everything right all the time. But she hadn't been prepared for the utter coldness in his eyes. Those same blue eyes that had once radiated pure affection, kind eyes she'd felt so much tenderness for, were frozen and extinguished, as though the magic of their previous encounters had been nothing more than a girlish fantasy, a stupid and unforgivable misunderstanding.

"Ciao, Vincent."

"Did you bring the photo?"

"Vincent, I'm so sorry." She searched his eyes for traces of lost affinity.

"How could you?"

"Please, Vincent, that wasn't my intention."

"Yes, it was."

"But I never meant t—"

"You stole my son from me."

"I never wanted to hurt anyone."

"But you did."

"I was scared."

"Of me? Of Germany? I would have given you everything. You and—Vincenzo." He said the name reluctantly, but not without tenderness. "A home. A future."

"I wasn't brave enough." Giulietta lowered her gaze. "I'm not like you, Vincent."

He was silent. The view from the observation deck was spectacular, but Giulietta barely noticed it.

"I thought about you a lot, Vincent. At night, alone, next to Enzo. I never forgot you. Do you know how lonely a person can be in a marriage?"

He didn't reply.

"Vincenzo mustn't know anything about this. Enzo, either. The family is all they have. Please, Vincent!"

Giulietta would have done anything to keep him from revealing the truth. But he was unmoved by her pleas. He'd already come to his own decision.

"He won't know. Best for everyone. For my family, too."

Giulietta was surprised and relieved.

"On one condition: I want him to go to college."

"Vincent, we're not—"

"You can take his father from him," he interrupted in a harsh tone, "but not his chance in life. At the general high school, as a foreign kid, he doesn't have a chance. He has to go to the college-preparatory school."

"He did in Milan, but here he has to learn German first. It's not easy. He's so gifted in math and physics, but he struggles with languages."

"I'll pay for a tutor. Privately. Discreetly."

"No. I can't accept your money."

"It's not for you. It's for my son." Vincent was insistent. "And I want to see photos of him. Regularly. Otherwise, I'll tell him."

The severity in his voice frightened Giulietta. She understood that he wasn't willing to negotiate. She had no choice but to accept his terms, though she wasn't sure how she would explain to Enzo that they could suddenly afford a private tutor.

She felt worthless. How could he be so dismissive toward her? As crazy as it sounded, she'd always thought of him as her man. The father of her son.

For my family, too. The words haunted her as she walked back alone, her toes soaked with winter slush. *My family.* In another life, he would have meant her when he said that. Her, Vincenzo, and Vincenzo's siblings.

36

April 16, 1969
Vincenzo's life is going to change without his knowing why.
I'm lying to my husband, to my son, to my brother.
I'm not doing it for Vincent. I'm doing it for Vincenzo.

Books. From floor to ceiling. Giulietta had never seen so many books in her entire life. In neat, organized rows like tin soldiers, lining shelves that spanned the entire length of the wall. *This apartment doesn't need wallpaper,* Giulietta thought. *The books are the decoration.* The old parquet creaked beneath the rugs; a grandfather clock ticked softly. Everything in Mr. Grimm's home exuded a distinguished calm. He was friendly and genteel from the very first meeting, with a neatly cropped white beard, vivacious eyes, and a firm handshake.

"Nice to meet you, Vincenzo."

His voice was warm and attentive. A voice that inspired trust and motivation. Vincenzo gave him a skeptical look, but allowed Giulietta to herd him into the strange apartment. Everything here was different: suddenly, he was in the Germany of the Germans. It seemed to breathe intellect, culture, and coziness, which was one of those words they didn't have in Italian. There was a piano in the living room, with a white crocheted blanket and a bust of Beethoven on top. There was nothing luxurious or showy about it; everything was very modest, but it still held riches of a kind no money can buy: education. Grimm was a retired secondary school teacher. German, Latin, and ancient Greek. When Vincent had first come to Munich after the war as a refugee, Grimm and his wife had given him a room. They were like parents to him. Vincenzo, of course, knew none of this.

Grimm invited his guests to join him at the living-room table, and got straight down to business. "That general secondary school in Hasenbergl is absolutely scandalous. People there still think they have to cram knowledge into students' heads by force. Even with physical violence, if need be. But learning has to be fun. *Non scholae, sed vitae discimus!*"

Vincenzo didn't know any Latin. Grimm smiled at him amiably. "Well, I'm afraid I've never learned Italian. Even though I've been to Rome, of course. But we'll understand each other all the same."

Giulietta hoped so. What else could she do? She didn't have a choice either way. Vincenzo kept his expression perfectly neutral—he didn't want to let his guard down, to be the poor foreigner who needed extra help, to have to be grateful for assistance that he would never have needed back home. But Giulietta sensed that he secretly knew Grimm meant well. The fact that Vincenzo remained seated meant that he was giving him a chance. Grimm stood up and retrieved a book from one of the shelves. *Italian Journey*. Giulietta had never heard of it. She'd read a few of Goethe's poems, but she hadn't known that the great German had lived in Italy.

"The roots of European culture lie in the Mediterranean," Grimm told Vincenzo. "Ancient Athens, Rome—your forefathers! We're more alike than different, you and I!"

The next time, Giulietta accompanied her son just to the front door. After that, she let him go on his own. And waited at home until he returned, bearing a new book each time. She cooked for him and asked him all about it: which words he'd learned, what Grimm had said, whether he'd enjoyed it. Knowing that Vincenzo was with Grimm was like watching him step into a new world that had remained closed to her—a world he was allowed to learn everything about, apart from the secret that it had always been his world as well, from the very beginning. Had he been just another faceless guest worker child, the keys to that world would have remained forever out of his reach.

As Giulietta manned the counter in Giovanni's store, serving Italian, Greek, and Turkish mothers, she thought about their children and how they would likely never make it to the other side of the invisible door that separated Germans from foreigners. They might be every bit as intelligent as Vincenzo, but talent was nothing without support. And money.

Giulietta wrapped the Gorgonzola in paper, wished the customer a nice afternoon, and then noticed the torn stitch on her sleeve. The dress had seen better days.

When had she last done any sewing? Ever since Rosaria decided to spend the winter on Salina with the baby, Giovanni had been commuting back and forth between the North and South. While he was down there, Giulietta ran the shop. The door to the back room was never locked, but the sewing machine stood motionless.

Vincenzo, however, rode his bike to Schwabing, Grimm's neighborhood, every afternoon after school. It took him thirty minutes at first, then twenty-eight, twenty-six, twenty-five.

The more he learned the language, grasped its logic and beauty, the less he could sit still in his desk at school as he impatiently awaited his afternoons at Grimm's living-room table. Because what he discovered there, apart from German grammar, was the unexpected sense that, for two hours a day, this cold country had opened up its doors and reached out to shake his hand.

Granted, he wasn't lacking for food, a roof over his head, or a loving family. It was more like his homeless spirit had found a place of refuge. It wasn't just the language that now served him as a weapon in the schoolyard; what he really found in Grimm's books were answers to questions that nobody in his family knew anything about. Grimm lifted him into spheres whose existence was only known to those for whom the world wasn't good enough the way it was—the world of ideas. Werther, Faust and Parcival, Eichendorff, Ovid and Homer became his internal allies against the external world where he had no friends.

Goethe and Schiller showed Vincenzo a different Germany than that of the blond conquerors. Theirs was a land founded not on blood and soil but on the universal beauty of the ancient world, a generous, gleaming nation that had a place for him, a non-German. As a human being among other human beings. What Grimm called the German *Gemüt*—another word without a direct Italian equivalent, somewhere between disposition and soul—no longer seemed so foreign to Vincenzo; it suddenly felt like a reflection of himself.

> *Whereat my soul extended wide*
>
> *its wings toward skies to roam*
>
> *And through the silent countryside*
>
> *My soul went soaring home*

As Vincenzo flourished under Grimm's care, Giulietta met Vincent at inhospitable tram stations every Thursday at 7:30 p.m., no matter the weather, and delivered photos of the boy as promised. Each time, Vincent took the photos without looking at Giulietta and drove off. He never invited her into the car, not even on the night when she met him in a torrential rainstorm. Giulietta returned home, soaked, furious, and racked with guilt; yet the very next night, she stole yet another photo out of the family album, cropped Enzo and herself out neatly, and set it aside for the following Thursday, so she could present Vincent with more of the scraps he'd laid claim to.

It felt like she was cutting pieces out of her own heart. Giving away the only treasure she had, despite knowing that he didn't belong to her alone. More like he didn't even belong to her in part, and it was doubly painful for her to see Vincenzo pulling away from his family more and more. Even when Enzo called him over to work on the bike or play soccer—things he'd once done with enthusiasm—he would just shake his head, engrossed in a book Enzo didn't understand. And when Giulietta asked him what he was reading, he would simply tell her the title, without bothering to describe the content. As though he assumed that she, the little Italian seamstress and sausage seller, could not possibly join him on his new path.

Once, Giulietta followed him in secret. Not to spy on him, but to find out whether Vincent was watching him. She bundled up in a heavy coat and a head scarf and took the tram to Schwabing, reaching Grimm's street ten minutes before Vincenzo. She positioned herself on a street corner that gave her a view of Grimm's building, and turned away as Vincenzo came speeding up on his bike. He locked it to a streetlamp pole and went inside. Giulietta didn't see anything unusual. Neither Vincent's car nor Vincent himself. She waited for two hours in the freezing cold. Her heart raced. Then Vincenzo emerged from the building. Giulietta checked the street. Nobody around. Vincenzo unlocked his bike and rode off. Giulietta was annoyed with herself for her own mistrust, and for the fantasies that had driven her out here. Vincent probably didn't have time to follow Vincenzo around, she told herself. She peeled herself away from the wall she'd been leaning against and headed for the tram station. Then she saw him. He was standing in a phone booth, staring in the direction Vincenzo had just ridden. He stayed there until a woman holding a child knocked on the door of the booth in annoyance. Giulietta ducked between two parked cars. She heard his footsteps on the asphalt as they approached, went right past her without noticing, and hurried away.

In July, the first man walked on the moon. Giulietta, Vincenzo, Enzo, the college students, and countless friends clustered around the black-and-white TV that night, gaping at the unbelievable images being transmitted back to Earth in real time.

"Porca miseria," Enzo grunted in acknowledgment. "The Americans beat the Russians!"

The college students were silent, torn between contempt for the imperialist pigs and barely concealed admiration of their pioneering technological achievement.

"The Americans?" Vincenzo laughed. "Bah, it was the Germans. Wernher von Braun. He built rockets for Hitler."

The students pounced upon the new information and were soon knee-deep in wild conspiracy theories. Enzo poked Vincenzo in the side.

"Did your tutor tell you who invented the telegraph? Marconi. Your name! What would Hitler have done without the telegraph, huh? Smoke signals? Carrier pigeons?"

"Papà, why don't you just learn proper German?"

"When, wise guy? Between my double shifts at the market?"

Giulietta was worried the two of them would start squabbling again.

"They're flying to the moon," Vincenzo cried, "and you drive your forklift down to the end of the hall and back. How can you be content with that?"

"I do it for you," Enzo countered, "so you can have it better someday. Earn your own money first; then you can start running your mouth!"

Enzo got up angrily to fetch himself a beer. He knew Vincenzo had surpassed him long ago, and it filled him with shame.

"What about you?" Giulietta asked, trying to lighten the mood. "What do you want to do with your life?"

Vincenzo didn't reply. No matter what he said, it would only make everything worse.

Ultimately, it was Vincenzo who found his father a better job. During his daily journey to Schwabing, he passed a construction site for the new subway connecting Munich to the Olympic Park. They were looking for workers. Real men, willing to get their hands dirty underground. Vincenzo brought Enzo to the construction office. Translated for him. Enzo presented his Italian master craftsman's diploma and his letter of recommendation from Iso, but the German foreman was mostly interested in his biceps.

Fifteen minutes later, Enzo had his new employment contract in hand. They paid better than the wholesale market, plus extra for dangerous work or night shifts. Knowing German wasn't important. The United Nations of Guest Workers labored away under the earth, burrowing like voles beneath the streets and houses of Munich, day and night. The tunnel had to be finished in time for the 1972 Summer Olympic Games. Enzo was proud of his new job, because he was finally building something again, not just carrying boxes from A to B; he was diligent and fearless, and a few well-timed punches were enough to win him the respect of the others. He still didn't take German classes, though. There was no time for such luxuries.

Giulietta sensed that a storm was brewing. At one end of the table sat Enzo in his sweaty shirt, spooning his *pasta e fagioli* in silence; at the other was Vincenzo with a book beside his plate, memorizing Goethe while he ate.

The evening news ran a story about how Platform 11 of Munich's main train station had become one big stage for a couple of hours: politicians, journalists, diplomats, representatives of the Federal Employment Agency, and a brass band had assembled to welcome a train arriving from Istanbul, from which a shy young Turkish man named Ismail emerged in bewilderment. The spotlights were thrown onto the exhausted, unshaven, haggard man as the minister—or maybe it was the head of the Employment Agency, anyway, some bigwig—had solemnly shaken his hand and awarded him a television.

Ismail learned that he was the one-millionth guest worker. It wasn't technically true, because the one-millionth guest worker had crossed the border in 1964; it was a Portuguese guy, and he'd been given a moped. But that had been in Cologne, and 1964 was a long time ago, and they still needed workers, so in order to have something to announce again, the politicians decided to declare a new "millionaire." Ismail was the "millionth guest worker from Southeastern Europe," which meant mostly Turkey, but also Tunisia, for simplicity's sake. That was where most of them came from these days. The president gave a long speech in which he welcomed the foreign laborers and described them as an immeasurable boon, for they aided the German economy in achieving its tar-geted growth rate and helped older Germans in conquering the retirement-benefits mountain.

Ismail blinked into the cameras, intimidated, not understanding a word. What nobody said into the microphone was that, as soon as Germany had finished achieving said growth rate and conquering said retirement-benefits mountain, everyone expected Ismail to disappear again, quietly and without brass-band accompaniment.

As Enzo labored below ground, Grimm took Vincenzo to enroll at the Luisengymnasium, a college preparatory school. Giulietta went with them, wearing her best dress. The school director, an old friend of Grimm's, shook Vincenzo's hand and welcomed him to the school. Vincenzo didn't even have to take an entrance exam, though he'd tried to insist upon one. He knew he could handle it, and he wanted to show everyone how much he'd learned. Instead, the director told him of his love of ancient Rome. Vincenzo began to realize that, even in Germany, relationships were more important than résumés. The only thing he didn't know was who it was he actually had to thank for his good fortune.

"Mr. Grimm, one more question," he said as they said their goodbyes out-side the school gates.

"Yes?"

"How much did Mamma give you per hour? I want to pay her back someday."

Giulietta's heart stopped.

"Nothing," Grimm said, obviously uncomfortable. "You know, humanism isn't just lip service. It's a philosophy for life."

Vincenzo gave him an embarrassed look. "I'll pay you back."

"By making something of yourself!" Grimm laughed.

Giulietta was the only one who spotted the man on the opposite side of the street, stepping out from the shadow of a tree he had been lurking behind.

37

The sun rose just before we reached Rome. Now I was really feeling the lack of sleep in my bones. I looked up from the diary. Plane trees lining the road, trash beneath the rusty guardrails; a different era flashed past outside. Vincenzo and I sitting inside a time machine, silent, united in foreignness. It took me a moment to return to the present. Vincenzo was smoking. His rough skin, his delicate features, the gray, still-curly hair. In Giulietta's diary, he was an open book—his mother's loving gaze was my keyhole to his soul. If I hadn't known who he was as a child, he would have been such a stranger to me now that I could never have seen him as a father.

"Will you read to me?" Vincenzo asked without looking at me.

"I dunno."

"That's my mother."

For the first time, I sensed a note of vulnerability in his voice. He picked up his crumpled package of cigarettes and rolled the window down. Offered me one. I shook my head. The fresh morning breeze wafted in from outside. The pages of the book fluttered, and something fell out. A photo, cut out of a larger image—Vincenzo at maybe fifteen, with wild, dark locks. He was sitting in a bumper car, wearing a blue duffel coat and an Oktoberfest scarf draped around his neck. His expression for the camera was skeptical. I saw a man's large, hairy hand on his shoulder. His father's hand. But Enzo himself had been cropped out. I handed Vincenzo the photo. He took it, looking perturbed. It vibrated between his fingers on the rim of the steering wheel, danced silently in his hand, refused to reveal its secrets. Half a lifetime lay between the two Vincenzos. What had turned the one into the other?

"What's that?" Vincenzo pointed to a sheet of paper taped into the diary. I unfolded it. It was a letter.

Dear Ms. Macaroni,
It is our great pleasure to inform you that you have won first prize
in our readers' competition. We will be publishing the sewing pat-
tern for your modern wrap dress in our next issue . . .

Vincenzo smiled.

"You remember that?"

He nodded. Puffed on his cigarette. "Why are you interested in this?"

"You aren't?"

"It was all over a long time ago."

Over to him. It was his life. To me, it was like it was all happening now. For the first time. A time is only over once you've lived through it.

"She hung the letter up in the shop," he said, mostly to himself. "Like an announcement."

"Did it help her? Customer-wise, I mean?"

Vincenzo was silent for a moment, miles away. "She always ran the place when Giovanni was down south. He and Rosaria were half here, half there. And most of her customers were guest workers. Patching suits, an occasional wedding dress, but not what she really wanted to do. Her customers couldn't afford nice clothes—they were saving up to buy a house in their home countries."

"What about you? Did you want to go back or stay?"

Vincenzo looked at me, his guard back up. "Why do you want to know?"

"Just asking."

"We were there, but we never really settled in."

"Giovanni did."

"Yeah."

The conversation died. He didn't want to show his hand. And I didn't want to show him that I'd started thinking of his family as my own. I turned back to the diary. Abruptly, he started talking again of his own accord.

"Summer 1970. That was when we settled in."

I gave him a questioning look.

"The Game of the Century, remember?"

"I wasn't born yet," I responded dryly.

"Oh. Right." He had to grin. "World Cup semifinals, Italy against West Germany. In Mexico. Do you like soccer?"

"I like the stuff around it. Open-air screenings and stuff."

"Best game of all time. Everyone was sitting around their TVs. Nobody was out on the streets. Except the guest workers. We put a television and some chairs out on the sidewalk in front of Giovanni's shop. It was still forbidden to sit outside. German hospitality was an indoor thing. But we just did it. Open-air screening. We were the pioneers." He grinned wryly. "That was back when Germans still thought pasta meant egg noodles with Gouda cheese, when Tuscany was known only to Tuscans, not a German colony. Anyway, we sat outside and cheered for Italy. We nearly had it, but they scored again at the end of regulation, one–one, went to extra time, Beckenbauer limping around the field with a broken shoulder, and Italy ended up winning four to three. You can't even imagine what that meant to us. In the bars, the Italian waiters all threw down their aprons and ran into the street. We celebrated all night! People were screaming at us out their windows to be quiet. But we didn't give a shit. Suddenly we weren't just the little spaghetti-munchers, we were the winners! That was the moment when everything changed. We changed. And we changed Germany. We started walking through the streets with our heads held high. Gelato shops were trendy then, and all of a sudden—*that* summer—you could get a cappuccino in Schwabing. Not the kind with whipped cream—the real stuff, with foamed milk. And the pecking order changed at school. Suddenly there were kids under us. The ones who had come later. The kebab-eaters. That's what we, the spaghetti-munchers, called them. I gave them the beatdowns I'd gotten from the Germans."

I was startled by how talkative he could be. When the conversation wasn't about his family.

"And you?"

"I got my first Vespa. Used, yellow, tuned. Enzo saved up his wages to buy it. Girls liked it a lot."

He said it curtly, without a trace of vanity. Vincenzo had been a hit with the ladies, no doubt about it—even today, he was still attractive. But he didn't seem proud of it; he acted almost like it wasn't important to him. Maybe because it was something he'd never had to work for. Because you can only be proud of things you achieve yourself. And maybe that was the secret, the thing that made him even more attractive to women: he didn't fawn over them. I pictured the teenager he'd been: an outsider, silent, but with piercing eyes, not loud, not the center of attention, and thus more interesting than the others. Because he seemed to know more than they did, because he had a secret they wanted to unearth.

"Latin Lover," I remarked, trying to provoke him.

"Those were wild times. And the German girls were suddenly into the darker guys."

"And you had no idea about Vincent?"

Vincenzo fell silent. The mere mention of that name was enough to shut the door he had briefly opened.

He shook his head. "Read to me?"

38

September 13, 1970
Vt. wants to know every detail. I clip our son out of photos and
feel like a thief. Vt. is so severe that I forget what it was like to
love him. But the longing never stops. It's getting more and more
unbearable. A "pragmatic arrangement," he calls it. As though
feelings were controllable, like technology. This won't end well.

Vincent invited Giulietta to dinner. The diary didn't explain why he stopped
meeting her at the tram station, only that their secret encounters gradually
changed. He risked suggesting public places, perhaps because nothing untoward
was happening anymore, only routine handoffs of the most recent photos
and questions about Vincenzo's progress at school. Maybe because he thought
nothing could go wrong as long as he kept his feelings under control. And
maybe he was deluding himself, and he had no idea they were steering toward
an unavoidable collision.

One meal at Tantris cost as much as Giulietta spent to feed the entire family
for a week. But she'd resigned herself to the fact that he was the one to pick
the location—and pay the bill. The restaurant had just opened, and it looked
spectacular. Asian sculptures lined the entrance; the slanted, exposed concrete
walls were illuminated in red; spherical yellow lanterns floated above the tables.
The food here wasn't merely about meeting a physical need; it was an expression
of desire, a celebration of a lifestyle: fusty old Germany had discovered the art of
fine living. Unlike the other revolutions, this one started among the rich, then
spread to everyone else later. She would have loved to tell her brother about

it—if only she could. He would have been excited, but she felt out of place. If Vincent had told her they'd be going to the most expensive restaurant in town, Giulietta would have worn a different dress. One where she'd have been immune to the scrutiny of high society. The women's gazes were more dangerous than the men's. She was still beautiful, and men tended to focus less on the clothing than on what was underneath it. But women could tell cheap material from quality. Despite the perfect cut of Giulietta's dress, it couldn't quite conceal its origins as Vincent led her through the rows of tables to the one he'd reserved. Women's eyes passed judgment in a matter of seconds, with a deadly mixture of envy and intuition. A pianist played quiet jazz behind them.

All at once, a man in a three-piece suit stood up and greeted Vincent in a formal tone. A bigwig, Dr. So-and-So from the supervisory board. He introduced his wife, and Vincent introduced Giulietta. With her first name—that was it, not "a good friend," not "my wife." He did it with confident nonchalance, whereas Giulietta wished the earth would open up and swallow her. What was he thinking? How could he feel so safe? Maybe the doctor's wife wasn't really his wife, either? And then, for one brief moment, Giulietta thought about what it would be like if he actually did introduce her as his wife.

He brought her to the table, pulled out her chair. They nodded discreetly to the people at the neighboring tables in greeting, as if it were the most natural thing in the world, even though the whole thing was completely outrageous.

Once they sat down, Giulietta withdrew the envelope with the photos and handed it to Vincent. He stuck it into his jacket without comment and ordered the wine without asking Giulietta's preference. Giulietta watched.

"I'll mail them in the future," she said.

Vincent gave her a surprised look.

"If you want to punish me, do it right. Send me away; tell me you never want to see me again. But don't invite me to dinner just to sit with me in silence."

"Giulietta, we have an agreement," he responded quietly. "That's a promise one has to keep."

It always made her feel small when he showed off his moral superiority.

"And I'm keeping my promise," he continued. "Our son will go to college wherever he wants, to study whatever he wants, no matter what it costs."

Giulietta had had enough. "As you wish," she said, and stood up to leave. The people at the nearby tables glanced over.

"Giulietta. Please. Stay." He got up and took her arm.

"What for? All we're doing is hurting each other."

"Please." His voice softened. She remained standing. "Is that dress one of yours?"

She nodded.

"It's perfect."

She didn't react to the compliment.

"Does your husband let you make dresses now?"

She thought for a moment, then took her seat again so she wouldn't be in the waiter's way, with the other customers gawking at her.

"I don't make dresses. I sell cheese and sausage. I fill in for Giovanni, who's renovating his house on Salina."

"Why are you letting other people hold you back again?"

Giulietta hated it when he poured salt in her wounds, though it was also the first time in months that he'd asked her about her own life. "I owe my visa and my job to Giovanni. I owe it to Vincenzo to give him a mother. People in our family are there for each other. Aren't yours?"

He regarded her thoughtfully for a long moment. "You were my family. The promise we made to each other back then—I meant it."

The feelings she'd worked so hard to put away flooded back. Had all of his coldness been an act, a defense mechanism? She couldn't help taking his hand. "I never wanted to leave you. That had nothing to do with you. You have to understand that, Vincent. Otherwise, you'll never be happy."

The waiter interrupted them to fill their wineglasses and suggested foie gras as an appetizer. Vincent leaned down to his briefcase and withdrew something: a Venetian gondola made of black plastic, with gold accents and colorful lamps. The kind they sold tourists in Venice.

"I brought you something. It lights up when you—" He switched it on and set it beside Giulietta's plate. The tiny string of lights twinkled in every color of the rainbow. He grinned. The young Vincent, the one she'd missed so much, suddenly flickered to view in his eyes. Giulietta couldn't help laughing.

"Did you go to Venice?"

"I did."

The thought gave her a pang in her heart. Nobody traveled to Venice alone. The city she'd never seen, the city he'd wanted to take her to in the Isetta, all those years ago.

"What's wrong? Don't you like it?"

"Sure I do."

He frowned, as if only now realizing that the gift might hurt her.

"I thought about you the whole time. The shellfish didn't agree with Marianne. She was in the hotel with an upset stomach, and I went out alone. Wandered up and down the alleys. It was foggy over the canals, like in Milan."

She stopped avoiding his gaze. "You don't know how often I dreamed of Venezia. What it would be like now if I'd said yes back then."

There it was again. That softening in his eyes.

"What do you think our lives would be like now?" he asked.

"Maybe you wouldn't be as hard on yourself. Or on me."

He gave her a self-deprecating smile. "And you?"

She shrugged. She was afraid to even picture it.

"You'd be as beautiful as you are now."

"You wouldn't be as romantic anymore, but you'd be a little more easygoing."

They smiled at each other.

"And you," he said, "might actually be able to believe that happiness wasn't just something for other people."

"And then?" she asked.

"Then we'd be sitting here, eating and drinking wine, but we'd have the same rings on our fingers."

His wedding ring caught her eye. It was nicer than hers, of course. She felt like bursting into tears but managed to remain as composed as ever. Then they ate and drank wine, chatting about this and that as though they'd always been together, one couple among many sitting here, as though the whole world were an orange-colored festival of the senses. They never mentioned Vincenzo, or their spouses, or anything else that didn't exist in the here and now. They sought refuge in the lie that they were the same people they'd been before, unchanged at their core, unhurt and eternally young, as though they'd never made those life choices, as though their pasts and their families out there were just one possibility among hundreds. The thrill of the immediate moment.

When they left the restaurant at eleven o'clock, he tenderly tucked her coat over her shoulders, and she took his arm without thinking about it. They walked like that to his Iso Rivolta. The warmth of his arm, the familiar voice, their steps in harmony.

"Vincent, I don't know what's real anymore. When I wake up tomorrow, I'll think this was all a dream."

"So, what if we just leave for Venice right now? We'll be there by sunrise!" He sounded the way he had back then, unshakably optimistic, always ready to take the next step.

"Quit it, you're torturing me."

He stopped walking and gazed at her. "I'll drive you home." His tone was matter-of-fact again.

They glided through the night without speaking, in his warm cocoon of a car, safely isolated from all things difficult and unresolvable. The radio was playing the Beatles' last album, *Let It Be*. Giulietta held the gondola on her lap and thought about the time she'd ridden on his motorcycle in Milan, snuggled against his back, the scent of his leather jacket in her nose, intoxicated by the wind in her face as the city lights flew by.

He parked on the corner, away from her front door. The way he had back on Via Lodovico Il Moro. When he turned off the engine and they looked at each other, everything was suddenly perfectly easy. He wasn't the one who made the first move; nor was she. It just happened, like a wave that swept over both of them and gently lifted them up. She closed her eyes. Not kissing him would have been impossible; letting it happen was the most natural thing in the world. The scent of his skin, his hands running through her hair, then deeper—he felt the same as before, only slower, more knowing. It was overwhelmingly familiar and yet completely new. Tenderly, he drew her scarf down and kissed her neck. She put her fingers on his lips, uncertain. Not because she didn't want to return his caresses, but because she suddenly felt self-conscious: if he was looking for the twenty-year-old she'd been back in Milan, he wouldn't find her. She'd been a wife and mother for a long time; maybe it was officially too late. She closed her eyes so as not to show her fear. Then she felt his hands on both sides of her face, his lips on her forehead; something quieted inside her, and all at once, there was nothing to think about and no barrier between them.

Suddenly, she heard something. She opened her eyes. A flash of blue streaked across Vincent's face. Two police Volkswagens raced past them, tires squealing, and jolted to a stop beside the parked cars. Blue light bathed the empty street in an eerie glow. Four cops leaped out and stormed into a building. Giulietta's building. They were armed.

"What's going on, Vincent?"

"Stay here."

He took her hand, but she tore away, opened the door, and ran.

She heard shouting in the stairwell. Muted blows, commands, screams. The door to her apartment had been smashed open. The police dragged the college students out of their rooms by their long hair and put them in handcuffs. "Fucking pigs!" Roland yelled. In the middle of it all stood Enzo in his undershirt, clueless as to what was happening, but standing like a protective bear in front of Vincenzo, who'd been awakened by the commotion, only to find himself in the middle of a nightmare.

"No understand!" Enzo shrieked.

A policeman ordered him up against the wall, but he refused to take one step away from his son. Giulietta arrived just in time to explain that they were guest workers, not Communists, and the police contented themselves with searching their room. The little girl was standing in the middle of the living room, screaming; her mother was too stoned to defend herself. Vincenzo picked the girl up and comforted her.

"Shh, shh, don't be scared; they're not going to hurt us."

As the police led the handcuffed students to their cars, Giulietta followed them downstairs, holding the sobbing girl. Outside, she saw Vincent standing there, beside the startled neighbors in pajamas. He took a step toward her. She signaled for him to keep his distance. Enzo came out and put an arm around her. At that moment, Vincenzo ran into the street. He was too agitated to notice the man in the crowd who couldn't take his eyes off him.

"Vincenzo!" Giulietta exclaimed. "Come back!"

Vincent turned and disappeared into the darkness.

39

Vincenzo braked hard. A gas station somewhere in Tuscany. Without a word, he got out of the car, slammed the door, and went into the attached convenience store. I watched him go. The vehicle crackled, overheated; something gurgled under the hood. I pulled out the ignition key, grabbed the diary, and followed him.

A few minutes later, we stood at the shop window, gazing outside. Drinking espresso. Neither of us said a word. Outside in the sun, his Alfa Romeo stood out amid the modern cars.

"What do you have against him?" I asked. "He really did love your mother."

Vincenzo drank his coffee in silence.

"She loved him, too," I added.

He reached for the diary, which was sitting in front of me, and flipped through it. Then he took out a photo and stared at it, apparently shocked. It was of Giulietta and Vincent in a café in Munich; based on the clothing, it was probably sometime in the early 1970s. They were laughing into the camera a little uncertainly, as though they'd asked the waiter to take their picture and then changed their minds, but he'd already hit the button and captured this brief moment between exuberance and regret.

"You know this picture?" I asked.

He shook his head, unable to peel his eyes away.

I watched him, realizing. "You never saw them together, did you?"

He shook his head again. Placed the photo back into the book.

I gazed at him for a long time.

"What?" he asked.

"I never had a photo of you and Mom, either."

He avoided my gaze and stared outside. It was hard for me to gauge how deeply he'd been affected by whatever happened—or, rather, didn't happen—between him and my mother. He was sad, anxious, unreconciled. I opened my bag, took out the photo Carmela had given me on the terrace, and showed it to him.

"Where'd you get that?"

"From your wife."

His eye twitched slightly. I could only guess at what was going through his mind. Anger at his wife, probably, and admission of failure.

Outside the window, a family on vacation goofed around as they took a selfie with their ice cream. We'd be in the background of the shot. The second picture of us, I realized. Thirty years after the first.

While Vincenzo got gas, I called Robin. He picked up this time.

"I'm on my way back," I said. "I'll be there this evening."

"Okay," he said.

"How was your meeting with the Italians?"

"Very nice."

"Hey, listen, Robin, I know I acted like a total—"

He didn't let me finish. "I signed."

"What?"

"The contract."

"What contract?"

"Julia, they like your sketches. I mean, yeah, a few things need to be changed here and there, but that retro look—"

"You brought them my—Robin, those were just rough drafts. And I told you I didn't want to sell my soul!"

"Listen. Your sketches belong to the company. You don't want to work with them, no problem, I'll do it alone."

His words hit me like a punch in the face. "You can't just throw me out of my own—"

"Yes, I can."

"We're equal partners!"

"You can sue me if you want, but you'll never win. Just accept it."

I was speechless. I would have thought him capable of a lot of things, but not this.

"Robin, we've always made all of our decisions together."

"Yeah, until you bailed on me. The show must go on."

His voice was cool. Provokingly relaxed.

"The collection bears your name. The label will still be called that."

"You can't take my name away from me!"

"You'll have to think of a new one, then."

"That's my label!"

"The label will remain as we discussed. Just with a new design team. Nobody's irreplaceable."

"You are such an asshole."

"It's just business, Julia. Don't take it personally."

Vincenzo glanced at me, his brow furrowed.

"Fuck you." I let the phone drop, wishing I could smash it against the nearest window. The ground seemed to crumble beneath my feet.

"Did something happen?" Vincenzo asked.

I averted my eyes and got into the car.

We spent a while sitting there in silence. I tried not to cry. I was determined not to show weakness.

"Business or personal?" he asked eventually.

"Just business."

That wasn't true, obviously. My company was me, and I was my company. Or had been. I felt like a dog that had been kicked out the door. Out my own door. It had never been my own, of course. Everything was on credit. But it had been mine on a different level, way more than it had been his. My name, my designs, my clothes. How did he expect to keep it all going, with no soul and no personality? Did he really think his new friends could just copy the thing that defined my fashion, the thing that had won us the competition, by hiring some random designer? One who would just have to sit in the nest they'd built and do whatever the new bosses told her to?

I'd never considered Robin a great artist, but at least he'd always pretended to understand that personality was the only thing that couldn't be bought. And now he'd sold himself and our baby to people for whom personality was just a marketing tool. Nothing unique, nothing inborn, everything replaceable.

"I busted my ass for that company! Always at my limits, always a hundred and fifty percent, just for a little applause. What the hell is the point? In the end, you're back with nothing again!"

The words came tumbling out; I couldn't hold back any longer. I cursed Robin, cursed my industry, plotted revenge. I wasn't going to just let them kick me to the curb like a dog. No, I was going to fight for my baby, tooth and nail. Robin would beg me to let him stay, and in the end, he'd be the one leaving the company, not me. As soon as we got to Munich, I would get myself a lawyer. But the more worked up I got, the more helpless I felt. Realistically, I hardly had a chance of winning in court. I felt a chasm opening up within me. I was ashamed of myself for acting like this in front of my father. I was actually crying to him, of all people. As though I needed him.

Vincenzo listened to me. He was there for me, plain and simple. It took me a while to realize that he was neither judging me nor pitying me—that he actually understood every single word I said.

"There's a lot of Giulietta in you, you know."

I stared at him in silence.

"That's our family," he said. "Talent isn't a gift. It's a curse."

I could sense that he wasn't just referring to his mother. Or me. He was talking about himself.

"Did she succeed in the end?" I asked.

"How do you mean?"

"Just—in being happy?"

He was silent. Then he pulled out the diary and handed it to me.

"Why don't you just tell me the story yourself?" I asked.

"Because I don't know anything about her. Giovanni had that book hidden away the whole time, unbelievable."

"But you had a good relationship, I thought."

"She and I were one."

"So, the way she and Vincent secretly . . . You didn't know about that?"

He shook his head. "Not till after her death."

"When did she die?"

He flinched. "Read to me. Please."

40

*For days now, Vincent has been all I've thought about. The more
I try to break free, the tighter his hold becomes on me. I feel like
a fly in a spider's web.*

After that secret, interrupted kiss, Giulietta didn't have time to see Vincent again. She had to fight to stay in the apartment with Vincenzo and Enzo. The rental contract had been with the students, and the arrest nullified the family's sublease.

One Monday morning, there was suddenly a man in the kitchen—heavyset, in a hat and a loden coat—demanding to know what Enzo thought he was doing there. Enzo, who had just returned from the night shift, tried to throw the intruder out. His German wasn't good enough for Mr. Plattner and his Bavarian dialect to understand. Plattner, the landlord, took Enzo for a squatter.

Giulietta was at the store when Enzo called. She dropped everything and ran home immediately. By the time she arrived, Enzo had calmed down, but the landlord put up an even bigger fuss now that there was finally someone who could understand what he was saying. The condition of the apartment was the first problem; the second was that any sublease not expressly approved by the landlord was illegal. Giulietta didn't know that the students hadn't told him about her. Nor had she known that they'd been charging her half the entire rent—for a single room! Plattner gave them until the end of the month to get out—after all, he said, he wasn't a monster. When Giulietta translated that for Enzo, he went straight to the bedroom and started packing. He said he refused to spend another day giving Plattner the satisfaction of showing off his generosity.

"Where are we going to go?" Giulietta asked.

"We'll sleep at the shop if need be. God will provide for us somehow."

Giulietta hurried back to Mr. Plattner.

"We're respectable people. No politics, no drugs. We're a family. We're Catholic! You're Catholic, too, aren't you?"

He was, of course, but he didn't see why he should have to play the Good Samaritan. Business was business, and foreigners were foreigners. He didn't have anything against them; he simply preferred to rent to Germans. One never knew, after all.

Giulietta ran to the closet and withdrew their residence and work visas from a folder. "My husband works for the subway! My son is preparing for college!"

Plattner wasn't interested.

Then Giulietta offered to cover the entire rent.

"You can't possibly afford that," Plattner grunted.

"Never mind, friend," Enzo said, and pulled Giulietta away. Better to move out than allow themselves to be humiliated any further. They both went into the bedroom to pack their things. After a minute, the landlord followed.

"All right, well, if you insist . . ." He spoke to Enzo, not Giulietta. "Just twelve months for now . . . but no noise. No cookin' with garlic. Okay?" He sounded like an adult talking to a three-year-old. "And we'll hafta raise the rent a little, say by two hundred marks. All right, Mr.—uh—"

"Marconi," Giulietta said.

Enzo signed the rental contract on the stove, and Giulietta promised to transfer the deposit in the morning. When Plattner left the apartment, she hurried to the bathroom before Enzo could see that she was crying. Every time she had the courage to break free and seek out her own happiness, something happened that pushed her right back into the family's lap. It was as if she were cursed. The evil eye her mother had always warned about—perhaps it belonged to Mamma herself.

Then Vincenzo came home from school, and she told him that he was getting his own room. He looked surprised and asked how they were going to afford extra rent. Enzo assured him that, as long as he and Giulietta both worked, they'd manage. What Giulietta didn't tell Vincenzo was that there wasn't even enough in their bank account for the three months' deposit. They'd have to borrow the money, probably from Giovanni.

Enzo opened a good bottle of wine—which he rarely did—to celebrate their stroke of good fortune. Even Vincenzo got a little. He'd hardly ever seen Enzo as happy as he was that day. Giulietta was glad to see him in such high spirits. Glad for him, not for herself. Her mind was on Vincent. As she, Enzo, and Vincenzo raised their glasses and toasted their new apartment, she thought about the house where Vincent was sitting down to supper with his wife and daughter.

The very next day, Giulietta discovered why she'd actually gotten the lease. Giovanni was back on Salina, and she couldn't reach him on the phone. The connection failed a lot in winter, when storms damaged the only cable connecting the island to Sicily. The line was back in service the following day, but the bartender told her that Giovanni had gone to Sicily to meet with farmers and winemakers. Giulietta briefly considered asking Vincent for the money but then discarded the thought immediately. The only other name she could come up with on short notice was Erna Baumgartner, the widow who'd rented them the shop. When Giulietta told her what had happened, Erna didn't hesitate for a second. She went to the bank and brought the money straight to the shop.

"Just pay it back when you can." Then she asked the name of the landlord. "Plattner?" She made a face.

"What?"

"Ohh, he's a sly one! I know that type!"

"What type?"

Erna opened Giulietta's eyes. As it turned out, the neighboring apartments were Plattner's as well; a Turkish family lived in one, a Greek family in the other. The entire building belonged to him, the guy who supposedly didn't rent to foreigners. In reality, he loved renting to foreigners. But not out of kindness. Because the old building was legally protected by the city, he picked tenants he assumed would run it into the ground. Once the property was sufficiently dilapidated, he could apply for special permission to tear it down. Then he could build another property on the same site, with lower ceilings, more floors, and newer floor plans, so that he could make more money off his apartments—renting to Germans this time, of course. And everyone knew that people from the South didn't take care of their places, and they'd be going back to their own countries soon anyway.

"What do I do now?" Giulietta was horrified.

"Go to the bank, send him the deposit, then the contract's official. And then get workin'." Erna laughed.

That same evening, Giulietta and Erna reached out to Hatice, the Turkish mother, and Giorgos, the Greek father. If everyone worked together, they could prevent the building from being demolished. The next day, they began renovating. At their own expense. They needed to whip the old building into shape before Plattner got wind of it. They'd start with their own apartments: the broken tiles, the frayed electric cables, the calcified water lines. Then they'd move on to the rotting standpipes.

Giulietta cleaned. For days, she scrubbed the filthy floors in the students' rooms, pulled ancient newspapers out from behind the radiators, and sealed the windows with material from her workshop. She closed the store for a week. She knew Vincent would come looking for her there. And she sent a letter to his office address, which was listed in the phone book. She asked him to be patient. One extra week. Then they could see each other. A couple days to sort her thoughts. To make a decision.

But then Giulietta did what she'd always done, what most people do when life forces them to make a decision: she didn't. She let things run their course and marveled that the world didn't end.

She and Vincent must have met up at some hotel one afternoon—where exactly, her diary didn't say. All she wrote was that it was wonderful. Breathtaking. And that "*Que será*" was on the radio as they made love. Other than that, she simply described how she went home that evening, stopping at the market on the way to buy fresh fish for dinner. How she gazed in wonder at the illuminated stands and lanterns in the blowing snow, how the city seemed to fall silent. How, for one moment, before the fear and the guilt caught up to her, Giulietta Marconi, the unimportant little guest worker's wife, was the happiest human being alive.

They got together whenever they could. Over lunch, after work, sometimes even at night if Enzo was working. Nobody knew about it—they stole away from their lives and fell upon each other greedily, as though trying to make up for all that lost time. They were old; they were young.

Sometimes at night, she lay beside Enzo and thought that it was finally time to tell him, that she owed him the truth. But then life went on down its usual path. There was furniture to buy, there were walls to paint, and Vincenzo brought home a report card that filled them both with pride. Giulietta didn't decide to keep the secret; she simply put off thinking about how and when she would tell Enzo, over and over again, so as not to destroy the fragile joy that she shared with Vincent. They savored every minute life granted them together, and found themselves in two worlds, commuting back and forth between them as though sleepwalking.

Maybe, Giulietta told herself as she took the bus home in the rain, it wasn't something she had to be ashamed of—not the exception, but the rule. Maybe most people lived in multiple worlds at once, even though it wasn't obvious as they ran through the rain in their gray coats. Maybe that was the only way any-one could handle the bleak reality of existence—by occasionally escaping into another world that seemed real at first but felt like a dream shortly thereafter.

Interestingly, Giulietta wrote more about Vincenzo than about her secret trysts with Vincent—maybe for fear someone else might read it, but certainly out of motherly concern as well. Every line of her diary radiated her deep love for her son, and her amazement at how much like his biological father he was becoming.

Having his own room for the first time in his life did him good. He was on a roll at school, and life in Germany had finally started to feel more natural. Not that he liked everything about it, but when something bothered or infuriated him now, it wasn't because it was foreign and made him wish he could leave. It was because he wanted to change it—there and then.

The brief period of reconciliation and understanding with Enzo gave way to new, loud arguments at the dinner table, most of which were about a new sub-ject: war. Not the war Europe had survived, but the one the US had gotten into in Vietnam. The books the college kids had left behind were now in Vincenzo's possession. Initially, he hadn't been particularly interested in the topics them-selves; it had been more of a detective-like, almost ghoulish curiosity about whether the books full of note cards and scraps of paper would give him some explanation of how they'd ended up in prison. But then he discovered answers to questions he hadn't dared ask, questions that stoked the embers of a flame within him, a flame passed down from a different time. When, out of nowhere, Vincenzo began quoting the *Communist Manifesto* at dinner, it reminded Giulietta of her father. The story of an eternally recurrent battle between the free and the enslaved, between the working class and the bourgeoisie, in the villas of ancient Rome, the automobile factories of Detroit, the construction zones of West Germany, and the destroyed villages of Vietnam. Enzo tolerated it all patiently until Vincenzo attacked him directly.

"Before you insult us workers, go get a job yourself!" Enzo shouted.

"I'm not insulting you! Far from it. I just think you should stop allowing yourselves to be exploited!"

"Let me tell you something about exploitation, my boy: Unlike the Roman slaves, I get extra pay for nights and weekends, health insurance, and pension insurance from my employer, so that if something happens to me, then you and Mamma are taken care of. And what the Americans are doing over there is a disgrace, but don't forget that the Americans were also the ones who freed Sicily from the Nazis!"

"How can you be a worker and still vote Democrazia Cristiana? In 1971? You're digging your own grave!"

"Because Communists are godless people. You saw those college students. They don't work! Did you see the way they treated that little girl? They have no values! In your Soviet Union, bad people like that would have been sent to the Gulag! Do you know what the Gulag is?"

"Everything you know, you get from the tabloids! You've never read an actual book in your life! You can't even speak proper German, and you've been here for more than two years!"

Enzo ripped the Marx book from his hand.

"If you think these books are going to help you get anywhere in life, just remember where the college students landed. This is poison! You should be reading your textbooks! Math, physics, biology, that's what you need in this country!"

Enzo slammed the Marx book to the floor. Vincenzo retrieved it angrily, and then threw it in Enzo's face. They came at each other.

"Stop!" Giulietta shrieked. "Have you two lost your minds?"

After a long, awful moment, Enzo pulled himself together; Vincenzo ran to his room; and Giulietta wept.

It went like that every night. It was never really about the Gulag or the Vietnamese children. It was the reenactment of an old battle, the reopening of wounds Enzo and Vincenzo had inflicted upon one another years ago. Giulietta sat there, watching, thinking about Vincent. Enzo was easy to understand. He was fighting for his honor, his position as a father. Vincenzo, whose rejection of Enzo bordered on contempt, was only aware of his own intellectual superiority, not of the hidden root of their differences.

Giulietta could understand her son's feelings up to a certain point, but there was something inside him that she couldn't grasp. It seemed as if the battles between him and Enzo were really about the irreconcilable differences within Vincenzo himself, a genetic and familial blend that was more explosive than Giulietta was willing to admit to herself.

When did a person stop being a child? Vincenzo was sixteen now, and Enzo still thought firm discipline was enough to keep his youthful rage in check. Giulietta, who had believed that love would preserve the bond between her and her son, began to doubt whether it would be enough.

And since she herself desired freedom more than anything, she decided it would be best for Vincenzo if she gave him all the freedom he needed, even if it was hard for her. She knew she couldn't stop him. She let him say, think, and do whatever he wanted. She permitted him to go wherever, with whomever, for as long as he liked. She looked away once when he brought an absolutely shocking girl home with him and locked himself in his room with her.

The only thing she didn't allow him was the truth, because it frightened her too much.

41

The summer of Giulietta's affair with Vincent—that was what it was, an affair between two married adults who were escaping to a brighter world through the darkness of a hotel room—seemed endless. Just like back in Milan, it was as though a window had opened and all she needed to do was fly through it. As though the present were actually the fulfillment of a promise she'd nearly lost faith in.

They usually met at the newly opened Holiday Inn on Leopoldstraße, which was too expensive for anyone from Giulietta's circle, and too garish for anyone from Vincent's. Munich's conservative establishment avoided the giant concrete palace with its shrill underwater nightclub, where actual sharks circled around the guests.

Vincent and Giulietta never went to the restaurant there, just ordered room service. They arrived and left separately, and they planned their next meeting each time so that they wouldn't have to telephone. When Giulietta took the tram to the hotel, she always crossed the Münchner Freiheit, a square in Schwabing that the new subway had turned into a massive, craterlike gorge. The tram clattered across on spindly stilts protruding from its depths. At night, when Giulietta gazed out the window of the eighth floor of the Holiday Inn, she could see the lights of Europe's largest construction site—the Olympic Stadium, with its futuristic pavilion roof. Just a few blocks away, Enzo and his friends continued digging the subway tunnel, from Münchner Freiheit to Olympic Park, like subterranean moles.

When they were together, time slowed. Seconds became minutes, minutes became hours, hours stretched into eternity. And suddenly it was November.

Vincent stood at the window, silhouetted against the already-dark afternoon sky. "Where do we go from here?" he asked Giulietta, who was perched on the bed, rolling on her stockings. "When I get home and Marianne takes my coat, I feel like I'm cheating on you. On you, not on Marianne."

Giulietta got up and snuggled against him from behind. "You can't do it, either, can you?"

"Do what?" he asked.

"Leave your wife and daughter."

Vincent turned to give her a solemn look.

"But we can't keep acting like we're not in a relationship."

When Giulietta kissed him goodbye that evening—she always left first and walked through the lobby alone—she knew that she couldn't put it off any longer. Before Vincent told Enzo, which she wouldn't be able to prevent forever, she would have to do it. She had to take matters into her own hands, before things got out of control.

On her way home, without discussing it with Vincent, she made up her mind to tell Enzo. To risk everything. She owed it to her husband. If she couldn't give him loyalty, she could at least give him honesty.

When she unlocked the apartment door, Vincenzo ran to meet her.

"Where were you, Mamma?" He was practically hysterical. "I called the shop, but Uncle Giovanni didn't know where you were!"

"What happened?"

"Papà was in an accident."

They went straight to the hospital. It was some time before the doctors let Enzo out of intensive care. When they saw him, he was encased in plaster from head to toe. His face was bruised. A scaffold had collapsed, crushing his shoulder, his leg, and several vertebrae. It was pure luck that he had survived at all. A Turkish guy had dragged him and another friend of theirs out of the rubble. The other man was dead.

Giulietta grasped his hand, bewildered. He couldn't speak yet, but he gazed at her with infinite gratitude. Gratitude that he was still alive.

"Amore," she whispered.

He nodded carefully.

Vincenzo was shocked to see his father so injured. He'd hated him, yes; he'd felt superior to him, but he'd never seen him physically weak. Enzo had always been the powerful bear nothing could knock down. When Enzo was discharged weeks later, Vincenzo supported him the whole way down the long corridor, so that he wouldn't have to submit to the shame of using crutches. Better dead than a cripple, he said.

Giulietta wrote Vincent a letter. His reply, in ballpoint on graph paper, lay neatly folded in her diary.

Munich, April 28, 1972

My beloved Giulietta,
Your feelings do you credit. Of course you must remain at your husband's side. Abandoning him right now would be unforgivable. You're right: romantic love isn't everything, nor is physical love. Companionable love, standing together in difficult times, matters more in the end.

And that applies to us, too. I waited eighteen years for you; I'll go on waiting for you. It's just another test—I hope and pray it's the last one. You and I are two halves of a whole.
Love,
Vincent

On May 8, 1972, the family watched the grand opening of the Olympic Park subway station. On television. Enzo put on his best suit, which was to say his only suit. He looked a little strange, all dressed up to sit on the couch, but no one dared crack any jokes at his expense. Hans-Jochen Vogel, the mayor, gave a speech. A reporter interviewed the foreman. The news anchorman described the grueling night shifts, the unexploded ordinance from the Second World War, the five dead construction workers, the line's punctual completion. He discussed the Olympics, Munich's welcoming the entire world, the new, friendly face of Germany. But nobody talked about the nameless moles from the South, without whom they'd never have achieved it all.

After some time had passed, Giulietta went to see Vincent again, of course. Not seeing him would have been impossible. But arranging their secret trysts grew increasingly difficult. Enzo lay at home on the sofa; Giovanni was working. And when Giovanni was in Italy, she had to run the shop by herself. He paid for his sister to get her driver's license so that she could drive the delivery van and take Enzo to physical therapy.

Vincent waited.

Giulietta kept her head up, but she was gradually beginning to lose her nerve.

"You have to start sewing again," Vincent said. "That always made you happy."

"I am, don't worry."

In reality, she hadn't made anything in a long time. She sewed, sure, but it was hems, collars, tears in the guest workers' shabby suits. She wasn't creating—she was just mending holes. Somebody had to feed the family.

The women in her family had always worked. She remembered how her grandmother, tough and fearless, had gone out on the ocean at night with the fishermen. Her mother had worked the fields with her father, and then done the neighbors' laundry in Milan for a few hundred lire. *Dolce far niente*, pleasant idleness, was an invention of the German tourists.

All over the country, the mood was changing. The colorful hippie years ended; cuts became straighter again; people wore plaid instead of flowers. The revolution had lost its innocence; the tone had sharpened; the fronts hardened. A bitter aftertaste of violence and melancholy hung in the air. Napalm on Vietnam, bombs on US barracks, police checkpoints in the streets, and the word "terrorism" over and over again in the news. In June, the cover of the *Bild* tabloid showed a nude man, brought down by police. Beneath it, the headline read, "Naked Terrorist Terrorizes No More." Baader, Meins, and Raspe of Germany's own Red Army Faction, all taken into custody.

Vincenzo, who was watching the TV news with rapt attention, exclaimed, "Did you see his car? There, in the garage, where the shoot-out was?"

The bullet-ridden automobile Baader had hidden behind was an Iso Rivolta GT. A Communist with a penchant for fast luxury cars. Stolen, of course. Giulietta gasped. *Unbelievable,* she thought to herself. Only 797 of that model had been built. The love of her life drove one; Public Enemy Number One had another.

Enzo's shattered bones couldn't break his spirit, but his inability to feed his family gnawed at his self-esteem. He fought, both against the pain and the idleness. He showed steely discipline in his physical therapy. Every morning, he got up at six thirty, ate breakfast with Giulietta and Vincenzo, and then left the house with the two of them. Same time, same place, just on crutches. When Vincenzo got onto his moped, Enzo went to Giovanni's shop with Giulietta. There was always something to be done, even if it didn't make them money. Workman's compensation was all well and good, but he couldn't possibly just sit around and do nothing.

On August 26, 1972, Enzo walked out of the house without his crutches for the first time. It was the day Giulietta's affair was nearly discovered.

42

Giovanni had just returned from his summer vacation on Salina in a generous frame of mind, and he went all out. The opening ceremony of the Olympic Summer Games was a huge event, one the entire world would be watching, and he decided it wasn't going to happen without the Marconis.

They put on their best outfits and took the subway—Enzo's subway—to the new stadium. The cars were full to bursting; as they rode, Enzo proudly explained how the signals in the tunnel worked and pointed out the place where they'd disarmed an aircraft bomb. People spilled out into the terminal station, which was all pale, exposed concrete, decorated in gray and red. They followed the crowd past the TV tower and to the stadium, whose pavilion roof glittered in the late-summer sun like a silvery spider's web. Giovanni wanted to photograph the entire family with his new camera, but he couldn't manage to fit both his loved ones and the enormous tower into the frame. Giulietta couldn't help thinking about how often she'd snuck out here when everything was still under construction, bringing yet another photo torn from the family album.

"Come on, we'll take the picture somewhere else," she called to her brother.

The flags of 122 nations waved above the stadium as the audience streamed inside. The atmosphere was cheerful and boisterous. Munich was like an old house where someone had thrown open the windows, with a fresh breeze wafting through every room. The locals heard unfamiliar languages and saw people from countries they'd only visited in their fantasies, and for one magical moment, they forgot the walls, visible and invisible, that divided the world into East and West, North and South.

Greece was the first country to march into the oval; then the other 121 nations followed in alphabetical order. Countries Vincenzo had never heard of. Afghanistan, Ghana, Uganda . . . Each brought its own music and dance. They played folk songs, not military marches. It seemed less like a competition, more like one big international symphony.

White doves flew over the stadium. USSR and USA, Cuba and Canada—all were received warmly. When the Italians came in, Enzo, Giulietta, and Vincenzo all sang along. Finally, the German hosts entered. This year, however, marked the first time that the Germans didn't have one joint team. West and East Germany were competing under separate flags. The federal eagle against the hammer and sickle. The hostesses wore sky blue, pale green, and yellow—joyful colors for joyful Games. Munich, once the epicenter of Nazism, applauded its visitors enthusiastically, intoxicated by the colors of the world and the sense they were finally showing them a new, friendlier face. Giulietta felt an exalted gratitude for the opportunity to experience this day where there were no foreigners, where all nations were equal and celebrated together in peace. A day when people were just people.

"Clara!"

Giulietta whipped her head around. She recognized his voice immediately. A girl of about four ran down the stairs between the rows. She was wearing a blue dress, white socks, and a ribbon in her hair. Her mother chased after her. A tall, attractive blonde. At the top of the stairs was Vincent. He startled when he saw Giulietta. Everything happened much too fast. The mother caught her daughter, who had been running toward an ice cream salesman standing on the stairs not ten feet from Giulietta.

"Mamma, I want an ice cream!"

Giulietta looked away instinctively. Enzo gave the girl a friendly smile. The mother bought her an ice cream. Giovanni recognized Marianne. Vincent's former secretary. He glanced at Giulietta. Both of them held their breath. The girl went back upstairs, holding her mother's hand. Giulietta waited for a minute that felt like an eternity; when she turned around again, Vincent's family had disappeared.

Giulietta remained sitting. Vincent would have done the same, she knew. He'd surely have gone back to his seat, sat down beside his wife and child, and taken a lick of the ice cream Clara held out to him with a smile. She forced herself to keep staring at the parade, to resist glancing over her shoulder to scan the rows for him. There were eighty thousand people there, including the one who was closer to her than any other—yet who lived in another world.

Every day after school, Vincenzo came to Giovanni's shop to watch the Olympics live on television. He was most impressed by the swimming events—for the first time ever, the victor would be determined by an electronic judge, not a human one. When Larsson, the Swede, and McKee, the American, hit the end of the lane at the same time, the computer reported a difference of two thousandths of a second: 4:31.981 for Larsson, 4:31.983 for McKee, who stared at the electronic table in disbelief. Vincenzo calculated based on the distance traveled: the Swede had been 3.1 millimeters ahead. He remembered that day for a long time. It was the day when he realized how thin, how nearly invisible, the line separating winners and losers could be: 3.1 millimeters.

The line separating celebration from disaster was even thinner.

On the morning of September 5, it was all over the news: at 4:30 a.m., a Black September commando had invaded the Olympic Village and taken a group of Israeli athletes hostage.

The Games went on as scheduled all morning.

Vincenzo switched on the TV when he came into the shop for lunch. The cameras showed a masked man standing on a balcony with an AK-47. How had they managed to kidnap eleven top athletes with the entire world watching? But what really interested Vincenzo, even more than the "how," was the question of what would drive anyone to threaten other people's lives in the middle of a peaceful international event.

"Why are they doing that?" he asked Giovanni.

"They lost their homeland."

"Why?"

"Because the Jews went to Palestine."

"Why?"

"Because they were persecuted in Europe."

"So, the Jews lost their homeland, too?"

"Yeah, a few times."

"And now the Palestinians are coming to Europe?"

"Exactly. Nobody stays at home."

That night, the hostage situation ended in a bloody catastrophe; all the hostages died in a chaotic hail of bullets on the Fürstenfeldbruck airfield. The entire city was in shock. The hosts had failed to protect their guests. The most wonderful Olympic Games of all time turned into a dark stain on Munich's reputation. The rows in the stadium had once gleamed in every hue of the rainbow, but now everyone wore black. Beethoven's *Eroica* rang out instead of festive folk songs.

At Giovanni's shop, the usually lively guest workers sat staring at the television in silence. The ones from Arab countries knew dark times were likely ahead for them in Germany, even though they hadn't had anything to do with the incident. Unlike the Italians, who enjoyed a more secure status than other immigrants, the non-Europeans were always at risk of losing their visas. Some of them would soon be deported and return to their countries of origin, mostly dictatorships from which their years of exile had left them estranged. *Nobody stays at home.*

Around this time, Giulietta's diary entries grew shorter, drier, and increasingly hopeless. She went on seeing Vincent in secret as before, but she was less and less optimistic about their future. Her notes were mixed with newspaper clippings that painted a bleak picture. Public sentiment was turning not only against Arabs, but European foreigners as well. The steady economic growth that had begun in the 1950s slowed, until in 1973, it came to a ghastly stop.

Enzo had begun looking for work the minute he was off crutches. Giulietta typed his applications. She was trapped: as long as she was supporting the family on her own, she couldn't leave Enzo. She silently prayed things would get better. But nobody wanted to hire Enzo. The first rejections were due to his physical limitations—broken vertebrae meant his days of jackhammering underground were over. Enzo could have applied for disability benefits, but he was too proud. So, he went to a doctor and asked for a medical certification that he was completely healthy. But even then, he had no luck. The subway was finished; the city had spent an enormous amount of money on the Olympics; the economy was weakening. Enzo tried for less-physical jobs as a mechanic, and eventually even reapplied at the wholesale market, but none of his interviews went anywhere.

"See," Vincenzo said. "You should have learned more German."

"Language isn't the problem! I can repair engines anywhere—even in China!"

"Quit arguing, both of you," Giulietta exclaimed.

"It's not me," Enzo said. "Look at the others. Are they having any luck?"

And he was right: even Germans were starting to worry about job security. Back in the 1960s, when a guy had lost his job, he'd simply shrugged—he knew he'd find something else immediately. There'd been a surplus of jobs. But now, something was shifting, to everyone's surprise. An autumnal hangover settled over the country. As the revolutionaries of '68 came to the sobering realization that their ideals had shattered in the face of reality, workers suddenly felt replaceable. Had capitalism won?

But it was more than that. If 1955 was the year Germany had opened its borders to other Europeans, 1973 was the year Europe realized it was dependent on the rest of the world. And yet again, everything was about cars.

It started with the Yom Kippur War, a conflict that Giulietta, Enzo, and Vincenzo weren't involved in, yet whose consequences they still suffered. It took place at the eastern end of the Mediterranean. In order to get the US to stop supporting Israel, Arab countries restricted their oil output, making the world economy's jet-black circulatory system grind to a halt. Gas doubled in price almost overnight.

On November 25, 1973, Giulietta, Giovanni, Enzo, and Vincenzo took a walk down the empty highway toward Italy. It was a Sunday, and only bikers and pedestrians were allowed on the street, creating a strange atmosphere somewhere between carnival and apocalypse. A defiant Porsche driver raced past them, followed by cops in a pair of hopelessly underpowered VW Beetles.

"The future belongs to electric cars," Vincenzo said.

"Bah," Enzo replied. "Wars come and go. Soon the oil will be flowing again."

The German government responded to the oil crisis with an announcement that shocked the guest workers: they were stopping the hiring program, closing their borders to foreign job-seekers. They shuttered their recruitment offices in Southern Europe, Turkey, and Northern Africa. It was the end of an era. Fourteen million people had come to West Germany as guest workers since 1955. Many had gone back home as planned. But three million had stayed.

Giulietta served espresso in the shop as they watched Willy Brandt on TV. Vincenzo, Giovanni, Enzo, and their friends from the wholesale market: Yorgos, Mustafa, Alema. Wordlessly, they smoked their cheap cigarettes under the fluorescent lights. The front window was fogged, and it was cold in the room, because the oil heater was off.

"However," the chancellor was saying, "it has become necessary for us to give careful consideration to the point at which our society's capacity for accommodation is exhausted, and determine when social responsibility and common sense dictate that the process be halted."

In other words, the "guests" were no longer welcome.

"Is there work in Turkey?" Enzo asked Mustafa.

The man shook his head. "Bullshit Turkey." He was Kurdish, and he saw no future in his homeland, neither for himself nor for his wife and two children still living there.

Likewise, Yorgos couldn't go back to Athens—he'd fled the military dictatorship.

"If we leave now," Enzo murmured thoughtfully, "the Germans won't let us back in."

"Get wife and children here," Yorgos told Mustafa. "Before is too late. And you also, Giovanni."

Vincenzo watched the adults in silence. *Nobody stays at home,* he thought.

That same evening, Giovanni called Rosaria on Salina. They argued for hours about who would have to give in, who would have to leave the place they considered home. At midnight, Giovanni came to Giulietta's. Vincenzo was still awake, sitting with his mother at the table and helping her formulate a cover letter for Enzo. The heat was off; they were wearing thick woolen sweaters. For the first time in his life, Vincenzo saw his uncle weeping. Giovanni's inexhaustible reserve of good cheer had run out.

"Move in with us, Giovanni," Giulietta said. "We need to sublet one of the rooms anyway. Then you can save the rent on your apartment."

"Thanks, but—no."

"She's not going to come, Giovanni."

"If I move out of that place now, that means it was all for nothing. No, Giulietta, no. I'd rather eat *pasta e fagioli* for weeks than give up our home. She'll come back one day, and the children will go to school here. She's as stubborn as a Sicilian donkey, but so am I. I'll wait until that damn island sinks into the sea!"

After months of rejections, with the country turning against him, Enzo started letting himself go. He never complained, but he stopped getting up early and spent the cold winter days in the apartment by the radio. It was the winter where "Angie" played everywhere they went. Even the Rolling Stones had grown melancholy.

Vincenzo brought home a brilliant report card that semester. His star alone was rapidly ascending. He even invited friends over: nice German boys who glanced around the apartment, looking slightly intimidated, and sometimes girls who secretly made eyes at him. Giulietta was delighted that he was finally meeting people. She'd been afraid that her two men—Vincenzo was no longer a boy, after all—would grow so far apart that the gap could never be bridged, but to her surprise, their relationship improved. Vincenzo helped Enzo however he could and spared him the shrewd commentary. They worked on Vincenzo's Vespa in the yard together, and occasionally even went for a walk in the snow. It almost seemed that Vincenzo was attempting to support the weakened Enzo by acknowledging him as his father. And Enzo was grateful to Vincenzo for not taking advantage of his weakness.

"I finally have my son back," he said once to Giulietta as they were getting ready for bed.

She wondered how it had happened, and then she understood: Vincenzo sympathized with his father because he finally saw himself in Enzo. Not the gifted college-prep student, but the boy he'd been not long ago, the one who couldn't find his footing in this country.

For Giulietta, traveling to meet Vincent felt more than ever like entering a different world. He worried about the economy, of course, but not about his own job. Quite the opposite, in fact: he'd been promoted to technical director. When the company moved to its new headquarters, right beside the Olympic stadium, he'd gotten a fancy new office on the nineteenth floor with a view of the Alps. In his world, wishes came true. Giulietta wondered why he still bothered to see her at all.

"You don't need me," she said in the silence of the hotel room. "You have everything."

"I need you."

"For what? All I do is tell you about my problems. That's what you have a wife for, not a lover."

"You're not a lover. You're my Giulietta."

"I'm not the same person anymore. I feel like I've aged a decade this year." She turned away from him, secretly glad they only ever saw each other in the semidarkness of the room, where she could pretend to be younger.

He turned her face to his and gazed at her openly.

"So what? I'm getting older, too. And growing old together is nice."

"Vincent, I may have to go back to Italy."

He gave a start. "Why?"

"This country doesn't want us anymore. Enzo is nobody here. Back home, at Iso, they always appreciated him. We're running out of money. If he doesn't find something soon, he's going back."

"And Vincenzo?"

"He can finish high school in Italy."

"What do you want?"

"I don't know anymore." She buried her face in his shoulder.

Desperate and insatiable, they made love.

43

In February 1974, Enzo took the night train to Milan. From Stazione Centrale the next morning, he rode the tram to Bresso, to the Iso factory. The sun barely penetrated the morning fog, but it did his soul good to be surrounded by his native language again. The Milan dialect, which he'd found so cold and smug when he first arrived from the South, now felt like a refreshing dip in the sea. He was home. If Iso would give him back his old job, he wouldn't hesitate to end his German adventure. And Giulietta wouldn't be able to hold out any longer. She'd finally have to admit that her fashion design dreams would remain dreams, even in Germany.

As Enzo disembarked and breathed in Bresso's familiar suburban air—coal ovens, fog, the scent of freshly ground coffee—his heart grew ever lighter. He strode through the factory gate. And stopped. The lot outside the hall, where the employees' countless *motorini* had once parked, was practically empty. It was nine o'clock in the morning; the early shift ought to have been well underway. Enzo heard birds chirping, a sound he'd never heard here before. No noise came from the assembly hall, no hammering, no rattling, no hissing. It was eerily still.

He opened the large metal door and entered the hall. Cloudy morning light shone through the large windows. There wasn't a soul in sight. Two chassis with motors and transmissions sat on the assembly line. Without bodies. Screws littered the ground, along with boxes, tools, an empty coffee cup. Before, everything here had been spic and span.

"Enzo!"

Pierluigi's voice echoed through the hall. His old friend from the assembly line. He emerged from the glass-front foreman's office. "What are you doing here?"

Enzo embraced him warmly. His friend had put on weight.

"What's going on here?"

"Didn't you hear?"

"I heard you were having difficulties, yes, but—"

"Difficulties? It's a disaster."

"But what happened? The new models, the Fidia, the Lele, those are good cars!"

"Very good, in fact. *Guarda che bella*, metallic blue with white leather!" Pierluigi gestured to a freshly assembled Iso Fidia. The majestic sedan was larger and faster than a Mercedes S-Class. "The four fastest seats in the world. Even John Lennon has one. Do you know how many we sold last year?"

Enzo shook his head.

"Twenty."

"But I thought you found that investor from New York?"

"Oh, stop! He ruined the company. He wants to bring in American management! Can you imagine? *Porca miseria!* The man knows cars about as well as a nun knows the Kama Sutra!"

Enzo was bewildered.

"We were a family, Enzo! But in the end, we were just too small. You don't need to build the best cars anymore—only the most cars. All that's left are the mass producers." Pierluigi shrugged in resignation. "Nowadays, who can still afford a car that uses as much gas as an ocean liner? At these prices? John Lennon, he's got the money, but take a look around. Sports cars are just gathering dust in display windows. The oil crisis destroyed us."

Enzo was speechless. They could never have afforded these cars, he and Pierluigi and their friends. But building them had filled their hearts with pride.

"The golden age of the Granturismo is over," Pierluigi declared, picking up a screw from the floor. "Such a shame. In a couple of years, our streets will be packed with sterile compact cars from Asia."

Enzo approached the sedan. A daring, confident design. He ran his fingers across the gleaming logo on the radiator, the mythical griffin, the Rivolta family crest.

"Why did you come, Enzo?" Pierluigi asked.

"No particular reason."

"How long are you staying?"

"Not long."

Soon after Enzo's return to Munich, Vincenzo came to the shop one day after school. Giulietta was in the back room, hemming a pair of pants. Vincenzo dropped his backpack.

"Have you eaten?" Giulietta asked without looking up.

"Mamma, I'm quitting school."

Startled, Giulietta removed her foot from the sewing machine pedal.

"I'm going to get a job. I don't need a diploma—tenth grade is enough for an apprenticeship."

"What are you talking about? You wanted to go to college!"

"And you wanted to become Coco Chanel."

He felt bad immediately. He went to her and laid a hand on her shoulder.

"Mamma, we can't all live on your patching clothes. You've always been there for me. Now, it's my turn."

Giulietta felt ashamed. Should she have kept the gravity of their financial situation from him? But how? He'd always seen through everything.

"You've only got one more year before you graduate!"

"Mamma, you started working when you were eighteen, too."

"But I wanted you to have it better than I did!"

She blamed herself the way she always had, wishing she could have offered him every opportunity.

"I'm bored with school anyway," Vincenzo said, guessing at his mother's thoughts. "I'm going to go see Papà and—"

"Stay here! You're going to finish school!"

The sharp tone surprised even her. She'd thought of Vincent, of course. He would never accept this.

"I don't want to see you sad, Mamma."

Giulietta stood up. "Vincenzo, until you're twenty-one, I decide for you. And I'm not sad because I have to make money. If you want to make me happy, go to college. Do you know what the greatest sin is? Wasted talent!"

She had tears in her eyes. Vincenzo gave her a kiss.

"Thank you for everything you've done for me. Now, I'm going to start paying you back."

He turned around decisively and left the shop. Giulietta couldn't stop him. It hurt her soul. Parents were supposed to provide for their children, not the other way around. At the same time, she couldn't deny feeling a certain degree of pride: her baby was all grown up.

She told Vincent as they were lying in bed.

"Impossible," he said as though shooting the word out of a pistol.

"He's made up his mind, Vincent. I can't stop him. But maybe I can at least convince him to learn a trade. If he could come work for you and—"

"Out of the question." Vincent got up.

"Then what should I do?"

"Come to my office tomorrow."

"With Vincenzo?"

"No. With Enzo."

Giulietta gave him a distressed look.

"I'm going to get Enzo a job."

"But—"

"And Vincenzo is going to college."

She was shocked at his generosity, but there was no way she could accept his offer.

Vincent read her thoughts.

"You don't have to say anything," he told her.

"But—we already sent an application once before, last year, and BMW turned him down. I mean, since the accident, Enzo—he can't work as well as he used to."

"Don't worry about it. I'll talk to the personnel director. He owes me a favor."

She hesitated.

He took her hand and squeezed it. "Do you want our child to have a future?"

Wind blew over the terrace outside BMW headquarters. It was one of those early March days with a hint of spring in the air. The trees were still bare, but the skies were filled with the twittering of migratory birds rather than the caws of winter crows. Flags fluttered outside the futuristic building beside the Olympic

Park. It had been constructed at the same time as the stadium, four silver towers of concrete, steel, and glass in the form of four cylinders. Faith in the future of the automobile—in a future *through* the automobile—in architectural form.

Enzo wore his suit. Giulietta had chosen a conservative blue outfit, no jewelry, flat shoes. She hoped Enzo wouldn't notice that her heart was in her throat. She'd told Enzo that she'd bumped into Vincent, the *ingegnere della Isetta*, while she was out shopping.

"He was just a boy in Milan," Enzo said.

"And now he's the *direttore tecnico*."

As Giulietta strode toward the entrance, Enzo swept his gaze slowly across the parked BMWs and then stopped.

"An Italian designed this car body. Michelotti. And this one is by Bertone."

"Come on, Enzo!"

Enzo refused to hurry and walked quietly to the entrance. She wasn't sure what was going on in his mind. He'd accepted the invitation silently, almost too easily. Swallowed his pride. That a man like him needed his wife to find him work.

The foyer looked like the set of a space movie filmed by Le Corbusier. Enzo walked indifferently to the sweeping reception desk, where a young woman in a plaid suit was standing. Oversized collar, blouse, scarf.

"Good morning. How can I help you?"

"Marconi, Enzo."

"Do you have an appointment?"

Giulietta went to help him, but he refused to let her steal his thunder. "Yes. With Dottore Schlewitz."

"Mr. and Mrs. Marconi are here."

Vincent's secretary led them into his office. *Another pretty secretary,* Giulietta thought. This one was young enough to be his daughter. Vincent got up from behind his desk near the window and came over to greet them. Seeing him here gave Giulietta a feeling of trepidation—he seemed so severe in his professional world, so full of authority. The office intimidated her. More than that, though, it was the little things she spotted even before he shook their hands: the model Isetta on the shelf. His gray flannel three-piece suit. The picture frame on the desk, which she could only see the back of. She didn't belong here, or at least her daytime self didn't, and Enzo was even more out of place. Vincent greeted her very formally, excessively so, she thought. He was better at hiding his anxiety than she was. Then he held out a hand to Enzo.

"I'm glad you made time to come out. Please, sit. Coffee?"

Giulietta nodded. Vincent led them to the green corduroy sofa set and called out to his secretary to bring coffee. Then he sat down with them.

"I was so sad to hear that the Iso factories had been sold. What a loss. I'm still driving mine. Fantastic car."

Enzo was silent. Tensely, Giulietta withdrew the folder with Enzo's résumé and cover letter from her bag. She could sense Vincent's confusion. Enzo didn't seem intimidated. He simply sat there and took the folder Giulietta held out to him.

"It's not easy for niche manufacturers in this day and age," Vincent said. "The fact that we're expanding despite the oil crisis is partly thanks to our foreign workers." He talked and talked, filling Enzo's awkward silence. "We understood how to use that potential. We offer interpreters right here in the factory, language courses, a company newsletter in several languages—we even have foreign foremen and master craftsmen now."

Enzo didn't say anything. The secretary came in and set three cups on the table. Espresso, not drip coffee.

"A little quirk of mine, from my time in Italy," Vincent said, and smiled.

Giulietta and Vincent drank their coffee. Enzo left his on the table. Giulietta grew uncomfortable. It felt like Vincent was applying for a job with Enzo rather than the other way around.

"Very good coffee," she said.

"So, you applied to BMW once before?" Vincent asked.

"Yes."

"We brought the rejection letter." Giulietta took the folder from Enzo's hand and found the letter.

"I've told our personnel director about what high-level work you did at Iso. When they hear the word 'handcrafted'—everything here is moving toward automation, you know."

Enzo watched him. Or did it just feel that way to Giulietta? She could barely take it. She never should have brought the two men together, she thought. They didn't belong in the same room. It was wrong to mix fantasy and reality—too disorienting. Too hard to tell what was real and what wasn't.

Vincent accepted the letter without reading it. Giulietta handed him Enzo's letters of recommendation as well.

"We've got the new plant in Dingolfing," Vincent said, barely glancing at the letters. "We can offer you a position in the assembly department there. For one year to start."

Giulietta smiled at Enzo in relief. He remained calm but didn't look pleased.

"It's ninety minutes from here," Vincent said. "By commuter train. There's a hostel for factory personnel as well, of course."

Vincent gave him a questioning look.

Giulietta could hardly stand the silence.

"No, thank you," Enzo said.

Giulietta's breath caught in her throat.

"Well, if you'd prefer to work in Munich—" Vincent began.

"No. I'm finished. Go back to Italy."

"Enzo! Che dici?"

Enzo got up and held out a hand to the thunderstruck Vincent.

"Goodbye, Dottore. *Piacere.*" He turned to Giulietta. "Come on; we're leaving."

She couldn't move for a moment, but then she jumped up. Shot Vincent a look indicating for him to wait. But Enzo politely bade the secretary farewell.

"Enzo, what's the matter with you? Do you have a job offer in Italy?"

The elevator doors closed. Enzo pressed the first-floor button.

"No."

"Why don't you want the job? If you don't want to go to Dingolfing, I'm sure he has something in Munich. We should be grateful that there's anything available at all!"

Enzo was silent.

"Why did you bother coming here?"

Enzo gazed at her for a long moment as the elevator glided quietly down.

"I just wanted to see him."

The elevator stopped. Her stomach twisted in knots.

"He doesn't even look that much like Vincenzo."

The door opened. Enzo went out to the foyer. Giulietta remained frozen in the elevator.

Outside in the parking lot, she ran after him. Shaken, she took his arm. "Enzo! What are you talking about?"

He spun around, looking determined. "Don't lie to me anymore, Giulietta." He gazed straight into her eyes.

Now Giulietta could see that he was quivering with rage and humiliation. How could he have known?

"I went to the doctor. In Milan. Back when you couldn't get pregnant." She was baffled.

"The doctor said it was because of me."

"What? Why didn't you ever tell me—"

"Because I—" He struggled to compose himself. "Because then I would have destroyed the only family that I could ever have."

Giulietta grew light-headed. Everything was spinning. She floundered for something to hold on to. Out of the corner of her eye, she saw Vincent come out the front entrance. He stopped and stared in their direction as Enzo grasped her arm firmly.

"I only ask one thing," Enzo said. "That you end it. For good."

The following days were hell for Giulietta. When something carefully hidden is suddenly wrenched into the light of day, the shame becomes an open wound. She felt naked. She was mute around Vincenzo, who didn't understand what was the matter with her. They ate at the dinner table in silence, with Enzo acting like nothing was wrong. He chatted about the weather, the news, Giulietta's birthday that weekend. She wished he would shout at her, accuse her, make a scene, because only then could she have countered his attacks, finally given voice to the unsaid. Unjust though it would have been, she longed desperately for an explosion that would incinerate everything. But Enzo never gave her the chance. And Giulietta would have severed her own tongue before allowing Vincenzo to find out. He would never forgive her for having lied to him all his life. She couldn't lose him.

Giulietta called Vincent, dialing his office number with quivering fingers from a phone booth at the wholesale market.

"He knows everything," she said, and heard Vincent gasp at the other end of the line. "I didn't tell him."

"How did he find out? And when?"

"I don't know. He won't say."

"And Vincenzo?"

He's thinking of his son, she thought, *not of me.*

"No."

"I'll be there for you both. I'll take care of Vincenzo. Promise."

At first, Giulietta didn't understand what he meant. He'd been taking care of Vincenzo for a long time already.

"I'll get a divorce if you want me to," he said. "But you have to have the courage to do the same."

Giulietta felt her knees shaking. "The entire family is coming over for my birthday on Friday. What do I tell them?"

"The truth."

44

Giulietta couldn't do it. Not before her birthday. A March windstorm swept through Munich, moody and surreal in its warmth, washing winter from the world. On Friday morning, she went to the hairdresser, and while the family waited for her at the shop—Giovanni had baked a cake himself—she secretly took a detour to see Vincent. He was waiting in the nearly empty parking lot outside BMW headquarters. The flags flapped wildly in the wind; twigs were strewn across the ground. Giulietta drew her scarf more tightly around her neck. She was restless, wishing she could have met him on a different day, not now when everyone was waiting for her. But he'd asked to see her today specifically. He seemed tense, but his face lit up when he saw her.

"I wanted to show you something. Won't take long."

"I have to get going soon."

"It's a present. Close your eyes."

Impatiently, she covered them with one hand. Vincent led her a few paces through the lot. It felt like an eternity. She peeked through her fingers. Sunlight blinded her.

"Now, open them!"

Giulietta took her hand away from her face. She didn't understand what he was holding at first. Something metallic glinted in the sunlight. She hoped it wasn't jewelry—a bracelet or a ring she could only wear in secret. He smiled and stepped to the side. And then she saw it. Behind him. A fiery-red convertible, glowing among the dark-gray sedans. An Alfa Romeo. Sensuous curves, gleaming chrome—1950s lines, from back when cars weren't merely smooth and practical, when they'd still had a face.

"Happy birthday."

He held out the key. It took her a moment to comprehend.

"No, Vincent, you're insane!"

He led her to the car. The black top was open; the dashboard glittered in the sun. Red lacquer, black leather.

"Look what it says there." He pointed to the beautiful three-spoke steering wheel. The Milan city crest, the snake and the cross, gleamed golden on the Bakelite hub, and in the semicircle above it, in fine letters, it said, "Giulietta."

It was the name of the car.

"It's a 1955," Vincent said.

The year of Vincenzo's birth.

He smiled.

"*Oddio*, Vincent, this is outrageous."

Her face flushed red. He pointed to an envelope sitting on the dashboard. She took it. Her hands were shaking. She opened it and withdrew two tickets. Opera tickets. *The Magic Flute*. La Fenice. Venice.

"Are you crazy?"

"We always wanted to go to Venice. The only crazy thing is to dream about it for this long without doing it."

She looked at the date. Tomorrow evening.

"Vincent, what am I—how am I supposed to tell them?"

"I told Marianne yesterday."

Giulietta was shocked.

"It's best for everyone."

Her head spun with fear. Every time she'd finally been about to do it, something had always happened. Like Enzo's accident. She was superstitious, even now; it was too deeply ingrained. Her mother. Sicily. Her entire life, which had confirmed over and over again that you could never escape yourself.

Vincent embraced her. His scent reminded her of the thing she had always loved about him: that he continually belied those accursed old beliefs about the impossibility of eluding fate. He proved it with his words, with his life.

She threw her arms around his neck, held him tight, and kissed him, breathless, confused, and overflowing with love. "I want to live with you, Vincent!"

"I want you, Giulietta. All or nothing." He gazed deeply into her eyes. She nodded.

"Tomorrow morning at seven o'clock," he said. "Here at the car."

Everyone was there. Giovanni had bedecked the shop with garlands. Rosaria, who was visiting, had brought the best Malvasia wine from Salina. Vincenzo and Enzo gave her a modern orange radio alarm clock. Everyone hugged her; everyone toasted her happiness. Wrapped in a fog, all Giulietta heard were the bells of the church nearby.

That night, as she lay beside the sleeping Enzo, she stared at the illuminated white numbers on the new clock, watching them flip down one by one. Zero-one-five-eight, zero-one-five-nine, zero-two-zero-zero. Like autumn leaves. Life ticked by, and nothing ever came back. Eventually, she got out of bed and tiptoed into the kitchen, where she sat down at the table and wrote in her diary. After an hour, she made herself a coffee. Nobody heard her. And then, all at once, everything was perfectly easy. Alarmingly simple, as though another will had taken hold of her. She went into the bathroom, packed the essentials into a toiletry bag, fetched two dresses from the closet—one light spring dress and one evening dress—plus shoes, stockings, and underthings. One small suitcase—she didn't want to take more than that. Last, she slipped her diary into her purse.

From the bedroom door, she cast one final look at Enzo. It was a look without regret, but full of sadness that she hadn't been able to give him what he needed. Then she quietly opened the door to Vincenzo's room, bent over, and kissed him on the forehead. His skin was warm; his breathing was even. Her heart burst with tenderness.

Giulietta eased the apartment door shut and crept down the stairs, keeping close to the edge so that the old wood wouldn't creak, before walking past her mailbox and opening the front door of the building. It was still dark; the air was cold and smelled of approaching April. Then she took off running as fast as she could.

They would see the sun rise over the Autobahn.

45

Warm wind in my hair. The window half-open, the sun above the hills, the cypresses. We were passing Florence. I set the diary aside and looked at Vincenzo.

"Didn't she leave anything? No explanation? No goodbye note?"

Vincenzo shook his head, eyes forward. Even today, he still didn't understand.

"What does she say next? Read it!"

I turned the page. The next one was blank. So were the rest. "That's it. The diary stops there."

I showed him the white pages. He looked away. Stared out at the road ahead.

"What happened then?" I asked.

"I don't know."

"What do you mean, you don't know?"

"I don't know, goddammit!"

He smacked the steering wheel. I jumped.

We were silent for a while. Then he opened the glove compartment and nervously fumbled out a couple of cassettes. Rummaged through them, chucked one on the floor, and put the other in the cassette player. I'd heard the song before, though I wasn't sure when and where. It moved me in a strange way. When I looked back at Vincenzo, I saw that he had tears in his eyes.

"'Time in a Bottle.' The single came out right about then. I listened to it over and over. Jim Croce, you know him?"

I shook my head.

"Cro-ce. Like Christ's cross. Italian parents."

I nodded, not following.

"He wrote it for his son. His wife tells him she's pregnant, and he writes this song. Jim Croce is twenty-eight or so, truck driver, not very successful as a musician. Nobody wants to release the song, and then all at once, he's famous. He's on the charts, but with a different song, not a sad one like this. Everything's going great, and then he's flying to a concert and the plane crashes. Nobody knows why—the sky's clear, the plane's okay, but they crash into the trees. He was thirty. And—" His voice broke.

I got a queasy feeling in my stomach. Slowly, I realized what he wanted to tell me but couldn't. Because every time he looked at me, he saw her as well.

PART 3

46

Giulietta never arrived in Venice. And she never returned. But she must have been happy in those last few hours of her life.

A radiant March day, a breeze over the Alps, the air smelling of flowers and melting snow. The top was down; Giulietta was behind the wheel. Vincent confirmed it for the police later. The car hadn't made any unusual noises. The Alfa Romeo had been nineteen years old, but perfectly maintained, a collector's vehicle with barely any miles on it.

The engine purred like clockwork as they wound their way up the Brenner Pass. They wanted to take the old road—not the newly built tunnel but the exact route he'd taken to Italy twenty years before. Giulietta leaned into the curves energetically, passed a Beetle, relished the Alfa Romeo's throaty growl. Only Italian cars made that sound: small cubic capacity, big opera. It was colder up here; there was still snow on the rocks, melting in the spring sun. Glittering rivulets ran down the asphalt.

When they got to the top, muffled in warm hats and scarves, they kept going without a break at the rest stop, onward toward the South. The light changed as though someone had replaced a bulb. Everything grew brighter, airier, more transparent. A light for all eternity. Vincent snapped a photo of Giulietta without knowing it would be the last one ever taken. Her dark curls peeked out from beneath the colorful head scarf and danced in the wind, her laughter, the sun on her skin, a moment of complete joy. There are only a few moments in life when one feels both free and safe. It's normally one or the other. Or neither. But this was a moment she wished would never end.

There were no witnesses to what happened on the pass, just that one photo, which Vincent later showed in court. As though her happy smile could prove his innocence. She hadn't missed the curve, he said, no, she'd braked; he'd heard it, the clack of the pedal against the metal, an unusual sound because the brake normally never touched the floor—the Alfa Romeo Giulietta had good brakes. Then Giulietta's scream, the sudden screech of steel against the guardrail, which held, though it was rusty and badly anchored; the car skidded along it for several feet, but the curve was too narrow. The convertible tipped to one side and rolled over the barrier, and if Vincent had been buckled in like Giulietta was, he would have tumbled over the edge along with her.

He was thrown from the car, he explained to the judge. A blessing in disguise. He managed to grab hold of a bush, which saved his life. He saw the red convertible career over the steep slope, and then it was gone. Suddenly there was no noise at all, just the wind above the rock ledge. The silence was the truly frightening thing, because beyond the ledge lay the abyss. Vincent knew that Giulietta was plummeting into that abyss, fully conscious, and there was nothing he could do to break her fall.

Vincenzo didn't learn those details until much later, as he was sitting in court, listening to Vincent's testimony. The day of her death, he knew nothing about any of it. He was merely surprised that his mother wasn't awake to make him breakfast like always, but he assumed she'd worked all night, and he didn't want to wake her. It wasn't until he returned home after school that he sensed something was wrong. Enzo asked whether he knew where his mother was. He'd already called Giovanni and her friends, but nobody had any idea.

By late afternoon, Giovanni grew uneasy as well. Vincenzo suggested they go to the police, but Enzo didn't want to. Vincenzo didn't understand why. Only later did he realize that it wasn't out of the usual distrust the foreigners had for Germans in uniform—it was out of embarrassment at going public with his dishonor. Apparently, he already suspected the truth.

But then everything became far, far worse.

Enzo ordered Vincenzo to stay home, then disappeared without saying where he was going. When he returned that night, he was as pale as a ghost.

"What happened?"

Enzo could only shake his head.

"What happened, Papà?"

Enzo went to Vincenzo and embraced him. His large hands gripped him so tightly that it alarmed Vincenzo. His father's powerful body was shaking like a terrified child's. Enzo burst into tears.

"She was in an accident," he said.

Not a word about Vincent.

Vincenzo felt like he'd been punched in the stomach. Numbness settled over him instantly, so that he registered the world from a distance, without feeling anything. Giulietta had been the sun that everyone revolved around. A universe without her was inconceivable.

The pathology lab, where Enzo had to identify her body. Enzo's protective hand covering Vincenzo's eyes so he wouldn't see his mother's mangled features. The doctor looking away. It all passed Vincenzo by like some terrible movie he wasn't in. Vincent's name never came up once, or not that he knew of. The only words that pulsed through his mind were "car accident."

If not for the question of guilt, it would have remained just that, an accident. But Vincent, in his helpless, furious bewilderment, set in motion an avalanche that would destroy the rest of Vincenzo's family as well. He couldn't believe what had happened, and he told the police right there on the scene that Giulietta could not have possibly been responsible for the accident. It must have been a problem with the car. A technical flaw. He gave them the name of the man he had bought the Alfa from. Stammered about negligence, about responsibility and accountability. As if, by finding someone to blame, he could somehow make things right again.

After two paramedics had loaded Giulietta's disfigured corpse into an ambulance to bring it to Munich, Vincent had the wrecked car transported there as well, to a mechanic he trusted. He wanted to prove that Giulietta had been innocent. And that he had as well. They checked the brakes meticulously: cylinders, hoses, drums, everything. Apparently, it wasn't the seller's fault, either. The brakes were in perfect working order. They were already packing up their tools when Vincent himself came over in an oil-smeared apron, pointing to the one thing they'd overlooked.

It was a thin brake hose, barely eight inches long. The hole in the rubber was clearly not from wear and tear—it was a clean, fresh cut made by a knife. Drop by drop, the brake fluid had trickled out of the hydraulic system beneath their feet as they drove up the Alps, until finally there'd been no pressure left in the brakes on the way down. Giulietta hadn't had a chance. Someone must have wanted them both dead. Someone who knew about the affair. Someone who knew about cars. Someone who was jealous. Someone who would rather see Giulietta dead than in the arms of another man.

The phone rang. Vincenzo answered it. Giovanni ordered him in a choked, trembling voice to come over immediately. The police were on their way to arrest his father, he said. Enzo came out of the kitchen into the hallway and asked who was calling.

"That's not true!" Vincenzo shrieked into the phone. "He had nothing to do with it!"

"Vincenzo, get over here right now!"

Enzo yanked the receiver out of his hand and listened to Giovanni. Vincenzo stared at his father in disbelief.

"Tell me it isn't true."

"Giovanni, are you crazy?" Enzo shouted into the phone.

The doorbell rang.

Over and over again.

Vincenzo was frozen in terror. Enzo silently gestured for him to answer.

Hesitantly, Vincenzo opened the door. Two policemen were standing there. Handcuffs and pistols on their belts.

"Good evening. Is Mr. Enzo Marconi at home?"

"No." Frightened, Vincenzo tried to push the door closed again, but the police held it open.

"Go away!" Vincenzo yelled.

Enzo stood in the apartment as though he had turned to stone. Vincenzo pressed his body desperately against the door.

"Help me, Papà!"

Enzo stared at the door like a condemned man waiting for his executioner. Somehow, Vincenzo managed to force it shut.

Enzo approached him slowly.

"Listen, my son . . ."

He took Vincenzo in his arms. Vincenzo shoved him away. The police banged against the door. Enzo held Vincenzo fast, forcing him to look him in the eye.

"Listen to me!"

"Assassino!" Vincenzo's fists flew out at Enzo. *"Assassino!"*

Enzo weathered the blows, not releasing his son.

Then the police kicked down the door and stormed into the apartment, guns drawn. They found Enzo and Vincenzo huddled on the carpet, locked in a desperate embrace.

47

Vincenzo carried his mother's coffin. Giovanni walked in front of him, the hard, black wood resting on his shoulder. The pallbearers on the other side were two older men from the village whom he didn't know. Taller than the others, he had to bend his knees slightly so the coffin wouldn't tip. Through his tears, he had only a blurry view of what went on around him.

He followed Giovanni's sluggish steps as though hypnotized, leather soles crunching on the asphalt, accompanied by the sounds of women whimpering and wailing behind him. Sounds he'd never heard before. It was as though their hearts had been torn from their chests. Rosaria's continuous sobbing, her mother's monotone prayers, and the shrill, almost insane screams of his grandmother, Concetta. Minutes felt like hours and seconds like minutes. The street never seemed to end; accompanied by the wind and the indifferent cries of the seagulls, they made their way, past the last few houses in the village, to the cemetery overlooking the sea. Clouds gathered above the island; brief glimpses of sunshine were followed by light showers, which they could see approaching from across the water. It was as though the heavens were weeping softly.

The white gravestones were weathered, with crooked crosses and Madonnas amid the loamy paths, their paint peeled away in the salty wind. He'd first visited this place with Carmela, as a thirteen-year-old, the night before Giovanni's wedding. It had been an adventure then, ghostly and romantic, the gravestones in the moonlight over the sea. Now, he was blinded by the much-too-bright light of day. He wished the sky would envelop him and hide his pain in darkness.

Giulietta wasn't getting one of those little shoebox graves, Giovanni had decided. Her grave would be on the side of the cemetery facing the sea, where it could be seen, he'd told the priest. The sea of their childhood, from which they'd been separated for so long.

"We come into the world empty-handed; we leave it empty-handed," the priest said. "And all that remains is the love we have sown in the hearts of those who were close to us."

No, Vincenzo thought. *What remains is a pain that no one can ever take away. What remains is what was left unsaid. What remains is a gaping wound.*

Giulietta's picture hung everywhere in Malfa. The death announcements were plastered in clusters—Giovanni had ordered more from the printer than the little town had walls. The black-and-white photo showed an enchanting young woman, as radiant as summer. But looking more closely, one saw a glimpse of unfathomable sadness even back then, as though her soul had always known. A life that ended before it really began.

Out on the piazza, the old people sat around talking about her, though hardly any of them had truly known her. If they knew anyone, it was her parents. And the ones who had distanced themselves from her father, the Godless Communist, back in the day, now whispered of a curse upon the Marconi family. After all, wasn't she a rebel like her father, one who'd rejected the laws that had held Sicilian society together since time immemorial?

Everyone remembered how she'd left her husband six years before, at Giovanni's wedding, and run off to Germany. A good man who had never done anything wrong, and now he was the only member of the family not at the funeral. In order to avoid a bigger scandal on the island, Giovanni had made his wife, his mother, and Vincenzo promise not to say anything about Enzo's arrest.

"It was an accident, understand? An accident!"

But no rumor, no matter how vague, could stay under wraps on Salina for long. Rumors were like vine pests, they said. They came across the ocean on the ships, from island to island, and eventually they spread everywhere.

Enzo's absence spoke volumes. It left a vacuum that soon filled with speculation, and to Vincenzo's horror, the very thing that was so inconceivable to him was obvious to the villagers, familiar from the old days. Adultery, violent death, and a husband absent from the funeral—they concluded even more quickly than the German police that Enzo had "punished" his disobedient wife. More horrifying still was that several of the old people saw the supposed murder not as a crime but as the justified restoration of family honor.

Soon, even Vincenzo caught himself thinking, How could she? A German! That wasn't just cheating; it was betrayal! Sure, Enzo was difficult, but hadn't he always been faithful? Hadn't he changed? Hadn't he stopped forbidding her from working and pursuing her *passione*?

Then again, had fashion really been her dream, or had she secretly aspired to something completely different? And hadn't it been hypocritical of her to decide they should all be a family again, but then start cheating on her husband? Why a German, of all people? Who was this guy, and how had he turned her head? Was it because Enzo was out of work? Shouldn't people stick even closer together in difficult times? Why hadn't her lover had the guts to come to him and Enzo after the accident? Why had he survived when Giulietta hadn't? Wouldn't it have been fairer if he'd been the one who died? If Vincenzo could see him now, he thought, he'd make sure that justice was done. An eye for an eye, a tooth for a tooth.

He was ashamed of these thoughts. How could he judge his mother? Didn't he have her to thank for everything? What did he know of her secret pain? So many times, he'd heard her weeping at night but never comforted her. Would that have kept her from leaving? Maybe he could have given her the support she hadn't found in Enzo.

But then, his sympathy turned to rage. He scolded her in his mind, using words he would have been mortified to hear spoken aloud. She had a right to do what she wanted, he told himself, but she'd had no right to lie to him. He was the person she'd taught that lying was wrong. How could she play happy family with him when she didn't believe it herself?

The gazes of the villagers bored straight through Vincenzo. Everyone expressed their sympathies, but beneath those flowery phrases, he sensed the poison of unspoken scandal: he was the son of a whore. And the son of a murderer.

That night, Vincenzo stood on the roof of the old house and gazed up at the stars. The wind had died down. Only then did he feel hungry. He hadn't eaten anything all day. He was cold. He thought about the things the priest had said at the gravesite. Helpless attempts to make sense of something senseless. A God who abandoned his creations with such indifference couldn't possibly be a God of love.

Giovanni climbed onto the roof and stood beside him.

"Why, Giovanni?"

They stared out at the pitch-black sea.

"I don't believe it. Papà loved her too much. He could never do that to her."

"Sometimes, people say 'I love you,'" Giovanni said, "but what they really mean is, 'I own you.' Like a person is a plot of land. But even the land doesn't belong to us. We serve it by cultivating it. Look at this, the house we're standing on. On paper, it belongs to Rosaria's mother. But these stones will outlive her. They'll outlive us all. We're here to safeguard the house for the next generation." Giovanni gazed at his nephew for a long time without speaking. "If Enzo couldn't have her, he didn't want the other guy to, either."

Vincenzo felt light-headed. "Did you know? That she wanted to leave us? For a German?"

Giovanni shook his head.

The sea was silent. In the distance, they could see the glow of Stromboli.

It was snowing in Munich. In the middle of April, daffodils in winter slush. Vincenzo shivered. He parked his Vespa outside the pastel-green police headquarters on Ettstraße. It was twilight; the bells of the Frauenkirche rang out for evening Mass. The doorman was eating liverwurst on a hard roll. Vincenzo despised him. Just because. Because he was a cop eating liverwurst on a hard roll.

The investigating officer had asked him to come in. On Good Friday! Vincenzo didn't know whether Enzo, who was still in custody, would be there. He'd made up his mind not to say anything. The empty hallways smelled like floor polish. Somewhere, ABBA's "Waterloo" played softly.

The officer smelled of cologne and sausage. His name was Detective Unglaub. His handshake was firm, somehow binding, but Vincenzo didn't like the look he was giving him, a mixture of sympathy and skepticism. Vincenzo preferred the skepticism to the sympathy. *He doesn't need to act like we know each other,* he thought. *He can save his pity for the kids in Africa.* Unglaub invited him into his office. Enzo wasn't there.

"I'm very sorry about what happened to your mother."

Vincenzo took the chair in front of the desk. He pulled a cigarette out of his pocket. Unglaub offered him a light, but Vincenzo lit it himself.

"I need to ask you a few questions."

Vincenzo was silent.

"Has your father ever been violent?"

"No."

"Has he threatened violence?"

"No."

"Was he jealous a lot?"

"Who gives a shit now? She's dead."

"Your father still denies committing the crime."

"What the hell does it matter what he says?"

"If I were you, I wouldn't take that tone in front of the judge."

Unglaub went to a cabinet to fetch a file, then pulled out a photo and set it on the desk in front of Vincenzo.

"Do you know this man?"

Vincenzo looked away immediately, as though the photograph itself were scandalous somehow. Then he looked again. It was the German who had given him the racetrack.

"Do you know him?"

Vincenzo shook his head, his mind spinning. Jesus, so it had been going on for that long!

The detective frowned. "He was in the car with your mother when the accident happened."

Vincenzo felt the blood throbbing in his temples.

"He gave a statement that the brake hose had been manipulated."

Unglaub studied his face. Vincenzo tried to keep it as neutral as possible.

"Let's see it. The brake hose."

The detective considered for a moment before taking another photo out of the file. It showed the twisted underbody of the Alfa Romeo. And in an enlarged view, the brake hose.

"Our laboratory investigation suggests that the brake line was cut with a sharp object. Likely a knife. Right there, that's a clean cut."

"That could happen in an accident."

"The cut is in an area that's otherwise undamaged. The car made impact headfirst."

Vincenzo felt sick.

"At the time of the accident, the brake fluid had already leaked out."

Unglaub took the photos from Vincenzo.

"I understand that you don't want to accuse your father. But he had a clear motive and—"

"Don't worry. When he gets out, I'll kill him."

He stubbed out his cigarette in Unglaub's engraved ashtray. "Oktoberfest 1973," it said.

"Where are my mother's things? Her clothes, her bag. I want them back."

"I can't return those until after the trial."

Vincenzo got up without a word and went to the door. The moment he put his hand on the doorknob, the detective called, "Mr. Marconi!"

His voice wasn't sharp. More confidential. Vincenzo turned.

"Wait just one moment, please."

The "please" struck Vincenzo as odd. He stayed where he was, his hand on the doorknob. Unglaub went to the cabinet and took out Giulietta's purse. Pain shot through Vincenzo's chest. The purse was intact, no blood on it. Unglaub set it on the desk and beckoned him over. Vincenzo hesitated. Unglaub removed something from the bag. A light-gray notebook with a cardboard cover.

"Your mother kept a diary. Did you know?"

Vincenzo went to the desk to retrieve the book. Unglaub held on to it for a moment. Looked him in the eye. As though to make sure Vincenzo could handle what he was about to see. Vincenzo wrenched the book from his hand and opened it. On the first page, sure enough, there was Giulietta's beautiful handwriting in blue ink, her name, her address, her sketches. Vincenzo's throat closed up. He shut the book. He didn't have the right. Unglaub gave him a searching look. He knew something. Vincenzo sat down and opened the book again. What he read then pulled the final rug from under him.

> Vincenzo's life is going to change without his knowing why. I'm lying to my husband, to my son, to my brother. I'm not doing it for Vincent. I'm doing it for Vincenzo.

Shocked, Vincenzo turned to stare at the detective, who had never taken his eyes off him as he read.

Vincenzo flew through the night. The cold sleet stung his face, but he didn't feel it. He knew only the feverish, furious pain in the depths of his soul, driving him out of his mind.

"Did you know?"

Vincenzo grabbed Giovanni by the collar. Giovanni's daily earnings, which he'd been taking out of the register, rained across the floor.

"No!"

"She always told you everything!"

"Vincenzo! There are things better left unsaid!"

"Stop lying to me!"

Erna Baumgartner stormed inside.

"Vincenzo! What are you doing?"

He ignored her.

"Go to the police, Giovanni," Vincenzo shouted with tears in his eyes. "Read her diary yourself!"

"What does that change? Does it bring your mother back?"

Vincenzo shoved Giovanni away. His back slammed into the wine shelf, sending bottles crashing to the floor. Erna shrieked.

"You're such a coward, Giovanni," Vincenzo hissed as Giovanni got to his feet. "You're lying to yourself!"

Erna took Vincenzo's arm kindly. "Vincenzo. I'm so sorry for your loss. If you need anything, no matter what—"

"Get out!"

"Vincenzo, this is my shop," Giovanni exclaimed, turning red. "Apologize to Erna this instant!"

"Out!" the boy roared.

Frightened, Erna stumbled backward through the door.

Vincenzo ran up the stairs of the old Schwabing apartment building and hammered on his former tutor's door. Grimm opened it, wearing striped pajamas. He appeared to be nursing the flu.

"Vincenzo? My word, you look—"

"Did you know?"

Grimm was alarmed at first. Then he understood. The truth flashed across his face before he could pretend otherwise. Vincenzo stood there, drenched, shaking.

"Why don't you come inside?"

In the background, Vincenzo heard Mrs. Grimm's voice.

"Did you know who my father was?"

Grimm hesitated. Then he said, "Yes."

A word like a kick in the stomach. Of course, Grimm had known. But having him say it to his face made the betrayal even worse. How pathetic the man seemed now, a guilty conscience in pajamas.

"Vincenzo, come in."

"You knew the whole time, and you sat there, babbling about truth and goodness and all that Humanist bullshit!"

Grimm's wife came to the door, unsettled and scared.

"What happened?"

"Maybe it would be best if we called your father," Grimm said.

"Why doesn't he have the balls to come see me?" Vincenzo's voice echoed through the stairwell. "Fucks my mother while I'm memorizing fucking Goethe!"

Grimm put a hand on his arm.

Vincenzo slapped it away.

"Liars! You're all a bunch of fucking liars!"

Vincenzo stormed down the stairs and ran outside into the sleet.

48

The cars racing past were from another era. The airstream, a slap in the face every time. I wasn't really here, parked on the shoulder of the Autostrada. I was in a different time, before I was born. Vincenzo had simply stopped driving, between two tunnels in the Apennine Mountains, and gotten out of the car. Now he was leaning against the rusted guardrail, smoking a cigarette. His exhausted, unshaven face in the midday sun. He suddenly seemed older. Thinner. Unexpectedly lonely. The story he'd told had upset him too much. The hazard lights on the Alfa Romeo Montreal blinked wearily.

"Did you look for your father?" I asked.

"No."

"You wanted him to come to you."

He looked at me in surprise, as if wondering how I could possibly get it. I gave him an ironic look, which made him realize that I knew exactly what he'd felt. The kid in me had been able to bury her father, but never the longing for him to come find her.

"It's a curse," he said. "Like a condition you inherit." I could hear the guilt in his voice, though he didn't apologize. "And now it's too late. You're not a child anymore."

"It was different for you," I said. "You had two fathers who would have done anything for you. I had zero."

"They didn't want me. They wanted my mother."

We stood there in silence.

"What did you do, then?" I asked him.

"What did I do? Got into trouble. Flipped out. Skipped school, did drugs, stole cars, you name it."

He tossed his cigarette away and went to the car.

I counted back. March 1974. I was born three years later.

"And Enzo?" I asked. "Are you still in touch?"

He shook his head. "He's persona non grata. To the entire family."

"What, so you never saw him again?"

"Well, I saw him one more time. At trial."

49

It took months before Enzo's case came to trial. In early December, Enzo sat ramrod-straight before the judge. The crucifix on the wall and the Advent wreath on the bench were the only adornments in the bare courtroom. He was wearing his best suit and a pair of standard-issue glasses he'd been given in jail. His eyes had gotten bad. His gaze was fixed on the man who would pass judgment upon him. He wiped the sweat from his brow as the German interpreter sitting beside him announced his plea.

"I loved my wife, Ms. Giulietta Marconi, very much, and I would never have hurt her. I, Enzo Marconi, plead not guilty."

Enzo cast a beseeching glance to the side, at his son. Vincenzo looked away. He had long hair now, a beard, and a Led Zeppelin T-shirt. He was nineteen, though he looked much older. He'd been called as a witness. He'd smoked a joint that morning because it was the only way he could get through the ordeal. The only thing that still united him and Enzo was their shared distaste for having intimate family secrets exposed to the public. Vincenzo finally understood why he and Enzo had always fought: the family was built on a lie, and Vincenzo's real family could never exist. He would have lost his mind completely that year if not for Giovanni, but even his beloved uncle hadn't been able to stop him from screwing up. From smoking dope day and night. From bombing his college entrance exams. From hanging around with the wrong crowd. From stealing. From being insufferable to everyone who wanted to help him. He was like a boat whose line had snapped in a storm, now drifting out to open sea. And he didn't care one way or the other.

Vincent was the very last witness called to the stand. The receptionist at BMW headquarters testified before him. Vincenzo liked her brown suede shoes with her red-and-black checked suit. The prosecutor, an overachiever in beige, pointed to Enzo.

"Are you sure that this is the person you saw in the company parking lot?"

"Yes," she said firmly. "I was taking a smoke break, and people like that, you don't normally see 'em outside headquarters."

"What do you mean by 'people like that'?"

"Um. Southerners, like. And he seemed odd to me, cos he hid behind the cars. To watch Dr. Schlewitz. And the lady."

"Mrs. Marconi?"

"Yeah. It was a real noticeable car, that red Alfa Romeo Dr. Schlewitz was showing her."

"And when you went home that evening, was the red Alfa Romeo still there?"

"Yeah."

"Could someone have manipulated the Alfa Romeo during the night?"

"Sure. Parkin' lot's not locked or nothin'."

Vincenzo looked daggers at Enzo. But Enzo simply sat there. Bearing it all in silence.

Then they called up Vincent. The man who should never have been in the picture. Had he not been, Giulietta would still be alive. And her son would never have been born. Vincenzo watched him closely. At first glance, he didn't see any similarities between the two of them. Maybe the build—they were both on the skinny side. The area around the nose, the thin lips, the hurried way of talking. Other than that, he was a respectably clad German who had clearly enjoyed a great deal of success, but still appeared humble and composed.

Having his private life exposed weighed on him, Vincenzo could tell, but Vincent seemed comfortable addressing the court. He spoke himself, not through a lawyer. To Vincenzo, who sat there in a rebellious slouch with his hair in his face, it seemed like the judge and Vincent came from the same world. As though the two of them were the only ones in the room who could go out for a nice beer after the trial concluded. Fancy prep schools, Vincenzo thought. Munich University. Think liberal, live conservative. Pedigree wasn't always something you could tell by a tie or a haircut, but you could sense it. There was a German word for these kinds of guys, a word they didn't have in Italian: *Spießer.* Squares.

"Do you swear to tell the truth, the whole truth, and nothing but the truth, so help you God?"

"I do."

The district attorney rose. Another square, but without the liberal trappings, Vincenzo thought. At least he embraced what he was.

"Dr. Schlewitz, did Mr. Marconi know about your relationship with his wife?"

"Yes."

"Mrs. Marconi told you that?"

"I heard him ask her to end it for good."

"So, you've met before?"

"Yes. I offered him a job."

At the defense table, Enzo balled his fists, sweating.

"And that was when you heard him ask her to end the affair?"

"Yes."

"Did he threaten you in any way?"

"No. I think he just wanted to see me. Then he got up and left."

"And then what?"

"Then—shortly after that was when the—accident happened."

"How long had your affair been going on at that point?"

"Around three and a half years. But we met back in 1954."

"If your relationship had been going on for that long, why didn't Mrs. Marconi leave her husband sooner?"

Vincent struggled to answer.

"In her diary," the district attorney went on, "Mrs. Marconi describes you as the love of her life."

Enzo shifted miserably in his seat.

"Were you afraid of how Mr. Marconi might react?"

"How do you mean?"

"Did Mrs. Marconi describe her husband as particularly jealous?"

Vincent looked over at Vincenzo. Their eyes met only briefly. "Yes. But also as a loving family man."

Vincenzo hated this. A stranger talking about his family. At that moment, he hated his mother, too. What else had she told Vincent about them?

"When you left for Venice," the district attorney continued, "had Mrs. Marconi decided to get a divorce? Or was it just a brief escape?"

Now Vincenzo hated the lawyer, too. Why air all this dirty laundry now, when it was already perfectly obvious why Enzo wanted to send them both to their deaths?

"I don't know."

He seemed honest, at any rate.

"Were you planning on leaving your wife?"

"That isn't relevant here!" Vincent lost his temper for the first time. Irritated and uneasy, he glanced toward the spectator area—only briefly, but it was enough for Vincenzo to identify the woman he was looking for. Vincent's wife was blond, withdrawn, elegant. She was sitting straight, with her bag on her lap. *Very brave of her,* Vincenzo thought, *to show her face here as the betrayed wife.*

"Thank you very much, Dr. Schlewitz."

The judge dismissed Vincent from the witness stand.

During the break, Vincenzo stood near Giovanni. The Germans clustered at the other end of the hall. Giovanni tried to distract Vincenzo through conversation, asking whether he was coming to Salina for Christmas, mentioning the great Barolo wine he'd just gotten from Piedmont, telling Vincenzo to keep away from the new political demonstrations. In turn, Vincenzo told his uncle all about the radical leftist prisoners who were on hunger strike to protest their solitary confinement, about the death of Holger Meins, about how Sartre had visited Andreas Baader in prison. Vincenzo was glad not to be alone. He waited to see whether Vincent would approach him. But Vincent was nowhere to be seen.

On his way to the restroom, Vincenzo heard a couple arguing in the stairwell. Quietly, but sharply. Vincenzo glanced down over the railing and saw Vincent and his blond wife. Now he could see that she was heavily pregnant.

"We made a promise to one another," she said. "In sickness and in health."

He nodded, agitated and confused. Eyes downcast, he begged his wife to forgive him. Apparently, they, too, were seeing each other for the first time at trial. Maybe he'd moved out, Vincenzo reasoned, after the affair had come to light through the accident.

"I can't forget this happened," she said, "but the only way we can ever have a future together is if you leave your past behind. Once and for all. Can you promise me that?"

"Promise," he said, and she took his hand. He leaned his head against her shoulder. Then the bell rang to call everyone back into the courtroom.

The judge announced his verdict on December 23. Everyone in the courtroom stood up except Vincenzo. It was obvious which way things would go. He just hoped the sentence would be stiff, because he never wanted to see Enzo again.

"Enzo Marconi, the defendant," the judge read out in a faint Munich accent, "has no alibi and a clear motive, and thanks to his professional background as a mechanic, he had the necessary knowledge to cause failure of the brake system in the vehicle that was involved in the accident."

You've got it good, Vincenzo thought. *After this, you can go back to your nice house with your wife and children and say to yourself, Thank God I have a better life than the people I have to deal with every day.*

"An unemployed guest worker's jealousy of a well-situated German rival is highly plausible," the judge went on.

Enzo gritted his teeth as the interpreter whispered in his ear.

"Additionally, the defendant's specific cultural background must be taken into consideration. So-called honor killings are, unfortunately, not unusual in Sicilian tradition."

All eyes were on Enzo. At that moment, Vincenzo almost felt a little sorry for his father—or should he say ex-father now? Or maybe it was less sympathy than an instinctive understanding, a shared dislike of German resentment. They were foreigners in the eyes of the judge, but in Enzo's and Vincenzo's eyes, the judge was the foreigner, not they. It was outrageous that a foreign country's justice system was allowed to decide his fate!

"Taking all of the evidence into consideration, the court comes to the following *conclusione*: as the prosecution has failed to demonstrate proof of guilt beyond a reasonable doubt, the principle of *in dubio pro reo* applies. The court finds the defendant not guilty of premeditated murder due to a lack of evidence."

Vincenzo couldn't believe his ears. A ripple of outraged murmuring went through the courtroom. The district attorney shook his head in incomprehension.

Even Enzo himself couldn't believe it. He gazed at the judge as though he were an angel of mercy. The judge wished everyone a merry Christmas, cleared his files from the bench, and left the room. Enzo shook his interpreter's hand euphorically. His eyes sought Vincenzo's. *Son, I'm innocent!* they said. *What does that judge know,* Vincenzo thought. Screw the German justice system, where they threw stoners in jail but let murderers go free!

On the morning of December 24, Enzo returned home. The first thing he'd done upon his release was buy a Christmas tree. Vincenzo heard the key in the door, the banging of the tree as he set it in the hall, his heavy breathing, his winded voice.

"Vincè? Are you here?" He hauled the tree into the living room.

Vincenzo emerged from his room. He'd already packed his bag.

Enzo gave him a surprised look. He tried to embrace him.

"My son—"

Vincenzo pushed past him to the door.

"Wait! Vincenzo! *Amore mio!*"

Vincenzo simply left him standing there. Enzo may have won the trial, but he'd lost his family.

Vincenzo wasn't sure where to go. The melting snow soaked through the soles of his summer shoes. People hurried through the streets, making last-minute purchases for Christmas Eve before the stores closed. Nobody was in a festive mood; everyone looked annoyed. Bumped into each other, cut in line. *The Christmas spirit,* he thought. *Such a lie.*

He went to a department store to warm up. Wandered aimlessly through the lingerie section. Nobody noticed him. The hit of the season, Udo Jürgens's "*Griechischer Wein,*" was lilting from the speakers. The lyrics about dark-eyed men with their southern music rankled Vincenzo.

And now they're singing about us, he thought. *The state wants to get rid of us, no money for the schools, but we're good enough for schmaltzy songs. Foreign, southern, lazy, we sit around in the taverns, drinking wine, and then when we're drunk enough, we dance the sirtaki and rape a German girl. Or go ahead and kill her, according to "Sicilian tradition."*

The song went on. Greek wine and blood, swarthy strangers longing for their faraway homes.

Vincenzo didn't ever dream of home. He wasn't even sure where home was supposed to be. Not here, not there, not anywhere. Who was this Jürgens guy, anyway? *And why the Greeks? What about us? We were here first!* But who was "we"? Vincenzo had cut his ties to "them," but he certainly didn't belong with the Germans, either.

But the song was relentless, evoking the sea and wind, the old houses waiting for the migrants to come back.

Suddenly, Vincenzo burst into tears. He hated himself for it, but he couldn't stop. A saleslady asked him if he was all right. He ran outside.

If he no longer wanted to belong to the ones who didn't belong here, where did he belong? Could he decide whom he belonged to, or was that predestined, a question of blood? If Enzo could never be his father no matter how much he'd wanted to, was it because of the foreign part of him, the German part? What about him was even German? Vincenzo carried the German inside him, the intruder into his family, and he would never be able to cut him out, because that would mean killing part of himself. Was that the good side of him or the bad side? If his mother had had the courage to give up everything for that man, there had to be something special about him, right?

By sunset, he'd found the address in the phone book. The streets in Bogenhausen were completely dead. Vincenzo felt uncomfortable. A neighborhood he didn't belong in. The precisely trimmed hedges, the expensive cars outside the villas, the silence. He was hungry; he hadn't eaten all day. Church bells sounded in the distance.

50

He'd pictured a bigger house somehow, more ostentatious, a villa with a pool, maybe. This was more of a bungalow, large but practical. *Not bad, actually,* Vincenzo thought. He could imagine living in something like that. He read the nameplate on the front gate but couldn't work up the courage to ring the doorbell. He jumped over the gate instead. It clinked softly. He snuck around the house. The pine trees rustled above him; the snow crunched beneath his feet. He was leaving tracks, he realized. *Crap.*

Then he heard soft music through the window. Bach or something. *"Jauchzet, frohlocket,"* intoned the choir. The living room was all lit up; the Christmas tree was decorated. *Strange,* he thought, *their tree is smaller than ours.* He'd expected a giant Nordmann fir with petit bourgeois ornaments. He was standing in the yard, about twenty feet from the window, but in the dark, he was invisible. His shoes were completely soaked.

Vincent's wife was setting the table for three. A girl ran into the room, maybe five or six years old. She had blond pigtails and was wearing a blue dress. *Adorable,* Vincenzo thought. *My sister. Half sister.* Vincent ran after her and scooped her up, which made her laugh. Vincent beamed at the little girl and swung her in a circle before they disappeared into the kitchen again.

The sight sent a pang through Vincenzo's heart. He stood there as though frozen to the spot, holding his suitcase in his clammy hand, but eventually he got too cold. He went back around to the front. There was a doorbell. He thought for a moment, then pressed the button. Instantly, he regretted it and started toward the gate. Behind him, he heard the door opening. He turned around.

A halo of warm light radiated from the hall. The little girl was standing in the doorway.

"Who are you?" she asked.

Vincent came to the door as well. He recognized Vincenzo immediately. Took the little girl's hand.

"Honey?" the woman called from inside.

Vincenzo simply stood there, shivering.

"Vincent? Who is it?"

Vincent carried his daughter back into the house, leaving the door open a crack.

"It's one of the trainees," Vincenzo heard him say. "He has to repair something—the Iso. I'll be right back."

"I want to come!" the child exclaimed.

"Stay inside, honey. It's cold out there."

Vincent came out of the house in slippers. "Come on. I'll show you to the garage," he said loudly enough for his wife to hear, and then pulled the door shut behind him.

Vincenzo already despised him for that. Vincent made a silent head motion to follow him.

Vincent closed the large door behind them. As the flickering fluorescent light slowly came on, Vincenzo saw a new BMW—a big family sedan, dark blue—and the gorgeous Iso beside it. All at once, he recalled the scent of the factory-new leather, the way the dashboard glittered in the sun, and his respect for the stranger who'd let him sit in this very car, back when he was just a boy, barely able to see over the steering wheel.

"Please. We can speak privately in here."

Vincent unlocked the BMW. Not the Iso. Sat in the driver's seat and opened the passenger door. Vincenzo hesitated, glancing around, but then sat down with his bag on his lap. Vincent shut his door quietly. Vincenzo left his half-open.

"Please excuse me. My wife knows nothing about this."

Vincent could only manage to hold his gaze for a few seconds. Vincenzo's eyes drifted over the wooden dashboard. The car smelled new. He opened his bag and withdrew the little car he'd brought with him, and handed it to Vincent. It was the red Ferrari from the racetrack Vincent had given him for Christmas so many years ago.

"Merry Christmas."

Vincent blinked.

"I kept it, without telling anyone. When my mother gave back the racetrack."

"That's yours." Vincent's voice trembled.

"I don't need it anymore."

"Vincenzo, I'm so sorry about what happened."

Vincenzo didn't react. Toyed with the switches on the dashboard.

"I'd love to invite you in, but my family—"

"The family you were going to leave."

He held Vincent's gaze, unblinking.

"I read all about it. She kept a diary."

It took Vincent a while to process the information. Vincenzo removed a crumpled pack of cigarettes from his jacket pocket and offered one to Vincent. French, unfiltered. Vincent waved it away, bewildered. He was grasping for words. Vincenzo lit his own cigarette and pulled out the ashtray.

"I wish I could turn back time," Vincent said. "But you don't always get everything you wish for, you know."

Lame, Vincenzo thought. *Dear old dad explains the world.* He merely shot him an *Oh, really?* look.

"How's your father?" Vincent asked.

Thanks a lot, Vincenzo thought. *"Your father." That certainly answers that question.*

They could see their own breath. The windows began to fog.

"What's her name?" Vincenzo asked abruptly.

"Who?"

"The girl. My sister."

Vincent didn't reply. As though revealing the girl's name would create a connection that could never be allowed to exist. He laid his hand on Vincenzo's shoulder. "Vincenzo, if there's anything I can do for you, then—"

Then what? Vincenzo thought.

"I know, Vincenzo. I know I should have been in touch, all this time after the accident. It wasn't easy for me, either, trust me."

Vincenzo got out.

"Where are you going?"

"To ask her myself. What her name is."

Vincent jumped from the car. "Wait! Please!"

Vincenzo stopped. They gazed at each other across the hood. The fluorescent light hummed.

Vincent went around to Vincenzo. "I know where you're coming from, but for now, my family needs a little peace and quiet. We just can't do it right now. This is the first time we're back together. Please understand, this was hell for them."

Vincenzo sensed his desperation. He wanted to protect something. Vincenzo could understand that. But what he didn't understand was why he wasn't part of it. Family, that was other people. And besides, what sort of family was Vincent trying to protect? That family was ruined anyway. What he wanted to protect was a lie.

"I did move out, you know, after I told your mother I would. But then after what happened . . . and Marianne was pregnant, as it turned out."

He looked at Vincenzo for a long time. "One small child, one on the way. We have responsibilities, too. Marianne didn't deserve what I did to her. She was generous enough to give me another chance. But only on the condition that I establish clear boundaries. Do you understand?"

"Vincent! Dinner's ready!" It sounded like a command.

"Listen, Vincenzo." Vincent put an arm around his shoulder. "I promised your mother that I would support you through college. I'm going to keep my word. I don't want you to lack for anything."

"So that I'll shut my mouth and let you all eat your roast turkey in peace?"

"No, Vincenzo, that's not how I meant it!"

Like a dog, Vincenzo thought, *who gets bones from the plates but has to stay outside.* He grinned sarcastically and stomped his cigarette out on the garage floor.

"Vincent!" Marianne's voice was louder now, more worried.

"Someday when you have a family, you'll understand," Vincent said.

"No. I'll never understand. I'll never be like you. Fuck your money!"

He jerked the garage door open with a crash and stormed out to the street. Vincent hurried after him.

"Vincenzo!"

His wife came to the door, alarmed by the noise. Vincenzo made eye contact with her, briefly. Vincent came running up. Vincenzo spat at his feet, turned around, and left.

Behind him, he heard the little girl's voice. "Daddy, who was that man?"

51

That man was my father. He seemed vulnerable now, leaning against the rusted guardrail with his head down like that. I could see the young person in him—and to my own horror, I saw myself as well. Vincent's words echoed through my mind: *People remain strangers only until one has heard their stories.* But there was one thing I still didn't understand: How could someone who'd been rejected by his father treat his own child the same way?

"How could he do that?"

Vincenzo took a deep breath and then shrugged. That old disappointed anger was still simmering inside him.

"He wants to put things right with you," I added, because I couldn't think of anything better to say. I wanted to help him somehow.

"It's far too late," he said.

"Better late than never."

I felt the urge to hug him. But I couldn't. What a ridiculous twist of fate, I thought, that I was standing by a guardrail in the middle of nowhere and had almost maternal feelings toward someone who really ought to have been taking care of me, not the other way around.

I don't remember which of us was the first to start grinning crookedly. His lips quirked in that same wry way I'd seen on my own face.

"When you first called me, you and Giovanni," he said, "I behaved like an idiot. A complete idiot. I didn't want Carmela to find out."

"Why not? She knew about me, didn't she?"

"It's none of her business. You're part of *my* life."

"No," I replied. "I'm not."

He seemed surprised at my sober tone. I didn't back down. It was just a statement of fact.

"You're like your mother," he remarked. "Mercilessly honest."

I didn't tell him that wasn't true. Behind the grown woman was a lost little girl who wished her father would put his arms around her. But I would still rather have died than have shown him that. I got my pride from him, not from my mom.

"I wrote letters to your mother," he said. "She sent them all back. Unopened."

I was surprised. "She never told me that."

"Did you ask?"

"No."

We fell silent for several minutes. Stared out at the landscape. Then, after a while, he quietly said, "Thanks."

"For what?"

"For coming."

I leaned against him very gently, almost imperceptibly, because I was afraid it would kill the moment if I was too obvious. From the way his body remained perfectly still beside me and he nearly stopped breathing, I could tell that he had the same fear.

"We should get going," he said then, before opening the hood and topping up the oil.

I called Vincent. Clara answered. He was doing better, she said. He was looking forward to seeing us. I promised we would be there in eight hours. She thanked me. It was genuine, but I could sense that she was tense as well. She didn't mention the half brother she was about to meet for the first time.

Vincenzo held out the keys.

"Ever driven one of these?"

My eyes went wide.

"Nope."

"Get in."

I sat down behind the steering wheel. *A time machine,* I thought.

"When's it from?" I asked.

"Seventy-four."

The year Giulietta died.

"But you didn't buy it back then?"

"No, I restored this one. Watch out, the clutch and the brake are really close together."

After testing the pedals, I impulsively removed my shoes. Handed them to him. He accepted them without comment, smiling skeptically. I turned the key in the ignition, and the old animal roared to life. I hit the gas. I wasn't used to this much brute power—I was happy if my asthmatic wreck of a car started at all. I could sense Vincenzo's anxiety; he was the exact opposite of a good passenger. But he kept his mouth shut, which I appreciated. It took me a while to tame the beast, but then it was wonderful. A car that was truly alive—everything about it was direct, raw, and unfiltered. He turned the radio on. Italian ad jingles, a barrage of staccato from a present day I wasn't interested in.

"So, then what?" I asked him. Christmas 1974—he must have met my mother shortly after that.

He was silent, searching for a different station.

"Did you ever see him again?"

"One other time. Together with your mother."

"She told me she didn't know anything about him."

Vincenzo didn't respond.

"Did you tell her who your actual father was?"

"I didn't have a father anymore. *Basta.*"

He fumbled with the radio. *Control freak,* I thought. If he couldn't be behind the wheel, he had to at least take charge of the radio dial.

"You know what the really ironic thing is?" he asked. "If it had worked out with Vincent, I mean if he'd made me part of his family that Christmas, you would never have been born."

"Why not?"

"Because I'd never have met your mom."

"Why? How did you two meet?"

I knew Tanja's version of the story, but I wanted to hear his.

"After that, I completely shut down. Wanted to get away from everyone. Kept moving around, a few nights here, a few nights there. I crashed with weird people—for a while, I just wanted to die. Your mother was my salvation."

"Where did you meet for the first time?"

"At her commune. I just happened to be hanging out there with a friend, a guy whose couch I'd slept on, and he had to leave his apartment. So, we were over at your mom's place, sitting around drinking with her, and she said, 'Hey, there's an extra mattress here, you can stay awhile.' To this day, I still don't know why she did that. Maybe because I was just as pissed at my family as she was at hers. The other guys in her commune were runaways, too. But none of them were working class. They were all bourgeoisie kids with Nazi daddies."

52

Tanja

When Vincenzo saw Tanja for the first time in January 1975, she had shoulder-length black hair and was wearing a tight black turtleneck without a bra. She was sitting at a large wooden table, typing. A crumpled pack of cigarettes lay beside her typewriter. The air was smoky. It was cold—the squat house didn't have heat. One of the windows was broken and had been covered with a banner. There were mattresses on the floor. Someone had scrawled "The Pigs of Today Are the Schnitzel of Tomorrow" on the torn wallpaper. Punk rock was blaring from an old stereo. Six people were at the table, all in coats and wool sweaters, all older than Vincenzo. He leaned against the wall and watched them. Someone had brought him along; nobody took much notice. And that was perfectly fine with him. He was haggard, emaciated, and when he looked in the mirror—which he rarely did—a pair of sullen, fiery eyes stared back.

But though his cheeks were sunken and his clothes were torn, his mind was razor-sharp. He'd broken off contact with his family, but despite his loneliness, he was filled with a grim, intense feeling that he had his finger on the true pulse of life. Perhaps that was what drew him to Tanja and the commune: the wintery figures outside on the streets were the living dead. Satiated, but frozen. Inside the squat house, everyone was hungry. They were burning. They were at war.

The first time Vincenzo heard the words "urban guerilla," they came from Tanja's lips. He liked the phrase immediately. And he liked Tanja immediately as well. She was the radical opposite of his mother: she did what she cared about, accepting zero lies and zero compromises. At barely twenty-four, she already had a graduate degree in political science. She wanted to become a journalist, and she had started writing for underground leftist magazines. Her mind was brilliant; she debated men and women, young and old alike, and she always had the better arguments. Tanja was never satisfied with superficialities. She got to the root of things, and she had an opinion about all of them. Radical, yet reflective. Impulsive, but out of conviction, not emotion. Until that point, Vincenzo had only been peripherally aware of current events in Germany, but she put them into a context in which everything suddenly made sense. Even his own life.

"The individual," she read as she typed, "attributes his position of weakness within society to his own lack of ability, but it is state-organized repression that has drummed that idea into his mind from a young age. The system thrives upon our fear of becoming who we could be!" Then, with almost religious fervor, she quoted a text from a revolutionary magazine.

"We must perceive each individual's distress as a call to free ourselves through anti-imperialist struggle. We must understand that we have nothing to lose by destroying this system, but everything to gain through armed revolution: collective liberation, life, humanity, identity."

Ulrike Meinhof had written the text in prison. Vincenzo knew the terrorist only by her blurry black-and-white image on the "Wanted" poster Giovanni had hung up in the shop to show that he was on the right side of the law. Yet the words spoke straight to Vincenzo's heart. Because they offered him, who no longer belonged anywhere, a new "we," a reflection of his own rage, of his own sense of being lost. Meinhof legitimated the desire for destruction that had been eating Vincenzo up inside.

"Today, we know that one cannot face the armed ruling class unarmed," the guy sitting beside Tanja read on as he helped himself to her pack of cigarettes. "Organized violence is a necessity in the class struggle!" Just as she stood out with her intellect, he dominated the room with his physical presence. He was very tall, with long, unwashed hair and a mustache, and wore an old leather jacket with a fur collar. Every so often, he slipped an arm casually around Tanja's shoulders. The two were the unofficial royal couple of the commune. She called him Olaf, but nobody knew his real name, not even Tanja. He was an illegal, an active agent for whom the commune had offered to act as a safe house. It was only now that Vincenzo understood what that meant: unlike those who passively rejected the system, Olaf was a soldier in an underground army that everyone talked about but hardly anyone knew personally. Of course, he might be a government spy, who knew? His face wasn't on any of the "Wanted" posters. But Olaf knew about operations before they even happened.

"How serious are all of you about changing society?" he demanded.

The others hesitated.

"The idea is good, but killing another person in the name of an idea—," one said.

"The left has failed," Olaf broke in. "Instead of fighting the police state, you're tearing each other apart! The Communist League, the Marxist-Leninist Party of Germany, the German Communist Party, the Communist Party of Germany/Marxists-Leninists—total bullshit! Critical solidarity? Empty words! Do you know what you all are? Intellectual chickenshits!"

"And the RAF? What's your vision for society? The only thing you guys are interested in is getting your own people out of jail!"

"It's not jail! It's solitary confinement! It's torture!" Olaf slammed his fist against the table.

Everyone fell silent.

Tanja jumped in. "What has peaceful protest achieved? Nothing. State repression continues! Exploitation of the Third World! The wars! You can't talk to the Auschwitz generation. They shot Ohnesorg just for protesting—they'll shoot us, too. Unless we arm ourselves. Bringing those responsible to justice is a legitimate strategy!"

"So, the ends justify the means, you're saying? What gives you the right to decide whether another human being lives or dies?"

"How many people would have been saved if Hitler had been assassinated?" Tanja shot back.

Vincenzo listened with fascination.

"Every liberation movement requires sacrifices," she continued. "Cuba. Bolivia. In Algeria, one million people died for independence. Our resistance isn't aimed at the innocent little people—it's aimed at the big corporations. The banks. The justice system!"

When nobody else spoke, Olaf took the reins. "Who's with us?"

Nobody moved. Tanja cast a challenging look around the group.

Vincenzo raised his hand.

53

"Why did you join them?" I asked.

We'd passed through the tunnel and were heading toward a toll station. Bologna. We'd been driving for six hours, but we were still only halfway there. Vincenzo gave me a look that suggested he'd been asked that question too many times already.

"Why did your mother?" he retorted.

"I asked about you."

"I was a little asshole, and I wanted to become a bigger one," he said. "No, seriously. Who was I? Nobody. Can you imagine that? You're hanging around in the suburbs somewhere, you've dropped out of school, your family has gone to hell in a handbasket, you turn on the news and you see the big shots. The stars and politicians in their limousines. How did they get there? Are they really more deserving, or just better connected? But then you discover a way to get on the news. What I liked about the urban guerillas was that they were in the minority, but they didn't let anyone debase them. They fought back. You don't have a chance, so use it!"

I wasn't sure whether I heard a sarcastic note in his voice, or whether he still genuinely believed what he was saying, even after all these years. He handed me the toll card and rolled down the window. As I had never been to Italy before, this ritual struck me as odd. The filthy card slot, the weird computer voice, the bored-looking guy in the tollbooth. How many thousands of cars did he process every day? How could he possibly spend his whole life cooped up like that? He mumbled something I didn't understand, but when he saw the Montreal, his eyes lit up.

"Che bella macchina! Complimenti, signora!"

"Grazie."

I passed him the handful of coins Vincenzo gave me. The men exchanged compliments and talked shop. One excited, the other cool. I was apparently riding in some kind of Italian national shrine, like Sophia Loren on wheels. Then the person behind us honked, and the barrier went up. I weaved my way into the traffic headed toward Modena.

"You know," Vincenzo continued, "we were the elite. Everyone else was sleepwalking, extras in someone else's dream, but *our* eyes were open. We were campaigning for a more just society. One that didn't divide people into those who owned everything and those who had nothing."

He fumbled out his cigarettes and handed me one. "Don't you ever have the feeling that the world has gone deeply wrong?"

"You sound a little like Mom, you know."

He raised an eyebrow but didn't reply.

"Besides the fact that capitalism won," I went on, "I've never had the patience for politics. I had to take care of myself."

He grinned at me wryly. "Capitalism won because of people like you."

I had to grin back.

He took a drag on his cigarette, and then turned serious. "Truth is, I really just wanted to impress your mom."

"What'd you do?"

"Did I kill anyone, you mean?"

I simply gave him a curious look. If the things my mother had said were true, it seemed possible. Not that Tanja was an innocent, but unlike her, he'd actually done time.

"I was the lookout. That was all they'd let me do. At first, anyway. In exchange, I got a roof over my head and a mattress."

"What about Giovanni? Did he know where you were?"

"Yeah. He came over once, trying to get me back on the straight and narrow. Brought me this gigantic basket of food, like he thought he had to save me from starving to death. 'These aren't good people. This isn't how you go about it. What are you going to do when the cops come? They'll deport you! Come back home . . .' I threw him out. But I kept the food. And shared it with the others."

"Who fell in love first? You or Mom?"

"Me. Your mom was—out of my league, you know? She'd been to college; she knew every book in the world; she was pretty; she was unbelievably well spoken. And I thought to myself, *What good am I to them, anyway? What can I do?* All I had was the rage inside me."

"But she didn't see you as a foreigner."

"Sure she did. But that's what gave me an edge. Totally undeserved!" Vincenzo laughed. "Italy in the seventies, that was like paradise to the Left. Paris sixty-eight was the center of the student protests, but Northern Italy, the car factories, that was the center of the workers' struggle. It was a civil war out there! Lotta Continua, Sinistra Proletaria, Brigate Rosse . . . Here, people didn't just talk—they went on strike, they shot people, they died. They kidnapped Fiat managers, put bombs in factories, set police stations on fire."

"Why here specifically?"

"Because the Italians have always distrusted the government. They're anarchists at heart. West Germany banned Communism; here, they were the second-strongest party in Parliament! The biggest threat to the Democrazia Cristiana! If the revolution had a chance anywhere in Europe, it was in Italy. If you ask me, that was the only reason they accepted me into the commune—I was Italian. All of a sudden, I wasn't a spaghetti-muncher; I was the avant-garde!" He grinned.

"Racism in a different form."

"Of course it is," he laughed. "They asked me all kinds of questions about who I knew—Moretti, Berlinguer, Feltrinelli—I had no idea who any of them were. But I quickly realized that the less you say, the more interesting girls think you are. Just scowl mysteriously and smoke a joint, that was enough."

I smirked.

"Except for Olaf. It wasn't enough for Olaf. He thought I was just a ragged little wannabe. Which I was. Until . . ."

He paused.

"Until what?"

"Until I got sick of just being the lookout. I wanted to tear something down, too."

54

Everyone got fake IDs except Vincenzo. He hadn't gotten up to anything serious—he wasn't on any lists; the cops weren't looking for him. Still, he was utterly fascinated by the gray ID cards Olaf and Tanja snagged on one of their first missions: one piece of paper, so much power. The documents allowed people to change their names, reinvent their appearances, lose their identities. The night Olaf handed out the IDs with the manipulated photos was a kind of sacred initiation ritual from which Vincenzo was excluded. He was reduced to the role of silent observer, just like on missions when they only trusted him to stand lookout on the corner. Tanja, though officially responsible for propaganda, was allowed on the front lines. She was Olaf's right hand, spokeswoman, and lover. And even though everyone else slept with everyone, the two of them were a couple. Vincenzo was invisible to Tanja.

Late at night, as Tanja screwed Olaf, Vincenzo read her writings. He found them strange at first—written in lowercase, devoid of emotion—but striking in the crystalline clarity with which they put urban guerilla tactics into a larger context: shoplifting was a necessary expropriation measure through which the people recovered what belonged to them. Passport theft was an act of resistance against the fascist state. Bank robberies served to destabilize the capitalist system in order to trigger the uprising of the masses. Tanja quoted Mao Zedong, Ulrike Meinhof, and the South American Tupamaros. In one article, she celebrated the kidnapping of the head of Berlin's Christian Democratic Union party as their greatest success since the imprisonment of the Red Army Faction leaders. For the first time, she wrote, militant leftists had brought Chancellor Schmidt to his knees and forced the release of their jailed comrades. Tanja didn't explain what her comrades had been arrested for. Apparently, when both sides claimed the high ground, morality was merely a question of perspective.

Language can clarify or obscure, Vincenzo thought. These people sounded so self-righteous, focusing their spotlight so much on *one* thing, as though trying to distract from something else. Vincenzo wondered what it was they were hiding, what Tanja was really feeling. And why he couldn't stop thinking about her.

The misunderstanding between himself and Tanja lay in the fact that they were against the same thing—the state, the system—but they hated it for different reasons. Vincenzo, the working-class immigrant, felt betrayed and excluded; Tanja, the rebellious middle-class girl, saw changing the country as her calling, even her obligation. Background didn't matter; nothing mattered except their common goal, opposing populist fascism. But the roots of the soul go their own way, and ideology makes a person just as blind as love.

Vincenzo was supposed to keep watch while Tanja and Olaf scoped out a department store as a potential target for attack. It was a foggy winter night; a ghostly soup had settled over the city; traffic lights blinked, forlorn, out of the white nothingness.

But Vincenzo followed them, defying orders, and brought a stack of tabloid papers he'd stolen. Why not just burn the store down then and there? It was a good opportunity: smash the windows, light the newspapers, disappear into the fog.

"I decide what we do and when," Olaf said. "Go back to your post."

Vincenzo refused. He wanted a say in things. Olaf didn't take him seriously. Tanja tried to calm them down and argued it would be better to rob the department store than set it on fire. Just as Olaf and Vincenzo were about to start brawling, two cops emerged from the fog. Asked what they were doing. Demanded IDs.

They ran. The cops followed. Vincenzo had the car keys in his pocket, and he jumped behind the wheel. Olaf and Tanja got in quickly, and Vincenzo barreled straight toward the cops at top speed. They dove out of the way. Vincenzo sped down Leopoldstraße. Olaf yelled at him. "Idiot!" "Loser!" Vincenzo glanced around. All quiet. But then, a police vehicle shot toward them from the opposite direction, lights flashing, tires screeching as it spun around. Vincenzo stepped on the gas. The streets were nearly empty, but he could barely see anything. He raced through the fog with the patrol car hot on his heels. A second siren sounded—they were trying to trap him using a pincer move. Vincenzo killed the headlights and sped up even more. Invisible, through the soup. Tanja screamed. Olaf shouted. Vincenzo remained calm. He hit the brakes and veered sharply onto a side street. Then he accelerated, and the sirens faded behind them. When they got home, even Olaf had to admit that the disobedient kid was great at one thing—driving. He'd found his niche.

Vincenzo put new license plates on the getaway cars—inconspicuous Fords and compact Audis provided to them by a guy named Slobodan—and took them to be repainted. After each mission, he scrubbed the car inside and out to remove fingerprints, then drove the vehicle to a scrap merchant. Soon, the others began entrusting him with courier jobs: secret messages from prison, packages he wasn't allowed to open. Once, he drove all the way to Turin, to a mechanic on the *periferia*, where two young guys with no names gave him weapons. AK-47s and Berettas. He stuffed them into a recess inside the car body and ferried them across the border. Secretly, he took a pistol for himself and hid it inside his mattress.

Then he stole his first car. The Fords and Audis were too sluggish for his taste. It took him thirty seconds to jimmy the lock and hot-wire the vehicle, in broad daylight, right there in the street. It was a white Alfa Romeo Giulia, the perfect getaway car: a four-door, and faster than the cops' BMWs. Olaf didn't like the Italian car. When it came to anything automotive, he was a total German snob.

"If you want something fancy, at least get a Benz. Something reliable!"

In reality, he was mostly angry that Vincenzo had acted on his own again. Tanja separated the two of them before they could come to blows. They were about to conduct their biggest mission yet, and they had no time to lose.

55

They'd already discarded this particular mission as too dangerous, but recent events demanded a swift act of vengeance. The RAF siege of the West German Embassy in Stockholm had ended in catastrophe: rather than exchanging hostages for the twenty-six RAF prisoners, Helmut Schmidt had ordered police to storm the building. Four dead, two on each side. On the evening news, Chancellor Schmidt had declared that the state would no longer allow itself to be blackmailed.

That required a response. The unforgiving logic of escalation: either do nothing and accept defeat, or turn things up a notch. Now, more than ever, they felt like part of the larger game. Important. World-changing. Which meant they needed more money. Vincenzo was never told where the bounty from their operations went, but he wasn't dumb.

The little fishes' robberies were to help get the big fish out of prison.

Their target was a bank branch in Milbertshofen, halfway between Hasenbergl and Schwabing, between Giovanni's guest-worker neighborhood and Grimm's genteel German one. Tanja had done the recon: there were no security guards, and the nearest police station was seven minutes away. No violence, they all agreed. Not after the Stockholm debacle.

Everything went as planned at first. There were four of them: Olaf and another guy went in with stocking masks and guns, Tanja guarded the door, and Vincenzo waited in the getaway car. The white Giulia. He left the engine running. Watched the street in the rearview mirror. No cops. Then he heard a gunshot. Tanja ran inside. Another shot rang out. The three of them ran outside and scrambled into the car. Tanja had blood on her hands.

If Vincenzo hadn't stared at her, it wouldn't have happened. The blood shocked him. He took his eyes off the street, though only for a second.

"Go!" Olaf exclaimed.

Vincenzo slammed on the gas pedal, choking the engine. Immediately, he turned the key again. The starter whined, but the damn engine didn't kick in.

"Fuck! Fuck! Fuck!" Olaf shouted.

Vincenzo tried again. No luck.

Then the guy ran out of the bank. Jeans and a brown leather jacket. He aimed at the car. Tanja drew her Beretta. A bullet shattered the glass. Tanja shot back. Vincenzo ducked, cursing as he turned the ignition and pumped the gas. The engine didn't start. Olaf fired. The windows shattered. Shells flew through the car.

"Go, goddammit!" Olaf roared, smacking him in the head.

Vincenzo turned the key once more, as hard as he could. It broke off in the ignition, but the engine finally sprang to life.

He slammed on the gas and sped away.

He glanced in the rearview mirror. The man in the brown leather jacket collapsed onto the street.

"Where'd he come from?"

"Jesus Christ, shut up and drive!" Olaf growled, and then turned to Tanja. "Where the hell did he come from? You said they didn't have guards there!"

Tanja was uninjured but white as a sheet. Olaf's neck had been grazed, and he had his hand clamped over it to stop the blood. Vincenzo had glass splinters in his face.

"That wasn't a security guard," she said. "That was a cop."

"What the hell?"

"He just happened to be there! Cops go to the bank sometimes, too!"

"Shit!" Olaf turned to Vincenzo. "This is your fault, Spaghetti," he snapped. "Your fucking special car! If you hadn't taken this shitty Alfa Romeo, this wouldn't have happened!" He slammed his fist against the dashboard, hard enough that the wood paneling broke. "Italian piece of shit!"

"Calm down," Tanja called from the back seat. "It's not his fault."

"We said no blood!"

"But that was a pig!"

"He wasn't on duty, though!"

"Then why did he have his goddamn gun on him?"

"You're out," Olaf snarled at Vincenzo. "Next time, I'm getting the car."

Vincenzo stared at the shattered windshield in silence. He hated screwing up. He thought about the cop.

He parked the Giulia in a garage, removed the license plate, and threw a tarp over it, cursing. Tanja tended to Olaf's neck. Nobody said a word. Olaf and Tanja retreated to their room with a bottle of wine and locked the door. Soon Vincenzo heard the two of them, going at it harder than usual.

Later, sometime past midnight, Vincenzo sat down at the table and took the accursed starter apart. It was unusually quiet in the apartment—everyone was asleep; no music was playing; the only noise was the hum of the refrigerator. Behind him, he heard the lock on Olaf's door click. He recognized the sound of Tanja's bare feet on the creaky floorboards as she quietly padded past on her way to the refrigerator.

Only then did he see that she was naked except for her black glasses. She fetched a bottle of wine and glanced at Vincenzo coolly. Her long hair fell into her face.

"It was the starter," Vincenzo said.

She looked at the small electric motor in his oil-smeared hands.

"It's from Bosch. Quality German craftsmanship."

Tanja let out a short laugh. Then she approached him, slowly, until she was close enough that he could smell the disturbing scent of sex on her skin. She set the bottle on the table and twisted the corkscrew in.

"Why are you so angry?"

He wasn't sure how to respond.

"You're the only one who never says anything about his family," she said before yanking out the cork. She filled Vincenzo's empty glass, gazing at him.

He was speechless at first; then he wanted to say something, but Olaf emerged from the room. He was naked as well.

"All good?"

Tanja didn't reply. Olaf picked up Vincenzo's glass and chugged it. So that there was no mistaking who was the boss around here. Vincenzo sensed that Tanja didn't appreciate it any more than he did.

"Leave the kid alone. Come on," Olaf said, taking her hand.

Tanja obeyed. But before she left, she turned back to Vincenzo and kissed him. On the lips.

"Buona notte, Vincenzo."

Olaf stopped in his tracks, looking confused.

"You two got something going?"

She regarded him calmly. "None of your damn business."

Vincenzo startled. The air was thick with tension. Olaf stared at Tanja. Then he slapped her across the face. Vincenzo leaped up, but she shoved him aside. She didn't want help. Didn't need any. She gazed into Olaf's eyes, perfectly composed, perfectly under control. "So, you're jealous? *You?*"

Vincenzo wanted to clarify that he hadn't touched her, but she gestured for him to stay out of it.

"We have an agreement," she said. "Freedom in all relationships. No power dynamics, no ownership."

She poured wine into Vincenzo's glass and then took a sip of it.

Olaf glowered at her. "Wasn't my intention."

"If we want to change society," she said, "we have to start with ourselves."

"Sleep with whoever you want, then," Olaf snapped, humiliated, and went back into the room.

Tanja removed a cigarette from Vincenzo's pack and lit it.

He was confused. Why was she acting like this?

"Are you guys actually together, or is that just—kind of—"

Tanja smiled at him. There was a hint of superiority in her eyes, which he didn't like, but at the same time, he thought he sensed a complicity there as well. She left without answering his question, and without kissing him again. She disappeared into Olaf's room but kept the door open. Vincenzo was left by himself. Did he and Tanja really have a connection, or had she just used him to get back at Olaf?

Vincenzo lay awake all night, puzzling. He closed his eyes and saw her before him, naked and unfamiliar. Her long legs, her small, firm breasts. Her righteous rage, her cool heart. He didn't understand her, but he admired her. No matter what happened, Tanja never let anyone get under her skin. He liked that, and he wanted to take a page from her book. He decided to plan a mission of his own. And he wanted Tanja to be part of it.

56

He waited for the right moment, and then he struck. Olaf was sleeping with another woman; Tanja was alone.

"Got something to show you," Vincenzo told her.

After midnight, Vincenzo parked the stolen Giulia on a nice street in Bogenhausen. The villas were dark. Tanja was uneasy driving around with their busted windows, but there was no stopping Vincenzo. He was almost fanatical in his determination.

"Where's the guy work?" Tanja asked.

"Some BMW hotshot," Vincenzo said, and took his Beretta out of the glove compartment.

"Where'd you get that?"

Vincenzo shrugged and clicked the safety off.

"What are you planning on doing?"

In Italy, militant leftists had kidnapped a Fiat manager and an Alfa Romeo engineer in order to get ransom money. But Vincenzo was planning something else.

"Don't worry. We're just taking back what's ours." He sprang over the fence and held out a hand to Tanja. The front gate rattled quietly. She took his hand, and he led her up the driveway to the garage. The windows of the bungalow were dark.

"He'll be home at this hour," she whispered.

"By the time he wakes up, we'll be gone."

Picking the lock on the garage was easy enough. The door swung upward with a soft squeak. The two cars were waiting there in the darkness: the blue

BMW and the silver-gray Iso Rivolta. Vincenzo pondered a moment before breaking into the BMW while Tanja kept watch outside the garage.

"You drive this one," he said before turning to the Iso. He peeled back the weather strip on the window and slid a wire inside.

"But what about the getaway car?"

"We'll leave it there. Come back for it later."

He really only wanted the Iso. But now greed overcame him. He wanted to take whatever he could.

"No, people will notice it!" Tanja hissed.

He ignored her and unlocked the driver's side door. Sat behind the wheel. Paused for a moment. Memories came flooding back. *Funny,* he thought, *it all seems so much smaller than it did back then.* The wooden steering wheel, the instruments, the leather seats. He ripped the ignition wires out and short-circuited them. Sparks flew in his hand. The starter made a grinding sound, but the engine didn't turn over.

"Hurry, he'll hear you!"

"Get in the BMW!"

The car refused to start. Maybe it had been sitting idle for too long, and the battery was dead. Tanja saw a light go on in a window.

"He's awake! Let's go!"

Vincenzo didn't want to give up. He kept trying, feverishly, stubbornly.

"Fuck, come on!" Tanja tugged his sleeve. He pushed her away.

Then the car started. The deep rumbling of the eight-cylinder engine echoed through the garage. Vincenzo grinned and started getting up to work on the BMW.

"Jesus Christ, drive! Forget the BMW! The guy's coming!"

Tanja shoved him back behind the wheel of the Iso, ran around the car, and got in on the passenger side. Vincenzo thought for a moment, then put the car into first gear and hit the gas. All at once, he saw Vincent running up the driveway. He braked hard.

Nobody moved. Vincent was wearing a robe over his pajamas and aiming a pistol at the driver. Blinded by the headlights, he had no way of knowing who was inside.

Vincenzo held his breath. Tanja began to panic.

"Go! Run him over!"

Vincenzo froze.

Vincent slowly approached the driver's side door, clutching the gun in both hands.

Vincenzo couldn't see whether it was real. He reached into his jacket pocket and drew the Beretta.

"Out of the car!" Vincent called. Then he recognized Vincenzo. He kept the gun pointed at him as his expression slowly turned to shock.

Vincenzo pointed his own gun back. Time stood still. Nobody dared breathe.

"Shit, go!" Tanja screamed.

Vincent took a step back.

"Do you know him or something?" Tanja asked.

"No."

Vincenzo slammed on the gas. The Iso broke through the wooden gate. He veered onto the street, tires squealing, and sped away. What he was fleeing wasn't Vincent, but the gaping abyss within himself.

He would be capable of killing his own father.

His hands were still trembling when they reached the garage and got out. Tanja recovered quickly enough, but Vincenzo went straight to bed and pulled the blanket over his head. He didn't want to see anyone else.

When he awoke the next morning, he was alone in the squat. His eyes were swollen; his limbs were stiff. He shrugged on his jacket and went down to check the damage on the Iso.

As he walked into the garage, he saw Olaf and Tanja standing by the car. They were arguing.

"You idiot," Olaf snapped at him. "What was the point of that mission?"

"My business."

"The pigs seized the getaway car. Your shit was in it."

"Nothing was in it," Tanja protested.

"Your fingerprints!"

Vincenzo inspected the front of the Iso. The fence had shattered a headlight, but other than that, there were just a few minor dents and scratches.

Olaf grabbed his arm. "We're not car thieves, kid," he said. "We conduct our operations so that we can free our comrades from solitary confinement! This isn't some lame college-protest group. We have a chain of command here!"

"If I wanted to obey orders, I would have joined the army," Vincenzo shot back.

"What's the car worth?" Olaf demanded.

"The Iso is mine."

"Bounty belongs to the collective."

Olaf opened the door to get behind the wheel. Vincenzo grabbed him and yanked him back with a force that surprised Olaf.

"There are rules around here, kid." Olaf scowled at him.

"I make my own rules."

Olaf gripped him by the collar.

"Stop, both of you!" Tanja exclaimed.

Olaf slammed Vincenzo against the car. Vincenzo stumbled, but then ran at Olaf and rammed him like a wild bull. Olaf kicked him, and the two were soon locked in a furious fistfight. Tanja stopped trying to intervene. She stood by and watched until Vincenzo emerged victorious. He was smaller and skinnier, but Olaf was no match for his determination. Olaf, nose bloodied, curled up on the ground.

"Goat fucker!"

Panting, Vincenzo looked at Tanja.

That evening, Olaf was gone. Nobody knew where he was. Vincenzo sat on the mattress in Tanja's room, rolling a joint as she tended to his split eyebrow. All at once, when he felt her breath on his skin, he couldn't help kissing her. She wasn't surprised. Merely wary. The connection between them wasn't explosive like the violence that morning; it spread cautiously until it became a certainty. Carefully, she tugged his T-shirt over his head and settled over his hips as he lay back against the mattress and unbuttoned his pants. He loved her confident movements, the experience she seemed to radiate. He felt safe with her. It was the most wonderful thing Vincenzo had felt since his mother's death had thrown his life into darkness. A door opened somewhere deep within, and his body was flooded with light.

Then the cops arrived. Without warning, they broke the door down and stormed the apartment. There were ten of them at least. Vincenzo and Tanja startled awake. Fortunately, some housemates in the kitchen resisted arrest, yelling loudly, which gave them the valuable seconds they needed. Completely naked, they clambered out the window onto the overhang, and then over a wall onto the next roof. Flashing blue lights lit up the night. Shouts echoed from buildings all around; dogs barked—it was like the movies. Tanja took Vincenzo's hand, and her firm grip gave him an intoxicating sense of invulnerability. They dashed from roof to roof like comic-book superheroes.

The Iso was still in the garage. They got in and drove off. No underwear, no passports, no money, nothing. Vincenzo sped to Giovanni's shop; darkness enveloped the line of stores across from the market. They ran naked to the door; he broke it open, and they went inside without switching the light on. Vincenzo grabbed some money from Giovanni's secret hiding place under the register. Tanja stuffed salami and cheese into a bag.

"I don't suppose your uncle has clothes anywhere around here?"

Vincenzo thought for a moment before opening the door to the back room and turning on the light. The fluorescent bulb hummed, flickering. The sewing machine sat silently on the little table. Beside it lay a nearly finished blouse, as though Giulietta had merely stepped away from her work and would complete it in the morning. Tanja stepped into the room, marveling. Enthusiastically, she touched the beautiful clothes on the stands and finally put some on.

"How do I look?" she asked Vincenzo, laughing. And then realized he was standing there, frozen in place.

57

They had to make it to the border without hitting a police checkpoint. The Autobahn was deserted. Tanja was wearing a loose blouse and a plaid skirt with a wide belt, the last outfit Giulietta had made for herself. Vincenzo had on an unbuttoned blue shirt beneath a corduroy suit that was far too large for him. He took the rat run he'd used when bringing the weapons back from Turin—a small border station near Mittenwald, left unguarded at night.

Then came the old Brenner Pass, which was strangely still in the wee hours of the morning—no cross by the side of the road in memory of Giulietta. Through South Tyrol at dawn, the cool air and the gleaming mountain peaks; then the sun rose, and they passed Verona. Onward through the Po Valley, down the Autostrada del Sole, past Florence, Rome, Naples. Down bumpy regional highways full of potholes, farther and farther south. They stopped only to get gas and to trade off behind the wheel, napping en route. Coffee, cigarettes, imperialist cola. At noon the following day, they arrived, drained, at Reggio Calabria, the most southerly port on the mainland. Luckily, they didn't have to abandon the car: a vehicle ferry had recently begun offering service to the Aeolian Islands.

The ferry line went from Reggio to Milazzo on Sicily, and then from there to Lipari, Stromboli, and Salina. No German police would find them there, at the end of Europe, where time had stood still for decades. The deckhands watched with curious interest as they guided the Granturismo onto the ferry—a much-too-young, oddly dressed couple in a far-too-expensive car. The Iso was dusty inside and out; because it didn't have air-conditioning, they'd traveled the rough roads with the windows down. As the ship's propeller churned the water and the ferry pulled away from the dock, they knew they'd made it.

Late that evening, they reached the empty harbor. Theirs was the only vehicle that got off on Salina. Tanja, exhausted, slept in the passenger seat while Vincenzo searched for the road to Malfa he'd taken in the little Ape all those years ago. The cliffs were eerily silent; the sea shimmered in the moonlight. Then the lights of the village appeared in the darkness.

The rumbling of the V8 engine echoed from the old stone walls fading in the yellow glow of the streetlamps. Vincenzo remembered how he'd run through these alleys with Carmela. He wondered what she looked like now. Nothing had changed in town. Twenty years from now, it would still look exactly the same. Only Rosaria's parents' house, on the street leading to the little fishing harbor, wasn't the crumbling pile of stones it had once been. The walls had been repaired and plastered white; it had windowsills, flower beds, and a TV antenna. This was what Giovanni put his money from Germany into.

Vincenzo got out, sweaty and overtired. A cool, salty breeze greeted him. At the harbor, the surf crashed dark against the rocks. The Iso was crackling and popping beneath the hood. They'd reached the southern edge of the continent, just before Africa. Before them, foamy sea; behind them, scorched earth.

A light went on in a second-floor window. Vincenzo recognized the silhouette of his aunt, who was peering out suspiciously. When she saw him, she ran down in her nightgown. "Vincenzo, what are you doing here?" She regarded the large car and the sleeping girl in the passenger seat with confusion. "And who's this?"

"My fiancée," Vincenzo lied.

When they awoke the following morning, their minds still on the road, the whine of the engine continued to echo in their ears, but everything here was hauntingly quiet. Only the muted sound of the breakers penetrated the closed windows. They found themselves lying on a large, old, dark-brown bed that groaned as though three generations had already been conceived and died in it. The walls smelled damp. Sitting up made Vincenzo dizzy. He fell back onto the bed.

"What's wrong?" Tanja felt his forehead. He was burning up. Dazed, he became dimly aware that Rosaria opened the door without knocking and brought in a tray of coffee, oranges, and cookies. She opened the windows and leaned over him, looking worried. Said a few words to Tanja in broken German. The coffee was hot and bitter, and what happened after that escaped his memory.

Vincenzo plunged into a world of fever dreams, a confusing flood of memories, fantasies, and contradictory emotions. He lost all sense of space and time, of day and night, of the figures at his bed and the ones in his head. Tanja held his hand at night when his eyes flew open, and he spoke to his mother in Italian; when Tanja responded in German, he looked distraught. As the summer sun sank behind the curtains, he suddenly saw Vincent standing in the room in his plaid slippers, a gun in his hand. He saw the blue police lights illuminating the walls as he escaped through the bedroom window with Tanja. He saw Enzo's eyes desperately seeking his in the courtroom. And he saw Giulietta's diary in his own hands.

Everything welled up inside him and coalesced into a desperate, bottomless rage against everyone who'd betrayed him, who'd taken from him the only person worth living for. He cursed their mentalities: the ignorance of the guest workers and the arrogance of the bourgeoisie, the Sicilians' servility and the Germans' coolness. Vincenzo also cursed Olaf for his empty babble and his impotent violence, and he hated himself for having made himself a stooge.

Vincenzo's past burned on the funeral pyre of his fever. Here, at the end of the world, there were only the moist heat, the sweaty sheets, the dust dancing in the sunbeams that shone through the windows, the piercing chirps of the grasshoppers, and the roar of the surf. Tanja stayed by his bed day and night, together with Rosaria; Rosaria's mother, Maria; and Vincenzo's grandmother, Concetta, who was overjoyed to have her grandson back. Occasionally, Rosaria's little daughter, Marietta, came running over as well, curious about her older cousin. After escaping into an exile of anger and violence, Vincenzo now returned home to the women's nourishing, nearly forgotten lap.

"Do you know the story of Oedipus?" he asked Tanja.

"The one who slept with his mother?"

"Who killed his father."

"What about him?"

"Nothing."

"What made you think of that?"

"What if I had done it?"

She shrugged. "He would have deserved it. He killed your mom."

He was silent. He didn't say which father he meant. He was terribly relieved that he hadn't pulled the trigger that night in Vincent's driveway. He could never have lived with the guilt.

On the first day he was finally back on his feet, still very weak but hungry again, he ate lunch with the women at the table. Rosaria had made squid in tomato sauce. Before he'd even finished eating, his grandmother took him and Tanja firmly by the hand.

"Come on, I have something to show you."

Concetta wore black, as she had since Giulietta's death; though physically a shadow of her former self, she radiated as much determination as ever. She lived in a room Giovanni had renovated for her—the old *magazzino*, once used to store the field equipment. Now it held a wrought-iron bed, a large wardrobe, and the makeup table from her Milan apartment. It smelled musty. Only a faint echo of sunlight streamed in from outside, from a world that had given Concetta nothing but disappointment, loss, and betrayal. She invited Vincenzo and Tanja to sit down—Tanja on her bed, Vincenzo in the only chair—and said to Vincenzo in a decisive tone: *"Devi sposarla. Non basta essere fidanzati."*

Tanja gave him a questioning look.

"She says we should get married," he translated, and attempted a wry smile.

"Tell her the truth," she retorted.

Concetta looked to Vincenzo for translation. He hesitated. Old and frail though his grandmother may have been, she was still the undisputed matriarch. In her world, she alone decided who was worthy of becoming part of the family and who was not. It was she, not Giovanni, who had cast her son-in-law Enzo out forever.

Right now, though, Vincenzo didn't have the energy to discuss the significance of civil marriage.

"Yes, we're getting married soon, don't worry."

"Isn't she Catholic?"

"Sì, sì," he replied, though he had no idea what religion Tanja was, if any. It didn't matter to him, since he'd lost his own faith in God. And there was little point in trying to explain to Concetta that there was no way a loving God would allow the Americans to throw napalm bombs on Vietnamese children. Or have his mother die before she'd had a chance to live. Concetta removed a ring from her finger. Vincenzo recognized it—as a child, he'd admired it on his mother's

finger, and been slightly afraid of it as well. Heavy silver, crowned with a square seal. A First Communion gift. After Giulietta's death, Concetta had retrieved it, and now wore it herself in honor of her daughter. Tanja had no idea what was happening as Concetta grasped her right hand and slid the ring onto her finger with the tender, unflinching authority that only grandmothers have.

"*È della mamma di Vincenzo,*" she said, and gestured to Vincenzo, who was just as speechless as Tanja.

"Tell her I can't accept it."

Concetta smiled at Vincenzo, who was paralyzed, incapable of translating. Tanja got up and removed the ring. "No, Tanja, wait!" Vincenzo could understand her reluctance, just as he knew that rejecting Concetta's generous gesture would insult his grandmother deeply. Tanja held the ring out to Concetta and asked Vincenzo to tell her that she appreciated the thought, but she couldn't accept the gift, because she wasn't part of the family. Vincenzo hesitated. He knew his grandmother would see Tanja's directness as an affront. And that she would only tolerate the German girl here with a ring on her finger. So, he mistranslated, saying that Tanja would be happy to wear it, out of love, but she believed that wearing the dead mother-in-law's ring would bring bad luck. Concetta didn't reply. In stony silence, she took back the ring, then went to her makeup table and laid it tenderly in a drawer. After that, she never looked Tanja in the eye again.

That evening, Vincenzo and Tanja fought for the first time. Tanja wasn't willing to compromise her principles of radical honesty through lies. If his relatives couldn't accept her as an emancipated woman who defined herself by herself rather than by her husband, then they would simply have to hide somewhere else. She refused to wedge herself into the role of caring companion she'd landed in overnight, when they'd only slept together recently. After her experiences with Olaf, the last thing she wanted was to be trapped in a relationship. Vincenzo pleaded with her to stay. He tried to explain that he was just as much of an outsider here as she was. It wasn't entirely true, however. Even though part of him had adopted revolutionary ideals, another part had never left his family's Italy. They argued to the point of exhaustion.

Concetta, Rosaria, and Rosaria's mother listened to the argument from the kitchen with concern—an argument in a language that now seemed even harsher, more foreign, and more threatening than ever. Until finally noises rang out from the guest room that everyone in the world understood as the language of reconciliation.

Tanja used the only phone booth on the island to call a lawyer in Berlin, the one who also represented their imprisoned comrades. He advised them to stay hidden until the situation had blown over somewhat. No arrest warrants had been issued for them thus far, but every other member of the commune was in jail, including Olaf, and there was no way of knowing whether he'd tip the police off. *He*, not Vincent, had told the cops where she and Vincenzo lived. Vincent hadn't even reported the theft of his expensive car. He'd simply spread a cloak of silence over the entire affair.

Once Vincenzo's fever broke, he and Tanja went down to the beach. He was still a little wobbly. Clouds billowed high in the sky; the sun beat down with powerful warmth. They clambered over the stones barefoot. Down here, it was more obvious that the green island had once been a volcano: instead of white sand, their feet hit hard, black rocks. Vincenzo, weary to his very bones, was filled with the desire to leave everything behind. Not to have any more responsibilities. To simply exist in the company of Mother Earth, the sea, and four women.

"You think they'll find us here?" Tanja asked, staring out at the water.

He shook his head and lifted his shirt to draw his gun from his waistband. Tanja looked alarmed. But he didn't intend to shoot it. He wanted to throw the damn thing into the sea.

"Wait!" Tanja stayed his hand. "Who knows what else we'll need it for?"

"Why bother?"

She blinked at him in bewilderment. As if that were up for debate.

"Tanja. Have we changed anything?"

"If we stop fighting, they win."

"We have AK-47s. They have tanks, planes, armies. Who are we? Society couldn't give a shit about little fish like us."

"Not if we force them to take notice of us. Be sand, not oil, in the machinery of the world!"

Vincenzo shook his head firmly.

"People don't want a revolution. They want everything to stay the way it is. And these guys like Olaf, or Baader and Meinhof, they don't care about society. Or the working class. Or the Third World. They only believe in themselves."

He'd touched a sore spot. Tanja was slowly beginning to suspect the same thing, though she couldn't yet admit it.

"What about you?" she asked. "What do you believe in?"

"Nothing anymore."

He wound up and launched the pistol into the water. Then he stripped off his clothes and ran naked into the surf. Tanja followed him. The sea enveloped him, tossed him back and forth in the rolling waves, until he surrendered to them and stopped feeling lost, sensing that he was part of this massive, eternal breath. He closed his eyes, dove down, and allowed the sea to take everything from him that hadn't been himself.

Later, they lay side by side on the black rocks, their bare skin drying quickly in the sun. Vincenzo had died and been reborn. He reached for her hand and found it effortlessly, felt it return his gentle pressure as he clasped it. His heart was pounding, but his mind was more calm than it had been in a long time. The sky and the silhouette of his dark, curly head reflected in Tanja's pale eyes.

"You and me," he said. "We don't need anything else to be happy."

"But I don't want to be happy."

Vincenzo stared at her in astonishment. "You would rather be unhappy?"

"No. I want to have a purpose. A goal. I want to know what I'm living for."

"Maybe there's no such thing. Maybe it's all just one big coincidence."

"What's the matter with you?"

"It's true. And it could all end tomorrow."

Tanja straightened up and gazed out at the sea. He kissed her neck and ran a hand through her hair.

"We can just do it all day and all night."

She laughed. Then she grew serious.

"We hardly know each other, Vincenzo."

"This is our chance. No old burdens. We can forget the past."

"What about your family? This island is full of past."

"We'll just reinvent ourselves."

He drew her to him.

"I dunno." She hesitated. "We can't place demands on each other," she said. "I don't want to end up in another relationship like the one with Olaf. I mean, he'd screw anyone with a pulse, but when I did the same thing, he got possessive. It should always feel free."

"Of course." Vincenzo kissed her. Her delicate shoulder blade. Her pale skin in the sharp sunlight. "Anything you want."

She gave him a fleeting kiss before getting up and jumping into the water. He watched, praying he would never be driven away from this paradise.

As they walked back to the village, the church bells began to ring. The Easter procession was coming in their direction. A Christ figure wrapped in black swayed on the men's backs. They marched through the village, with the old priest leading, followed by women dressed in black. Automatically, Vincenzo recalled his mother's funeral. Rosaria waved them over. Her mother and Concetta were there as well.

Vincenzo and Tanja joined the march. They went up the hilly country road with even strides, through vineyards and caper fields, to the Church of the Madonna del Terzito—where, according to the old folks, the Virgin Mary had once appeared to a pair of farmers. A second procession was approaching from the other side, bearing the Madonna on their own shoulders. She, too, was wrapped in black velvet. The two groups met on the street in front of the church. The sun emerged from behind the April clouds. The ministers removed the gold-embroidered black cloths from Christ and his mother, then leaned the figures toward each other; the Holy Mother seemed to be clasping her resurrected son in her arms.

58

The island was one giant exhalation. The fields lay fallow beneath the vast sky, rolling toward the sea in gentle waves. Wine, capers, and olives interspersed with wild bushes, herbs, and cacti. Everything twisted and sprawled; lizards whirled around in the dirt. Yellow moss on the stones, old walls eroded by salt, derelict houses. Island of emigrants, island of absence. Vincenzo spent entire days wandering the dusty streets to find the places of his past, disturbed and intoxicated by the memories flooding his senses. The numbing scents of pine trees, wild thyme, and rosemary—the smell of the last summer of his childhood. Palms and eucalyptus trees whooshed in the wind, the endless sea glittering behind them. When he closed his eyes, he could still picture every detail of the wedding: the white tablecloths in the windy field, his mother's red dress, Giovanni's suit . . . and the old stone wall where he'd had his first kiss.

His grandparents' house was still there, to the extent that it could still be called a house. Little more than the foundation walls peeked out from the undergrowth, black and sodden and overgrown with wild vines. The roof had collapsed long ago, and inside, it smelled damp and moldy. Someone had used it as a toilet. The field where Giovanni and Rosaria had celebrated their marriage was scarcely recognizable, overtaken by wild shrubs, weeds, and enormous thistles. *Nature is merciless,* Vincenzo thought. *It swallows everything and forgets what was. Everything of value exists only in memory.* When Vincenzo returned to the village, the sun had already disappeared behind the mountain; rusty lanterns gleamed gold atop the walls.

"What are you?" a fisherman asked him in greeting. "A foreigner or an emigrant returning home?"

Vincenzo wasn't sure how to respond. The villagers divided everyone into categories that he rejected. Foreigner and native, emigrant and returner, master and slave. Vincenzo didn't want to be any of those. And to his delight, he soon discovered that villagers afforded him a certain "jester's license." To them, he was *il tedesco*: he was young; he was different; he stood out, and so he couldn't be expected to follow the written and unwritten community rules too closely.

Around here, his foreignness was no longer a source of subtle indignity—it was admirable. *Complimenti*, they said when he told them about Germany; down here, his life in the wealthy North sounded like the fulfilment of a dream the islanders had been denied. The ones who still lived here belonged to the stubborn, melancholy caste of the left-behinds, the ones who hadn't made it onto the ships bound for America or the trains to Germany. The most courageous or desperate among them had long ago left for parts unknown in search of the dignified life they had never found in their native land. Their abandoned houses were crumbling now, and the yards where their children had played were overgrown with time.

Though it made no sense for a restless twenty-year-old, Salina somehow struck Vincenzo as the ideal refuge: the part of him that was still a child was loved unconditionally in that special Mediterranean way, while the part of him that was old beyond his years could reinvent himself. Here, he wasn't just the things society saw in him—the foreigner, the guest worker's kid, the prodigy. He was just himself, a stranger in a wild landscape that reflected his own soul.

Tanja, on the other hand, was the biggest scandal on the island. Every woman in the village was outraged at her shamelessness for lying nude on the beach, while every man fantasized about the beautiful German woman. When she walked down the street, people of both genders averted their eyes. She heard their spiteful whispering as she went by, and felt their veiled, lustful gazes on her back. As long as she passed for Vincenzo's betrothed, they had to leave her in peace, but her presence was an event that pushed the usual laments about unemployment, the ineptitude of the government, or the murderous Red Brigades into the background. It never occurred to anyone that the young couple might be somehow connected to the violence erupting on the mainland against the state and the police.

Then Giovanni arrived. Once he'd heard from Rosaria where the nephew who'd robbed him had escaped to, he'd seized the first opportunity to head south. He emerged from his rickety delivery van unshaven and weary, kissed his daughter when Rosaria put her into his arms, and then went straight to Vincenzo and slapped him. *"Deficiente!"* he grunted, and hugged him. Vincenzo was glad to see him again. He grinned at his uncle, half-wry, half-embarrassed, as Giovanni showered his little girl with kisses and pet names.

Giovanni joked with Tanja over lunch, but Vincenzo couldn't tell what his uncle really thought of his *"fidanzata."* In the afternoon, when the heat let up, Giovanni took Vincenzo on a walk to Giulietta's grave. Vincenzo mentally prepared himself for a barrage of questions. How could he waste his life and his talent like this? What were the police accusing him of?

But Giovanni didn't mention the past as they walked toward the old cemetery overlooking the sea. Unlike Tanja, who immediately launched into a discussion of anything problematic, the Marconis—particularly Giovanni—preferred to leave things unsaid, allowing everyone to save face no matter how grave their offenses. Giovanni praised the unparalleled beauty of Aeolian Mother Earth, the silvery light on the olive tree leaves, the scent of the sirocco blowing from Africa, and the incomparable taste of the local olives and the cactus pears. He vowed to return for good one day. Vincenzo knew him well enough to know that his enthusiasm would fade a day or two after his arrival, giving way to glorious stories about Germany, which he admired, though still didn't love.

Finally, they stood at Giulietta's grave in silence. The white paint on the angel had already peeled a little in the salty air. It was the first time Vincenzo had come out here, and a wave of grief and despondence washed over him. Giovanni nudged him in the side.

"What are you going to do now?"

"No idea."

"They came to see me," Giovanni said.

"Who, the cops?"

"They said if they found you, they'd deport you. If you ask me, as long as you're out of the country, they're not interested in you. So, stay here awhile."

"I don't want to go back anyway."

Giovanni pondered. "What are you going to do here?" Vincenzo shrugged. "You wanted to build cars once upon a time, remember?"

Vincenzo turned away. "Forget it, Giovanni. I'm a failure."

"Nonsense. You're twenty! Do something with your life. You want to make the world a better place? Stop causing trouble and start the revolution with yourself!"

Vincenzo snapped that if his family hadn't screwed up so much, he would be at college by now, in Milan, maybe London, instead of suffering for the sins of others.

"Quit blaming everyone else," Giovanni retorted. "You're an adult now. Either you pull yourself out of the muck, or you stay stuck in it."

"What do you expect me to do? No high school diploma, no money, no nothing."

"Get your diploma here. There's a *liceo* on Lipari."

"If I enroll there, they'll find me."

"Bah, the Italian cops don't give a shit about you. You're not that important."

"What if they send me to the military? You expect me to kill for this fascist state?"

"So what? At least they'd teach you discipline!"

"Look who's talking. Didn't you leave Italy to avoid the draft?"

"At least I tried to find a job!"

"What job am I going to find on this fart in the middle of the sea? Everyone's left this place because there's no work here! Don't you get it? I'm screwed, I have nothing!"

"You have yourself. Your mind." Giovanni lowered his voice. "And you have a woman."

Vincenzo searched Giovanni's eyes and then shrugged.

"I barely know her."

"Do you want to marry her?" Giovanni asked with unusual directness.

"Maybe."

Giovanni gave him a searching look.

"You need to get this girl pregnant fast. Otherwise, she'll leave you."

Vincenzo raised his eyebrows skeptically.

"You got yours pregnant, and she left anyway."

Giovanni smirked at him and shrugged.

"Women. What can you do?"

He put an arm around Vincenzo, and they walked back to their house, to their women.

Well after midnight, once Tanja had fallen asleep, Vincenzo got up, snuck out of the house, and wandered through the alleys to sort his thoughts. A cool wind wafted in from the sea; a dog barked somewhere; there was trash lying around. It felt as if the entire village had been abandoned, and now only the walls were left to tell the stories of the people who had once lived here, who had dreamed of a better life elsewhere.

The idea of "making something of yourself" tortured Vincenzo, the suggestion being that a person wasn't something already. As though a person were only somebody when "the world," whoever that was, recognized and rewarded the achievement through a monthly salary, a car, and envious neighbors. Logically, then, anyone who didn't have all of those things was nobody. His mother had drilled into him how talented he was, how he could have it better—so much so that he'd developed an instinctive reluctance to fulfill her expectations.

Giulietta's death hadn't taken that burden from his shoulders. If anything, it put even more pressure on him. Moreover, his childhood dream of becoming an automotive engineer was no longer undiscovered terrain through which he could surpass his father, the assembly worker—it was already the successful domain of a different father, one he despised.

After that fateful night outside the garage, following in Vincent's footsteps seemed completely out of the question, no matter how much of the man's talent he'd inherited. He wondered whether professional success was something he actually wanted, or whether bourgeois society had simply conditioned him to think that. He thought back to his old tutoring sessions with Mr. Grimm, to *Wilhelm Meister's Apprenticeship*, and reflected on how hollow the ideals of the educated bourgeoisie seemed when confronted with real life, that battle for existence, dirty and unjust. The entire idea of going to the office every morning and then coming back to his suburban home every night struck him as wrong and dishonest.

If it was true that there was no right life in the wrong one, he thought, then he would have to make a far more radical choice, namely, to make no choices at all, to refuse to commit to anything. What he really wanted was something totally different, not a plan so much as a feeling, a desire that had absolutely nothing to do with what people expected of men his age.

Vincenzo had considered suicide more than once and wouldn't have minded dying on one of Tanja's political "missions." What made him think so little of himself, while everyone else had always seen him as something special? Other people admired something they themselves didn't have—knowledge, a talent. But why should a person be proud of his own talent? He was born with it, just like he was born with his shortcomings, with blue eyes or brown. *People can only be proud of what they've achieved under their own power,* Vincenzo thought.

Perhaps it had been his time in Germany, or the shameful secret of his parentage, that had convinced Vincenzo he didn't belong anywhere—neither with his classmates, nor with the proletarian father he looked down on, nor with the biological father who had rejected him.

The only person he'd felt a deep connection to had been his mother. Nobody could replace her, not even Tanja. When it came down to it, he was alone in the world. There was only one way for him to truly be part of a family, Vincenzo decided: to become a father himself. Children would be the proof that his existence wasn't pure coincidence. That it had a purpose. That he'd leave something behind.

He clambered over a wall into the overgrown yard of an abandoned house—a beautiful, majestic building, not a squat little thing like his grandparents' place. He crept quietly across the broken tiles on the terrace. Flower patterns in the moonlight. They clicked beneath his feet. He forced the door and stepped inside, where it stank of bird shit and musty damp. Bats fluttered in the darkness. *It wouldn't take much to bring the house back to life,* he thought. The walls were old but stable; the roof had holes, but it hadn't fallen in. It was a place just waiting to be filled with voices. Vincenzo wasn't sure what he would do on Salina, but it didn't matter where he lived. He had to put down roots to keep from losing himself completely.

At dawn, he crawled into bed. Shivering, but aflame with his vision, he nestled against Tanja's warm, sleeping body. Whispered into her ear that he loved her. She rolled over, ran a hand through his hair, mumbled something, and drifted off again. Vincenzo didn't let up. "Tanja, I want to live here with you. I want to have children with you. I want to marry you."

Surprised, she opened her eyes, sat up, and switched on the lamp.

Vincenzo told her about the abandoned house. About the tiles on the terrace and the unborn children. She listened for a while, half-skeptical, half-amazed, before finally interrupting.

"Vincenzo, I want to get out of here."

"We can't go back."

"But we can keep going."

"Where?"

"Farther south. Algeria, Cuba, Bolivia. We can actually do something there. Not in this godforsaken village where nothing will change in a hundred years."

"How do you plan on getting across the border without a passport?"

"We can buy passports. What would I do here?"

Vincenzo stroked her bare shoulder tenderly. "I love you."

"I love you, too," she whispered.

Tanja thought for a moment and then lit a cigarette.

"What am I supposed to do here, Vincenzo? Cook for you?"

"Obviously." He grinned ironically. He couldn't picture Tanja as an Italian mamma, but why should the things he loved about her—her free spirit, her convictions—stand in the way of having a family? They would do things differently than their parents had. They'd redefine themselves and raise their children to be truly free. They'd show the world what was possible.

The more he talked, the more skeptical Tanja became. What had she gone to college for? She saw herself as part of a larger movement, where people throughout the world were fighting for the same ideals. As soldiers of a revolutionary army. And she'd seen Vincenzo in their ranks, too. Why was he doubting everything all of a sudden?

No, Vincenzo replied, he still believed in a more just society where everyone had the same opportunities. It was just that—he couldn't put his motivation into words. He fell silent. He felt alone, more alone than ever.

Tanja sensed the shame beneath his silence. She tried to encourage him: he wasn't bourgeois; he didn't need a house or the millstone of a family around his neck, not yet. He was still so young; he had so much potential; it was time for him to make something of himself . . .

"Don't tell me how talented I am! I'm sick of hearing it!" He got up, walked out of the room, out of the house, slamming the door behind him and leaving Tanja alone.

59

Vincenzo didn't get far. Where was he going to go, after all? Without his passport, which had surely been confiscated by the German police along with everything else he owned, he was nobody. And without a future with Tanja to look forward to, the gnawing fear that he was a loser weighed on him more than ever. It wasn't the self-doubt that had plagued his mother all her life, though—deep down, he felt superior to everyone else. It seemed to him like the world was a play that had started before he arrived, and even though he had a ticket, every seat was already taken.

By dinner, Vincenzo was back at the family table. He didn't say another word to Tanja about children. After the evening news—Giovanni had brought down a German television—they showed a documentary about Vietnam. The Viet Cong was outside Saigon; the US army was near defeat. Everything was in chaos. The Americans flew South Vietnamese orphans out in gigantic cargo planes. Tanks and helicopters filled the aircraft on the way over; on the flight back, hundreds of small children. The war orphans were going to be placed with foster parents in the US—"Operation Babylift," they called it. The first of the planes crashed shortly after takeoff—155 dead.

Vincenzo was enraged. He shouted at the Americans with such vitriol that Giovanni had to turn the television off. Tanja didn't understand why he was getting so emotional.

"The war is over, Vincenzo."

"Nothing's over!" he exclaimed. "What right do they have to steal those children? What will become of them? Where are they going to be in twenty years?"

"They're orphans. They're taking them to a better life."

"Criminals. Child thieves. What the hell are they even doing in Vietnam?"

"The Vietnamese are Communists," Rosaria put in.

"Oh, and I guess they eat little kids?" Vincenzo snapped at her.

"Do you know how many children Stalin murdered?" Giovanni shot back.

"Stop fighting!" his little daughter cried.

Vincenzo slammed his silverware onto the table, stood up, and left.

Tanja stayed at the table.

Later, Giovanni and Rosaria argued. He wanted to take her and their daughter back to Germany so that she could finally start school there.

"She's with her own kind here," Rosaria said.

"The teachers are asses here. They haven't seen any of the world. How are they supposed to explain it to the children?"

"I'm tired of traveling back and forth, Giovanni. So is she. She needs to know where she belongs."

"You want me to give up everything I've achieved in Germany?"

"You've forgotten your roots, Giovanni. I'll wait here until you return."

Giovanni drove back to Germany. Alone. Soon, summer heat settled over the island. Some days, they'd get sand between their teeth, carried across the water from Africa on the sirocco. Tanja came up with a plan. If she had to stay here, she could at least stop wasting time. And if changing the world using weapons wasn't an option from here, she could at least change it using words. She started writing her doctoral thesis. An old Olivetti typewriter she got from the village junk dealer, books she had comrades mail her from Germany, and a spot on the covered terrace, surrounded by the laundry Rosaria hung—that was all she needed. She got a friend in Germany to send her a typebar with German accent marks; Vincenzo installed it for her.

The clacking of the typewriter became part of the house. As soon as the sun came out from behind the clouds, Tanja was out on the terrace in a bikini and a dark-brown hat that had belonged to Rosaria's father. Concetta took Vincenzo aside and demanded he make his fiancée see reason: whatever she was writing there, she ought to do it in the house and properly dressed, stop tarnishing the family name.

Of course, Tanja did no such thing; in fact, resisting the old Sicilian women spurred her on. Tanja saw asserting her identity in this society shaped by shame, religion, and obedience as part of the struggle for liberation. The bikini as a political manifesto of personal authenticity. What Vincenzo considered respect for the customs of one's hosts, she called subjugation to the patriarchal regime. But though Vincenzo defended his family to Tanja, he also protected Tanja from his family. He treasured her free spirit, her intelligence, and her courage to be herself. And he was her man—or at least he wanted to prove to her that he was.

Tanja took care of herself, though. She repurposed an old coffee grinder, and every evening, she ground fresh grain to soak overnight; in the morning, to the Italians' bewilderment, she'd mix it with almonds and fruit from the garden. Little Marietta marveled at the enormous bowl full of mush that the Germans apparently consumed every morning. She wanted to eat some of it, too, because she was convinced that this "muesli"—a word nobody had ever heard on the island, and none could pronounce—was the secret reason why Germans were bigger than Sicilians. And she wanted to be big someday, tall and strong. Rosaria's mother, meanwhile, was convinced that eating so much in the morning ruined a person's stomach, and kept to her single espresso with two spoons of sugar.

Fall arrived early that year. Don Calogero, Carmela's father, came down from Palermo to supervise the grape harvest. Rosaria asked him to hire Vincenzo as a seasonal laborer, but only a few workdays came of it. Too few grapevines had survived the pests.

The noble Malvasia, the liquid gold that had brought fame and fortune to the island a hundred years before, now provided only a modest living to a handful of farmers. The older generations' knowledge hadn't been lost, but without organized distribution and the northern vintners' modern methods, the few barrels that were pressed remained on the islands unbottled—the wine only got as far as Lipari and Filicudi. It was unfiltered, dark, and not yet adapted to the palates of the masses. Vincenzo helped with the harvest, but Don Calogero quickly saw that farming life wasn't growing on him. Technology was the only thing he was enthusiastic about, and there wasn't much of that out here, on this archipelago at the edge of time. The women still stamped the grape must with their bare feet.

When the first storms swept across the island in November and torrents of rain flowed through the alleys, Vincenzo winterized the house. He fixed the rotting windows, sawed, hammered, and nailed. Back in Germany, the Baader-Meinhof Gang was on trial, and Niki Lauda became the Formula One world champion.

They celebrated Christmas 1975 alone with the old women, because Rosaria had gone to Munich with her daughter, Marietta. Tanja hadn't expected the winter storms to be so bad. The wind whistled through every crack in the walls, and they were cut off from the mainland for days at a time when the ferries couldn't dock on account of the high waves. *C'è mare mosso,* they said. Ugly sea.

When the sun set at five o'clock, Tanja and Vincenzo sat by the dim lamps, reading whatever books they could get their hands on; they spent whole evenings deep in discussion, usually of world politics, never again mentioning the real questions. They secretly knew that, despite the intellectual connection they shared, the one thing they would never agree on was family. Unspoken words created a gulf between them, which they filled with wild, unbridled sex that only made them hungrier for the things they couldn't give each other.

Vincenzo was sure Tanja would change her mind once he was in a position to feed a family. He blamed himself, not her. The thought of his relatives seeing him as a parasite was an affront to his sense of self-worth. They, like Rosaria and the two old women, were living off the money Giovanni sent from Germany. He needed money of his own. He needed work. He needed a place in the world, the thing that gave a man footing and structure. "Give me a place to stand, and I will move the Earth," Archimedes had said. Vincenzo knew now that he couldn't expect anything like that from Tanja. She gave him wings but not roots. He suspected that, as a man, he could find such a place to stand only in the world of men, not in the world of women.

Concetta had gone to church every day, rain or shine, to pray a rosary for Vincenzo. All winter long. And one day, when the orange trees were in bloom again and the migratory birds set off for the North, something happened. It was the April 7, 1976, edition of the *Giornale di Sicilia*, which the fishmonger wrapped around the purchase Vincenzo was making at the harbor. The black-and-white photo on the crumpled second page electrified him. Vincenzo unwrapped the fish from the newspaper right there at the harbor.

The photo showed a man in his forties with a plaid cap, aviator sunglasses, and a determined expression. Vincenzo's childhood hero, the man who was to the Sicilians what Niki Lauda was to the Austrians or James Hunt to the English. The only internationally ranked Sicilian race car driver. A living legend. Nino Vaccarella.

Every May, the oldest and toughest race in the world, the Targa Florio, was held in Sicily. Once a year, the island's serpentine country roads became an insane racecourse as Ferraris, Porsches, and Alfas tore through the old villages at unimaginable speeds. There was nothing protecting the drivers or the fans, apart from a few hay bales and the occasional rickety crash barrier along the worst of the nine hundred curves. Onlookers formed an honor guard by the roadside, farmers crossed the track on donkey carts, and children stretched out their hands excitedly to feel the fireballs roaring past. Sometimes a Maserati would race into a flock of sheep. The whole thing was more like an out-of-control public festival than a world championship—which was exactly what made it so famous.

Back then, if you'd asked an American or a Japanese person what they associated with Sicily, they'd say two things: the Mafia and the Targa Florio. For Sicilians, it was the one spectacle of the year (apart from the Easter procession) that yanked the villages out of their slumber. The international car-circus had descended upon the island annually since 1906, a day when poverty and hopelessness could take a back seat to high-society ladies and death-defying drivers—who were real men back then, rock stars on wheels: Tazio Nuvolari, Stirling Moss, Wolfgang von Trips, Clay Regazzoni, Jackie Ickx . . . and Nino Vaccarella. He was the undisputed local hero, "one of us," a teacher from Palermo who had made it to the top through sheer driving talent alone. In 1964, he'd won 24 Hours of Le Mans in a Ferrari; he'd won the '65 Targa Florio in a Ferrari and the '71 in an Alfa Romeo; and he was competing again this year, even though he was already in his forties—the only Italian anyone thought had a chance of ending the German drivers' recent dominance. The Germans were younger, their Porsches more modern, but nobody knew Sicily like Vaccarella.

When Vincenzo saw Vaccarella's picture, he knew what he was going to do with his life. He remembered when he was nine, standing in a bar in Milan with Enzo and his buddies as they celebrated Vaccarella's victory in Le Mans. He also recalled how the world had seemed to him back then: an open field of possibilities. If Vaccarella could do it out of nowhere, with no connections and no money, he could, too. After all, there was one thing in the world that he knew he was truly exceptional at. Whenever Vincenzo had wheels under his butt—whether the soapbox of his childhood, the moped of his youth, or the stolen cars of his urban guerilla days—nobody else could hold a candle to him. It was the one area of his life where he'd never been beaten. In the intoxicating rush of speed, he could leave all his humiliations behind.

He didn't have much time, as the race was coming up fast—they'd already started ferrying the cars to Palermo from the mainland. He was well aware of what the women would think of his plan: his aunt would fear for his life; his grandmother would say that the racing world was a cesspool of vice; and Tanja saw Vincenzo as a misunderstood intellectual, not a daredevil.

But as crazy as it was, the dream felt to him like liberation from his fathers' dual shadows: there was nothing he despised more than them, but nothing he loved more than the machines they made. Determined not to follow in their footsteps, he didn't want to go to college like the one, nor become a manual laborer like the other. No, he would never end up at a drafting table or on an assembly line—he belonged behind the wheel. Vincenzo against everyone else. Holding neither a pencil nor a wrench, but his own life, which could very well end at the next curve.

Vincenzo brought the fish home without mentioning the plan to anyone. The determined staccato of Tanja's typewriter echoed from the terrace as Rosaria prepared the fish with thyme, rosemary, salt, and olive oil, and Concetta dozed in the semidarkness of her room. Vincenzo knew where Rosaria hid the cash Giovanni brought her—in the cantina, behind the Malvasia bottles. He took only what he would need for two weeks, packing one change of clothes into a worn plastic bag he slid under the bed. Then he put on his old sneakers and strolled into the yard, where the Iso Rivolta slumbered beneath a tarp, hidden from the evil eye that neighbors might cast upon the luxury car. He pulled down the tarp and wiped the dust from the car, polishing the lacquer lovingly.

Over dinner, he mentioned with perfect nonchalance that he'd found work in Palermo. A construction job. It would last only a couple of weeks, and he'd bring the money back home. The news startled Tanja, but Rosaria was proud that her nephew had finally made a manly decision. The work would do him good, and they could certainly use the money now that they had two extra mouths to feed.

Vincenzo avoided any hard questions by leaving for the ferry to Milazzo before anyone could stop him. Tanja accompanied him to the harbor. She resented his abandoning her there by herself, but she tried not to let it show. She wished him luck; they kissed goodbye; and he promised to return by the end of the month. Then, under the covetous eyes of the deckhands, he steered the gleaming Rivolta onto the rusty ferry—a far-too-young man with a far-too-big dream.

60

The ferry glided across the calm night sea. As the lights of the small island disappeared on the horizon, Vincenzo suddenly grew afraid of losing Tanja. He'd lied to her because he hadn't wanted to justify himself. Deep down, he still didn't feel strong enough to address her misgivings. He wanted to come back with something concrete, a success that would legitimate his plan.

He'd followed the Targa Florio year after year in the papers and on television; he knew the loophole he could use to his own advantage. In 1973, the dangerous and chaotic race had lost its world championship status and become a national event. The cars were still overpowered and the safety measures more ridiculous than ever, but the reclassification made it possible for private drivers to qualify as well.

Vincenzo was aware that nobody would take him seriously without identification, connections, or racing experience. But there was one person who might help him get onto a racing crew, if he believed Vincenzo had talent. And that one person was Nino Vaccarella. Vaccarella wouldn't turn him away, Vincenzo assured himself, not when he himself had gone from a nobody to a living legend. He would return with contract in hand, would earn his own money legally for the first time in his life, would show Tanja that he was enough of a man to make her his wife. He still admired her too much to consider himself her equal—but now that was going to change.

Vincenzo kept watch over the Iso Rivolta, which sat on the ferry amid the dented Fiats and Renaults. The conspicuous car was a risk, of course, but it was the only thing that would allow him to cut a *bella figura* in front of the drivers. Without the car, he was nothing. He didn't sleep a wink until the ferry reached

Sicily at dawn. Cautiously, Vincenzo maneuvered the Iso down the rusty ramp onto the pier. Milazzo was still asleep; the morning air was clear; no carabinieri were in sight. Left in peace, Vincenzo took the coastal road out of town, then the freeway heading toward Palermo.

In Campofelice, just past Cefalù, he found himself on historic asphalt already: the country highway was the long straightaway on the circuit. Here, the race cars would reach their top speeds. Marshals were busy putting up advertisements. Campari, Martini & Rossi, Fernet-Branca. Farmers were unloading straw bales from their donkeys. A red Alfa Romeo shot past at an insane speed—a few drivers already practicing, in the middle of regular traffic. The children by the roadside waved excitedly.

Vincenzo tried to decide how to go about his plan. His mother's voice echoed in his mind: "There's no greater sin than wasted talent." But where she'd blamed herself for not having lived her life, Vincenzo blamed the world for not recognizing and fostering his gifts. His mood vacillated between youthful megalomania and a profound sense of failure, and the closer he got to his goal, the more his idea seemed doomed to fail. The only thing that gave him a sense of security was the car he was driving—built by Enzo, bought by Vincent. He hadn't managed to achieve anything in life except for stealing this car. He felt like a charlatan.

In the middle of the hilly, May-green landscape, the empty bleachers at the start and finish lines stretched toward the heavens. It was the calm before the storm; half the pits were still closed, while mechanics stood outside the others, smoking. An engine revved somewhere; mechanics rolled a Lancia Stratos off a truck. A flock of sheep grazed nearby.

Vincenzo turned onto the pit lane and drove slowly past the garages. Lancia, De Tomaso, Alfa Romeo . . . He tried to look as nonchalant as possible as he got out, but contrary to his expectations, nobody was interested in his car here. A mustachioed mechanic called out that he needed to move his vehicle. Vincenzo approached him and asked about Vaccarella.

"Who are you?" the mechanic retorted. With all the confidence he could muster, Vincenzo replied that he'd come to speak with Vaccarella. The mechanic eyed him mistrustfully, but here the expensive car did its job. "Nino's on the track." In Sicily, there was no telling who might belong to the kind of family you didn't mess with. The mechanic turned and walked away. Vincenzo went to the track. He waited.

Nino Vaccarella knew every curve of this course like the back of his hand, but he still drove the track over and over before the race, practicing for days on end, memorizing every switchback and summit. It was that modesty, that respect for the magnitude of his task, that had taken him to the top.

Vincenzo observed a dozen young men in plaid shirts and jeans at the edge of the pit line, smoking and chatting. All at once, the group sprang into action when an open-top car raced over before braking hard. Vincenzo recognized the model, an Alfa Romeo Tipo 33. A red beast with a twelve-cylinder engine snarling viciously in the back and "Campari" written on the sides in white. The motor sounded like a ravenous circular saw, an angry, infernal howl with the transmission wailing sharply beneath it. A cockpit of bare metal, a hard seat, a tiny steering wheel—this wasn't a car; it was a coffin on wheels.

The driver's helmet read, "Vaccarella." As he climbed out of the car and silenced the five hundred furious horses, the group of young men launched themselves at him, and now a few women joined them as well. At first, Vincenzo thought they were looking for autographs. Vaccarella took his helmet off and spoke to them calmly. Vincenzo moved closer, trying to catch a glimpse of Vaccarella, but he was immediately pushed aside. Then he heard what the men were saying and realized they all wanted the same thing from Vaccarella that he did!

The energy and volume they unleashed took his breath away. It wasn't the competition that frightened him—he would gladly have taken on any one of them—but the mirror they held up. He'd been prepared for practically any-thing: that Vaccarella would be too busy to see him, that he'd brush Vincenzo off arrogantly, that he wouldn't show up at all. But none of his mental scenarios had included other men his age with the same reckless dream in their heads. In a flash, he realized how self-absorbed he'd been, both on the island and in the years before, and how unprepared he was for the world at large. Vincenzo, who'd always felt different from everyone else, for better and for worse, suddenly understood that he was just one of many, that talent didn't entitle a person to happiness, that nobody was waiting around for him.

Silently, Vincenzo watched the other boys crowding around Vaccarella. They had one big advantage over him: they were Sicilian kids, with simple clothes and flat caps. They were like Vaccarella. The driver seemed to enjoy fielding their questions and faced their hotheaded temperaments with the calm, understanding, and love that only a person who had once been one of them could manage. And Vincenzo, with his inner turmoil, his Milanese dialect, and his German upbringing, was once again the outsider.

He left without even trying to compete. On the pit line, he saw two young Italian Porsche drivers—the lucky ones who had actually made it into the cockpit. In their racing coveralls, they looked like Vaccarella at first glance, but their posture and the way they spoke to the mechanics betrayed their social class. Vincenzo recognized them as jeunesse dorée, people whose fathers had taught them the world was all theirs.

But Vincenzo didn't want to give up. Unlike a few years ago, when he'd cursed the world for his unhappiness, he now realized that dwelling on the past was self-sabotage. Damning Enzo and Vincent to hell wouldn't free Vincenzo from his own hell. Just the opposite: thinking about them day and night was his hell. And now, he was determined to pull himself out.

Vincenzo approached the mechanic outside the Alfa pit.

"Can I work here as your assistant?"

The man regarded him with a sneer. "Where are you from?"

It was the usual question down here in the South—where you were from was more important than where you were going. Vincenzo hated the ritual. No matter which answer he gave, it was always wrong. "I'm not trained, but I know my way around cars."

"You have a strange accent. You from the North? Milanese?"

"No, I'm from here," Vincenzo lied. "And I'll work for free."

And that was how Vincenzo took part in his first race—albeit not in the cockpit, but as a foot soldier to the foot soldiers. He wanted to be closer to Vaccarella than the fans while he waited for the right moment to approach the man, and he was prepared to work his way up from the very bottom. But the mechanics didn't let him anywhere near the cars; he was just the errand boy for engine oil and coffee. The action on the track barely registered, so immersed was he in the chaos of the sticky pit that stank of gas, sweat, and exhaust, where there was never enough of anything, and something was always breaking and forcing them to improvise, where the top dogs pushed him around and humiliated him. But Vincenzo had something to prove, and he clung to his dream.

The race was crazier than ever. A driver was killed when his car veered off course at the end of the straightaway. Two Alfas had to drop out, leaving only Vaccarella to represent the team. He drove as though in a trance, winning by a slim margin. When he descended from the winners' podium with trophy in hand, he announced into the reporters' microphones that this race had been his last. He dedicated the win to all Sicilians.

Vincenzo packed his dirty clothes into the Iso. The afternoon heat faded; the team celebrated. Vincenzo was dog-tired. He hadn't managed to talk to Vaccarella. But he'd learned a lot. He'd learned that it wasn't just about the driver's talent or the mechanic's skill; rather, it was the understanding between them that mattered. They used different languages to talk about the same things. The driver felt something in his body that the mechanic could measure only in grams and milliliters, in fine-tuning the attenuator, the oil pressure, or the weight distribution. The secret to success was the art of translating from one language to the other. Vincenzo resolved to come back the following May. He had a year to prepare.

"Bella macchina," a voice said behind him.

Vincenzo turned around and saw a man in unassuming gray pants and a white shirt. It was Nino Vaccarella.

"Such a shame they went under. *La Iso*, those were the golden years." There was a hint of melancholy and bitterness in his voice. He extended a hand to the stunned Vincenzo. "Ciao! What's your name?"

"Vincenzo."

"Where are you from?"

Vincenzo told him nothing about his past and everything about his plans for the future.

Vaccarella listened attentively. "You're different from the others," he said afterward. "You've got brains. Why don't you go to college?"

"Why shouldn't a race car driver have brains? I can do more than just drive fast. I know how to make the car faster, too."

"Ah, you're a technician, like that Austrian with Ferrari," Vaccarella replied. "Lauda is good, but he doesn't just have brains—he has money, too. He bought his way into his first cockpit."

Vincenzo blinked. He hadn't known that.

"See these new drivers?" Vaccarella pointed to the twenty-year-olds standing beside their silver Porsches. "That's the future. Now that the Targa isn't a championship race anymore, they're buying themselves cars. They get all the best materials, and let me tell you, the days where talent was enough are over. In the future, whoever has the biggest budget will win."

But Vincenzo wouldn't accept that. The world needed other people, too, he insisted. People who made it on talent alone. People like him, Vaccarella.

"That's Italy," Vaccarella replied. "What matters here isn't what you know— it's who you know. If you want my advice, kid, get your diploma and find yourself a normal job. Take care!" He smiled and began to walk away.

"Wait!"

Vaccarella turned around.

"What's the real reason you're quitting? You're still the best."

Vaccarella gazed at him for a long moment. The evening sun reflected in his eyes.

"My son's just come into the world. You can't keep doing this job once you're a father."

Then he got into his Fiat and drove home.

Vincenzo made the return journey that night in his oil-smeared clothes, with a near-empty tank, barely any money left, and one or two fewer illusions. People say our dreams give us wings. But though that was perhaps true for his mother, Vincenzo's own wings were weighed down by her failures, and he felt more like Icarus. He began to realize that his challenge wasn't flying higher than everyone else—it was taking his first steps on the ground.

As soon as he parked the Iso outside Rosaria's house at dawn, he could sense that something was wrong. It wasn't the lack of wind or the calm surf. It was a different stillness, a new absence. At first, he thought perhaps Tanja had left, but when Rosaria came out to meet him with reddened, helpless eyes, he knew immediately what had happened.

61

The white angel marking Giulietta's grave seemed to have been waiting patiently for Concetta to be buried beside her daughter. Silence lay over the cemetery by the sea. Unlike Giulietta's funeral, nobody collapsed into loud lamentations; none of the black-clad widows clawed their faces. Though Concetta's life had been one long complaint, she'd gone out of the world quietly and unobtrusively, as though she hadn't wanted to bother anyone with her demise.

Only a handful of mourners stood in the midday sun. Concetta's childhood friends were already dead; she'd been away for most of her life, and upon returning to the village, she'd retreated to the shadow realm of her grief. Giovanni had traveled down from Germany. Tanja stood at Vincenzo's side. She had one trait that he greatly appreciated: however complicated things were between them, if Vincenzo was in danger of stumbling, she made sure he didn't fall. Maybe her strength was what scared Vincenzo. It wasn't fear of being dominated, but fear that she wouldn't need him as a protector, that she'd ultimately abandon him.

He wondered what his grandmother would say if she were gazing down from Catholic heaven at the strange couple by her grave. And he wondered what would become of the two of them. If family is the place that gives us a sense of identity in this strange world, if family is the corset holding the fragments of our selves together, then who do we become without it? When a life ends, what remains? What had Concetta left behind that would outlive her? Nothing—except her children, and only now, as he watched the gravediggers lower the coffin into the dry ground, did Vincenzo understand how painful Giulietta's death must have been for her. People could outlive their parents without feeling guilty, but not their children. The essence of life lay in passing it to the next generation.

He looked over at Carmela, who was standing on the opposite side of the grave. She'd developed into a beautiful woman, with sensuous lips and large olive-green eyes. She returned his gaze. The wind blew her black locks into her face. She'd come from Palermo with her parents. He wondered whether she remembered that kiss on the old stone wall. The last day of his childhood.

His mother had fled to Germany with him the following morning, and he hadn't seen Carmela since that night. The thought of having kissed those lips struck him as strange and indecent now. He tried to push the memories aside, but the numbing song of the crickets in the grass carried him back to that unforgettable summer.

The old stone wall was still there. Behind it lay the olive grove where the wedding guests had partied the night away as his hand secretly explored Carmela's small breasts, with their firm, curious nipples. It was his first time, and he'd never forgotten the way Carmela suddenly moaned and surrendered to his touch, how the intensity of her response had frightened and aroused him in equal measure. How close they'd been back then, still children, and how distant she seemed now. He grew light-headed. He was ashamed of himself for thinking these things at his grandmother's grave, while standing next to Tanja and his family, and he was seized by the fear that they could read his thoughts. He avoided Carmela's eyes.

Later, when the family gathered at the house, Vincenzo and Carmela sat on the old wall again. Lizards skittered across the weathered stones. The wind had picked up, and white crowns of foam adorned the waves; in the distance, a ship sliced through the endless blue. Carmela's hair smelled the same as before. Without either of them having said a word, there was electricity in the air. Vincenzo noticed how different her eyes were from Tanja's. Tanja's gaze was a clear, incorruptible mirror, while Carmela's deep-green eyes drew him into an unfathomable abyss. He was turned on, and yet something inside him grew calm in Carmela's presence.

"Did you think about me?" she asked.

"Yeah."

"How many girls have you kissed since then?"

Vincenzo smiled mischievously.

"You? How many boys?"

"A few. But none of them kissed as well as you did."

Tanja was down on the street, looking for him. When she saw the two of them, she turned and went back to the village.

"Do you remember what you told me that night?" Carmela asked.

"What?"

"That every star might be a departed soul."

"I said that?"

"I don't believe things like that anymore." Carmela laid her hand on his. "I'm sorry I wasn't at your mother's funeral," she added. "I lost my nerve."

"It's okay." Vincenzo preferred not to be reminded.

"I didn't want to believe it. What they said about your father. It isn't true, is it?"

"Forget about him." He got up and held out a hand to her.

The next morning, Carmela and her parents headed back to Palermo. She gave Vincenzo a furtive kiss on the cheek before getting into her father's Lancia. Tanja saw it but didn't say anything. They waved as the black sedan disappeared down the dusty road, and then returned to the silent house. Rosaria began cleaning the kitchen; Tanja sat at her typewriter to compose a piece about Ulrike Meinhof's suicide in Stammheim; and Vincenzo breathed in the delicate scent that Carmela's perfume had left on his cheek.

It faded by evening, but after that, Vincenzo sought in Tanja the fiery feeling he'd found with Carmela. They desired one another, clung to each other, but they began to grow apart without admitting it to themselves.

He had to see Carmela again.

62

Carmela

"We are no longer driven by the hunger for food, but by the hunger for freedom, love, tenderness, new forms of work, and social intercourse."

Tanja sat naked in bed, her typewriter on her legs, and read from a German newspaper. The church bells sounded through the open window. It was midnight. Vincenzo lay naked beside her with a hand-rolled cigarette in his mouth.

"'In the past,'" she read, "'it was the envy of the hungry that the bourgeoisie suspected beneath their abundantly set tables; today, it is the madness of the failures who cannot find their way in careers and consumer society.'"

Vincenzo ran a hand over her skin. He took the newspaper from her.

"Hey!"

She grabbed the paper back and went on reading, this time to herself.

"Who writes this shit?"

"Joschka Fischer."

Vincenzo got up, annoyed. "He's the one who's a failure. Those idiots in the Sponti movement just talk about themselves all day while people are dying horrible deaths somewhere else."

"Uh-huh. And you? You wish you were bourgeois yourself."

"Me?"

Tanja regarded him soberly. "*You* failed. You defeated yourself."

It was something he both hated and admired about her: she saw things for what they were, and she could sum them up with perfect directness. Very un-Italian.

"I want to build something with you," he snapped. "But you tear everything down! You have to criticize everything; you're never satisfied!"

"Satisfaction is a bourgeois value," she replied, lighting an unfiltered cigarette. "Satisfied people have never changed society."

She was right, as always, but Vincenzo didn't care. All these words were making his head explode. He wanted her intimacy, not her opinion. He wanted her skin, her breasts; he wanted to possess what didn't belong to him. She put on her hat and started typing. He grabbed his pants and left the room.

He poured himself a glass of wine in the kitchen, where Rosaria and her mother were sitting at the table in their nightgowns.

"Why did you get engaged to her?" Rosaria's mother asked. Italians can also be direct in the absence of the person under discussion.

"Because I love her," Vincenzo replied.

"Mamma, they're not engaged." Rosaria had seen through their little game, and she was sick of it.

"*Santa Madonna!*"

"That's how they do things in Germany." Rosaria shrugged. While in exile, she'd learned that cultural differences were like the weather. Why pass judgment on something you couldn't change? But Rosaria's mother stared at Vincenzo as though he were a stranger. He drained his glass of wine and left.

Late that night, they made love ravenously and insatiably. After that, there was a powerful June storm, sheet lightning over the dark sea, wet cacti in the wind. The water ran down the windowsills and gurgled through the alleys in torrents. They lay in bed and smoked. Then, Vincenzo got up and opened the window. The cool droplets pattered against his chest. They'd reached out for one another but hadn't found each other, and they didn't know why.

The next day, the air was fresh and clear. Vincenzo pulled the tarp from the Iso and sped aimlessly up and down the island, along weathered guardrails between the rocks and the sea, shattering the silence, past cacti, startled seagulls, and fleeing rabbits. Nothing but vast sky above him. A wild rush of absolute freedom—but not the freedom he was looking for.

He called Carmela from the bar at the harbor. He was in luck: she was home. She was happy to hear from him, if not surprised. Her voice exhilarated him. He promised to visit her. Not a word to Tanja.

It was a calculated risk. He'd leave the Iso on the island; he could move around discreetly without the stolen car. He told Tanja he was going to Sicily to look for work as a mechanic. Lying to her was astonishingly easy. In the morning, she waved with her hat as he, packed light, boarded the bus for the harbor. Before he was even around the bend, she went back into the house, holding a book. The hydrofoil departed punctually; the sea was calm; nobody took any notice of him. He took it as a good omen.

From Milazzo, he hitchhiked to Palermo. A small truck picked him up, and he rode in the bed, which was full of cactus pears. In Palermo, he got directions to the university. It was easy to find, not far from the harbor where the big ferries departed for Naples, Cagliari, and Tunis.

A group of anti-fascist students had set up information tables and banners near the entrance. One of them was shouting into a megaphone about supporting the Lotta Continua radicals. A loud argument erupted and soon turned physical. Vincenzo avoided the crowd; where there were leftists, there were plainclothes policemen. The Red Brigades had just committed their first assassination, a revenge killing of a prosecutor in Genoa. The state's response was brutal. A student pressed a flyer into Vincenzo's hand. He threw it away without reading it. Sat down on a wall a little farther off and waited.

Vincenzo wasn't prepared for the emotions that seeing the university students would trigger in him. Not because of the politics—he'd grown indifferent to them, almost alarmingly so. What cut him more deeply was seeing people his age who were in no way more intelligent than he was but had access to knowledge and thus to a place in society that would remain out of his reach. He tried to accept it with nonchalance, with his holey T-shirt and long hair amid all these button-downs and briefcases—even the leftist with the megaphone had his hair neatly parted on the side. But he couldn't quite manage to shrug it off.

The only thing that kept him from wallowing in self-pity was the bold, unfulfilled dream he still had in his head. He would show them all one day, as the triumphant victor on the racetrack. The world he identified with now was a world these bookworms didn't know the first thing about, a world of thrills and heroic battles, man versus man. These scrawny little lawyers' kids could only dream of such things.

But Vincenzo was clever enough to know he was only dreaming, too—he had nothing but raw talent and delusions of grandeur.

Then Carmela came outside. She'd seen him first. Laughing, she ran toward him, her black hair dancing on her shoulders, and when she kissed him on both cheeks, he was suddenly home. She looked amazing. Her full lips didn't need lipstick; her green eyes gleamed darkly; she was wearing a light linen dress and a flowered scarf around her neck.

He didn't know why, but something about her drew him irresistibly. Maybe it was the way she looked at him: Her gaze was free of judgment, of evaluation, of questions. She was simply there. For him.

"Come on, we're leaving town!"

She swung herself onto her Vespa, started it, and laughed. He got on, and she drove off.

It was like they'd only seen each other yesterday. No "What took you so long?" No "What have you been doing?" Tension crackled between their bodies. He gripped the luggage rack for support at first, but then he sensed that she liked it when he put his arms around her hips. She wore no helmet, and her hair flew in the wind, taking him back to the day they'd driven across the island in the little Ape, her hair fluttering against his cheek.

It was one of the first hot days of the year. Vincenzo wiped away the thoughts that held him back from embracing everything about this moment. The sun at his back, the sea spread out along the coastal road to Cefalù, the rattling of the Vespa, the way her body tensed up when she went around a curve. He blocked out everything else. She stopped outside an old gate in a stone arch. It hung rusty and crooked on its hinges, and squeaked softly when she opened it.

"I always come here when I want to be alone."

"Does this belong to your father, too?"

"Yes."

The vineyard lay on a gently sloping hillside. Vincenzo could see the sea gleaming in the distance, behind the pines. The ground smelled lush and fruitful.

"You've got it easy," Vincenzo said. "All you have to do is inherit."

"My father might sell everything. He wanted a son, you know. Women work the fields, but the padrone is always a man."

"What do you want to be, then?"

"Dunno." She shrugged.

"But you're in college."

"For my parents. What about you?"

Without waiting for an answer, she strode ahead to lead him through the grapevines that lay golden in the afternoon sun. The wind was still; everything was at rest; the crickets chirped. His career plans were no more important to her than her own. He liked that.

She doesn't have to become anything, he thought. *She's already everything.*

They walked to an old house in the middle of the field. Ochre walls, closed windows. It was larger and more imposing than the houses on Salina. Carmela opened the rotting wooden door and went inside. He followed. Sunlight streamed in through the collapsed roof, but the air was pleasantly cool. It smelled like straw.

"This is where my grandparents used to live. Today we store hay and equipment in here."

Vincenzo walked through the room, fascinated. The chirping of the crickets echoed through the window slats. He glanced around. Carmela walked to a window, stopped, looked at him. The light that shimmered through the slats enveloped her in a magical glow. She was all silhouette, dark, waiting. The cricket sounds were suddenly deafening. Vincenzo held his breath. She leaned against the window. Though he couldn't see her face, he felt the heat radiating from her body.

He went over and pressed his chest against her breasts. She received him with a soft moan; everything was completely natural. He knew what he needed to do; he didn't think about it anymore. She closed her eyes and waited for him. When his lips met hers, her body arched upward. She grasped his neck and pulled him close.

"*Amore* . . . I waited for so long . . . *amore mio.*"

She tugged off his T-shirt and unbuttoned his pants. It was as though it had always been like this. They simply picked up as adults where they had left off as children. They gave themselves over to their bodies, which found each other effortlessly, because they spoke the same language.

Vincenzo stayed for a week. He even slept on the couch at her parents' house, leaving every morning and returning in the evening. He told them that he was taking the bus to Cefalù to work for a master mechanic he'd met at the Targa Florio. And he really did take the bus, but he got off at a stop along the way, where Carmela picked him up on the street. Then they'd drive to her grandparents' old house and make love.

Every day for seven days, one long, flowing dream, an intoxicating rush with no yesterday and no tomorrow. Carmela let herself fall and pulled him with her. She was everything he'd been missing in Tanja. Perhaps she didn't have Tanja's intelligence, but Vincenzo was continually amazed at the cleverness of her hands, her instinctive knowledge of where he wanted to be touched and what he needed. She took him as he was, light and shadow, lust and sudden sadness, laughter and pain—it was all one. Once they knew every single inch of each other's enchanted bodies, he went back to Salina, fulfilled and confused, back to his family, back to Tanja.

Once again, lying came easily to him. He told them about Antonio, the master mechanic in Cefalù who had taken him under his wing, and gradually let on that he didn't just want to be a mechanic, but a race car driver. He cast himself in a critical light—he needed to learn humility, he said—and adorned his tale with details until he almost believed it himself. As though the Vincenzo who was apprenticing under Antonio as a mechanic were one of his other selves, no less valid than the one whose experiences had coincidentally been real.

The truth was that he couldn't wait to see Carmela again. Before long, he returned, and they repeated their magical encounter in the old house, even more thrillingly and unforgettably than before. Carmela put him under a spell, freed his senses, and yielded to him in a way he found addictive. It went on like that for weeks, months, in the dazed heat of the Sicilian summer. He commuted between the big island and the small one, hiding each part of his life from the other.

He and Tanja kept having sex, which didn't strike him as unusual, but something changed. To his surprise, the affair didn't increase the distance between the two of them—it made them more relaxed around one another. He still found Tanja's pale, slim body beautiful, but his desire weakened. Or rather, shifted to Carmela. On the other hand, his interest in intellectual discourse with Tanja was rekindled. Her incorruptible judgment, her clear assessment of situations, and her spot-on sarcasm were the intellectual anchors that helped keep him from getting lost in his Sicilian family with its unwritten laws.

At night, when he lay awake beside Tanja, who was reading a book by lamplight, and yearned for Carmela's sensuality, part of him wondered why he didn't simply leave Tanja and make his relationship with Carmela public. But another part of him took it for granted that the German was his *fidanzata*, or rather, still considered him her *fidanzato*, her fiancé, protector, and companion. Then he laid an arm over Tanja, nestled against her hips, and slept like a baby.

Tanja was also the only person who didn't want to talk him out of his dream of becoming a race car driver after Niki Lauda crashed on the Nürburgring that August, and nearly burned alive in his Ferrari before the eyes of the two amateur filmmakers who captured the whole thing. It wasn't particularly unusual back then—one or two drivers died every season—but Lauda was Vincenzo's idol. The cool strategist among the hotheads, the gifted man among playboys.

The images circulated around the globe. Vincenzo and Tanja saw them in the bar, repeating over and over again in slow motion, the sea of flames and the horrifically long seconds in which Lauda was fully conscious and on fire, unable to free himself. Rosaria and her mother pleaded with Vincenzo and prayed rosaries, and even Giovanni called from Munich to try to talk sense into him.

Only Tanja encouraged him not to give up. She even predicted that Lauda would survive through sheer willpower and would return to the track to defend his title.

Niki Lauda's heroic comeback earned him Vincenzo's deep respect but prompted new doubts about his racing dream. How was he ever going to make it in such a brutal sport? And the more insurmountable the gap between his current situation and the goal he had set himself, the more frequently he quit early on his training runs through the empty roads, seeking out other, more effortless thrills with Carmela instead. When they were together, the rest of the world fell away.

Autumn clouds over the sea. Endless blue, a transparent rush of light and colors. Even October was still warm. Commuting between two women became second nature for Vincenzo; he didn't want to give up either of them. It didn't even seem like cheating to him—it was shockingly simple, a natural state that fit him like a glove. And as long as nobody knew, it was like it wasn't happening. When he was with Tanja, there was no Carmela, and when he was with Carmela, he forgot Tanja. Life was good, he thought every time he crossed between the islands, unbelievably generous and vast.

One day, just after he'd returned from Sicily and was washing dishes in the kitchen with Tanja, she said, "Move in with her if you want."

Vincenzo gave a start.

She gazed at him calmly. "If that's genuinely what you need," she said, "just be honest with me."

There was no point trying to deny it. He froze in shame.

"You're free. I won't stand in your way." She took the plate he was still holding and dried it.

He didn't know how she'd found out. And he wasn't entirely sure whether the open-mindedness Tanja professed was really the product of her revolutionary convictions, or whether she simply didn't want to show weakness. She didn't act like she planned on leaving him, nor did she pressure him to leave Carmela. She simply kept writing her dissertation and becoming friends with Rosaria. She and Vincenzo still made love regularly enough, and as far as he could tell, she wasn't seeing any other men besides him.

She remained calm, but Vincenzo grew increasingly nervous. He didn't say a word about it to Carmela at first—which was easy enough, since they didn't talk much during their secret trysts, preferring to let their bodies communicate for them. But then his body began unmistakably telegraphing what he'd lacked the courage to say out loud. All of a sudden, he couldn't get it up anymore. Not with Tanja, which he would have understood, but with Carmela. She was as erotic as ever, and he hadn't stopped wanting her, but his body refused to obey orders, which made him frantic. Carmela responded with gentleness and understanding. She embraced him tenderly and stroked his chest, until he abruptly began to cry. A wave of sadness crashed over him, and he wasn't sure where it had come from. He left early and went back to Salina.

To his own astonishment, he told Tanja about what had happened. She replied with a Freudian interpretation that annoyed him, and then she reminded him of his actual goal, racing, which annoyed him even more. For reasons mysterious to him, his anger at Tanja's imperturbable nature made him horny. They made love, wild and unreconciled.

Afterward, she told him that she believed in him, and that he was the only thing standing in his way. She said he could make all of his dreams come true—he just had to take the first step. To break the long journey up into small stages.

He simply needed to go see Antonio, the master mechanic in Cefalù, for real. To practice the circuit in his car, to study every curve like Vaccarella had.

They were all things he should have been telling himself, and it dawned on him that he'd been distracting himself this whole time. That he'd escaped into lust as a way of protecting himself against failing in the world he actually wanted to be part of. If there was one thing he'd always felt good doing, besides driving fast, it was making love. He was one of the few men at that time who was capable of not only taking pleasure, but giving it as well.

He was a tender lover, curious, passionate, and long-lasting. He'd never understood why, instead of "*fare l'amore*," the Germans used words like "*ficken*," which sounded devoid of passion. More bourgeois terms like "have intercourse" or "sleep together" didn't do it for him, either. Sex wasn't something one "had," like a car or a dentist appointment. It was something sacred and healing, something that gripped you and transformed you, something you surrendered your rational mind and your ego to—and definitely not while sleeping. Women loved that about him and had as hard a time leaving him as he did them. The mirror Tanja held up to him that night was a sobering one, and once again, he couldn't help admiring her mental clarity. Just as Carmela gave him roots, Tanja gave him wings.

63

It wasn't until the harvest began that Vincenzo realized how quickly fall had arrived. Don Calogero came to Salina to oversee the harvest of his Malvasia fields. Rosaria sent Vincenzo to pick him up at the ferry with instructions to ask as politely as possible for a chance to work for him again. Vincenzo could hardly say no, since maintaining his secret affair with Carmela meant avoiding irritating her father at all costs.

He stood on the Santa Marina pier, watching the approaching *aliscafo* slowly lower its wings into the water, and racked his brain for ways to keep Tanja away from him. Under no circumstances could Calogero find out—for Carmela's protection, among other things.

Calogero greeted Vincenzo with almost fatherly warmth. He was eager to get straight to the fields, without wasting any time. Vincenzo drove him there on a borrowed Vespa to avoid questions about the stolen Iso. Here, on the western edge of town, the vines extended to the edge of the cliffs overlooking the sea, their leaves a vibrant green. Golden light on golden wine. Ernesto, the leaseholder, was waiting for them.

The first task at hand was to determine when it would be best to harvest— the grapes had to remain on the vine for as long as possible in order to develop their characteristic sweetness, but they also couldn't wait too long, or else the grapes wouldn't get enough sunshine over the two weeks they spent drying on the rooftops. The ideal window was just a few days in length, and once they'd started harvesting, things would need to move very quickly. Don Calogero spent only a little time talking to Ernesto before making a decision, and then laid his arm around Vincenzo to stroll with him through the trellis of ripe grapes.

"Tell me, Vincenzo, what do you want to do with your life?"

"I want to be a *pilota*, a racing driver. You know that."

"They're all playboys! Parties, girls, drugs. That's not your world."

"I don't care. I'm interested in the technology, the speed, the challenge."

"You're a Marconi," Don Calogero said. "Your grandfather was a man of honor. He preferred to die on this land with his head held high rather than make false compromises."

Vincenzo didn't understand what he was getting at. "Once I've finished my training with Antonio, I'm going to compete in the Targa Florio next year. The rules—"

"You have to choose, Vincenzo."

"I *have* chosen."

"It's a question of your honor." Don Calogero plucked a grape and tasted it. "And my daughter's honor."

Vincenzo froze. The don went on walking calmly. Tore a withered leaf from a branch.

"These vines have been neglected. The leaseholder is an idiot. But if they were well cared for and managed, this could be a gold mine. It's excellent soil."

He turned around and cast an unmistakable look at Vincenzo, who was standing paralyzed among the vines.

"You're too smart to throw your life away. I don't have any sons. And if you're running a family business, you don't have to do military service."

Now Vincenzo understood. Calogero had already thought everything through.

"But the two of you have to get married."

Resistance was futile. Don Calogero never took his eyes off him. Vincenzo searched frantically for an escape route.

"I can't leave Tanja. She needs me."

"A man has to make decisions," Calogero said. "Sometimes that includes painful ones."

Vincenzo hated being driven into a corner. Don Calogero coming at him like this made him think walking away from everything—Carmela, that was, since the vineyard didn't interest him anyway—would be better than bending to the man's will.

"Thank you for the offer. I'm honored. But I'm not a farmer. I'm only happy when I'm driving fast."

"You're a Marconi," Don Calogero said, shaking his head. What he didn't say out loud, but which Vincenzo heard loud and clear, was that Vincenzo needed to keep his hands off Carmela from now on if he wanted to go on living.

"Where do you get this restlessness, Vincenzo?" he asked thoughtfully. "Still that same story with your mother?"

Vincenzo was silent.

"Starting a family would be the best way of honoring her memory. She would have wanted grandchildren."

A cool sea breeze wafted through the vines. Don Calogero left Vincenzo standing there alone.

Rosaria knew, of course. Her mother, Carmela's mother, they'd all planned this whole thing out. It had been stupid of Vincenzo to think he could live the same way here that he had in Germany. The familial net was closing around him. He tried to call Carmela from the bar in Santa Marina, but her mother answered, again and again. And Vincenzo always hung up.

Once the grapes were dried and had been left to ferment, Don Calogero left the island. The sun was setting behind the dormant volcano by six o'clock these days, and the first storms were sweeping across the island. The sky turned gray; Stromboli and Panarea disappeared on the horizon. Rosaria taught Tanja how to knit. Vincenzo felt like an addict going through withdrawal. The old house was smothering his soul. Everyone knew everything; gazes weighed heavily upon him, but nobody mentioned Carmela.

The tough old veil of sin and guilt settled over their conversations at the dinner table. Concetta's ghost. Tanja seemed to be the only one who wasn't affected. Maybe because she didn't have it, that dark gift imbued into every Sicilian child at church, through the sweet Communion wafers of a forgiving God. But forgiveness required the thing the person did to be a sin, and every cell in Vincenzo's body resisted the voice inside him whispering that seeing Carmela had been a mistake. How could that be a sin, when it had allowed him to reunite and reconcile deeply with the life God had given him? Those afternoons in the old manor with Carmela had been like a rebirth. And now he was slowly dying.

Tanja finished her doctoral thesis in December. She went to Lipari to have it bound and mailed to the PhD supervisor who had been supporting her all this time. When she returned, the family received her with a celebratory dinner. Rosaria made *orecchiette al ragù di pesce* and *involtini di totano con finocchietto selvatico*, using her mother's recipes. Vincenzo opened their best wine, and for a moment it seemed like they could forget everything that had driven them apart, that they could actually become the family he had dreamed of.

Tanja was unusually quiet that evening. When Vincenzo wanted to make love, she merely gave him a tender, contemplative kiss and fell asleep. The wind picked up overnight, tearing and rattling at the windows, but the predicted rain didn't fall.

The following day, Tanja gave little Marietta her typewriter and packed her few clothes into an old suitcase. Vincenzo, who had been repairing the wind damage to the terrace roof and came in with mussed hair, didn't notice what she was doing until she was already finished.

"I don't owe you an explanation," she told him.

"You can't just leave."

"Sure I can."

"Tanja, I haven't gone back to see Carmela."

"I'm not leaving because of her. I'm leaving because everyone knows, and nobody talks about it. I'm leaving because there's nothing left for me to do here. Because we have nothing left to give each other."

She made the bed and then picked up her suitcase.

Rosaria came in and realized what was happening.

"Tanja, wait," Vincenzo said. "I know you don't want to become a Sicilian housewife. Of course. Nobody's expecting you to. I want something more for myself, too." He took her arm to stop her from leaving the room. "We had plans. We had a vision. Do you really want to give all of that up? If we can't change ourselves, how can we change society?"

"I have changed myself, Vincenzo. But things around here won't be any different a hundred years from now. And be honest—you don't give a shit about society. The only thing you care about is yourself."

He tried to wrench the suitcase from her hand.

"They'll arrest you at the border!"

Tanja didn't release her grip. "I've been in contact with a comrade in Naples. They're going to get me a new passport."

"What, so you already planned this whole thing?"

"Let me go!"

He blocked the door violently. They yelled at one another until Rosaria finally separated them, screaming. Then they stood facing each other, panting, until Vincenzo realized how pointless it was.

"I'll drive you to the harbor," he said in a choked voice.

"The ferry might not be running in this wind," Rosaria remarked.

The thought of being stuck on the island spurred Tanja on. It was a brief, totally botched farewell. Rosaria wept. Her mother said she'd known from the beginning, and it was better this way. Vincenzo tore the tarp from the Iso. It blew away, across the street, over the wall, out to sea. He didn't chase it.

In the car, he hoped against hope that he could change her mind.

"You're two different people," she said. "And neither one can win. You'll always be torn between two worlds. Two countries, two women—I can't live with that."

"Me, neither."

"You'll have to learn."

When they reached the harbor, the sea foam splashed over the large stones behind the quay wall. The ship wasn't there.

"The *aliscafo* is still in Lipari." The harbormaster's meaty face was burrowed into his raincoat. "They'll come if the wind lets up. If it doesn't . . ." He shrugged.

The other passengers accepted the news with stoic equanimity. The sun was already behind Monte Fossa. It was getting cold. Vincenzo and Tanja went to the bar and had a coffee. Silent, lost in their own thoughts. The other passengers followed them one by one, letting the draft in.

The last glimmer of light disappeared behind the dark clouds, and the *aliscafo* still wasn't there. The wet lanterns on the pier. The even roar of the sea. A storm without rain. The waiting passengers, crowded into the bar. The coffee, the cold feet, the fogged windows, the faces full of everything of which Tanja had had enough.

"It'll be here."

"I'm telling you, it's not coming."

"It is."

Their exchange expressed Tanja's impatience and Vincenzo's tiny glimmer of hope that the tide might still turn in his favor after all.

They crossed to the car, which was parked by the pier. The wind had died down somewhat, but the sea was still churning. Still no rain. Vincenzo started the car and let it idle as he switched the heat on. The windows fogged over quickly. Tanja wiped a spot clean so she could keep an eye out for the ship. The engine rumbled, a warm, muted bass against the thundering breakers.

Vincenzo searched her eyes for uncertainty, hesitation. It was impossible that they'd never see each other again.

"Will you write me?"

"Of course."

"I need you," he confessed. "Don't leave me."

It made her cry. She'd never seen him so vulnerable. He pleaded, clung to her, pulled her close. Sought her lips. She avoided them at first. Then she kissed him. Unbuttoned his pants. Lowered herself onto him. One final, desperate flare.

Then the *aliscafo* arrived. It danced at the pier, the waves tossing the little boat back and forth as Tanja stepped onto the swaying gangway. Two sailors held out their hands and pulled her on board. Then they closed the door and tossed the lines overboard.

Vincenzo stayed at the pier, watching the cold lights of the ship as it disappeared, whirring, into the night. Then the rains came.

64

"That was our last time."

Vincenzo blew a cloud of cigarette smoke through the open window. I didn't respond. We passed warehouses, a collapsed bridge, furniture outlet stores. The Autostrada continued straight as an arrow through the wasteland of the Po Valley in the sluggish midday heat. This was where Italy showed the ugly flip side of its legendary beauty.

"When was that exactly?"

"December twenty-first, seventy-six."

I counted forward. Nine months. He smiled at me.

"If it hadn't been stormy that day . . ."

His smile was so tender and warm that I grew bashful.

"So, I was an accident."

"You weren't an accident. You were a child of passion."

Tears sprang to my eyes. Tears I didn't want him to see. He took a tissue out of the glove compartment and gave it to me. My mind was racing.

"You mean she didn't leave because you and Carmela—"

"No. I stopped seeing Carmela after her father's ultimatum."

"But if you'd had the choice, you wouldn't have."

"That's completely theoretical! The fact is, it was over, and your mother took off because she couldn't stand being in the village any longer."

That wasn't how I'd heard it. In the version she'd told me, she'd left because he cheated on her, and she preferred to live honestly alone than compromised with someone else.

"Did you love her?" I asked.

"Yes." He fell silent but then added, "But sometimes you love the idea of a person more than you love the actual person."

I needed to get out of the car. I took the next exit.

"Where are you going?"

Control freak, I thought. "I'm hungry."

"But there's nothing around here!"

We were somewhere outside Verona. Plains all around us, tiny villages, crumbling farms, endless telegraph lines. We looked around and finally spotted a small Ferris wheel near a country highway at the edge of a village. A tent, a carousel.

"They'll probably have something there."

The tiny fair seemed like it was from a different era. Rusty iron, faded paint, drooping garlands. "Luna Park," an iron sign said in colorful letters. There was an empty carousel with pink ponies, the dwarf Ferris wheel with a couple of empty gondolas, a shooting gallery with blue teddy bears, and a sausage stand playing bad pop music. The ground was muddy, and the party seemed to be over. There were no children around, just a couple of workers in heavy vests dismantling everything. Iron hardware clanked as the men loaded it onto old trucks. Vincenzo asked the tired-looking guy manning the sausage stand if he still had anything available. He was closed, he said, but there was a little left over for the staff.

"*Würstel.*"

We ordered a sausage each, plus coffee, and watched the old carousel owner clean his pink ponies as though he had all the time in the world. I liked him somehow. He looked like Geppetto, the carpenter in *Pinocchio.* It was refreshing, just standing there and not saying anything. It doesn't work with most people. Vincenzo was good at silence. I was happy to be on the road with him, neither here nor there, without his wife or my mother. We would never have really gotten to know each other in a place that one of us considered our terrain. And I sensed that he was glad to be here, too. I had the fleeting thought that maybe I wished I would never get home.

I didn't have to ask any more questions. When the food arrived, Vincenzo picked up where he'd left off. He wanted to finish his story.

65

Vincenzo had screwed up and lost both of his women. As generous as the summer had been to him, the winter had thrown him mercilessly back into cold, hard reality. He'd overreached, spent too long on the fence. People who can't decide eventually get decided about.

"Don't cry over her," Rosaria's mother told him. "She wasn't good for you."

"Be quiet, Mamma!" Rosaria exclaimed. She'd grown fond of Tanja, more so than anyone had expected. The house felt empty without the creaking of the grain mill, the clacking of the typewriter, the sound of the German language.

Vincenzo stopped eating, stopped sleeping, spent his nights wandering from one room to the other. Ran in the rain to the beach where he'd sat with Tanja, blaming himself, tearing himself apart. His casual gait, that arrogant nonchalance, the pride of the dispossessed to whom the world belongs, had given way to the slouch of a loser. Everyone else his age had found their path; they were at college, living in shared apartments, starting families. Vincenzo didn't have a girlfriend, a job, or even a high school diploma. All he had was a car that wasn't his. He spent hours on the terrace with his transistor radio, listening to Deutsche Welle. Followed every detail about the RAF, torn between hope and the fear of hearing Tanja's name.

Rosaria brought cookies and coffee. After a while, she couldn't take it anymore. "Call Carmela," she told him.

Vincenzo shook his head. He hadn't chosen her, and he knew she hadn't forgiven him for that. Carmela was the kind of woman who didn't do things halfway. Her love had been complete, and Vincenzo's love had been divided.

"Go see her!" Rosaria insisted. "Win her back."

"But I don't want to be a farmer, you know? With Tanja, I was free. With Carmela, I'd be her father's slave!"

Rosaria sighed. "Then, what do you want, Vincenzo?"

"To be left alone!"

He became insufferable. If he hadn't helped Marietta with her homework every afternoon, Rosaria probably would have thrown him out. When she wanted to clear Tanja's typewriter away, Vincenzo fell into a rage. The little girl was the only one he allowed to touch it.

"This *macchina* can only write German words," he said, and began teaching Marietta the language of the far-off country where her papà worked.

Rosaria called Giovanni, hoping he could make his nephew see reason. She pulled the telephone and its long cord out to Vincenzo, who was smoking on the terrace.

"Oh, Vincenzo!" Giovanni always sounded cheerful, even when he wasn't.

"What's going on?"

"Listen. When you're young, being lovesick is nice for a week or two, but then it's just self-pity. Be glad, now you're free and can concentrate on your own crap."

"How are things in Germany?"

"How do you think? Bad. People are scared. Spending less money. Unemployment is rising, and Tanja's friends"—his term for the RAF to avoid having to say that hated name—"are creating chaos. Police everywhere."

"Why don't you come back, Giovanni?"

"They're changing the laws. Maybe they won't let me back into Germany anymore. We Italians are still better off than most, but who knows what will happen next. The Turks are starting to bring their families over. You could still come."

Vincenzo was silent. He'd always thought he and Tanja would return together eventually. What would he do in Germany without her?

"Listen, Vincenzo, you need to wake up. You have to go back and get your damn diploma. You should go to college, like your mother wanted! If any of us can succeed, you can!"

"Don't worry, Uncle Giovanni."

"But I am worried! You should start worrying more, too, instead of just screwing everyone in the neighborhood without a care in the world!"

Ah, so that was the way the wind was blowing—straight from Don Calogero's house. Vincenzo simply hung up. The family was really getting on his nerves. He understood Tanja better than ever.

At night he was seized with panic. When he lay in his cold room, with the sea thundering angrily against the rocks, he saw his fathers standing before him, calling him a loser, a charlatan, a nothing. He heard his grandmother slinking through the house, a silent, dark accusation; and in the end, Giulietta came to his bed and tenderly laid her hand on his sweat-soaked brow. He startled awake and flung the window open. What suffocated him was the fear that his life would end as unfulfilled as hers had.

When he stared at the television in the drafty, smoky bar, he saw—whether in soccer, Formula One, or politics—only winners and losers, the beloved and the despised. He was desperately afraid of being among those who got left in the dust. Not the guys here, the normal ones, the invisible ones merely existing in their dark, damp houses. No, the ones who dared to step into the public eye—athletes, artists, visionaries—only to fail in front of everyone. Briefly part of the world, and then quickly forgotten again. But then he thought about his idol, Niki Lauda, who had nearly burned to death in his Ferrari before escaping death's clutches through sheer willpower and returning to the racetrack. Just to show everyone that he alone decided whether he could be defeated or not.

After a sleepless night in February, when the sea was calm and the ships were running, Vincenzo left the house at dawn, packed a small bag into the Iso, and took the first ferry to Palermo. He had to forget Tanja. More than that, though, he had to show her, Carmela, and everyone else that they'd underestimated him.

In Palermo, he swore to himself, he wouldn't ring Don Calogero's doorbell. If he saw Carmela again, it would be as a man who had succeeded on his own. As a man who was somebody. A winner.

He found Nino Vaccarella back at his old school. *Il preside volante,* they called him, *the flying principal.* Vaccarella actually remembered Vincenzo. When Vincenzo told him that he'd driven the track every week over the past summer and memorized every curve—he lied about his best time, of course—Vaccarella couldn't just send him away. He himself was done with that circus, he said, but he knew someone who knew someone.

Two days later, Vincenzo was at a pizzeria with Claudio, a roughneck car-dealership owner and the head of a private racing team. Their original driver had just broken his neck skiing. Vincenzo believed that his run of bad luck had finally turned for the better.

"Without Nino," Claudio said, "the Targa just isn't what it was. Now that it's only a national championship, a lot of second-class drivers take part. So, you're in luck." He grinned cheekily.

Vincenzo didn't particularly like him, but what did that matter? The guy needed someone young and crazy to get his car to the finish line as fast as possible, and Vincenzo needed a car. His Iso was a luxury vehicle, not a speed machine.

The car was a converted street vehicle, a red Alfa Romeo Giulia GTA with a roll cage and a racing gearbox. They took the country highway to Cerda, and when they rounded a curve, the start- and finish-line spectator stands suddenly came into view, smack in the middle of the silent landscape. Claudio had Vincenzo get behind the wheel and then hit the stopwatch. Vincenzo flogged the Giulia down the street as though the devil were chasing him. When he moved into the passing lane and nearly slammed into a truck coming in the opposite direction, Claudio shouted, "Stop! Now!"

He got out, threw up by the side of the road, and then turned to look at Vincenzo.

"You're driving for me. But every scratch you put on my car, you're paying for personally."

"I don't have any money."

"You have the Iso. I'm keeping it as collateral."

Vincenzo slept in the workshop and tinkered with the car at night. He knew more about the mechanical side of things than most drivers, and even more than some mechanics. He wasn't satisfied with the car as it was. His detailed suggestions for improvement drove Claudio's mechanics insane. They called him *testardo teutonico*, stubborn Teutonic fool. But he didn't care. He was burning the candle at both ends.

The changes he made at night to the attenuators, the fuel injection, and the differential, he tested on the track the following morning. His favorite time to drive was between five and seven o'clock, when the sun was rising and the road was still empty. Each time, he hit the brakes a little later as he approached the curves, until all five of his senses could perceive that limit where his tires lost traction, the fine line between life and death.

"You've got it," Claudio said at last, and clapped him on the shoulder. "You've got the butt instinct."

They went to Vaccarella's cobbler on Corso Vittorio, a taciturn, old-school Sicilian. As he measured Vincenzo's hands, Claudio pointed reverently to the black-and-white photos on the wall. Race car drivers of the past fifty years. All wore buckskin driving gloves, the kind they only made here. Giulietta would have loved them, Vincenzo thought.

A week before the race, Vincenzo went to the post office and sent Rosaria two tickets for the race. One for her, one for Carmela.

May 15, 1977, was a day that went down in history. But not in the way Vincenzo had pictured. The morning before the race was one big, chaotic festival. Children ran around touching the roaring vehicles; people sold baked goods; groupies in leather skirts crowded around the drivers. And Vaccarella was there, relaxing and chatting with friends. Claudio had been right: the drivers weren't the death-defying knights of old anymore. They were a bunch of wild daredevils. Maybe this was Vincenzo's big chance. Their risk-taking versus his intellect. Rosaria had made the journey and came to the pit line in order to sneak a medallion of the Madonna into Vincenzo's car.

"Is Carmela here?"

"Of course." Rosaria smiled and pointed to the stands. "Her parents, too."

"I told you not to say anything to Calogero!"

"Carmela wouldn't have been allowed to come otherwise. Sorry. But they all have their fingers crossed for you."

Vincenzo slipped on his new buckskin gloves and went to the car. He avoided looking toward the stands. He squeezed himself into the roll cage behind the wheel, and then everything happened very, very fast. Ignition, mixture, instrument check. He moved with a practiced logic, becoming part of the machine. He narrowed his thinking, sharpening his concentration on his immediate surroundings, until instinct took over and he entered into a state of crystalline focus where everything else faded into the background. He loved this feeling, the sense of perfect inner calm with the engines roaring all around him.

He screwed up the start. A bad omen that drove him to risk everything. Having to catch up from the back meant having everyone else's dust blocking the view ahead. Only instinct could tell him whether a passing maneuver would succeed or end at the nearest tree. Vincenzo's secret weapon was that he knew every single curve and the distance between, even if he couldn't see them. He drove at a ludicrous speed, motivated not by a will to victory so much as a fear of losing. By the second round, he'd already made up the time he'd lost. When he crossed the finish line for the third and fourth time, his mechanic's board showed that his times were the fastest in his class. By the fifth round, he'd passed the other Alfa Romeos, but he went on going like a bat out of hell, with no thought to sparing his tires.

That was when the accident happened. Vincenzo was right behind the yellow Osella, an open-top beast with a BMW engine, one class above Vincenzo's Alfa Romeo, a purebred race car that was absurdly overpowered for the curvy rural roads. Even so, Vincenzo was able to stay hot on its heels because the back half of the Osella's body had flown off in a collision. The engine, the transmission, and the tires were completely exposed, but the driver went right on racing. Vincenzo knew how dangerous that was: without the tail planes, the car lacked downforce. On the curves, which were covered with a fine film of dust, the driver was already balancing a dangerously fine line. Pure instinct stopped Vincenzo from taking advantage of his opponent's weakness and passing on the sharp curve to the right. Instead, he remained behind the Osella and thus witnessed the moment its wheels lost their grip and the car spun off the asphalt into the mud, went flying, and turned several pirouettes before slamming into a group of spectators at full force.

For a fraction of a second, Vincenzo was tempted to keep driving, but then he hit the brakes, got out, and ran to the scene of the accident. It was a bloodbath. Injured people lay in the grass with twisted arms; scraps of yellow car body hung in the trees. The Osella had been contorted into a grotesque clump of metal, and the driver was unresponsive. Everything was unnaturally quiet, frozen in shock. Then the survivors began to scream.

The race was halted immediately. The drivers all got out of their cars as the horrible news spread from village to village. Once it became clear that two spectators were dead, many were injured, and the driver was in a coma, everyone knew that this dark day marked the end of a spectacle that had outpaced itself. Ever-faster and more powerful race cars in the old villages of Sicily—it could only have ended badly.

As Vincenzo, consternated, parked his Alfa Romeo in the pit, Vaccarella took him aside. Ashen faces everywhere. No music, no awards ceremony.

"What did I tell you? Go home, get your diploma, learn a proper trade. Stop before this happens to you. And find yourself a good woman."

Vincenzo cursed the day and the hopes he'd placed in it. His career was over before it had even begun. That evening, the newspapers went out with headlines reading, *"È morta la Targa."* The oldest car race in the world had been destroyed by its own madness. Vincenzo left in a rush. He couldn't look Carmela in the eye.

66

My father was me. Different stage, same play. On the racetrack or on the runway, it was always about whether you'd found your place beneath the stars or had to fight for one. And about how much harder it was for someone who had to pitch their tent far from home.

The workers tore down the carousel. Old Geppetto had a hard time keeping up. I wondered how many times he'd assembled and disassembled the thing over the years, and how many more times he'd have to before he could finally take it down for the last time and go home. Life was a circus, and we were acrobats on the tightrope. Without a net.

"Shall we keep driving?" Vincenzo asked.

I didn't know how to tell him I was scared to arrive back home, where a plunge into nothingness awaited.

"Seems to run in the family," I remarked.

"What does?"

"Having to fight tooth and nail for our dreams."

"Would you rather have inherited a fashion empire?"

Vincenzo grinned at me wryly. I smirked.

"Legacies are prisons," he murmured, and then ordered two more cups of espresso. "They break a lot of people. Too heavy a burden. You and I had to invent ourselves. It makes us free."

"I've been reinventing myself again and again for a long time. Rolling that stone up the mountain over and over gets pretty goddamn tiring. One of these days, I'd like to reach the top. And stay there."

Vincenzo gazed at me with unexpected affection. It made me uneasy but also felt good. He understood where I was coming from, and he wasn't giving advice. I told him about the years I'd spent making the rounds through trade fairs and fashion shows, the successes, the setbacks, the power dynamics within the industry, the frustration of being dependent on people I despised. The feeling of never being good enough, of always having to go one step farther. The end of one show was the beginning of the next. Like filling a bucket with a hole in it: everything you pour in runs out the bottom again.

"What are you going to do when you get back to Munich?"

I shrugged. "Go to war. Or give up on the whole thing. Maybe I should have just sold out. The path of least resistance. What do you think?"

"No."

"Why not?"

"That's not you."

"How would you know?" I grinned at him skeptically.

Vincenzo fixed me with a solemn, penetrating gaze. "I was in a similar situation back then. Talented, but everything I touched ran through my fingers like sand."

"So, what did you do then? After the race?"

"Life decided for me. You decided for me."

67

Vincenzo shuffled through the village in torn jeans, drank at the bar, smoked weed in the piazza. His racing fever had been extinguished; the wunderkind of yore had fallen into a black hole called reality.

"You've become a *fannullone*, a do-nothing!" Giovanni scolded when they saw each other again that summer.

Giovanni had come to Salina to buy wine, olives, and capers from the farmers, and to argue with his wife. Vincenzo didn't care what his uncle thought of him. Giovanni had succeeded in life, so it was easy for him to say things like that.

"Try it out somewhere else," Giovanni urged him. "You can race in Germany, too!"

"Where the police are looking for me!"

"Well, then, stay here and learn to do something else!"

"I can't do anything else!"

"My God, Vincenzo, stop putting yourself down so much. This isn't like you!"

"Yes. This is exactly like me. A loser. There have to be both, winners and losers—that's how the cosmos stays in balance. You landed on one side; I landed on the other."

"You're not a loser," Giovanni grunted. "You're an idiot!"

The one productive part of Vincenzo's life was the afternoons he spent with Marietta, teaching her German using Tanja's typewriter. As Giovanni and Rosaria argued over whether their daughter should attend *la scuola secondaria* in Germany or Italy, Vincenzo devotedly taught her correct pronunciation of the unvoiced *"ch."* They particularly enjoyed inventing long, snakelike compound nouns.

"Schreibmaschinentastatur." Typewriter keyboard.

"Schreibmaschinentastaturreinigungsmittel." Typewriter keyboard cleaner.

"Schreibmaschinentastaturreinigungsmittelfabrikbesitzer." Typewriter keyboard cleaner factory owner.

"Schreibmaschinentastaturreinigungsmittelfabrikbesitzertochtershochzeitskuchen." Typewriter keyboard cleaner factory owner's daughter's wedding cake.

But in the evenings, when his little cousin was in bed, Vincenzo hung out at the bar with the other unemployed guys, and in the morning, while she was in school, he slept.

Rosaria called Calogero in Palermo. She knew that the only person who could pull Vincenzo out of his hole was Carmela. Calogero was glad to hear from Rosaria, because he and his wife were having a huge problem with their daughter. Carmela hadn't taken Vincenzo's abrupt disappearance well. She accused her father of interfering, of having driven Vincenzo away. In revenge, she'd moved out, and was now living with an Indian guru named Satyan—or, rather, a fat Sicilian guy named Salvo who'd given himself a new name, like everyone else in that orange-attired group.

"Isn't it awful?" Calogero exclaimed into the phone. "They have no respect for their elders anymore! And everyone sleeps with everyone else!"

Rosaria remained calm. "So, what's Carmela's new name?"

"How should I know? I couldn't care less!"

"Listen," Rosaria said. "This is what we're going to do."

The following week, Rosaria went to Palermo. She found Carmela, who now went by Shakti, and talked to her. They argued, shouted, cursed men, collapsed weeping in one another's arms, and in the end, Rosaria returned to Salina with a letter. She put it on the table in front of Vincenzo.

Vincenzo didn't even touch it for several days. When he had finally imbibed enough liquid courage to open it, he couldn't believe what he was reading. He hadn't thought he was worthy of her love. He called her.

Two days later, Carmela appeared at the door with a backpack over her shoulder and a kitten in one arm. Her colorful, floor-length dress smelled like an Indian bordello. Rosaria threw it in the washing machine while Carmela and Vincenzo poured milk into a bowl for the cat, amazed and grateful that they didn't need words to reconnect. No explanations, no apologies. Their love was like a suitcase they'd forgotten on the train platform, and when they returned from their journeys, it was still sitting there.

Don Calogero arrived by ferry the next morning. His wife threw her arms around her lost daughter, sobbing. Carmela refused to speak to her father. He bore it with dignity and took Vincenzo by the arm.

"Come on, let me show you my new car. A Citroën CX. *C'est merveilleux!*"

The village dozed in the noontime heat as Calogero's Citroën glided slowly down the main road. Dogs slept in the shade of the houses; the sea was a leaden mirror.

"The Italian car industry is going down the tubes," Calogero said. "Striking has become a national pastime. The Communists are ruining the country."

Vincenzo wondered what the old man actually wanted from him. And almost as soon as they'd left the village, he got down to business.

"You two are young. You're wasting your time as though it were infinite. Those gurus talk about reincarnation, like after you die you come back and get another chance, like life is some kind of game. It's fine for them to say those things to get girls into their beds, but the truth is banal: when it's over, it's over. And you stand before your maker, who demands accountability."

"Carmela's done with that guru. She wants—"

"Listen," Calogero broke in. "Two months ago, they found cancer in my lung. Carmela doesn't know. The doctor didn't try and give me any false hopes. My days are numbered."

Vincenzo was shocked. "That's horrible. But isn't there anything they—"

"It's not horrible. Death is a gift. It teaches you everything about life. To distinguish between what's important and what isn't."

Vincenzo grew uneasy. He hadn't been expecting that response.

"They say that love is what counts. But love comes and goes. Feelings are everything to you young people, but when you get older, you understand that family and the earth are the real constants."

Calogero parked the Citroën near the edge of the village, where his vineyard began before sloping down to the coast. The grapevines were askew, rotten, and neglected. He got out and went down to the field to inspect his plants. Vincenzo was filled with almost paralyzing empathy. He followed.

"All you have to do is cross the old vines with the resistant varieties from America. The vine pest is at the roots. You cut it off here, right at the bottom, and put the old plant on a healthy root. It takes some time, but eventually they grow together. Come here, look!"

Vincenzo edged closer. The idea that this was a man who was about to die unnerved him. But Calogero brooked no sympathy—he was worried only about the grapes.

"Carmela will inherit this land," he said. "It's not worth a lira if it isn't cultivated. But it could be revitalized in a couple of years. The Malvasia will return to its former greatness. All it needs is a strong young man. A man with a good head on his shoulders. A vision. German discipline."

Vincenzo swallowed. "Don Calogero, I—"

"The South is neglected. Reactionary. It needs people like you. People who have been other places. Who have a modern mind-set. Who can breathe new life into the old country."

"I can't." It wasn't even because he didn't want to—he didn't think he was capable. Big goals scared him. He felt doomed to fail. All he wanted now was to get through the day. The least possible amount of responsibility.

Calogero turned and gazed sternly into his eyes. "You have your grandfather's blood flowing in your veins. Nobody loved the land as much as he did. It's time to come home, Vincenzo."

"I'm deeply honored, Don Calogero, but—"

"Giovanni will sell the wine in Germany. You've seen how successful he is. You just have to know what people are missing. They have money; we have taste."

Vincenzo fell silent. How was he supposed to refuse a dying man?

"You won't get any respect for your dreams, Vincenzo. People only respect you for what you have. That was your grandfather's undoing. He was the best farmer on the island, but the land didn't belong to him, so they could treat him however they liked."

Vincenzo could hardly argue with that. Don Calogero was right. Talent alone was merely a promise. And very few promises were ever kept.

"Don't misunderstand," Calogero said firmly. "I'm not doing this for charity's sake. But if you think you can have Carmela without our blessing, you're a hundred percent mistaken. The only way you'll have her hand in marriage is if you can feed your family."

A light breeze rustled the vines, driving away the midday heat. Calogero gazed out over the island and breathed in its lush, summery scent.

"There isn't a more beautiful place on Earth, not even America. Picture it: Your house is here. Your children are running around in your fields; nobody can chase them away. A man has to know where he belongs."

It was tempting. Not the wine, but the roots.

Vincenzo spoke to Carmela. It was too soon; it was too much. But the more they thought about it, the more they realized they had no other choice. They couldn't keep living off Rosaria. If they wanted to be together, they needed a house. Ground beneath their feet.

Rosaria loaned them the money for engagement rings. In September, Vincenzo signed the lease for Calogero's fields. He would have to hire workers for the harvest, and he would have to learn things he had no idea about yet. The grapes lay golden in the sun and the air was magically light, but Vincenzo had an odd feeling in his stomach. As though gravity were pressing him to the ground. The family had just sat down at the dinner table to raise a toast—Calogero opened their best bottle of Malvasia—when the telephone rang. Rosaria handed the receiver to Vincenzo.

"Congratulations," Giovanni said. "Your grandfather would be proud of you."

"*Grazie.*"

Then a pause.

"Guess who I saw on Leopoldstraße yesterday?"

"You didn't."

"I did."

Vincenzo was electrified. "How is she?"

Giovanni was silent.

"How is she?"

"She's round. Very round. I thought you should know." Giovanni's voice sounded meek.

Chills ran down Vincenzo's spine. "Was anyone with her?"

"No, she was alone."

"Did you talk to her?"

"Briefly. I congratulated her and asked who the lucky father was. Just making conversation, you know, I didn't think that . . ."

"What did she say?"

"Nothing. She just looked at me and—didn't say anything."

Vincenzo stared at the others at the table. Rosaria, Carmela, and Calogero gave him questioning looks.

"Vincenzo, listen to me," Giovanni exclaimed into the receiver. "Don't do anything stupid, now. Stay where you are!"

Vincenzo hung up.

"What's the matter?" Rosaria asked.

"Nothing."

Vincenzo didn't say a word about the call, just racked his brain anxiously. They toasted; the women served swordfish *caponata*; then they all went to bed. Vincenzo lay awake all night. At four o'clock that morning, when everyone else was fast asleep, he slipped out of the house. He got into the Iso and took the first ferry off the island. As he stood at the railing and saw the lights of Salina at dawn, that fragile green oasis in the sea that had so generously given him a home, he began to cry. His life had been one long string of goodbyes. The minute he found a home, he had to leave it. But this time was different. He had a family now.

He sped down the dusty southern roads like a man possessed, headed for Naples. From there, he took the Autostrada del Sole, up the entire Italian boot, driving for one day and one night. He pumped himself full of coffee and cola, stopping only at gas stations, taking brief naps in the car, moving on whenever he saw police. Standing still scared him. As long as he was in motion, he felt safe.

The next morning, he called Giovanni from a phone booth in South Tyrol, feverish and yearning. "Do you have her address?"

"Vincenzo, don't come! It's crawling with police here. Didn't you hear about the Schleyer kidnapping?"

He'd seen the images on TV. The checkpoints on the highway. The whole country in a state of emergency. But he was worried about Tanja, not himself.

"They're just checking who's leaving, not who's going in!"

"Are you insane? They're checking everyone, especially guys your age!"

"Who am I, though? A little fish, a nobody."

"In a stolen car!"

"Don't worry about it, I'll be fine. Just get me her address, got it?"

"Vincenzo! Don't cross the border!"

Vincenzo hung up.

He knew the border. He'd smuggled guns across it several times. The important thing was knowing where not much was going on. Never take the main highways the trucks use—they had dogs at those checkpoints. He left the Brenner Highway near Meran and took the freeway to Timmelsjoch, up ridiculously windy roads to elevations over eight thousand feet. A lunar landscape, rocky and lonely, full of chasms and empty Mussolini bunkers. The bored cops waved him through. Slowly, he rolled toward the Austrian checkpoint. The young border guard glanced briefly at the German license plate and stopped him.

"Anything to declare?"

"No, nothing."

His perfect German. His poker face.

It worked.

The guard waved him through. He drove off very slowly, not wanting to draw attention.

Once he was out of sight, he hit the gas and careened down the serpentine roads as though on wings. Now the German border was all that was left.

Mittenwald was small enough; that had always worked. Better safe than sorry, though. The stolen car. He took the rural highway until just before the border, past small creeks and bed-and-breakfasts, before turning onto a forest road and leaving the Iso in the woods. *You can tell Germany by the smell,* he thought. Pine forest and wet moss. He waited until it was dark and then set off. Turned around for one final look at his beloved Iso. He'd left the keys in it. Whoever found the car was one lucky duck.

He tripped over a root and sprained his foot. Nothing broken, but it hurt. Maybe it would have been better to drive after all? The Iso had always brought him luck. He hesitated for a moment, but then kept going, ever northward. He tried to use the stars for orientation, but they were hidden behind the dense trees. He'd lived for years beneath the clear coastal sky, and now there was nothing but forest and darkness all around. He got lost. Cursed. Second-guessed himself. Until he finally hit a barbed-wire fence.

The border ran straight through the woods. He glanced around. Nobody in sight. He climbed over the fence, tearing his pants on the barbed wire, and jumped down on the other side. Germany!

Just one meadow separated him from Mittenwald. The lights, the church tower, the river. He heard a country highway beyond the far shore. He could try and hitchhike.

Suddenly, a blinding glare. A flashlight shining in his face. He hadn't heard them coming. Two cops with a German shepherd. He stopped where he was, deciding to play innocent.

"Evening!"

"Evening," he replied. Bavarian accent, that always helped.

"What are you doing here?"

He shrugged. "Out for a walk."

The dog barked at him. He was scared of dogs.

"Uh-huh. ID, please."

"Sure, just a second."

He acted as though he were looking for it. Buying time.

"I must have—I think I left it at home."

The cops can smell a lie a mile off. It's in their blood. A butt-o-meter for lies.

"And where is home?"

Vincenzo hesitated. His first mistake.

"Not from around here, eh?"

"No. I'm from—Munich."

His hands were shaking. He stuck them in his pockets. Racked his brain frantically for a way to get out of there. The woods were behind him. The dogs would be faster. The river? He could swim faster than a dog.

"Italian?"

The accent. Dammit. Gone too long.

"No."

His second mistake. They didn't believe a word he said anymore. And they knew that he knew it. There's always that moment when you look the other person in the eye and realize they've caught you in a lie, and you know that continuing to lie would only make things worse.

Vincenzo sprinted toward the river. Automatic reaction, fight-or-flight response, pure fear—his third mistake. He was faster than the dogs at first. Jumped down the embankment and waded into the river, but it was shallower than he expected. The dark water barely came up to his hips. The dogs behind him. By the time he got halfway across and could finally swim, an animal had caught up. A stabbing pain shot through his leg as its sharp teeth sank in. He fought with the wet beast, which writhed furiously and snapped at his flesh. He kicked and flailed, screamed in terror, and dove underwater. Then the cops grabbed him and yanked his arms behind his back so violently that it nearly dislocated his shoulders.

Salami. Giovanni brought salami.

"Goddammit, you were supposed to bring me Tanja!" Vincenzo shouted, and kicked the table.

"Quiet down," the guard called from the door to the visiting room, "or you're goin' back to your cell!"

"No problem, it's okay," Giovanni replied to placate the guard, and took Vincenzo's hand. He was sweating.

"Get me her number, Giovanni," Vincenzo said.

"What you need right now is a lawyer, you idiot!"

Vincenzo ran his hands through his hair frantically. His head was bloody from slamming it against the cell door. He hadn't eaten a thing. Just torn himself to shreds with self-accusation and made plans to break out. His prison was in the middle of Munich; Tanja was right nearby—yet more distant than ever.

"What good would that do me? Who am I to them? A foreigner, a criminal."

"Goddammit, stop whining like a child!" Giovanni slammed his fist onto the table. "Act like a man!"

Vincenzo jumped to his feet, prepared to shout back at him, but then he bit his lips and fought back the tears that sprang to his eyes. He slumped into his chair again.

"Giovanni, I'm going to be a father. I haven't achieved anything in life except for this baby. Find her. I'm begging you!"

Giovanni was sympathetic.

"*Va bene.* I promise."

68

I wasn't sure whether to believe him. In his eyes, he was a victim; in my mother's, he was a deadbeat, and she had done the best she could in a terrible situation.

"I thought you didn't want to see me."

"Is that what she told you?"

"Well, she didn't tell me you were in prison until later. In the beginning, it was always, 'Papà is in Italy.'"

Vincenzo's eyes narrowed to mistrustful slits. "Of course I wanted to see you! Your mother didn't want you to see me behind bars."

I pondered. Might be true. If she'd asked me, I would rather have seen him there than not at all. I studied Vincenzo's face. That strange mixture of arrogance and vulnerability.

He turned away. *"Dai, andiamo."*

We left Luna Park and got into the car without speaking. He behind the wheel. I in my own head.

"How is Tanja?" he asked abruptly.

"Good."

"Do you have siblings?"

"No."

"Did she ever get married?"

"No."

"That sounds right."

He lit a cigarette.

"What about you?" I asked. "Are you happy with Carmela?"

He blew smoke out the window. Just as he was about to say something, my phone rang. I hesitated. It was my mother.

"Julia! Everything okay?"

"Yeah."

"Do you need me to pick you up somewhere?"

"No."

"Where are you now?"

"On the Autobahn."

"You're hitchhiking?"

"No."

"Are you alone?"

"No."

She didn't ask any more questions. She knew. And she was scared.

"Julia, I wanted to tell you . . . Please, can you forgive me?"

I waited. To see whether she was going to say anything else. I could feel her falling apart at the other end of the line.

"I had to do it, Julia. Burn all the bridges. Sometimes radical forgetting is the only way you can move on."

So that was what she called it. Radical forgetting.

"That was self-centered of you."

"Yes."

We were silent for a while. Vincenzo glanced over nervously.

"We're headed to the hospital," I said. "To Vincenzo's father."

"Which hospital?"

I thought for a moment, trying to decide whether I wanted her to come. Whether I wanted the two of them to see each other. Whose side I was on.

"Bogenhausen."

I ended the call with an uneasy feeling. As though I'd betrayed them both. Vincenzo didn't say anything. I took one of his cigarettes.

"You think she'll come?" he asked.

"Dunno."

He lit the cigarette for me.

"When did you see her again, back then?"

The memory clearly made him uncomfortable. "Giovanni found her number. Called her. She didn't come, though."

"Had I been born yet?"

"Yes. I didn't see her again until the trial."

I felt dizzy. "She told me she visited you in prison."

"You don't believe me?" His tone was sharp now.

I didn't respond, which hurt him. I didn't want to be unfair, but I also didn't want to be lied to again.

"Listen," he said. "Your mother told you what she told you. And you came down to hear my side, right? We'll be in Munich in four hours, so we have until then. Or I can just shut my mouth. Up to you."

He was even more upset than I was. His story wanted to break free from the prison of his memory. But how reliable was it? Most lies, I thought, weren't actually lies so much as sins of omission. Nobody wanted to be at fault. Everyone had their story where they'd given love but not received it. Perhaps the other half of Vincenzo and Tanja's story was also the part missing from my own story about myself—a life where I was loved more than I could have ever imagined.

69

Vincenzo's flight was at an end. The vast sky over the sea had narrowed to a bleak box. Another German word: *"Untersuchungshaftzelle."* Pretrial detention cell.

"Untersuchungshaftzellengenosse." Pretrial detention cellmate.

"Untersuchungshaftzellengenossengeschwätz." Pretrial detention cellmates' idle chitchat.

He went halfway out of his mind.

When he saw Tanja again, they weren't allowed to talk to each other. Only about each other. He sat at the defense table; she was on the witness stand. She was wearing a hand-knitted poncho, and despite her shorter hair, she seemed more feminine somehow. She didn't accuse him of anything, merely said they knew each other from their time in the commune—but she was also doing that to save her own neck. The policeman they'd shot outside the bank had survived. Now, he was here in court. Luckily, he'd only been grazed on the thigh—but he recognized Vincenzo. Olaf and Tanja had worn stocking masks. Vincenzo, the driver, hadn't.

"Mr. Marconi," the prosecutor barked at him, "are you still trying to tell me that you didn't know the names of your accomplices?"

"That's correct."

"The injured party has testified that you were behind the wheel. You can't possibly have driven and shot at the same time!"

"I did."

"I don't understand," Vincenzo's public defender said during the break when they were alone. "You don't want to identify the bank robbers—okay, I can't force you to, even though that would reduce your sentence. But why don't you admit that one of them did the shooting? Why are you taking responsibility for a crime you didn't commit? When the eyewitnesses—"

"Because it's true. I did the shooting."

Vincenzo got seven years. Grievous bodily injury and accessory to robbery. Mitigated by the fact that he admitted the crime and showed remorse, and that the victim hadn't suffered any permanent damage. With good behavior and a little luck, he could be out in four, maybe five years. When his daughter was starting kindergarten. He didn't even know her name.

Shortly after he was sentenced, Tanja visited him at Stadelheim Prison. A place without color. The walls were gray, the floors, the cell doors, the bed frames, the sheets, even the food. It was 1978; outside, it was spring.

"Thank you," he said softly.

"For what?"

"For naming her Giulia."

"With a *J*. Julia."

"Julia."

They gazed at each other for a long moment. Searching for what was still there. Missing what was lost, wondering where it had gone.

"I'm the one who should be thanking you," she said.

"For what?"

She glanced at the guard outside the door before leaning across the table. "For your testimony," she whispered.

He wasn't overly proud of it. It had been the only choice. What was he supposed to do—take his child's mother away from her?

"Take care of Julia," was all he said.

She nodded. "I found a job. Full time. An editorial collective. We're doing an alternative city paper. The *Blatt*. Independently managed."

"Good."

"Did you hear?" she whispered. "The Red Brigades kidnapped Aldo Moro. In Rome. Same strategy as with Schleyer. Germans must have been involved."

Vincenzo didn't reply. He'd seen it on television. The shot-up Fiat, the dead bodyguards. The wife, the children, the pope appealing to the kidnappers' sense of humanity. The demonstrations, the K9 units and helicopters combing the entire country. He now felt nothing but contempt for the radicals.

"Why didn't you bring her?" he asked.

"I don't know. Do you want her to see her father in prison?"

"Why not? You've always been big on honesty."

"She's still too young. When she's older. When she'll understand."

"Bring her to see Giovanni sometime. Rosaria's finally coming back. With Marietta and the baby. They're going to go to school here."

Tanja nodded, but Vincenzo knew she wouldn't go.

"I ended my engagement," he said. "To Carmela. The wedding's off. Everyone says I'm crazy."

He searched her eyes for a reaction.

"It was the right decision." That was all she said.

"Do you have a photo of Julia?" he asked.

"I'll send you one. Do you need anything else? Food? Medication?"

"The photo."

"Okay."

She got up to leave.

"Tanja."

"Yeah?"

"Do you have a boyfriend?"

"No."

She was honest, he thought. She would have told him. Wouldn't she?

"Come back soon, okay?"

"Okay. Ciao."

"Ciao."

True to her word, she brought him the photo. Julia in a little knit cap, peeking out of a baby carriage. Large, dark eyes, curious and genuine. She didn't look much like Tanja, but she didn't resemble Vincenzo, either. What he saw in her was Giulietta. He hung the picture on the wall above his bunk. In the shabby cell he shared with a Yugoslavian who heard voices and hammered on the door every night, the photo was his only bright spot. His final vanishing point.

On good days, the Yugoslavian was a funny guy who knew a lot of jokes. Not just dirty ones, either. Subtle, philosophical ones. He was in for manslaughter.

"What about you? Political stuff, huh?"

Vincenzo nodded without looking at him.

"Asshole. Police state here, thanks to people like you. Like Yugoslavia! Was nice Germany before. Now everything shit."

Vincenzo might have fallen apart in that melting pot of failures. What killed the prisoners' hopes of ever leading a normal life again was the isolation. People fell and had nobody to catch them. You had to stay on the gangs' good side—the Italians here, the Turks there, the Yugos somewhere else. The Germans were the only ones who didn't stick together. Vincenzo tried not to get dragged into anything. But if you wanted them to leave you alone, you had to pay. Cigarettes, money, or sex. Vincenzo kept his head above water through salami and red wine. Giovanni visited every Monday.

At night, when the Yugoslavian was asleep, Vincenzo conversed silently with the ghosts he could no longer escape, the restless souls whose lives had remained unfinished. His mother, who had brought him to his father's country without ever truly arriving there herself. His grandfather, who could never be his own master on the land he loved and worked.

Vincenzo talked to them as though they were sitting on his bunk, and came to perceive their story as the eternal search for a place one was allowed to stay, a place where one's own existence would no longer be called into question. And it finally dawned on him that his "place" was neither a house nor a country—it was a person. He wasn't alone anymore. He had someone worth living for, a person he loved more than himself. He had to stop toying with his own life as though it weren't worth anything. He had to take care of himself. Because he was needed.

He couldn't disappoint her. Those little eyes, full of all the hope in the world. Reflected in them, he no longer saw himself as the last link in a loose chain. The natural order of things, disrupted by his mother's death, had been restored. The love he himself had longed to receive was now something that flowed through him, from generation to generation. For the first time in his life, he viewed responsibility not as a burden but as a task that awaited him, that connected him to life. He could stop searching—all he had to do was assume his intended place.

The nightly conversations with Julia's picture on the wall gave him unexpected motivation. He might have despaired of not being able to watch her grow up, but he was missing only the first few years. He had to avoid losing himself in anger or self-pity—he had to accept his punishment and make the best of it. Use his time productively instead of wasting it like he had when he was free.

Did prison suck? Yeah. Was it worth fighting against? No. Was there a life after it? Sure. The meaning of life? He was here to turn shit into gold.

The prison library had everything he needed. He registered for high school equivalency exams and started hitting the math and biology books as if he were a pimply teenager again. Read every book he could get his hands on. Vincenzo rediscovered his old friends—Goethe, Schiller, Eichendorff—and found he truly understood them now.

Unfazed by any distance,

You come flying over, the hypnotized

Butterfly craving the light,

And finally it burns you.

And until you understand it,

this: Die and become!

You will remain but a melancholy guest

On the dark earth.

Every night, the last thing he looked at was the photos on his wall. The Yugoslavian's was decorated with blond pinups from the Pirelli calendar, but the space above Vincenzo's bunk showed a perfectly straight row of Polaroids in chronological order: Julia on Tanja's lap at the typewriter, Julia's first steps, Julia's first birthday cake. Tanja came irregularly, always alone, sometimes not at all, but she kept her promise and sent photos regularly.

When Vincenzo closed his eyes, he saw the striped blanket on Tanja's sofa, the brown dishes on the table in her shared apartment, the wooden coffee mill, the black-and-white cat. He lived with them, taught Julia her first words, repaired a broken stroller, and put her to bed—until the shrill 6:00 a.m. alarm bell jolted him back to reality. Clean the cell, breakfast, yard.

Every time Tanja went too long without writing or failed to visit, he fell apart. Those were the only moments when he saw himself as an angry, innocent victim. But one photo of Julia in her mother's arms was enough to remind him why he was doing time.

Once, when he went to the visiting room to wait for Tanja, the last person he'd ever expected to see was sitting at the table—his German father. Quiet, withdrawn, as though embarrassed to be seen in this place. Vincenzo turned to leave, but Vincent got up.

"Wait! Just one minute!"

Vincenzo eyed him disdainfully.

"How are you?" Vincent asked. He looked different. Smaller, somehow. The graying temples. The cautious expression.

"Fabulous."

Vincenzo had been bracing himself for a string of self-righteous, upper-middle-class questions about how he could ever let himself sink so low. But then he realized Vincent had come because he felt guilty.

"I brought you—" He gestured to the briefcase on the table. "Those are books. Automotive engineering manuals. Physics, too, totally up-to-date. I thought you might be interested."

Vincenzo didn't deign to glance at them.

"Mind your own business. You bring nothing but misery."

"Vincenzo, I want to . . . Not a day goes by when I don't think about your mother. I think she'd want us to—"

"How would you know what she'd want?" Vincenzo interrupted sharply.

Vincent flinched.

"Don't worry about me, jackass," Vincenzo said, and turned away. "I'll be fine."

"Vincenzo!"

He turned back.

Vincent went over to him and lowered his voice so that the guard couldn't hear. "The Iso. They brought it back to me. Customs did. They asked me whether I knew who had stolen it. I didn't tell them anything."

Vincenzo left without giving him the satisfaction of a thank-you. When he got back to his cell, the guard brought him the briefcase full of books.

"The guy left these for you. Don't you want 'em?"

"Is he gone?"

"Yeah."

One year later and twenty-two pounds lighter, he received his high school diploma from the warden personally. With distinction.

When Tanja came to visit, he brought the diploma along and laid it on the table in front of her.

"And I applied for a distance-learning course. Vehicular manufacturing. I'll be done by the time I get out."

He waited for her reaction.

She smiled at him. "That's great. Really!"

Her happiness was genuine, but something was missing. Maybe she couldn't reciprocate what he didn't say. The hope he associated with the educational plans.

"Aren't you glad?" he asked.

"Of course. Totally. That's awesome!"

"You look different somehow. Did something happen?"

Her eyebrows went up. "Didn't you hear?"

"What?"

"They shot John Lennon."

He actually hadn't heard. John Lennon was his favorite Beatle. Still, though, New York had as much relevance to his life as the moon.

"Some lunatic," Tanja said. "I think the CIA was behind it. They had him on the list for a long time."

Vincenzo nodded absently. "How's Julia?"

"Good. She likes preschool."

"I want to hold her."

"When she's old enough."

"When she's old enough!" Vincenzo blurted out. "When is she going to be old enough?"

Tanja turned cool.

"*Scusa,*" he murmured, pulling himself together. "I . . . Sometimes I go nuts in here. But don't worry, I'll be getting out early on good behavior—the warden told me himself. And the distance learning, that's just like normal college, you know? With a regular degree and everything. I'll be earning enough for all of us."

"Yeah."

He took her hand.

"Tanja. Trust me. Everything will be okay. You just have to be patient a little longer."

She nodded. Bit her lip. She had tears in her eyes.

Vincenzo, still holding her hand, got up from his chair and kneeled beside the table.

"What are you doing?"

"Will you marry me?"

She was completely caught off guard. "Vincenzo, are you crazy?"

"Of course. A man would have to be crazy to marry you!"

She laughed, half-touched, half-bewildered. Vincenzo beamed at her. She buried her hands in her face and wept silently.

He got a letter from her a week later. She wrote that she still cared about him, but nowadays people didn't need the state's permission to raise a child. That she was exploring alternative lifestyle and relationship forms. That marriage was an outdated institution. Vincenzo wadded up the letter and threw it into the corner, cursing.

There could only be one explanation for how she was acting. When he brought it up, she claimed she didn't have time for relationships, alternative or otherwise, but then changed the subject a little too quickly.

"Giovanni, you've got to help me convince Tanja!" Vincenzo shrieked into the pay telephone in the hall. "I can't take it anymore!"

"If you ask me, she just doesn't want to disappoint you."

"She was going to wait for me!"

"Vincenzo, listen to me. The most important thing is to get your degree. How many exams do you have left?"

"Dunno."

"Have they said when you're getting out?"

"Another year, probably. Listen, Giovanni, can't you just go check in on her, at her apartment? Bring her wine or whatever. I want to know who she's living with."

Giovanni sighed. "Vincenzo, what do you expect? She's young, she's attractive, she's German . . ."

"What the hell is that supposed to mean? Do you still believe Italian women are better? Such bullshit!"

"Vincenzo! What if you were out and she were in jail? You wouldn't have touched another woman?"

"No."

"Let me tell you something, genius. You don't have to know everything. Some things are better left unsaid. The way Germans are always talking everything out . . ."

"I want the truth, goddammit!" Vincenzo screamed. "Are you going to visit her or not?"

Giovanni didn't say anything.

"Kiss my ass!" Vincenzo slammed the receiver down and kicked the wall.

That evening, he stopped believing that he could hang on. And even if he did, there wouldn't be a place for him out there anymore. The empty space he'd left behind was already overgrown. Nobody needed him. He sat silently in front of the television with the Yugoslavian.

"We cannot digest any more foreigners," Chancellor Helmut Schmidt was saying on the news. "It will mean murder and mayhem."

70

On July 11, 1982, Vincenzo took the photos down from the wall one by one. Julia on a tricycle, Julia on a bicycle. Julia with pigtails, Julia in a cowboy hat. Julia grinning cheekily into the camera, looking more and more like Giulietta. Nearly five years he had missed. He slid them into his light-brown leather jacket and put on his scratched boots. The bell-bottoms and the turtleneck, now ratty, the same ones he'd been arrested in nearly five years before.

From beneath the bunk, he pulled out the gift he'd spent months building for Julia out of plywood scraps from the prison workshop—a Ferrari-red soap-box car. With rubber wheels, a steering column, and a hand brake.

The Yugoslavian hugged him goodbye.

"Forza Italia!"

Vincenzo gave him a questioning look.

"Tonight! World Cup finale! Germany against Italy!"

"Oh."

He didn't care. Tanja was waiting outside.

She stood on the far side of the street beside her small red Renault, smoking. It took Vincenzo's eyes a moment to adjust to the light. To the traffic. To a sky without walls. To Tanja's body as they embraced.

"What's that?" she asked, and pointed.

"For Julia."

They loaded the soapbox car into the trunk and drove to the preschool. Vincenzo waited in the lobby while Tanja picked Julia up from her class. He felt like an intruder into this innocent world of little shoes beneath benches, cute animal pictures above the coat hooks, colorful drawings on the walls. Julia

Becker. The name sounded foreign to him. Julia Marconi, he thought, that would have been right. But somehow it made him oddly proud that she had a different last name. Or rather, relieved. It gave him hope that his daughter would escape the Marconis' fate.

Then she came out of the room. Slowly, but not shyly, she walked up to him. She was wearing red corduroy overalls; her tiny hands were covered in dried paint.

"This is Vincenzo," Tanja said.

Julia regarded the strange man curiously and a little skeptically. How tall and grown-up she seemed! Vincenzo suddenly felt very small, overwhelmed by shame and immeasurable love.

As they walked to the car—Julia showed him the picture she'd finger-painted—everything was so easy and self-evident that Vincenzo could hardly believe it. Almost like a normal family.

"What's it like in Italy?"

"Nice. It's sunny there."

"Can we go to Italy, too, Mommy?"

"Sure, when you're older!"

They drove to Olympic Park. There were ice cream stands, roller skaters, and rowboats on the lake. Cloudless sky, mild breeze—summer was here. Vincenzo carried the soapbox up the rubble mountain and showed Julia how to steer and brake, and then Julia rode down, squealing. Vincenzo ran beside her, hanging on tight, but he tripped and somersaulted down the hill. The dry grass, the warm air, the light. "Again!" Julia screeched, laughing. Then they ran up and launched themselves down again. Tanja had to stop them, or they'd have driven straight into the lake out of sheer exuberance.

She worried about Julia more than necessary. Vincenzo sensed it but didn't let it stop him. He lifted Julia over his head, gripped her little hands, and swung her around wildly like a carousel, threw her high into the air and caught her. She giggled and crowed like she was at one with the entire world, and both of them forgot about everything but that perfect moment of happiness Vincenzo had spent so long waiting for. He was infinitely grateful to be alive.

Tanja took a picture of them with her pocket camera. It ended up being the only photo of Vincenzo and Julia together.

Later, they went to Tanja's editorial office, a storefront in Schwabing that smelled like tea and hashish. The *Blatt* was a last gasp of anarchy that had survived into the 1980s, the fading echo of a psychedelic guitar riff in a country that was dancing to German New Wave, a tiny oasis of leftist mavericks and caricature artists.

Julia ran straight to the big layout desk—snippets of paper with text, photos, classified ads, and comics. The walls were adorned with the front pages of the last several issues, a poster showing a peace dove, a call to a demonstration against the Pershing missile. Pershing, nuclear energy, deforestation—it all seemed unreal to Vincenzo. He didn't care who was in power as long as somebody gave him work. Work that would allow him to provide for his family.

"Ute, this is Vincenzo. Vincenzo, Ute."

"Hi."

The graphic designer at the layout desk was wearing a washed-out T-shirt with a printed peace sign, which to Vincenzo always looked like a Mercedes symbol.

"Heard a lot about you," she said, regarding him curiously.

"Ute and I live and work together," Tanja said.

Vincenzo raised his eyebrows.

"We're a collective," Ute explained.

"Oh," Vincenzo said uncertainly.

Ute laughed.

"Why are you guys laughing?" Julia asked.

"No reason," Tanja said.

Ute poured them some tea.

They stood around awkwardly for a while, until finally Vincenzo asked, "Are we watching the World Cup final tonight? Germany against Italy?"

Tanja and Ute exchanged glances he didn't understand.

"Where are you going to be staying now, anyway?" Tanja asked. "With Giovanni?"

He felt like she'd slapped him in the face.

"I dunno," he stammered.

"Do you need money for a boardinghouse?" Tanja asked.

For her, it had just been one afternoon, nothing more. He tried to keep his expression neutral.

"No, thanks."

He didn't have a pfennig to his name, but he wasn't going to beg her for handouts.

Tanja took him aside, out of Julia's earshot.

"Vincenzo, we have a daughter, but that doesn't mean we're together."

"Sure. I get it. You have your own life."

"We'll see each other on weekends, okay?"

Vincenzo nodded.

Even Julia sensed the leaden silence that filled the room. She looked up at Vincenzo and exclaimed, "Look, this is funny!" She pointed to an anti-cop cartoon.

Vincenzo went over to her. "I'll see you again soon, okay?"

"Where are you going?"

"Vincenzo lives with his uncle," Tanja said.

Vincenzo gave Julia a kiss on the forehead.

"Ciao, amore."

"Ciao!"

"See you soon," he told Tanja.

"See you soon. Are you sure you don't need any money?"

He walked through the door. Outside, he couldn't breathe for a moment. He felt like the rug had been pulled out from under him. He looked around. The sun was setting behind the buildings. He didn't know where he was or where to go. He hadn't even told Giovanni when he was getting out. So that he could be alone with Tanja and Julia.

A man bumped into him as he walked past. Vincenzo didn't pay much attention. Then he heard the man open the door to the editorial office. Vincenzo turned around and watched through the front window as the guy placed a box of paper on a desk. He had long hair and a beard, and was wearing a Palestinian-flag shirt and sandals. Not a revolutionary, more of a granola type. He handed out soft pretzels. Then he gave Tanja a kiss. She turned her face away so that it landed on her cheek—out of the corner of her eye, she saw Vincenzo through the glass—but the casual way he touched her hips was unmistakable.

Vincenzo froze. He balled his fists. *Goddammit,* he told himself, *pull yourself together! She's a free woman. It was almost five years. He was here, you weren't. He actually looks like a nice guy. Get out of here before he notices you.*

Just as he was about to turn away, Vincenzo saw the guy kneel down to give Julia a pretzel. Tanja positioned herself with her back to the window in order to block Vincenzo's view. She must have been getting nervous. The guy picked Julia up. Just like that, without even asking. Laughed with her, nibbled on a bit of pretzel with her. She obviously liked him.

Tanja saw the crash coming from a mile off. She hurriedly took the child away from him, but Vincenzo had already burst through the door. Everyone held their breath except for the guy, who looked clueless.

"Wait," Tanja said, and rushed to Vincenzo, Julia still in her arms.

He pushed his way past. He remained composed.

"Hey," he said to the guy, "you can do whatever you want with Tanja, but don't touch my daughter!"

"Vincenzo, calm down!" Tanja tried to hold him back. He shook her off. The guy began to understand who Vincenzo was.

"Hey, man. Just relax, okay?"

"I am relaxed," Vincenzo replied, fixing him with a steely gaze and grabbing him by the collar. "Did you understand what I just said? Say it!"

"What the fuck? Let go!" The guy tried to wriggle away from Vincenzo.

Tanja set Julia on the floor and took Vincenzo's arm.

"Vincenzo! Listen to me. Life didn't just stand still out here. You can't just assume you're entitled to things!"

"She's right," the guy said.

Vincenzo ignored him and regarded Tanja with disappointment.

"Slut."

She remained calm. The guy, on the other hand, seemed to think he had to defend her honor.

"That's enough! Get out!"

In a flash, Vincenzo spun around and slammed the guy against the bookshelf with brutal force. It tipped over, books spilling out. Tanja moved in front of Julia protectively. Now the guy was really mad.

"You have no business here. Get lost, you loser!"

Tanja was still trying to mediate, but Vincenzo saw red. He punched her boyfriend hard in the face, sending him tumbling against the desk.

"Are you nuts?" Tanja shouted.

Vincenzo glanced briefly at Julia, who was hiding in terror behind her mother's legs. He would have stopped there, but the guy grabbed his arm and dragged him toward the door. Vincenzo socked him in the stomach. The women tried to pull them apart, but it was hopeless. They fell to the floor, grappling wildly. A chair splintered. The women screamed.

Tanja scooped Julia up and carried her out of harm's way. Ute ran to the phone and—radical values be damned—called the police. Vincenzo ripped the phone from the desk, but she'd already given her name and address. Tanja's boyfriend whacked him in the neck with a chair leg. Vincenzo stumbled. The other man threw himself at him, but Vincenzo broke free with a yell and then whaled on him blindly until he went down, spitting blood. Only once he stopped moving did Vincenzo let up.

Tanja stared at him with cold rage. Julia was crying. Ute bent down to the injured man, who was curled up in pain. Vincenzo saw the uncomprehending fear in Julia's eyes and realized he'd made a horrible mistake. He wanted to go to her, to tell her she didn't have to be scared, but she clung to Tanja's leg in absolute terror.

"Julia . . ."

Tanja stepped in, blocking his path determinedly.

"Don't you touch her!"

His bloody hands trembled. Then he heard the police sirens. He racked his brain feverishly. The minute the cops came through the door, it was all over. He didn't have a prayer.

"Go through the bathroom!" she hissed.

Vincenzo forced himself through the bathroom window, jumped into the courtyard, and ran until his lungs were burning.

71

Giovanni was busy setting up the television when Vincenzo burst through the door. Italian flag on the cheese counter, the shop full of plastic chairs. A few soccer fans, all guest workers of Giovanni's generation, were already in there, waiting for the big game.

"Vincenzo!" Giovanni took in the bleeding nose, split eyebrow, torn shirt. "What the hell did you—"

"Don't ask! Just help me, goddammit!"

"It's okay, *non c'è problema*," Giovanni called to his guests as he hastily led Vincenzo to the back room.

Giulietta's sewing machine was still there. Giovanni rummaged around for alcohol to clean Vincenzo's wounds. His nephew meekly explained what had happened.

"You really are talented!" Giovanni snapped. "Every opportunity you get, you screw it up in spectacular fashion!"

"I wasn't going to sit there and let them treat me like a dog! What would Julia think of her father?"

"Well, now she thinks he's a violent goddamn idiot. *Bravo!*"

"Dammit, Giovanni, I need your help!"

"What are you going to do, hmm?"

Since he couldn't find any rubbing alcohol, he tipped a little grappa onto his Inter Milan scarf and dabbed Vincenzo's eyebrow.

"Fight for her! She's the only family I have."

"Bullshit. You have me."

"Then tell me what I'm supposed to do!" Vincenzo exclaimed in despair.

Giovanni pondered.

"You didn't exactly cut a *bella figura* today. But Tanja already made her decision a long time ago. In the end, the women are always the ones who decide."

"But the kid. The kid is mine!"

"What do you want to do, go to court? You'll never get custody. Who are you to the German judges? An unemployed foreigner with a criminal record."

"I'm her father!"

Vincenzo jumped up and started for the door.

Giovanni blocked his path.

"Use your head! If that man presses charges, they'll throw you right back in jail. Your moment of glory there, that was assault."

"What? It was just a normal fistfight. Plus, he started it. I was stronger, that's all."

Giovanni grabbed Vincenzo firmly by the shoulders and looked at him. "You need to get out of Germany."

Vincenzo considered. "Not without Julia."

"What, you're going to kidnap her or something? My God, you need to save your own ass. Immediately. We'll figure out the rest later. Wait here for me. I'll go get you a clean shirt, and then I'm taking you to Salina."

Vincenzo shook his head, panicked. "No! Once I leave Germany, I can't get back in. No, Giovanni, no!"

They reached the Brenner Pass shortly after ten. It was cool and dark in the cargo hold of Giovanni's delivery van. The blanket Vincenzo was hiding under stank of diesel. The old shocks squeaked. Giovanni rumbled over the speed bumps and stopped at customs. Vincenzo heard the muted voices of the Austrian officials. Giovanni, casual as ever. They chatted about the game. They knew each other. Several minutes passed. Silence except for the sports commentator on the car radio. Vincenzo was trembling in fear. Footsteps approached.

"Over! It's over! Three–one! The Italians are the world champions!" The commentator's voice cracked.

Giovanni slowly rolled onto the Italian side of customs. Vincenzo heard the Italian officers' shouts of celebration. The delivery van crept through without anyone stopping them.

Giovanni knocked against the steel wall. "Vincenzo, we made it!" he called. "We're in Italy!"

Vincenzo huddled beneath his blanket, weeping bitterly.

72

Decades later, an abandoned parking lot was the only indication that there had once been a border control station here. Trucks sped down the Autobahn without stopping. A different Europe, borderless, disenchanted. I was completely confused. Sorted my thoughts, my memories, my emotions. The stories didn't fit together.

"And you've never been back since?" I asked.

Vincenzo shook his head. He drove into the large, empty parking lot and shut off the engine. Abruptly, we fell silent. The rushing sound of passing cars, the hum echoing in my ears, drizzle on the windowpanes. Gray clouds hung low in the mountains. Vincenzo got out. He didn't go anywhere, just stood there with the rain running down his face, watching the cars drive by, into the tunnel, across the border.

I went to him.

"Mom said you hit her."

"No! That's not true!"

I couldn't remember. I could still picture our afternoon in the park, light and flooded with sunshine. What happened after that had sunk into darkness.

"I swear to you," he said.

"But why would she lie to me?"

"Do you remember any of it?" Vincenzo asked back.

I shook my head. "Only that it was awful."

He nodded and left it at that. *Maybe everyone has their own truth,* he seemed to be saying. *And maybe,* I thought, *our memories are just fortresses we build to protect us from ourselves.* I empathized with him.

"Why didn't you ever come back?"

He was silent.

"Why didn't you fight for me?"

He gave me a forlorn look. "You were in good hands."

It sounded like a question, not an apology. He turned away and ran a hand over his face in despair. Seeing him like this was unsettling.

"I didn't have the nerve," he said. "To your mother, I was just some lowlife."

I took his hand. "And I always thought you didn't want to see me."

"No. No!" He grasped for words. "Thank you for coming. Please forgive me. I'm sorry."

I stood there, distressed and soaking wet, barely able to process what he was saying.

"I'm not trying to justify myself," he said. "But you need to know that I always loved you."

He gripped my hands tightly.

I couldn't tell whether it was rain running down his face or tears. He was my father, but I wanted to hug him as if he were my child. I took his head in my hands and held it. He buried his face in my embrace, trembling all over. I was crying, too. We were standing in some shitty parking lot in the rain, and I suddenly felt like I'd arrived. Something I'd never allowed myself to do—just be there. My life, as brightly as it shone outwardly, was one long battle for existence. For a recognition that I could never receive, because no amount of success would replace what I had really longed for. Now, all of that fell away.

When we got in again, I glanced up at the old Brenner Pass road running through the craggy mountains. If Giulietta was still there, a restless spirit between worlds, she was looking down on us now. Her love had been with us the entire time.

A thunderstorm was coming down on the north side of the Brenner Tunnel. The sky darkened; the windshield wipers fought against the torrents of water pattering around us as though we were driving through a gigantic car wash. I was behind the wheel; the heat was on full throttle; our wet clothes were drying slowly. But we were safe inside our time capsule. Another hundred miles or so. With every number that ticked down on the odometer, the present day slowly caught up to us. We felt ever lighter, freed from the burdens we'd put behind us. I'd texted Clara to tell her we'd be there just after sundown. And asked how Vincent was doing.

"He's waiting for you," she responded.

When you come to Germany from another country, it often feels like gravity has a stronger pull here. There's a subtle kind of angst weighing on people, something other cultures lack. Or maybe it was just my own fears creeping back up as we closed in on our destination. Munich was where my own existence was currently going down the tubes. Nothingness was waiting for me. Sure, I'd made it without a dad. But I couldn't stop my dreams from running through my fingers, just like his.

"What will you do now, without your company?" he asked.

"Dunno. When we were on our way to see you, Giovanni said that Italians were masters of *bella figura*. Everything looks great on the outside, but inside, it's a disaster. He meant you, but . . . It's a perfect description of my life, too."

"Must be in your genes," he said, and grinned.

I couldn't help grinning back.

"Steve Jobs was thrown out of his own company, too," Vincenzo said.

"Yeah, but he was a multimillionaire by thirty."

"A couple years later, he came back and made Apple the most valuable corporation in the world."

"Honestly, I've had enough of corporations. I'd rather just run away to a deserted island."

"No, you wouldn't. Actually, you're furious. You want to murder your business partner."

He'd hit the nail on the head. I could hardly express in words how much I hated Robin for his shady move. The blow he'd dealt me had completely knocked me for a loop. I was still too hurt to fight back. But now I realized that my pain was just an echo of a much older wound. Life isn't a straight line—it moves in circles. Over and over again, we return to the start. But those older wounds were based on a lie. What I'd considered an axiomatic truth was actually nothing I needed to fear. My father had never left me and never died. He'd just been somewhere else for a while.

73

By sunset, we were in Munich, running on fumes. Vincenzo switched on the radio to distract himself. Migrant boats in the Mediterranean. The world had caught up to us. He was tense. I wondered if he was mulling over the same thing I was: whether he could forgive his father. Neither of us brought it up, though.

And then, finally, we were there. I didn't want to get out at first. He seemed to feel the same. Our time capsule sat in the hospital parking lot like a foreign object from a different dimension. Reluctantly, we left the Montreal—the warm cocoon—behind, like a secret that only we shared, and went to the front door.

I hate hospitals. Piles of concrete that smell like unhappiness. You always feel small and helpless there. The receptionist wanted to turn us away. Visiting hours were over. Too late. I tried piling on the charm, but then Vincenzo flew into a rage and kicked a trash can.

"My daughter and I just drove over six hundred miles, and my father is dying! Fuck your visiting hours!" He grabbed my hand and pulled me to the elevator. Somehow, I liked that.

Vincent's bed was empty. At first, I thought we were at the wrong door, but then I recognized his glasses on the nightstand. His jacket on the hook. The unmade bed. It made me uneasy. I'd been here just two days ago, but it seemed like an eternity; I wasn't the same person anymore. The night nurse came to the door. She wasn't surprised to see us and looked Vincenzo over with restrained curiosity.

"You're his son?"

Vincenzo nodded.

"He's been waiting for you."

We gave her a questioning look.

"Dr. Schlewitz is in surgery right now."

"Why? What happened?"

"Complications. You'll have to ask the chief physician. He came down especially for this—he's overseeing treatment personally."

"Is it risky?"

"Your dad's very strong. I brought him in for the operation, and he asked that I tell you—both of you—that he's going to make it."

She smiled, but I felt light-headed.

"Where's his daughter?" I asked.

"With her family. She was here the whole night. She'll be back as soon as possible."

All we could do was wait. We went to the vending area and called a pizza place. Ironic, I thought, that when my grandfather was young, he didn't know what a pizza was. I grew up on frozen pizza. Then came Turkish döner kebabs. What would be next?

"Che schifo," Vincenzo grumbled when he opened the box. "You call this pizza?" We ate it in silence, with vending machine coffee for dessert. Hospitals are the last German bastion that soy lattes haven't yet conquered.

"Should we call Giovanni and Rosaria?"

"No. This, here, is none of their business. It's between me and—" He pointed toward the empty bed without saying Vincent's name.

"What did he write in the letter?" he asked. "You said there was a letter in the bag that got stolen?"

"I don't know. I didn't open it. All I know is that he was adamant about wanting to talk to you."

Vincenzo's phone rang. It was Carmela. He spoke to her in Italian, and I wondered whether their marriage was a happy one.

"How'd you do it?" I asked when he'd hung up.

"What?"

"You know. Family. Success. You have everything you wanted now."

Vincenzo looked at me thoughtfully.

"Wanting something doesn't make it come about, you know. These things—they just happen. And all of a sudden, you become part of them."

"Was Carmela waiting for you?"

"No, she married quickly. After I'd called off the wedding—well, he was a contractor from Palermo. When I returned, she didn't want to see me. She was really hurt."

"What about you? What did you do?"

"Chased death."

74

After fleeing to Italy a second time, Vincenzo didn't stay with his family. He disappeared without a trace. He didn't want to be around anyone who knew him, who would remind him of what he once had been, wanted to be, or could have become. He wanted to be a stranger among strangers, neither speaking his mother tongue nor returning to his fatherland. Italy had its first privately operated television stations; a crazy guy had shot a young couple who were making love in a Fiat; and the new German government under Helmut Kohl was paying foreigners to leave Germany. That wasn't Vincenzo's world anymore.

In Palermo, he met up with a mechanic he knew from the Targa Florio who had converted an old Alfetta GTV into a rally car. They took a ferry to Finland. The Finns were holding a rally on ice, somewhere near the Arctic Circle. Careening across frozen lakes at ridiculous speeds. Frozen deserts.

For the next year, Vincenzo drifted around Europe, taking every rally driving job he could get. Third league, absolute risk, take the money and run. He wasn't driving to win anymore. He was driving to forget. The roar of the engines, the thrill of high speeds, racing as an addiction to numb his pain. Behind the wheel was the only place he could focus so much on the present that the past couldn't catch up to him. He didn't even love his cars now; no, he cursed them the way drinkers curse alcohol. Once, he rolled his car in the woods so badly that the vehicle was completely destroyed and the codriver broke his leg. Vincenzo walked away with just a few bruises. Dying wouldn't have bothered him, but death took no pity on him. Hell was the days between races.

Eventually, someone got into an accident, and Vincenzo was asked to fill in on the racetrack. Touring Car championships, big audience, the same old

Alfa-BMW rivalry. If Formula One was the advanced class, touring cars were the Circus Maximus. Not gentlemen drivers but gladiators fighting tooth and nail amid the jubilation of the masses. Vincenzo got a car from the previous year. A small, private racing team, enthusiasts with money to burn. He was a blank slate. Nobody took him seriously. Everyone in the league had talent, but what set him apart from the other drivers was that he had nothing to lose.

The other guys had a name, a wife, a family. They were attached to life. Vincenzo wasn't. At the crucial moment, he'd brake a second later, take the extra risk, keep driving with tires worn to the bone, long after the other drivers were changing theirs. One race after another, a circus touring across Europe. He never reached the podium, but he was getting closer and closer.

The following season, he landed a job with the Alfa factory team. The Alfetta was getting on in years, completely outclassed by the newer BMWs. But Vincenzo drove that car like a bat out of hell, and at the end of a crazy season—it was 1985—he was on the podium, with a garland around his neck and a silver trophy in his hand. It had all happened so fast, even he could hardly believe it. Three years of tunnel vision, closer to death than life, and suddenly his name was in the papers.

He hadn't won because he was particularly talented. It was because he was no longer afraid of defeat.

Finally, he went back to Salina. From the ferry, he took the country highway into town, on foot. It was a calm October day; the sea glittered silver. Rosaria's mother still lived in the old house. She welcomed him without asking what he'd done, and that was perfectly fine with him. She made him osso buco, and he went down to the beach. He felt freer and more relaxed than ever before. At last, he had nothing to prove to anyone. He laid the laurel wreath on his mother's grave.

He negotiated with the big racing teams over the phone. All of them wanted to sign him. Alfa Romeo, of course, as well as BMW, which filled him with mixed satisfaction. They offered him three years on the factory team and twice as much money as the Italians—more than he'd ever imagined. All he had to do was decide: Germany or Italy. Giovanni and Rosaria traveled down from Munich to celebrate his success with a big dinner. Vincenzo wasn't sure whether they were relieved at his success, or relieved of their own guilty consciences.

And then Carmela came. Unannounced.

"Auguri, Vincenzo," she said, and kissed him on both cheeks to congratulate him.

Vincenzo was caught completely off guard. He was sure she'd banished him from her life. And she looked so different! Not a *ragazza* anymore, but a *signora*. Expensive dress, Milanese designer purse, fluffed-up Kim Wilde hairstyle. She looked like a woman who had made it. And one who'd been hurt.

"What happened, Carmela?"

By sunset, they were back on their old stone wall. The wind rustled the grass; geckos twitched across the moss.

"You did it. I always knew you could." She meant it genuinely, without a trace of irony or malice.

"You're not mad at me?"

"I was. Furious. I cursed your name. But, I mean, bearing grudges doesn't help. It didn't make me any happier."

"I thought about you often, you know."

"I thought about you way more often." She smiled.

"Do you have children?" he asked.

She shook her head. "I got divorced."

Vincenzo blinked. "Why?"

"He was a pig." That was all she said.

"I'm sorry."

"You don't have to be. I should never have married him."

Vincenzo knew why she had. His rejection had humiliated her in front of everyone. She'd had no other choice if she wanted to defend her honor.

"I understand why you left, Vincenzo. She's the mother of your child."

"I haven't seen her in years."

Carmela was surprised. She had assumed he and Tanja were still together.

"I screwed that up, too," he said, and made a face.

"Remember Giovanni's wedding?" she asked. "We had our whole lives ahead of us. Anything was possible."

They gazed out at the barren, overgrown field before them. Their first kiss, the day when everything had gone off the rails.

"And now?" he asked.

"Now we have nothing left to lose."

"What if we just started over from the beginning?"

They got married in the same field, in the summer of 1986. Late that evening, when the guests were all full and dancing drunkenly, they sat on their old stone wall again, he in a black suit, she in a white dress. Like the marzipan figures on the wedding cake. They looked at each other and couldn't help laughing.

Vincenzo had followed Nino Vaccarella's advice to get out before it was too late. He'd turned down all the offers and rented a small apartment in Naples, where he worked for Alfa Romeo as a test driver. Not race cars, just normal street cars. He wanted to be alive when his children were grown.

They had bad luck with the first pregnancy, but the second one took. On a June night in 1988, he parked his little Alfasud outside the apartment building and opened the car door for Carmela. Cautiously, she handed him the two newborns. Carmela's exhausted smile; the fragile little bodies; the huge, amazed eyes. In the bar on the corner, fans were cheering as they watched Germany against Italy in the European Cup. Vincenzo couldn't care less. He held his twins close and kissed them tenderly. Carmela went on ahead with her suitcase to unlock the front door. He didn't see that she was crying tears of happiness.

75

I could have been jealous when he told me that, but all I felt was a quiet joy that his life had worked out after all.

"I don't know," he said thoughtfully. "I never forgot about your mother. Or you." He looked at me with restless eyes. The truth was that he'd remained eternally unredeemed.

"Did you ever see Enzo again?" I asked.

He shook his head. "Giovanni met up with him once. A long time ago. Here in Munich. He's repairing Vespas in a little auto shop."

"Don't you ever want to see him?"

Vincenzo shook his head. Cold. Unforgiving.

"Do you suppose he's still here or back in Italy?"

He shrugged. "Everyone talks about going back. Giovanni included. In 1992, when that refugee home was burned down in Rostock, everyone said, 'This isn't our country anymore.' But in the end, even Rosaria stayed. Their kids speak better German than Italian. They have German friends; they're FC Bayern fans; they even dream in German. This is their homeland."

"What about yours?"

Vincenzo laughed. "Homeland? Funny how there's no plural of that word in German. You don't get to have two homelands."

"If you had to pick one?"

"Whichever one I'm not in at the time."

He grinned and got up to buy two more coffees from the machine. "Before I finally married Carmela, I kept falling for German women. Tourists, coworkers. Maybe I was searching for Tanja in them."

"Do your kids know about their German grandpa?"

"No." He smirked. "But they worship German sports stars. Schumacher, Vettel, Schweinsteiger, Özil . . ."

My phone rang. I'd completely forgotten that my mother knew where I was. And with whom.

"We're waiting," I said curtly. "He's in surgery."

She was silent. I heard the wind rushing in the background.

"I'm downstairs."

Surprised, I went to the window. She was standing outside the entrance beside a streetlamp, wrapped in a thick scarf. She looked forlorn.

"Why don't you come up?"

"Is he there with you?"

"Yeah."

"Then—I didn't want to disturb you. I just wanted to . . ."

She paced back and forth indecisively. It annoyed me that she couldn't leave us alone, but I also felt sorry for her, standing out there in the dark, not daring to come in. Vincenzo signaled that he would let me speak to her in private, and then walked out.

"I know that he—" Tanja grasped for words. "That he perceives some things differently. He's very emotional."

I wasn't sure this was the time and place for a deep conversation. Or what she was expecting.

"It's not about what one person perceives and the other doesn't," I said. "What matters is what actually happened."

"There's never an objective truth when it comes to relationships, Julia. Everyone's trapped in their own version of the story."

She looked up at me, suddenly seeming very small.

"You were always talking about freedom," I said. "But you never gave me the freedom to see things for myself."

I took her silence as an admission of guilt. For a long time, she just stood there, gazing up at the window, with the phone to her ear.

"Have I lost you?" she asked.

Maybe, I thought. Something was broken and would never be quite whole again. But I couldn't banish my mother from my life any more than I could change our history. Suddenly, I saw Vincenzo approaching her. Tanja jumped.

Then she lowered the phone, and the two of them stood there, face-to-face. I still had my own phone to my ear, but all I heard was the wind. Neither of them spoke. Then I hung up. I felt like a child accidentally eavesdropping on her parents at night. It wasn't for me to hear.

He said something. Then she did. Then something happened. Even through the window, I could sense how uncertain and overwhelmed they were. Thirty years stood between them, two lives, two countries, and one lie.

She gave him a cigarette, and he handed her his coffee cup. Then they looked up at me. I waved. They waved back.

Later, Vincenzo returned. He was alone.

"So?" I asked. "How'd it go?"

He seemed deeply touched and a little confused.

"She's hoping you'll forgive her."

"Is she still there?"

"No."

I glanced at the clock. It was just after midnight.

"She took good care of you," he said. "I thanked her. And I said that you've become a woman she can be proud of."

He sat down next to me, a new light in his eyes. If he could forgive her after everything that had happened, I thought, then I would be able to, too. I snuggled against his shoulder and fell asleep.

I woke up just after four o'clock. It was very quiet apart from a few distant voices. Vincenzo had nodded off as well. Still bleary-eyed, I got up and walked down the hall. Bright fluorescent light shone behind the glass door to the ICU. A doctor was standing there, white coat and white hair, with a woman next to him. I didn't recognize her until I came a little closer: Clara. The doctor shook his head, and she froze.

The night nurse brought his effects. Shaving kit, wallet, pen, glasses. None of us wanted to take them. As if doing so would mean accepting that it was true. Vincenzo was devastated. Clara barely spoke and avoided looking at her half brother. We were all in shock.

Finally, I decided I would take the stuff, but Clara reached for it at that exact moment. When she did, a letter fell to the floor. The night nurse picked it up and gave it to me. My name was written on it in sweeping, slightly old-fashioned script.

I went to the window and opened it.

My dear Julia,

They're taking me into surgery in a moment. I promised to wait for you two, but it all happened so fast. The doctor says everything will be fine. I'll pull through, and I'm so glad you're on your way here. I can hardly tell you how excited I am to see you both. I hope Vincenzo's looking forward to it as well. How did he take my letter? I wish I could have told him sooner. I owed that to him—and not only to him, but to the father who was there for him when I wasn't. The one he thinks is a murderer.

Marianne only confessed her horrible deed to me on her deathbed. How she could live with such guilt for all those years is as incomprehensible to me as the thought of her being capable of something like that. I hope you and Vincenzo can forgive her someday. I can't.

Your grandmother, Giulietta, was the most precious thing life ever gave me. I wouldn't trade any of those few days we had together for the world. We cling to memories as though we can stop time. But in the end, we're left with nothing, apart from faith in a love that permeates everything and can bear anything, no matter how unbearable it seems.

For a long time, I considered myself an unlucky person, because I had lost Giulietta. Now I know that I was a lucky person because I had the chance to love her, both while she was alive and after her death. She lives on in you.

Your grandfather,
Vincent

Dawn was breaking outside.

"What's he say?" Clara asked.

"Nothing special," I replied, and folded the letter.

76

Behind the meadow, children played in a schoolyard. We were standing by the large windows of the public pool, watching the swimmers quietly doing laps in the hall. Vincenzo, Giovanni, and I. It was a sunny morning, not many people here, mostly older men and women. He swam here every morning—a German retiree with an Italian passport who belonged to a forgotten generation. He sometimes helped young Italians with government red tape, and he went to Mass on Sundays; other than that, not much happened in his life. Giovanni heard from him occasionally, though they still avoided one another. The swimmers all looked alike in their bathing caps, but when he came to the edge of the pool to rest, I recognized him even though I'd never seen him before. A small, sturdy Sicilian with bushy gray eyebrows. Giovanni knocked on the glass. Enzo, astonished, removed his goggles.

Impossible to guess what he was thinking at that moment. He dried himself off with routine movements, put on his robe, and came outside. He was shorter than I'd pictured. An old bear, ponderous, good-natured, and lonely. He stopped some distance away and regarded us with suspicion. It took the men some time to peer through forty years of slings and arrows to see what still remained. Enzo studied my face.

"*Ciao, Papà,*" Vincenzo said. There was an unexpected tenderness in his voice.

"*Ciao, Vincenzo.*"

Giovanni couldn't get a word out. Not because he was too moved, but out of shame for having misjudged his brother-in-law for half a lifetime. He gave Vincenzo a discreet elbow in the ribs. Vincenzo went to Enzo and embraced him. Enzo could hardly believe it at first. Outwardly composed, but deeply touched, he finally wrapped his arms around his son, stealing glances in my direction all the while. Vincenzo noticed.

"This is Julia. Your granddaughter."

Enzo approached me. He held out his hand, polite and affectionate.

"I'm Enzo."

"Julia."

He didn't let go of my hand.

"Show him the letter," Giovanni said at last.

I handed him Vincent's letter.

Enzo removed his reading glasses from the pocket of his robe and read.

An elementary school class stormed into the hall. The children launched themselves noisily into the water.

When Enzo had finished reading, he looked up wearily and handed it back to me. We held our breath. For a long moment, he gazed silently at the children in the water. Finally, he nodded sadly and said, "She was a mamma."

77

Two Years Later

Enzo wanted to be buried in the country that had become his homeland. All those years, Germany had treated him better than his own family. The guest workers and their children had become "people of immigrant background," and politicians were finally calling Germany what it had been for a long time, whether it wanted to be or not—a country of immigration. When Giovanni came here, Munich had a small handful of Italian restaurants. Today, there are more than seven hundred.

The face of Italy was changing as well. Tunisian immigrants from the other side of the Mediterranean were moving into the abandoned houses in the Sicilian villages. Europe gleamed and staggered, an old continent searching for a new identity.

"We Turks are the new Italians," Enzo's former apprentice said at his funeral. "And the Arabs are the new Turks."

I wondered when we would finally start simply thinking of each other as people, without asking who came from where. Then again, perhaps knowing where one comes from was a timeless, inextinguishable need. *A tree without roots,* Giulietta had said, *bears no fruit.*

It's true, too. In the past two years, things I would never have managed before have happened practically of their own accord. I opened my own atelier and fashion boutique, right around the corner from Giovanni's. It's small, but it's mine. I don't fly all over the world now—I work with local seamstresses and suppliers, creating sustainable, customized designs. Not in huge quantities, but each piece is unique and made with love. Where'd I get the start-up funds? No, I didn't want to inherit anything from Vincent. As it turned out, he had written us into his will, but Vincenzo refused his share, too.

"It's too late," he said.

Clara was surprised. Out of embarrassment, she gave him the Iso Rivolta, saying she didn't have any use for that "old Italian rust bucket" anyway. Vincenzo didn't tell her what it was worth. More than a new Maserati. He gifted it to me. That was my start-up fund. My chance to redefine myself again. What made this different from the other times wasn't what I was doing so much as how I was doing it. When I work on a design now, it's like Giulietta is right there next to me. The photo of her and Vincent in Milan hangs in my shop.

Marco, my admirer from the baptism, is around more often now. Pretty often, actually. It all happened fast. A little too fast, to be honest, but he's a wonderful man. Maybe the first one I genuinely trust. Today, we sped to an ultrasound appointment on his Vespa. The doctor says it's going to be a girl. There's no time for us to get married, even though Giovanni's telling everyone he's going to plan the biggest party of his life for us.

Vincenzo and Carmela separated, but they still live together. We Skype a lot. Tanja stopped by a few days ago, too. Vincenzo wants to come up to Munich for the birth, of course. And stay with us awhile. They'll probably fight over who gets to take care of the baby.

Sometimes I panic about how we're going to manage everything, but now I know that I was never really afraid of having a family. I was only afraid of passing something on that hadn't settled down inside me. Things can only scare you when you don't know them. The whole misunderstanding comes from thinking we have to achieve everything under our own power, instead of understanding that there are forces carrying us. We don't have to write the books of our lives alone. The people around us are our coauthors, and our children continue the story.

"What are you going to call her?" the doctor asked. We knew the answer immediately.

"Giulietta."

THE FAMILY TREE

GIULIETTA MARCONI, born in Malfa (Salina), 1935

GIOVANNI MARCONI, born in Malfa (Salina), 1935: *Giulietta's twin brother*

ENZO MARCONI, born in Malfa (Salina), 1932: *Giulietta's husband*

VINCENZO MARCONI, born in Milan, 1955: *Enzo and Giulietta's child*

VINCENT SCHLEWITZ, born in Gliwice, 1930: *Vincenzo's biological father*

TANJA BECKER, born in Darmstadt, 1951: *Vincenzo's girlfriend and Julia's mother*

JULIA BECKER, born in Munich, 1977: *Vincenzo and Tanja's child*

ACKNOWLEDGMENTS

I would like to thank the "Cultural Foundations of Integration" Cluster of Excellence at the University of Constance, who assisted my contemporary-history research and work on this project, especially Prof. Dr. Albrecht Koschorke, Prof. Dr. Sven Reichardt, Prof. Dr. Wolfgang Seibel, Prof. Dr. Rudolf Schlögl, and Christopher Möllmann as well as the Cultural Studies Research Group, Fred Girod, Christina Thoma, Daniela Göpfrich, and Nina Kück.

Lianne Kolf, my German agent, who always believed in the story, as well as her international coagents Andrew Nurnberg and Charlotte Seymour.

Susanne Kiesow, who discovered my manuscript underneath a large stack and edited it with loving precision.

Julia Schade and Cordelia Borchardt, who gave my novel the best possible home.

Liza Darnton, who gave my novel wings to travel around the world.

Jaime McGill for her brilliant English translation.

Michele Zatta (RAI) for his consulting work regarding contemporary Italian history.

ABOUT THE AUTHOR

Photo © Giò Martorana

Daniel Speck is an award-winning screenwriter for film and TV and a best-selling novelist. He was born in 1969 in Munich and studied literature, film history, and screenwriting in Munich and Rome. A passionate traveler, lover of Mediterranean countries, and builder of bridges between cultures, he draws his inspirations for his films and novels from the personal stories of people he encounters. His debut novel, *Anywhere but Home*, originally published as *Bella Germania* and translated into seven languages, was on the *Spiegel* bestseller list for eighty-five weeks. It was Germany's most successful debut novel of 2016 and was adapted by Speck into a television miniseries. In addition to teaching screenwriting in Germany and Italy, Speck is the author of the bestselling novel *Piccola Sicilia* and has written the screenplays for the films *Wedding Fever in Campobello* and *My Crazy Turkish Wedding* for which he received an Adolf Grimme Award and the Bavarian TV Award.

ABOUT THE TRANSLATOR

Photo © Saray Taylor-Roman

Jaime McGill is originally from Omaha, Nebraska, and spent eleven years in Berlin before discovering the endless summers of the American South. She has translated over a dozen novels, including works by bestselling German authors Jessica Koch, Oliver Pötzsch, Joline Hayes, and Emily Bold. When not working, Jaime can be found holding a bass clarinet, a cookbook, or a twenty-sided die.

Printed in Great Britain
by Amazon

78537393R00274